I0780342

CLAIMED IN THE CLOUDS

A COZY SCI-FI ROMANCE

THE FORTUSIAN MATES
BOOK 3

LISA EDMONDS

ALSO BY LISA EDMONDS

The Fortusian Mates Series

Sheltered in the Storm

Needed in the Night

Claimed in the Clouds

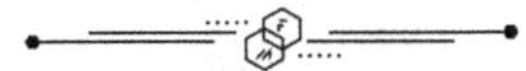

The Alice Worth Series

Heart of Malice

Heart of Fire

Heart of Ice

Heart of Stone

Heart of Shadows

Heart of Vengeance

Heart of Lies

Heart of the Pack

Heart of the Damned

Short Stories and Novellas

From the Ashes

Just For One Night

Blood Money

Ghosting 101

Perfectly Magical

Alice Worth and the Elite Death Machine

The Alice Worth World Novels

Mortal Heart

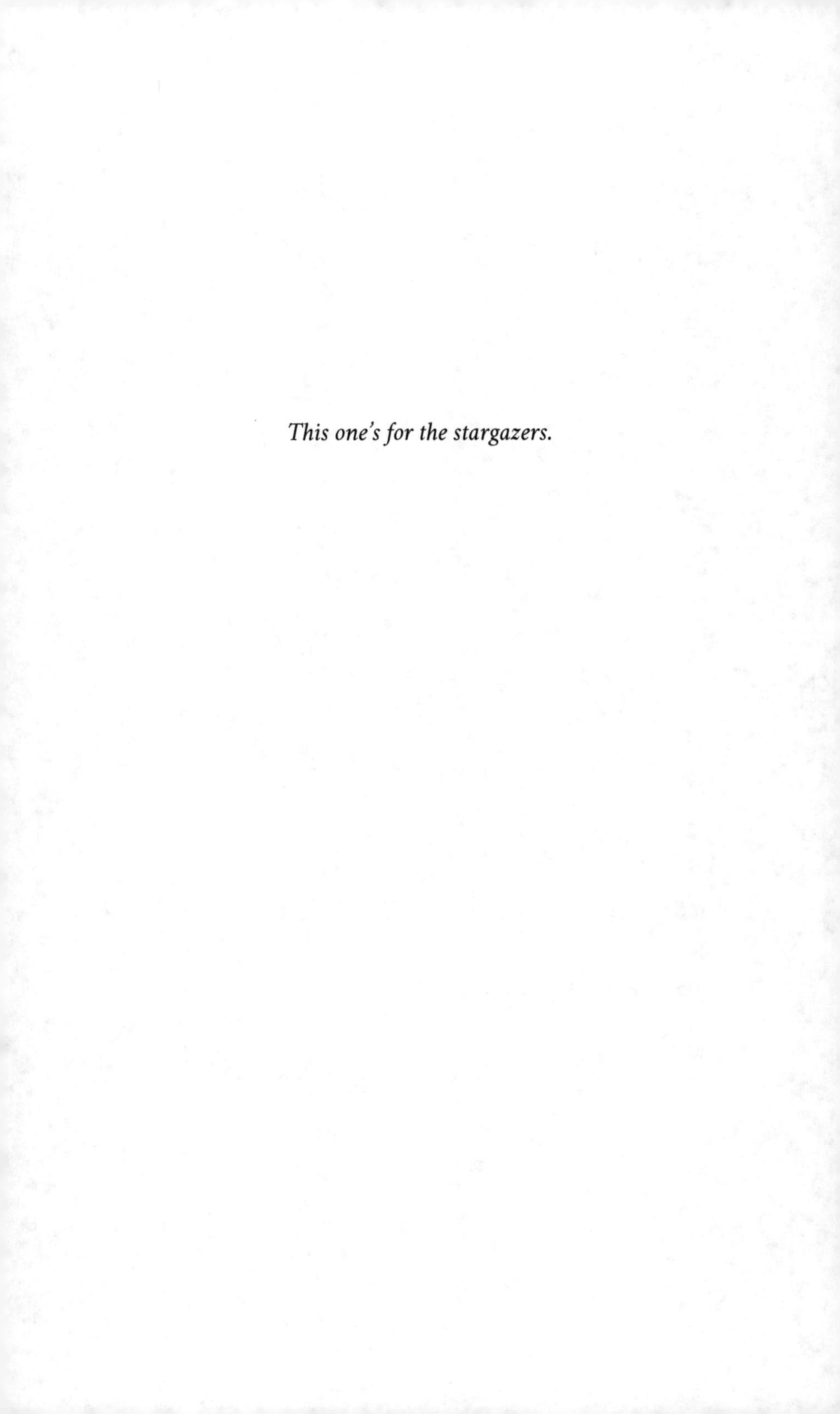

This one's for the stargazers.

CONTENT NOTES

This book, as with all other titles in this series, contains scenes that depict violence, death, physical intimacy, and some topics that may be disturbing to some readers.

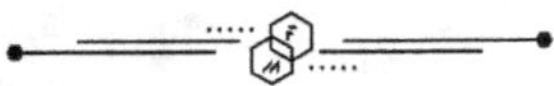

A complete list of content notes can be found **on my website at LisaEdmonds.com/contentnotes.**

CHAPTER 1
ELENA

DEATH CAME TO INGA POLAR STATION WITH MY NAME IN ITS POCKET.

Actually, it came for me about twenty-three kilometers from the station, which was about twenty-two kilometers too far to be survivable.

With an average air temperature of seventy degrees below zero and winds that often spiked from fifty kilometers per hour to three hundred in a matter of minutes, death was always close by on the ice planet Aloris—a grim shadow lurking just outside the airlocks, on the other side of the thick windows, and in the shimmering blue ice that extended as far as the eye could see in all directions.

I followed every procedure to the letter before I left the relative safety of the Polar Seven research pod. I triple-checked my survival suit from the top of my helmet to the soles of my boots. I studied the meteorological data and waited to leave until mid-afternoon, when the omnipresent dangers of life in the upper polar region of Aloris were at their lowest. The data showed my route from Polar Seven to Inga Station was clear and the eighty-kilometer journey should be uneventful—at least, weather-wise.

My cargo was one small travel case of personal items and ten carefully packed specimens of extremophilic fungi preserved in stasis containers. I suspected at least three of the specimens belonged to a previously unknown order of fungi, which meant I would be leaving Aloris on a high note.

Humming to myself to distract from my roiling gut, I carried my travel case and temperature-controlled pack of stasis containers to the airlock that led to the pod's tiny transport bay. Just for good measure, I checked my suit's status again. Green lights across the display inside the helmet's visor. Not that my tummy felt any better knowing that.

I switched the pod to unoccupied mode and opened the airlock.

The temperature-controlled bay contained a single small two-person crawler. The display in my helmet reported that the bay was nearly forty degrees colder than the pod. Still, the bay was a hells of a lot warmer than the air outside, and it protected the crawler from the roaring winds, brutal temperature, ice storms, and polar cyclones.

My data still showed optimal weather, but for visual confirmation I peered through the bay's small window at the gray sky and ice crystals swirling across the blue frozen expanse. A beautiful day by Alorisian standards.

I tapped my gloved middle fingertip and the pad of my thumb together twice to activate my suit's comms. "Regis to Walker."

After a beat, a familiar male voice responded in my helmet. "Walker here. Go ahead, Dr. Regis." The station's medical officer sounded brisk and businesslike, which meant he was within earshot of someone else.

I smiled to myself. We'd see how *businesslike* he'd be later tonight after we both finished our work in the lab.

"I've got an all-clear on weather, Dr. Walker," I said, matching his tone. "I'm heading back to base in the crawler. ETA one hour and fifty-five minutes."

"Understood. We'll track you." A pause, then, in a much lower-pitched voice, he added, "Forux will be happy to see you. Be careful, Elena."

There was the Arron Walker who liked to murmur in my ear when I shared his bed. I'd missed that voice and the body that went with it during my five-day stay at Pod Seven, along with Inga Station's sauna and my bathtub. The pod's sonic cleanser functioned perfectly well, but getting sanitized was far less enjoyable or relaxing than a long soak and scrub-down in hot water—especially if I wasn't the one doing the scrubbing.

I secured my specimen pack and travel case in the tiny cargo area, re-checked both my suit and the crawler's status lights, fastened and adjusted the seat harness until it was snug across my chest and lap, and rested my gloved hands on the controls.

Heart pounding, I studied the bay doors through the crawler's front window. Deep breaths, Elena. Deep breaths.

Six months on Aloris and a dozen round trips between an outpost pod and the main station, and still every time I opened a bay door and ventured out onto the ice, my anxiety skyrocketed. My fear of freezing to death wasn't the main reason I was leaving Aloris the day after tomorrow, but it was a big one.

As a mycologist, I spent half my working hours in the lab and the rest in the field. I'd lived on a dozen worlds in the past ten years and half of those had been inhospitable and even sometimes dangerous. A little peril had never kept me from doing field research.

I'd never lived or worked on an ice planet before, but I'd applied for a six-month stay at Inga Polar Station because extremophilic fungi absolutely fascinated me. The possibility of discovering new species and the promise of adventure and new experiences added to the planet's allure. Before my arrival, I'd fully expected to extend my stay another six months at least.

After less than a month here, and despite making several major discoveries, I knew I wouldn't request an extension. My body rebelled against living on this frozen world, where one breath—one mistake, one moment's distraction, one stroke of bad luck—meant almost certain death. I found life here exhausting for reasons that had nothing at all to do with how many hours I worked in the lab or in the field collecting specimens.

During my stay, I'd focused all my energy on analyzing the new species I found while counting the days until I got to pack up my meager belongings and get off this floating iceberg. The closer I got to my departure date, the slower time seemed to pass.

But then a month ago I received the best news I could have possibly hoped to get. After that, my last four weeks on Aloris flew by in a blur.

Now I was two days from boarding an off-world transport with Forux, my little Fylorian arval companion. All that stood between me and the fulfillment of a nearly lifelong dream were this trip back to the station and a last few shifts analyzing my samples in the lab.

The station wasn't going to come to me, though. And my window for safe travel would close all too soon. I took a deep, fortifying breath and activated the bay doors.

Creaking and wobbling in the wind, the doors rolled open on heavy-duty tracks. I'd probably never call any place "windy" ever again after living on Aloris. At the moment, my helmet reported the wind speed topped one hundred kilometers an hour, which qualified as a *calm* day in the polar region.

I squared my shoulders and piloted the crawler out of the bay. The moment it cleared the doorway, the wind shook the crawler's passenger compartment on the heavy track rollers. But the sky was light gray and not dark with an approaching storm, this was as strong as the wind was projected to get, and I had plenty of daylight to reach the station.

I reminded myself of each of those facts repeatedly as I closed the bay doors behind me and set course for Inga Station.

Flying transports were the typical method of travel on every planet where I'd lived. But on Aloris, crawlers were the safest and most common form of transport, especially away from the cities and interplanetary transport hubs. Small airborne vehicles were simply not suited to this harsh environment.

Slow and steady gets you where you're going on Aloris, physician Arron Walker had told me when I arrived at the station and gaped at the crawlers lined up in the bay. *Trying to get anywhere fast here just gets you dead.*

A lot of things got you dead on Aloris. Too many things.

Happily, an enormous long-range air transport would arrive at Inga Station the day after tomorrow to deliver supplies and pick up Forux, me, and our belongings. It would fly us to one of Aloris's four enormous transport hubs to begin our long journey to our next destination: Hyderia, the uninhabited conservation planet I had dreamed of working on since I was seventeen years old. The single-most difficult planet to get access to in all of Alliance space.

After thirteen years of study and hard work, I had earned permission and funding to conduct mycology research there for six months. Approval had come from the Ministry of Natural Sciences on Nyvor, Hyderia's sister planet, which governed the research stations on Hyderia. The posting was more than a dream come true. It was the chance of a lifetime.

Sometimes in the privacy of my quarters at Inga Station I replayed the congratulatory message I'd received from Minister Ganna from the Ministry of Natural Sciences just to hear her say *Your application has been approved* again. Those words played on a loop in my mind now as the crawler trundled over the ice at exactly forty kilometers per hour, the maximum speed allowed.

Slow and steady, slow and steady.

With one eye on the status indicators for the crawler and my suit—all reassuringly green—and the other on the expanse of ice in front of me, I rested my hands on the controls and listened to the wind howl.

The next hour passed at a truly glacial pace.

By the time I reached the halfway point, Pod Seven had long since disappeared in the rear viewscreen. I tried my best to focus on the thrilling specimens I was bringing back and how in less than an hour I'd be safe back at Inga Station and reunited with Forux and not think about the absolute nothingness surrounding the crawler right now.

Gusts of wind peppered the crawler with ice pellets that plinked off the hull like a sandstorm. I tightened my grip on the controls and kept an eye on the weather data. The forecast was still clear, with no cyclones indicated, but the wind indicator had gone from green to blue. The passenger compartment creaked and rocked on the track rollers.

I swallowed hard and tried to ignore the churning in my stomach. A blue light was fine. The crawler wouldn't tip; it was built not to. I was on course and nearly two-thirds of the way to the station. Arron and the rest of the team at Inga were monitoring the crawler's progress, ready to spring into action at the slightest sign of trouble.

Never mind that pretty much any kind of trouble out here on the icy expanse would kill me long before anyone from the station could reach me.

That last thought was not helpful, so I kept my eyes on the window and made a mental list of what I most looked forward to once I was off this planet. Sunshine. Wind that didn't sear my skin or make my bones ache. The ability to take a day trip to a lake or beach. Come to think of it, water in liquid form rather than as endless ice.

The sound of ice pellets scouring the hull made me add *rain* to my list. I missed the sound and feeling of rain as much as I missed the sun's warmth and skies in colors other than gray. Hyderia experienced lovely thunderstorms all year long, especially in its northern hemisphere's temperate rain forest. My future colleagues at the station there would probably think me strange, but I might just spend the first few storms outside to savor the sensation of raindrops on my skin—

An alarm blared, a light flashed red, and something huge and black and half as big as the crawler smashed through the front window.

It was all over in a blink.

One second, I was searching the horizon for my first glimpse of Inga Station's domes and daydreaming of a Hyderian thunderstorm…

…and the next, my ears were ringing, I tasted blood, and I was unbelievably, agonizingly, heart-stoppingly cold.

Everything was hazy and in slow motion, as if I was looking into the distance down a long tunnel or I'd been submerged in some viscous fluid. I blinked a few times and tried to make sense of what had happened.

My nearly unbreakable helmet visor was cracked on the right side. The roar in my head—or at least part of it—was the wind screaming through the crack. Ferocious cold poured into my suit through a rip in its right shoulder.

The right half of the crawler's passenger compartment was gone. If I'd been sitting on the seat to my right, I would be gone too. I stared blankly at the ruin of the compartment as if watching it on a viewscreen instead of sitting in the midst of the destruction.

Somehow, the crawler was still moving. Groaning and clunking, it trundled across the ice in the general direction of the station. The impact had thrown it off course, but the heavy track rollers seemed intact.

Blood pooled in my mouth and dripped down my chin. The air blasting into my helmet sprayed the blood across the inside of my visor.

How badly was I injured? Was I bleeding internally? I licked blood off my lower lip and flinched. No, I'd bitten my tongue during the impact.

Through the ringing in my ears and roar of wind in my helmet, I caught the sound of someone shouting over comms. The voice sounded like Arron, but I couldn't tell what he was saying. Probably some version of *Stay alive—we're coming for you.*

Stay alive. Sure, no problem. Damaged crawler, no protection from the cold or wind, broken helmet, torn survival suit, and still more than twenty kilometers from the station. This was my worst nightmare come true.

A bubble of terror and panic tried to rise. With effort, I stomped it down furiously.

You're damn right I'll stay alive. I didn't work this hard and come this far and earn an impossible place at a research station on Hyderia to die on this frozen rock.

I fumbled for the emergency repair kit in the pocket on my suit's right leg. The wind tried to rip the patch out of my gloved hand, but I got it into my left hand and slapped it over the rip in the right shoulder of my survival suit.

Pain nearly whited out my vision. My scream was inaudible in the howling wind.

Shit—I was hurt. My shoulder might be dislocated, or some bones might be broken. Shock and the brutal cold had muted the pain until I hit my shoulder with my hand. Now the agony was so bad that my stomach rebelled and I had to fight to keep from throwing up in my helmet.

When the pain faded enough for me to focus, I saw the patch had done its job and sealed the tear in my suit. The environmental system struggled to heat the frigid air trapped inside the suit.

Shaking uncontrollably, I pulled another repair patch from my pocket. I couldn't get a good grip on it. The wind stole the patch before I had a chance to use it. The next patch I *did* hang onto through sheer determination, but raising my right arm to try to affix it to my cracked helmet hurt so badly that I screamed again.

Despite the agony, I got the patch onto my helmet somehow and covered the crack almost completely. Cold air still streamed into the helmet through the tiny remaining opening. Not ideal, but I wasn't going to be able to raise that arm again to apply another patch.

Ahead, through the demolished front window and my blood-splattered visor, I spotted dark shapes in the far distance: two crawlers, one large and one small, traveling side-by-side. Rescue was within sight, but the distance between us seemed more than a light-year.

Gods, I was so cold and I hurt so badly. I couldn't tell if my suit was getting any warmer or not. That seemed like a bad sign.

"Elena." Arron's voice crackled in my helmet comms. It sounded like he was shouting, but the words were indistinct and barely audible. "Elena, gods-dammit…answer me."

I gritted my teeth and tapped my right middle finger and thumb together twice. No beep. The suit was too damaged on that side. I repeated the action with my left hand. *Beep.* A light sputtered to life on my helmet.

"Arron," I called, hoping he could hear me. "I'm alive. My suit is damaged. Hurry."

"You've…gear…up." Crackles drowned out part of his response. "Red…minutes to intercept…gear…Elena."

I stared at the distant crawlers in disbelief. Did he just tell me to shift gears and increase the crawler's speed above the safety limit?

This stretch of ice had been analyzed closely and the speed of the crawlers set accordingly. Going any faster meant the crawler's passage might create a resonance that could cause it to break through the ice or create hidden damage that would endanger others who used this path later.

The wind picked up again. The crackles in my helmet drowned out whatever Arron said next. The wind indicator went from blue to orange.

My thoughts were getting sluggish. I didn't *feel* cold, but my gut told me I was. That rip in the right shoulder and the crack in the helmet might not be the only damage my suit had taken. The approaching crawlers were still so far away that I had to risk increasing my speed to meet them as quickly as possible. They were probably already traveling at top speed.

All the gods above and below, get me back to Inga Station alive. I changed gears and accelerated.

Warning lights flashed across the control panel—the parts that still worked, that was. The crawler groaned and rumbled as if protesting being forced to go faster.

"I changed gears," I called. My voice sounded like it was echoing in my helmet, or maybe I was getting woozy. "Speed now fifty-five kph."

I would have given a lot to hear Arron's reply, or any voice at all, but the only sound in my comms was more crackling.

They probably couldn't hear me either, but I kept talking so I didn't get sleepy. "Something hit me," I said. "It was big and round, like a cylinder. I think it was a part of something that broke off. Maybe the crawler's scanners recorded the impact and someone can figure out where it came from. I hope the cylinder and the parts that broke off my crawler don't hurt anyone else."

Not that there was much else out here besides the station and its array of smaller research pods, but the wind might blow those debris a long, long way across the ice. They probably wouldn't do too much damage to a pod, but a small crawler like mine…might…

I forced my eyes open. I didn't remember closing them.

Everything was hazy, so I blinked until I could focus on the approaching crawlers. The endless ice made judging distance difficult, but my rescuers were close enough now that I could just make out two figures in helmets and survival suits sitting in each crawler.

I only had to hang on a few more minutes. Just a few more minutes.

"I'm awake," I said, because saying it aloud made it feel more true. "I'm awake. I'm alive."

But for how long? I couldn't feel my body anymore. Each time I blinked, time seemed to jump ahead several seconds or as much as a minute. The intercepting crawlers inched closer but the distance between us seemed to stretch with every sluggish heartbeat.

Through the growing fog, anger rose. That didn't help my body but it did clear my head a bit.

"I'm alive," I mumbled as darkness came and went. "I'm not going to give up. I'm not going to freeze to death on this gods-damned planet. I'm going to bring these samples back to the station, and then in two days I'm leaving to go study fungi on Hyderia. I'm not going to give up."

My eyes drifted closed. "I'm not going to give up," I repeated. "I'm not letting that spot go to anyone else. I worked too hard to get it."

The crawler ground to a stop and seemed to lurch several times. Shadows moved around me and I could have sworn I heard voices, but the noises might have been wind or my imagination.

When the fog lifted enough for me to open my eyes, I found a familiar human face hovering above mine. I seemed to be rocking gently.

"No one is going to get your spot," Arron promised, cupping my cheek with his very warm bare hand. He stroked my jaw with his thumb. "We've got you, Elena. You're safe."

I blinked up at him, too puzzled to formulate a reply.

Strange that he wasn't wearing a helmet. Where were we? Above him was a dark gray metal hull much too large and undamaged to belong to my little crawler.

Slowly—*very* slowly—my fuzzy brain started to make sense of my surroundings.

I lay in a hammock sling between rows of seats in the passenger area of the station's six-person crawler. The large engine thrummed powerfully and reassuringly as the vehicle trundled over the ice. My helmet and survival suit were gone, and I was in an emergency thermal bag that enclosed my entire body except for my face.

I wasn't cold, but I wasn't warm. I was mostly numb. At least my shoulder didn't hurt.

"Elena." Arron passed a medical scanner over my head and upper body and studied the screen. He set it aside and caressed my cheek again, his dark brown eyes peering into mine in a way that was far more medical officer than lover. "Are you with us?"

"Yes," I croaked. My throat was painfully dry. "I didn't die."

"No, you did not die," he said with an audible sigh of relief.

"You're in a crawler with Gavis and me, and we are on our way back to the station. We'll be there in about ten minutes."

"I think I'm missing some time," I told him. I was having trouble thinking, so my thoughts just came out my mouth. "And I feel very fuzzy."

"I know." His eyes tightened. "When I saw your broken helmet and all the blood, I thought you might be concussed or have internal injuries. Thankfully, your condition is mainly due to shock and hypothermia. You do have a badly fractured clavicle and damage to muscles and tendons in your right shoulder. Nothing we can't heal at the station."

What he didn't say—that if whatever had hit my shoulder had been a few more inches to the left, I would be dead—hung in the air almost as visibly as my breath would in the station's transport bay.

Arron found my hand and rested his on top. I couldn't feel his warmth through the thermal bag, but the weight was reassuring. "You did very, very well to survive," he said. "I'm proud of you. You fought like hell."

"I'm stubborn," I said with a ghost of a smile.

He returned my smile. "Thank all the gods above and below for that."

The rumbling of the crawler through my hammock sling was surprisingly soothing. I'd never found anything about a crawler the least bit comforting before.

"You didn't tell Forux about this, right?" I asked.

"No." Arron rubbed my hand. "Jakva distracted him with meat while we suited up and got away. But he's an empath, so I'm sure he knows by now you ran into trouble. He'll be waiting for you at the airlock."

My poor little Forux. I couldn't take him with me to Pod Seven because I had no way to protect him if something went wrong— which it *had*—so he would have been unhappy and clingy when I got back even if I *hadn't* just almost died. Now...well, I'd have a worried arval stuck to my side for the foreseeable future.

"And my samples?" I asked.

"I wondered when you'd ask," he said with a chuckle. "Right next to you, along with your travel case. Good thing you strapped them down in the cargo area. The case is in bad shape, but the pack of samples is fine and still temperature-controlled. Your discoveries made it back with you. You've set a record for the most new species discovered during a six-month stay at Inga Station."

He'd said it to distract me, but I didn't mind. I'd rather focus on my achievement than the grim reality of my close brush with death.

Warmth blossomed in my chest. Amazing to be able to feel personal and professional pride while lying in a medical sling, pumped full of painkillers and cocooned in an emergency thermal bag with only my face sticking out like an Ngaran moth larva.

"Well, there's another item for the *Awards and Accolades* section of my academic credentials," I said wryly. "So, what's the prize for setting the record?"

He tilted his head and pretended to give the question serious thought, though his eyes twinkled. "Well, it's not a *formal* award per se, but the very least we could do is take up a collection from the team and buy you and Forux a cabin upgrade on the cruiser from Aloris to Havel Prime. Give the little fluffball more room to run around during the journey."

"He would probably like that, but I'd settle for an extra coffee ration tomorrow." *And nighttime company tonight and tomorrow night.* Not that I said that aloud, given we weren't alone in the crawler.

Arron squeezed my hand as if he knew precisely what I was thinking. I managed to smile.

In all honesty, I doubted our habit of spending nights in each other's quarters was any kind of secret, but the unspoken rule at the station about relationships between researchers was that everyone pretended not to notice who slept where as long as it didn't interfere with our work.

Arron planned to stay on Aloris for a long time. A human born and raised on Earth, he'd left humanity's planet of origin after medical school to explore the farthest reaches of Alliance space. He loved Inga Station and everything about this planet. His field of research was thermophysiology. When he wasn't acting as the station's medical officer, treating hypothermia and the occasional broken bone or illness, he studied the effects of extreme temperatures on humans and nonhumans.

He was staying, and I was going. Once we'd established that, we simply enjoyed our time together without needing to worry about the future.

"Speaking of your imminent departure," Arron said, squeezing my hand, "a message came in about an hour ago from the director of research you'll be working with on Hyderia, a Dr. Husiorithae."

"Really?" I raised my head, then regretted it when pain flared in my shoulder and my vision swam.

"Really." He nudged me to lie back in the sling. "And it will be waiting for you *in your quarters* when you get released from the medical bay."

In other words, stay put, rest, and focus on recovering before worrying about Dr. Husiorithae's message.

"Thank you," I said, my voice soft.

We rode quietly for a few minutes. He alternated between comforting touches and checking the readouts on the medical equipment around my sling.

He should be wearing his helmet. The station's policy was to wear a full survival suit at all times when outside the facility. No exceptions. This rule had been drilled into me from the moment I arrived—by Arron most of all. And yet he was breaking it because he knew I needed to see his face and kind eyes.

We might have been good together if things were different. This wasn't the first time I'd parted ways with someone I cared about because our needs and wants and professional goals didn't align. Most of the researchers I knew faced the same dilemma more than once in their careers. We'd chosen a nomadic life, with all its joys and sorrows.

One of the few sensations in my numb body was a familiar twinge of heartache. The best cure for it was a cuddle with Forux when I got back to the station and then two final nights in Arron's bed.

I took a shaky breath. "I wouldn't have made it back to the station without you coming out to meet me, would I?"

"Probably not," he said, with a grim tightening of his eyes that said *No, you wouldn't have survived*. "But that's why the station's policy is always to have a crawler on standby and at least one driver ready to go at a moment's notice anytime someone's out on the ice. We've never lost a researcher due to a vehicle accident, and that wasn't going to change today." He rubbed my hand. "I wasn't going to let it."

He glanced toward the front of the crawler. "We're approaching the station now. As soon as we're secured in the transport bay, Gavis and I will carry this sling to medical. You need to stay in the thermal bag until we get to the emergency medpod." He raised his eyebrows. "You're not going to argue about walking there on your own, are you?"

The prospect of being carried through the station raised my hackles, but even I had to admit I didn't think I could stand up, much less walk.

"No." I sighed. "I just defied death, so I'm all out of defiance for the day."

He chuckled. "Knowing you, I seriously doubt that." He braced himself with one hand on the back of the seat as the crawler rumbled over the threshold of the station's enormous transport bay. When he met my gaze again, his expression had turned serious once more. "Hang on to that defiance, Elena. It saved you today."

My defiance had enabled me to achieve almost everything I'd done since childhood, but I didn't say that aloud. We didn't have that kind of relationship, and that was perfectly fine with both of us.

When we came to a halt and the engine powered down, Arron

rubbed my hand one last time and rose. "You made it. We're safe and home."

I managed a smile, but it faded quickly. *Safe* was relative, especially on this planet.

And *home?* Maybe for him, but not for me. I didn't know *where* home was, but it wasn't Aloris.

Maybe it would be Hyderia.

CHAPTER 2
ARDRUC

Tendrils of cold plasma in a half-dozen colors split the air around me, forming a blindingly bright curtain that resembled the tentacles of an enormous jellyfish.

"Computer, pause recording," I said.

The tendrils froze in mid-crackle.

I walked through the holographic electrical discharges, examining each as I cross-referenced its visual representation with the report on my datapad.

"Size, altitude, and location of this kora?" I asked without looking over my shoulder.

My research assistant, Dr. Makato Rg, hummed to themself before answering. "Forty-six by forty-six kilometers, Dr. Husiorithae. Highest point measured at forty-eight-point-seven-five kilometers." They provided the latitude and longitude of the center of the discharge, and then added, "The largest of five korae in the same cluster recorded at 2138 hours yesterday."

"Noted." I frowned at my datapad and turned. "The array recorded a total of nine clusters in forty-seven minutes?"

"Yes, sir." The very short, blue-skinned Ymarian atmospheric scientist folded their hands behind their back and met my gaze with their own three-eyed one. "I believe that is the most korae phenomena in the shortest period of time since my arrival. Very exceptional."

"Indeed," I said absently, my attention on my datapad once more.

"Sir." Rg coughed. "If you can spare me, I require a rest period."

I glanced at my wristcomm. The chronometer indicated we had been in the imaging lab far longer than I had realized. "Apologies, Dr. Rg. You are excused."

"Thank you, Dr. Husiorithae." Rg gave me a short bow and left.

Rather than rest during a single long sleep per daily cycle, Ymarian biology followed an ultradian pattern of six or seven alternating periods of sleep and wakefulness. Given their impeccable credentials and dedication to our shared interests, I had adapted to Rg's schedule. Occasionally, I became so immersed in my studies of Hyderia's unique upper-atmospheric electrical discharge phenomena, called *kora* or the plural *korae*, that I lost track of time. This was not the first time Rg had to remind me of their needs.

Rg's ability to analyze tremendous amounts of data quickly was their most significant contribution to our research. Their rest schedule allowed me to work and think in solitude throughout the day without the expectation of conversation or pleasantries. I would be the first to admit I excelled at neither of those skills.

Generally, I preferred to be alone in my lab with the data and scans collected by the massive arrays of imaging and recording equipment in orbit around Hyderia. And in the cavernous imaging lab, I immersed myself in the holographic replications of the spectacular cold plasma phenomena I had devoted my career to studying. Data was like the finest music to my senses. Science was my foundation and my balm.

To be able to research Hyderia's unique korae at the Nova Cal station was both the highest of honors and weightiest of responsibilities. No one knew exactly what caused the korae. I had amassed mountains of data during my two years here, but had not yet found the answer so many before me had sought. Far from being disheartening, that fact merely made me more determined to succeed where others had failed.

My wristcomm beeped. I snarled at the interruption, puffing smoke from my nostrils.

Incoming Message from Nyvoran Ministry of Natural Sciences, the screen read. *Designated Top Priority.*

My irritation evaporated. A rare call from the Ministry, at whose discretion I lived and worked on Hyderia, demanded an immediate answer.

I left the imaging lab and hurried to Lab One to respond. At my desk, I activated the main screen and stood at attention, shoulders back, tail coiled around my leg, and wings folded neatly.

The screen changed from the seal of the Ministry of Natural Sciences to the familiar reptilian features of Vice Minister Ganna.

"Greetings, Dr. Husiorithae," Ganna said, her expression very solemn. "I am sorry to disturb your very important work."

"Please do not apologize," I said. Her uncharacteristically grim demeanor caused a ball of unease to form in my stomach. "Why the urgent call? Has Dr. Regis been delayed?"

"My call is not in regard to Dr. Regis. I believe she is still due to arrive at Nova Cal at 1600 hours." Ganna bowed her head sorrowfully. "Rather, I am relaying a recorded message from your family on Fortusia, forwarded to me by your former colleagues on Engaren. My charge is to ensure you receive it."

I very nearly recoiled. The unease in my stomach turned to a much more visceral need to fight or flee. I fought to keep my expression neutral, as my wings fluttered and my tail lashed the air.

I had not stepped foot on my home planet for more than fifteen standard years. I had no inclination to do so ever again, and even less desire to hear whatever this message contained. Ganna's demeanor strongly suggested its nature.

I inhaled deeply. "I do not know anyone on Fortusia with whom I would care to correspond, Minister Ganna. You need not forward me anything, but I am grateful to you for alerting me that such a message exists."

She blinked with both sets of eyelids. "My charge is to ensure you *receive* it," she repeated, her expression now a combination of curiosity and mild disgust.

Ordinarily I would not care what someone's opinion of me might be. One did not rise in highly competitive scientific fields without developing a thick skin, and my dragon's-hide flesh was tough by nature. But Ganna chaired the committee that granted permission for researchers to live and work on Hyderia. My presence here was a privilege that could be revoked at any time and I would have no recourse.

Perhaps the facts of the matter might change her opinion about my reaction, but I had no interest in explaining myself to anyone. My past and my pain were no one's concern but my own.

As such, I had no choice but to capitulate as gracefully as I could manage, despite the bitter taste in my mouth.

"Thank you, Minister Ganna. Please send the recording." After a beat, I added, "And please pass along my gratitude to my former colleagues on Engaren for ensuring it reached me."

"I will do so." She leaned forward. "See Dr. Regis receives a warm welcome, Dr. Husiorithae. Everyone here at the Ministry looks forward to reviewing the fruits of her research."

"As do I," I said, because that was the expected response and not because Hyderia's fungi actually interested me. "I will ensure she has all she needs for her work."

She dipped her head in a traditional Nyvoran farewell. I followed suit.

When I looked up, her face on the screen had been replaced by the seal of Fortusia and the title *Sealed Communication for Dr. Ardruc Husiorithae—Top Priority Delivery Required with Receipt.*

And beneath that, the words *Notification of Death.*

I touched the screen. *Receipt Sent* flashed. Minister Ganna, my former colleagues on Engaren, and whoever else had forwarded this message until it tracked me down halfway across Alliance space had now fulfilled their Fortusian government-mandated tasks.

I could choose to play the message now, save it for later, or delete it outright. I discarded the second option immediately, and went so far as to reach for *Delete Message* before reconsidering.

In the handful of times I had mentally rehearsed a moment like this, I had deleted the hypothetical message without a pause and continued with my work. The night I escaped from the compound, I knew not only would there be no going back, but that I was severing all ties to the people who were my family by blood but were strangers to me.

No, not *strangers*—that was not the right word. I knew them well. I was their son and their brother. I had deserved so much more than what I had received. I had never deserved their scorn, cruelty, or abuse. Even as a young child, before I truly comprehended the full horror of my situation, I had known that on a deep level. It was *wrong*, no matter how frequently or forcefully they told me it was right.

And now one of those people who had been so monstrous to me had died, and I could not decide if I cared enough to find out who.

What puzzled me was why, even if my family had wanted to notify me of this death, their sect leader permitted it. The sect was anti-technology and anti-science with extremely limited access to both. But not only had the sect leader apparently permitted this communication, someone had managed to get it sent by a government official with enough authority to designate it Top Priority Delivery with Receipt, a costly endeavor.

Perhaps my curiosity won out, or I succumbed to some darker reason like I wanted to know one of my past tormentors had died. For whatever reason, I did something I had previously believed I would not do: I played the message.

My stomach knotted almost painfully as the Fortusian government seal faded to black. I planted my feet shoulder-width apart, folded my hands behind my back, coiled my tail once more, and raised my chin, as if facing a charging Hardanian war-pig or an academic review committee.

My father appeared on the screen.

Olme Fornuth, as I preferred to think of him, looked much older than I anticipated. The past fifteen years had not been kind to him. His wings drooped, his purple and red scale-patterned skin appeared sallow, and his feathers were patchy.

My father, mother, brother, and I were all genetically engineered using the DNA of the Fortusian equatorial dragon in combination with humanoid characteristics, but we differed in the colors of our skin and feathers.

I expected to feel anger at seeing him. Perhaps revulsion or bitterness.

Instead, I felt...nothing. Rather than flourishing within the confines of the sect, Olme appeared pathetic and broken.

Even so, I could not feel sympathy for him. He and my mother, Earra, had chosen this path and forced my younger brother and me to bend to not only their will but that of the sect leader. My brother had chosen to convert to the cult's ways. I had not, and had suffered so very greatly as a result.

Perhaps if Minister Ganna knew of any of this she would not have judged me so harshly for not wanting to hear the contents of this message.

Given it was Olme on the screen, I expected to hear Earra had died. That elicited a twinge, but only a brief one. My mother had been as harsh in dealing out punishments as Olme.

"Ardruc," Olme said. His voice startled me by how little it had changed, despite his appearance. He sounded and appeared stoic, though I noted a tightening of his eyes that indicated he mourned. "Your brother has died after a long illness."

Grief made my hearts ache and my throat grow tight. I had never disliked my brother. He had embraced sect life, but I had never sensed he truly believed like Olme and Earra and the others did. I had once hoped he might follow my lead and leave. It broke my hearts when he chose to stay.

But if I had thought for even one moment Olme had reached out with this news in an attempt to make peace, or even as a simple courtesy, I would have been mistaken.

"Our beloved leader has said you must return to your family now," he continued. "You will be married to your brother's wife."

My fists clenched. Like *hells* I would.

"You rejected the wife our beloved leader selected for you and turned your back on our faith and family for your love of *science*—" Olme nearly whispered the word "—but surely by now you must have realized there are no truths to be found in those studies." His expression hardened. "After your betrayal, Aora was bound to your brother, but now he is gone and she must have a spouse. This is your duty—"

"Computer, stop," I grated.

Olme froze in mid-sentence, his brow furrowed and eyes glowing.

Yes, that was the Olme I remembered: righteous and angry. Angry at my failings, my curiosity, my love of science, my betrayals —*my* betrayals, as if their decision to abandon all reason and fall under the sway of the sect leader, whose name they were considered unworthy to speak, had not betrayed my brother and me in the worst and most unforgivable ways possible.

My pain and grief were multiplied by the knowledge that if my brother had died from a long illness, as Olme claimed, his death was likely a result of the sect leader's anti-science teachings. Few illnesses were incurable on Fortusia, or anywhere in Alliance space.

My betrothal to Aora, a woman from the sect I barely knew, had pushed me to finally escape the compound. The sect and its leader had taken so much from me. They would not take my right to choose my own mate, or with whom—or *if*—I would have children.

I did not call my departure a betrayal. I called it my freedom. And on a rainy night at the age of nineteen, I had chosen freedom over the cruelly narrow life my parents and the leader wanted for me.

How deluded Olme and Earra must be to think they could make such a demand of me now and I would come crawling back to the compound to do their bidding.

"Computer, delete message," I said, my voice calm.

The computer beeped. The screen went dark.

I would grieve in my own way for my brother, but thanks to this message, I could finally close that chapter of my life. Any other messages that came my way, I would leave unacknowledged.

A weight lifted off my shoulders. I took another deep breath and exhaled.

Rg would not return to the lab for two hours. The forest called my name. I wanted to go for a walk, perhaps play my lat'sar to soothe my heartache. Or better yet, take to the sky. My wings longed to stretch and catch the wind.

But in a few minutes, a transport from Nyvor would deliver mycologist Dr. Elena Regis, a human scientist born and raised on Fyloria. I did not have time to retreat to the forest or the sky today, as much as I longed to do so. My duties as director of research for the Nova Cal station included welcoming a fellow scientist, escorting her to her apartment, and providing a tour of the facility.

According to my research, Dr. Regis was brilliant and insightful but distressingly prone to unusual leaps of logic. At least those leaps often lead to breakthroughs. Discoveries would help raise the status of this station and ensure its continued, though limited, funding.

I was not thrilled by her unorthodox methodologies. I had always found purely scientific methods to be the most worthwhile. But as our fields were very different, my own work and practices should not be affected by hers. Our interactions would be minimal. Perhaps I would ask for weekly or biweekly briefings simply to stay informed on her progress and otherwise ignore her.

Elena was the daughter of famed physicist Dr. Hilda Disen, chair of the heliophysics department at the most prominent university on

Fyloria. Elena seemed to want to distance herself from that connection and had chosen to use her artist father's last name rather than carry the weight of the matrilineal name Disen.

I could empathize at least somewhat with that impulse. My parents had no fame, but their adherence to the sect was a matter of public record. I had chosen instead to use *Husiorithae*, the second name of Earra's mother, my grandmother, who had not fallen under the spell of the sect leader, and who had gifted me my beloved lat'sar.

I set aside the unhelpful emotions caused by Olme's message, straightened my lab coat, and checked my reflection in the bank of screens above my desk. I appeared…unsettled. The feathers in my hair and wings were ruffled and my tail swished, as if I were a young male equatorial dragon either defending territory or courting a mate. Utterly ridiculous for an adult scientist and director of research.

I shook out my feathers, stretched and folded my wings, and stilled my tail. Now my reflection showed a thirty-four-year-old Fortusian scientist with smooth feathers and notable calm and confidence in his body language. Much better.

My sharp ears caught the familiar hum of the landing pad sensors directly above this lab change tone. The landing beacons had activated.

Elena was arriving nearly fifteen minutes ahead of schedule. Annoying, but I preferred an early arrival to a late one. The sooner I got her settled, the sooner I could return to the imaging lab and immerse myself in my research.

I took the steep stairs from the single-story lab's main hallway to the roof rather than the lift, as I found it cramped given my height and wings. The diminutive Nyvorans had not constructed the lift with Fortusians in mind.

The roof hatch opened, revealing the sleek gray Nyvoran Ministry of Natural Sciences transport on final approach. This hemisphere was currently experiencing summer, which meant comfortably warm temperatures. The cobalt blue sky was cloudless, the breeze gentle. Very pleasant weather for Elena's arrival, though perhaps for her studies she might have preferred clouds and rain. Her apparently beloved fungi thrived in the soil of Hyderia's thick forests, especially in such weather.

The short-range interplanetary transport landed on the pad. Once the engines and thrusters powered down, I approached the transport's side.

The door unsealed and lowered to form a ramp, revealing the interior of the transport—and a purple Fylorian arval with thick fur, two oversized eyes, four ears and four stumpy legs, and five fluffy tails.

The little monstrosity fanned out his tails and snarled at me. I showed him my own teeth, but he held his ground.

"Forux," a female voice scolded from out of sight inside the transport. "Be *nice*. We're trying to make a good first impression."

I blinked. Had Elena brought a *pet* to Nova Cal? A pet covered with fur that would befoul my pristine labs?

Dr. Elena Regis appeared in the transport's open doorway. "Sorry about that," she told me cheerfully. "He's my bodyguard."

For travel, Elena had chosen a practical and comfortable tunic shirt under a thermal vest, slim pants, and boots, and had styled her long blonde hair in a braid.

I might have considered her lovely by either human or Fortusian standards if I noted such things. My tail swished a few times before I wrapped it around my leg.

She settled the straps of an oversized backpack on her shoulders, leaned down to scratch the arval's head, and flashed me a quick smile. "Come on, Forux. Let's not keep the director of research waiting."

Without waiting for help, she wheeled two travel cases down the ramp by their handles. At the bottom, Forux eyed me distrustfully from behind her left boot.

Elena let go of her rolling crates, blew a few loose strands of hair out of her face, and smiled up at me. "Dr. Husiorithae, it's such an honor to meet you. Oh, wait." She gave me a perfectly executed small bow, a common form of greeting in my home region on Fortusia.

When she met my gaze again, her bright blue eyes sparkled. But when I did not return the greeting, a little furrow appeared between her brows. "I hope I did that right," she said.

I could not answer. I could not *think*. My breath caught in my lungs, my muscles seized, and my feet felt rooted in place, as if I had been too close to a bolt of lightning and experienced a shock.

Her rich, earthy scent filled me, pulled me under, and swept me away. All the world faded until all that remained was her. My skin tingled and my thundering heartsbeats filled my ears. The blood rushing through my veins became a roar. I had lost myself in a sudden riptide...but paradoxically, that tide had brought me to shore and a place of safety—of warmth and harbor, hearth and home.

I wanted her—gods, I needed her. My chest tightened as if I could not breathe without her scent in my nose. My cock and the tip of my tail stirred and thrummed in eagerness, ready to please her.

Realization was slow in rising, but when it did, it came with the same fight-or-flight sensation Olme's unwelcome message had caused. This all-consuming desire was the call of a true mate.

The fact I had never wanted this for myself did not matter. My body's response to her was physiological, innate, as natural as breath and bone. The call of a true mate promised pleasure and contentment and tomorrows full of joy.

No. I pushed back against the lure of her with all the strength I could muster. How could my body and soul know she was perfect in every way when we had been in each other's presence only moments? Had I not left my parents' compound because they tried to force me into a relationship I did not want? Olme's message had just reopened that wound.

And more importantly, I had chosen science as my path and passion. I did not want to be distracted—not when my privilege to live on Hyderia depended on focus and results.

I took a step back and fought to regain my equilibrium.

Professionalism and clinical detachment, I told myself, and forced my body to comply outwardly, even if my hearts raced and my stomach churned and my fingers tingled with desire.

I folded my wings, stilled my twitching tail, and clasped my hands behind my back so she could not see them tremble. And I puffed smoke from my nostrils as well, trying in vain to banish her scent.

An antigrav sled emerged from the rear of the transport and deposited a stack of crates on the far side of the landing pad, safely out of the way of the ship's thrusters. Her lab equipment and supplies, no doubt.

"Dr. Regis," I said, my voice rough. I cleared my throat. "I do not think Nova Cal will be an optimal place to conduct your research. I urge you to reconsider."

Her mouth fell open. Shock, confusion, and then anger crossed her face before she drew herself up to her full height.

"Well, I disagree," she said icily. "And more importantly, the Nyvoran Ministry of Natural Sciences seems convinced I'm well-qualified and an ideal choice for this post. Only two other mycologists have ever worked here, and that was decades ago. The fungi on this planet is virtually unknown."

Behind her, the transport's door hummed as it began to close.

Go, I wanted to shout. *Get back on that transport and go somewhere else—anywhere else. I am begging you.*

But I could not do that. She would have every right to complain to the Ministry, and I would have no explanation for my behavior that would not be humiliating in the extreme.

"Nova Cal is very isolated," I said. "There are only myself and my research assistant here, and we are very busy. I do not think you will be...content."

"You don't think I'll be *content?*" Elena put her hands on her hips. "You can't be serious. I'm a field researcher, not some spoiled tourist. I just spent six months at a polar research station on Aloris."

Forux growled. When the transport's door closed and sealed, I very nearly growled too.

"You weren't exactly enthusiastic in your response to my message introducing myself," Elena continued, "but you said you'd set up a lab for me and had an apartment waiting. And now you want to kick me off the planet?"

She took a step forward, her eyes blazing with fury and defiance. Our height difference did not seem to intimidate her in the least. I suspected very little did.

Her scent swirled around me again. Her anger had its own fiery fragrance too—one I liked, though I cursed myself for it.

"I've dreamed of researching on Hyderia since I was seventeen, Dr. Husiorithae," she snapped. "I have worked very hard for this. So whatever your problem is with me, too damn bad, because you're stuck with me."

The transport's engines powered up.

Elena grabbed the handles of her rolling crates and headed for the lift doors. "Don't worry about the rest of my gear; I'll come back for it myself," she said over her shoulder. "If you'll just show me my lab and where Forux and I are going to be sleeping, I can find everything else for myself."

I followed her to the lift to grant her access to the facility via the palm scanner. I would take the stairs myself.

"Speaking of your companion, I do not want fur in the labs," I said, my voice frosty.

"Neither do I," she shot back. "Arvals don't shed. He *does* bite, though, so I'd keep my distance if I were you."

I bite too, I wanted to say, but did not. Such a statement was neither professional nor clinical, and at the moment I was not sure if I meant it as a threat or a promise.

Once Elena and Forux were in the lift and headed to the main floor, I stalked across the landing pad to the stairway hatch.

The transport lifted off. The thrusters displaced air with a force that made me stumble, but at least that cleared Elena's scent from the area. In despair, I watched it rise above the treetops, circle, and accelerate toward the sky and the tiny, just-visible glowing dot that was Nyvor, Hyderia's sister planet.

As an atmospheric scientist, Hyderia had been my paradise for nearly two years. And despite what I had said to Elena, it was a mycologist's dream as well. But while she had found her paradise, I had unexpectedly lost mine—or had it ripped away.

For at least six months, I would be trapped in this small research facility with Elena, a human who had, for reasons biology could explain but I dared the universe to justify, triggered my instincts for a true mate.

Surely a deeper, fresher, and more miserable hell did not exist.

CHAPTER 3
ELENA

Trembling with anger, I watched Ardruc stalk back across the roof until the lift doors closed, cutting him off from my sight.

"What the hells is his problem?" I muttered to Forux.

As the lift descended to the station's main level, Forux circled my boots in agitation. My little arval's tails were fanned out, he'd flattened his ears, and he was growling. I hadn't seen him so angry in—well, ever.

"I wasn't expecting him to be joyful about my arrival, but trying to get me to turn right around and leave?" I fumed. "And he basically called me a tourist who needs babysitting? If he even *glanced* at the file I submitted to the Ministry, he should know I'm every bit as qualified to be here as he is."

Despite my exhaustion from the long journey from Aloris and nervousness about meeting the Nyvoran committee that supervised Hyderia's research stations, I'd been so happy to arrive on this beautiful planet after so many years fantasizing about living here. From the moment the Nyvoran transport descended through the clouds and I got my first look at Hyderia's forests, mountains, and seas, my heart had pounded so hard that if it had burst out of my chest, I wouldn't have been the least surprised.

And when I'd stepped out of the transport, my first deep breath of Hyderian air had filled my heart, body, and soul with joy. The air was clean, the scents of the forest sweet and rich, and the sunshine warm and welcoming. The view from the roof alone had nearly left me speechless with awe. Even Ardruc's grim expression when the transport door opened hadn't detracted from my happiness.

Maybe I'd allowed myself a few moments at the top of the ramp to notice how gorgeous he was, and how tall, and the textures of his scaly red and orange skin, and how brightly the feathers on his wings shimmered in the sunlight. Even under a lab coat, his broad shoulders looked even better than they had in his introductory message. And that *tail*...

All things I shouldn't notice about a director of research, but I had anyway—at least until I started down the ramp and put them aside. Ardruc might be a beautiful dragon man, but he was the DR, and a notoriously difficult one to work with at that.

Walking up to him felt like approaching the base of a cliff, except a cliff face was more expressive.

I'd worked with Fortusians before, as well as other species who were larger than humans, so his size didn't intimidate me. Neither did his golden stare or the way he studied me as if I were a specimen needing to be categorized and stripped of all my secrets.

I'd prepared for a frosty reception. His introductory message had been terse at best. According to the rumor mill within academic circles, he wasn't a cheerful person, or even particularly friendly, and he had a habit of being condescending. Clashes with colleagues had led to frequent relocations before he'd come to Nova Cal two years ago. The station's isolation seemed to suit him, as he had no colleagues to alienate. He was rather notorious for the number of lab assistants who'd come and gone during that time. His current assistant, Dr. Rg, had lasted the longest at five months and counting.

Still, I'd hoped I could forge some kind of congenial working relationship—especially since there were only three of us at the station. I'd even greeted him with a Fortusian bow, having practiced during my trip.

Instead of appreciating my friendly gesture, he'd recoiled like I was a diseased, slime-covered Aphrasian eel, and my hopes of a convivial workplace all but evaporated in a blink.

After that, I couldn't get into the lift and away from him fast enough. Judging by how briskly he walked back toward the roof hatch, the feeling had been mutual.

I adjusted the straps of my heavy backpack and made a face. At least he hadn't tried to share the lift with us.

The lift doors opened, revealing an empty, silent hallway lined with doors leading to several laboratories.

As I wheeled my crates out into the hallway, a door slid aside down the hall and Ardruc emerged. According to the station schematics I'd studied, that door led to a stairway that accessed the roof.

This long corridor also housed the station's medical bay and labs designed for a variety of uses. The other two sections of the T-shaped station were the residential wing, with apartments, a shared kitchen and hydroponic greenhouse, and recreational area, and another research wing where the station's enormous imaging lab was located.

Ardruc strode toward me, his face an expressionless mask and eyes glowing golden. Well, I'd take indifference over open derision. Maybe he'd warm up to me in time.

Or maybe we'd just ignore each other and focus on our own work.

"Your lab is at the end of this hallway," he said, his tone flat. He gestured over his shoulder. "Lab Three should be more than sufficient for your work. My assistant works in Lab Two."

My eyes narrowed. Lab Three was the smallest of the labs—less than half the size of Lab One, where I assumed Ardruc worked. I'd also assumed his assistant worked in the same lab and I would be assigned Lab Two. Apparently not.

"As for your quarters," he continued as he passed by, "they are this way."

He smelled smoky, which wasn't unexpected given his dragon DNA. He also smelled of ozone and something else I couldn't quite place but that reminded me of sun-warmed grass.

With a growling Forux at my side, I followed Ardruc to the end of the corridor and turned right.

He stopped at the first door on the left. "Apartment four will be yours. I live in Unit One at the end of this corridor. My assistant, Dr. Rg, occupies Unit Two. The third unit is reserved for representatives from the Ministry and other short-term visitors."

I flexed my hand at my side and didn't reply at first. According to the station's schematics, Apartment Four was a fraction of the size of the other apartments—a single living area with a bed nook and a small bathroom.

I didn't have much in the way of belongings, as evidenced by the two crates and my backpack, and maybe that had factored into Ardruc's decision to give me this apartment. Or maybe I would have ended up in the smallest quarters on the station regardless.

The smallest, least-well equipped lab *and* an apartment so tiny it made my economical berth aboard the cruiser to Nyvor seem luxurious by comparison. At least I'd *chosen* a small cabin on the cruiser rather than waste valuable funding on a larger suite. I apparently did not get a say in where I'd live at Nova Cal.

I'd worked in smaller labs, though, and slept in far less hospitable accommodations. And by all the gods above and below, *I was on Hyderia.* I'd sleep outside under a tree and conduct my research in a secondhand portable lab pod if that was what it took. Being here was a dream come true. Not even the galaxy's least friendly DR could detract from that.

"Thank you," I said finally. "I'm sure this will be sufficient for my needs."

Ardruc's nostrils flared. He puffed little wisps of smoke from his nose, took several steps back, and coiled his tail around his right calf. "Good," he grated.

Did my scent offend him? Surely not. But the way he'd recoiled when I walked up to him…was that because of how I smelled? That didn't make much sense, but I didn't have a better explanation. And even if he didn't like my scent, I'd think he would be better at hiding that just out of professionalism or simple good manners. Then again, good manners didn't seem to be one of his top skills.

I took a step back and pretended I'd just wanted to lean against the wall.

His golden gaze bored into me. "Are you certain you can move your equipment from the roof to your lab without assistance?"

"As long as there's an antigrav sled I can use, I'll be fine." I tried to sound cheerful when I added, "I spend a lot of time in the field, so I'm used to being self-sufficient."

"You will find antigrav sleds in storage room 1C," he said, his voice brusque. "At your earliest opportunity, please study Nova Cal's lab procedures, including my policies on resource management, reporting schedules, data organization, specimen collection and storage, and field research." His gaze raked me from head to toe. "And requirements for appropriate lab attire."

I'd skimmed the station's lengthy and extremely detailed procedures during my journey and planned to read them more thoroughly tonight before bed. Everything I'd seen during my quick review had seemed fairly standard, but I'd apparently missed something.

My eyebrows shot up. "There's a dress code?"

"Indeed." He folded his hands behind his back and raised his chin, assuming a haughty pose that immediately got my hackles up. "Nova Cal is an isolated facility, so visiting researchers may be tempted to become lax in following procedures and maintaining appropriate levels of professionalism. I have found requiring professional attire, including the use of lab coats during working hours, helpful in ensuring optimal performance and adherence to all policies."

Ensuring optimal performance and adherence to all policies? Was he quoting from the procedures, or did he actually talk like this? I was betting on the latter.

I might have met a stuffier, more officious, and more pedantic director of research or lab supervisor during my studies and academic career...but for the life of me, I couldn't think of one.

Still, I hadn't given up on easing the tension. "That sounds very logical." I smiled up at him. "I generally make it my practice to adhere to all policies and procedures wherever I work, even dress codes."

His brows drew together. "I would hope so, Dr. Regis. Policies and procedures exist for a reason."

And with that, my latest attempt to lighten the atmosphere and have a friendly conversation fell flat.

Well, Dr. Ardruc Husiorithae wasn't going to ruin this momentous day, much less run me off Hyderia like he had so many others. And if he thought he could, he was about to find out how wrong he was.

I grabbed the handles of my crates. "I won't keep you, then. If I need anything while I get settled in, I'll let you know."

"Please do," he said, while his tone and the way his eyes tightened implied he preferred I didn't. He backed up another few steps. "I will be immersed in my own research in the imaging lab until 1800 hours, and later I will be retiring to my quarters for the evening, but I am available at any time via station comms."

In other words, don't come to his lab or apartment in person.

Fine. We didn't need to be friends to work in the same station. I had my own lab and he had his. And as long as we could pass each other in the hall and common areas with a nod and a greeting, that would be fine too. Not great, not pleasant, and not nearly as warm and welcoming as my time at most other facilities, but fine.

I was on Hyderia with Forux. Nothing else mattered but that.

Ardruc turned on his heel and strode in the opposite direction into the station's other research wing. At the door of what I thought was the imaging lab, he scanned his palm and disappeared inside without looking back.

Silence.

I scanned my palm to access my apartment. Slowly, with a quiet grinding noise, the door slid aside. Add a creaky door to my welcome party. Forux bared his teeth.

I squared my shoulders and wheeled my crates through the doorway.

The apartment was as small as I'd imagined, but it had a skylight and a large window that overlooked the forest. It was clean, it had a comm panel and small food and beverage synth system, and the attached bathroom's shower was actually nice and had both sonic and water-based cleansing systems.

And in truth it wasn't *that* much smaller than my quarters at Inga. It was just its relative size compared to the other apartments that made it seem tiny.

"This is good," I told Forux, who'd jumped onto the little bed to survey his new place of residence. I left my crates in the middle of the living area and crossed to the window. "Oh, wow—just look at this view."

A burst of shimmering red kora spread across the cobalt blue sky like an enormous spider or twenty-armed Barmian fillesquid unfurling its appendages.

I gasped and pressed my nose and hands to the window, my gaze glued to the sky as my first in-person sighting of the planet's most famous natural wonder faded. "Forux, look," I whispered. "It's so beautiful."

He jumped down from the bed and joined me at the window. I picked him up and looked skyward just in time to see another kora blossom—this one multi-colored and even larger than the red one. My skin pebbled with goosebumps as I gaped.

I knew very little about the korae other than they were enormous upper atmospheric plasma discharges hundreds of kilometers long and no one had yet discovered how they formed. No wonder Ardruc studied these phenomena.

I tried to imagine him gazing at korae in awestruck silence, but I couldn't picture the dour dragon man expressing amazement. Well, maybe in private he looked at them in awe and wonder, the way I gazed at mushrooms, lichen, mold, and all other fungi.

Usually I unpacked immediately, moved all my equipment into my lab and got everything set up, and then explored my new station and its environment. But this time, all I could think about was getting my feet onto Hyderian soil and finding my first native fungi. Everything else could wait.

I paused just long enough to open one of my travel cases and retrieve a change of footwear. I unfastened my boots, toed them off, and perched on the side of the bed.

The bed squeaked when I sat down. And it creaked when I bounced lightly. I sighed.

I pictured Ardruc standing in the hallway outside this apartment with his chin raised, his hands folded behind his back, and his impassive golden gaze fixed on me, knowing full well he was giving me the worst accommodations on the station. And for a moment, just a moment, I envisioned Forux biting him right on the tail.

Had I wronged Ardruc Husiorithae in another life? Or was this how he treated everyone? Maybe so, if he went through lab assistants at a rate that bordered on legendary.

Well, he'd just found someone who wouldn't be cowed either by his smug superiority or a tiny apartment with a creaky door and a squeaky bed not much better than a cot. My defiance had kept me alive on Aloris, so I wasn't likely to be defeated by a grumpy dragon man. He wanted me off Hyderia, and I was going to stay. And if he wanted me to be dispirited, he'd find me cheerful every time we saw each other.

Newly energized, I put on a pair of comfortable shoes I'd

purchased years ago on Pallasia, let out a sigh of contentment, and left my apartment with Forux at my side.

The exterior door at the end of the corridor was right next to apartment one, Ardruc's residence. The scanner beside the door glowed red, indicating it was locked. The other apartment scanners, including mine, were green, meaning they could be opened by anyone's palm scan. In my experience, it wasn't common practice to lock one's door inside a secure facility, much less when there were only three people not just living on the station, but on the entire planet.

It was a small thing, but it felt significant—and more than a little insulting. Ardruc Husiorithae must not think much of his colleagues if he felt the need to lock his door.

I scanned my palm to open the exterior door and stepped outside onto the wide deck. Nova Cal was built on a platform about five meters above the mountain slope. I took a moment to take in the view of the valley and forest, and then hurried down the stairs to ground level. Forux dashed ahead of me to run in circles in the clearing. My little arval had been cooped up at Inga Station and on cruisers for much too long. So had I, in fact.

When I stepped off the stairs and stood on Hyderian soil, all my joy and disbelief filled my eyes with tears. I let out a little sob.

I was here. I was on Hyderia. The dream I'd had since I was seventeen had come true. And a wonderful warmth filled my heart as if I already felt at home.

The sky filled with massive bursts of korae in every color imaginable. I gasped and craned my neck to look skyward. The timing was obviously a coincidence, but I was happy to pretend the planet was as joyous at my arrival as I was. Sharing my happiness, Forux bounced on his little legs, yipped excitedly, and took off to run full-speed around the thick columns that supported the elevated station.

As much as I yearned to sprawl out on the grass and watch the korae, I wanted to find my first Hyderian fungi.

Behind the stairs, I crouched and found beautiful blue-gray

fruticose lichen growing on the shadowed, undisturbed soil. I ran my fingertips over it, feeling all the textures of the cup-like stalks. They were familiar, and yet different. Unique to this world and so beautiful.

I should take a sample, study it, uncover all its secrets, and give it a name if it didn't already have one. But there would be plenty of time for that. Today, I just wanted to take it all in.

After all, I planned to stay on Hyderia for a long, long time.

CHAPTER 4
ARDRUC

Dr. Elena Regis was the second-worst thing to happen to me since my arrival on Hyderia. The first was a broken leg after a fall during an ill-advised flight in high winds.

No, Elena might be the worse of the two misfortunes. My leg had healed thanks to the facility's medical equipment. There did not seem to be a cure for Elena.

My headlong dive into researching the physiology of true mates certainly offered no hope. For all the wonders of Fortusian medicine and genetic engineering, no method of permanently suppressing or eliminating the call of a true mate existed. Treatments could reduce the intensity for brief periods for emergencies, but none were designed for long-term use, and had serious documented side effects if used for that purpose.

After all, why would there be a *cure* for a circumstance the people of my home planet considered the best and most wondrous aspect of being Fortusian?

I wanted to roar with frustration. Instead, I gripped the edge of the imaging lab's computer terminal so hard that my knuckles paled and the metal creaked. Smoke poured from my nose and my tail whipped through the air behind me.

The door to the corridor chimed. I snarled. Had I not asked Elena to contact me via comms rather than come to my lab and interrupt my work?

I glanced at my wristcomm. No, this was likely Dr. Rg returning from their rest period. The past two hours had gone by in the blink of an eye as I searched for some form of deliverance from my condition.

I cleared the record of my searches, called up the same data and holographic korae Rg and I had been analyzing earlier, and rose from my seat to meet my lab assistant at the door. They habitually used the chime to request entry. I did not like to be startled when lost in thought.

I smoothed my hair, shook out my feathers, folded my wings, and tried to regain some semblance of professionalism. Above all, I did not want Rg to see how much Elena's arrival had disquieted me. The very thought of my secret getting out made my stomach heave and my feathers stand on end.

But when the door slid aside, I found not my assistant but Elena herself waiting.

She stood in the middle of the corridor rather than right outside the door as if giving me space. Maybe she had noticed me keeping my distance earlier and assumed I expected her to do the same. At least I saw no sign she had any inkling of why I wanted to avoid being close to her. And why would she? Humans had no biological mating imperative like Fortusians did.

She had changed from her comfortable traveling clothes into a very utilitarian jumpsuit and styled her hair in a neat bun. And she had a sheen of sweat on her brow and was breathing hard. She must be moving her equipment from the roof to her lab.

Just the sight of her hit me like a punch to the sternum. And her rich, earthy scent, stronger than ever because of her exertion…it would have sent me to my knees if I had not locked them the moment I saw her.

On Fortusia, mates knelt before their beloved. The image of

falling to my knees before Elena filled me with yearning and revulsion. And a deep, uncharacteristic, almost incoherent rage.

Of all the research stations on all the worlds, why had Elena Regis come here?

I was a scientist. I did not believe in fate or cosmic plans or any such ephemeral nonsense. And yet here she was, beautiful and infuriating and full of illogical ideas, and at my lab door despite my request that she use comms rather than approach me in person.

"I'm so sorry to bother you," she said before I had a chance to speak. Her expression was earnest and apologetic. "But my antigrav sled stopped working right outside the lift. I need to transfer my equipment onto a different one to finish moving everything into my lab and there are large crates I can't lift." She made a face. "If you have a moment, can you give me a hand?"

With effort, I unclenched my jaw. "There are several sets of antigrav nodes in storage room 1C that affix to the bottom corners of a crate to make it possible to move easily. I believe you will find them and the controllers in storage unit nineteen on the second shelf from the bottom." I studied her. "Which I could have told you if you had contacted me via comms." The second half of that sentence, *as I asked you to do*, hung in the air.

At least she had the grace to look abashed. "I'm sorry. I thought I'd walk over and ask for help since I was just around the corner." She peered over my shoulder before returning her attention to me. And she gave me, of all things, a bright smile. "And honestly, I also wanted to get a peek inside the imaging lab and tell you I witnessed my first korae earlier when I did a little exploring outside." Her eyes lit up. "They are *so gorgeous*—"

I did not want to engage in a discussion about the beauty of korae, or about anything else. I had thought I made that clear enough in our earlier conversation. Apparently not.

"Dr. Regis," I cut in. "I am very busy. Is there anything else you need?"

Frustration and annoyance flashed in her eyes before she took a deep breath and let it out.

"No," she said finally. "I'll go look for the antigrav nodes. And if I have any other problems, I'll use the comms to let you know." She glanced at the holographic korae tendrils over my shoulder again. "I'm sure the lab can analyze the korae in every way, but nothing's quite as good as really *seeing* them, is it?"

Despite my determination to keep this interaction brief, I frowned. "*See*, as in from the ground and with the naked eye?"

"Yes." As if lit from within, Elena nearly glowed with excitement. "It's the same way for me with fungi. I can take a sample to the lab, subject it to every test and analysis, and wring every scientific secret out of its cells, but there's nothing like seeing lichen growing on a stone in the forest or mushrooms on a fallen tree. You have to *see* them and listen to their natural environment to understand them and how they came into being."

I had never heard a scientist say anything less scientific or look so starry-eyed when discussing their subject of study. I felt quite certain I had not managed to keep my disdain off my face, but she seemed undeterred.

"Korae are breathtakingly beautiful," Elena continued. "I understand how they became your life's work." Her mouth quirked. "If my heart didn't already belong to fungi, I could see myself becoming an atmospheric scientist so I could spend my days studying something so miraculous."

I bristled at the implication that korae were *miraculous* rather than a well-studied and thoroughly analyzed scientific phenomenon. Calling something *miraculous* was only a few steps short of calling it *magical*.

"Korae are not miraculous," I said, and her smile vanished. I tried not to notice how the flash of irritation and hurt in her eyes and the way her mouth turned down made my chest ache and my skin prickle.

"They may seem so to a mycologist or someone outside the

scientific community," I added, "but they are very similar to upper-atmospheric plasma discharges observed on a number of worlds. The aspects that make them unique to this planet, and the fact we do not yet fully understand what creates them, do not make them inexplicable."

"I didn't say they were inexplicable." Her expression hardened. "Something can be quantifiable *and* marvelous. Isn't that the point of science? To see both?"

And therein lay our most significant difference, as I had already gleaned from reading her file and some of her published work. Elena's mind worked completely differently from mine. And yet my body believed she was my true mate. Science would be able to explain why if I consulted a physiologist back on Fortusia, but I had no desire to do so. I only wanted to be rid of her so I could work and live in peace.

"No, I do not think so." I took a step back. "Science is about data, analysis, and the search for theories that lead to conclusions and facts. Marvels and miracles and magic are something else entirely."

"What drives us in the search, though?" she challenged me, hands on hips. Her eyes sparkled as if she was actually enjoying our debate. "Data and analysis, of course, but we also need curiosity, imagination, and inspiration. Gut feelings. The chase of the wondrous and marvelous leads us to breakthroughs."

I shook my head. "Your thought process differs greatly from mine. I am grateful our subjects of study do not overlap. I would not want..." Very uncharacteristically, I let my voice trail off.

She raised her eyebrows. "Go ahead and finish the sentence, Dr. Husiorithae. Don't be shy about sharing your opinion now."

Shyness had nothing to do with my decision to truncate what I had intended to say. Why I had hesitated, I was not exactly sure. Maybe the knowledge I was as unlikely to change her mind as she was to change mine, or an uncharacteristic reluctance to risk insulting a colleague.

I gritted my teeth. "I have valuable work I need to be doing, Dr.

Regis. And no time to argue about the fundamentals of scientific inquiry."

"Let me guess," she said, as if I had not just overtly tried yet again to bring an end to this ridiculous conversation. "You're glad we study different things because you wouldn't want my way of thinking to influence yours." She smiled, but without humor. "I suppose it wouldn't do any good to point out we've published the same number of articles, have roughly the same kinds of accolades, and both achieved the seemingly impossible and earned permission to research here."

"What are you suggesting?" I frowned. "What relevance do our qualifications have to our discussion?"

"I'm suggesting there are many approaches to the kind of work we do, and I'm not the only person who thinks so," Elena said. "And I have the audacity to think that as living beings we should continually change and evolve and learn to do new things in new ways. Otherwise, we run the risk of never finding what it is we're looking for, whether that's new phyla of eukaryotic organisms or why the korae of Hyderia exist in atmospheric conditions that should make them impossible."

I was framing my retort when familiar footsteps echoed down the hall. Datapad in hand, Dr. Rg was approaching from the direction of their apartment, their eyes moving between Elena and me and expression quizzical.

I was suddenly aware that the feathers in my hair and on my wings were ruffled and my tail was twitching incessantly. I stretched my wings, settled them behind my back, and curled my tail around my leg once more.

"Dr. Rg," I said, making my tone very formal. "As you see, Dr. Elena Regis has arrived."

"Honored to meet you," Rg said, giving Elena a small bow. "I am Makato Rg. I look forward to discussing your recent publication on the prevalence of acidophilic filamentous fungi in recovering ecosystems. I find extremophilic fungi particularly interesting as well. I understand you recently worked on Aloris."

"I did," she said with a smile. Her joy grated on my nerves like a sandstorm. "I'm happy to discuss it anytime."

She glanced at my stony gaze and clenched fists, and her smile faded.

"Maybe later this evening," she continued, turning back to Rg. "Or tomorrow evening after you've finished your work with Dr. Husiorithae for the day."

"I look forward to it." Rg bowed again. "Welcome to Nova Cal, Dr. Regis."

"Thank you. And please call me Elena." With a wave, she headed in the direction of storage room 1C. "Later," she said cheerfully before she rounded the corner and disappeared from sight.

I stepped aside as Rg entered the imaging lab. Only then did it occur to me that they would notice I had not continued working on the korae analysis during their rest period as I normally would have done.

"A new arrival causes significant disruption and unfortunately reduces productivity," I said as Rg took their customary place next to the computer terminal. "I hope Dr. Regis immerses herself in her own studies and does not make a habit of visiting our labs during working hours."

"I am sure she will," Rg said, their tone neutral. They folded their hands behind their back and studied the holographic tendrils. "I am very interested in her research and look forward to hearing about it." They glanced at me and hummed. "After our scheduled work hours, of course."

What possible interest could Rg have in fungi? Their comments indicated more than a passing knowledge of the subject. Then again, what they did on their own time was no concern of mine.

I puffed smoke out my nostrils in irritation and to clear Elena's scent as best I could.

What a ridiculous human, watching korae from the ground with the naked eye and talking about *miraculous* things and *chasing the wondrous and marvelous* as scientific methods.

I snorted softly. Her thought process was even more undisciplined and unscientific than I had expected after reading her work. Even if she were not my true mate, I would want little or nothing to do with her.

Already it was clear she would be a distraction at best and a torment at worst. And I had experienced quite enough torment already in my life. I wanted peace. I wanted my peace *back*. The only way to accomplish that would be for Elena to leave.

According to my research, once she was gone, in time my body would readjust. There would always be an ache, but I could learn to live with that. Better to suffer an ache than sacrifice my principles and ability to reason, or worst of all, lose my place on Hyderia.

Yes, that was the only solution I could accept.

Regardless of any discomfort it might cause me, I must employ relentless, carefully calculated antagonism that stopped short of causing Elena to complain to the Ministry or her lab supervisor back on Fyloria. It would not be easy, but it must be done—preferably within the next few weeks or a month at most.

I puffed smoke again and picked up my datapad.

After all, I did not have a reputation for being nearly impossible to work with for nothing.

CHAPTER 5
ELENA

FOUR MONTHS LATER

The Nova Cal research station was so isolated, it might as well be alone in the universe.

Even so, I loved everything about the tiny and underfunded facility…everything, that was, except its director of research, who I would have ejected into space without a second thought given half a chance.

Luckily, my research required me to travel deep into the forest and away from the station for days or even a week at a time. Losing myself in the beauty and wonder of the wilderness filled my soul with peace—and healed old wounds no one saw or felt but me.

Well, and Forux.

My little companion leapt onto my shoulder, balanced himself, and growled. He never liked to sense my thoughts turn dark, especially in the forest, where he and I felt most at home.

I leaned my head against his soft purple fur to feel him rumble. "Sorry, friend. You're right: I can't be sad today. We're going back with a lot of good specimens. No time to think about you-know-who."

Forux curled his lip to show his teeth. He didn't need to understand my words to know who I meant. My emotions told him exactly who had invaded my thoughts five hundred kilometers from the station.

Forux growled again, louder this time.

"Okay, okay." I scratched his head. "Let's get packed up. We need to be in the air in less than two hours or we won't get to the station before dark."

He jumped down off my shoulder and stretched as I contemplated the dozen containers spread out across the blanket I was sitting on. Not exactly a scientific way to look over the specimens I'd collected during this three-day trip, but I didn't feel particularly scientific at the moment. I wanted to examine my prizes with the same kind of wonder I'd felt exploring as child on Fyloria.

Back then, I'd wandered the forest endlessly, marveling at the richness of variety of fungi and dreaming of what other species existed in the universe. Those were joy-filled days—

—right up until I returned home with my prizes to face my father's distracted attention and mother's utter disdain.

I sighed.

Forget intrusive thoughts about Director of Research Dr. Ardruc Husiorithae from five hundred kilometers away; my mother could ruin my mood from halfway across the galaxy.

Before Forux had a chance to growl at me again for my dark thoughts, I picked up my most significant find of the trip: a specimen I suspected might be an entirely new order of fungi. I wouldn't know for sure until I got back to my lab, but the equipment I'd brought with me had classified it as such based on its apparently eccentric oospores.

More than that, though, this mushroom was truly lovely, with two intertwined light blue stems, dark lines that looked like veins, dark blue fronds around the edges of the net-like cap, and another splotch of dark blue in the center of the cap.

After carefully removing it from its bed and putting it in a specimen container for scanning and analysis, I'd immediately taken out my datapad and stylus and drawn it by hand from various angles so I could really marvel at its beauty.

The rich soil, humidity, and minerals of Hyderia's thick temperate forests made it a mycologist's dream. The variety and colors of the mushrooms, lichen, mold, and other fungi transformed me back into that wide-eyed child who'd thought every specimen of fungi she found was the most perfect and beautiful sight in the galaxy. That deep contentment was one of the main reasons I'd fought so hard for permission and funding to study here, despite Ardruc's unfriendliness.

"If this *is* a new order of fungi, I plan to name it after you," I told Forux. "*Basiforuximycota*. Would you like that?"

Forux looked up at the sky as if wondering why I wasn't hurrying to start walking back to the transport. He knew I didn't like to fly after dark, even at relatively low altitudes. I only had to walk a little over a kilometer, but the sharply uphill journey cut through dense forest with no path and would be slow going.

I packed up my specimens, blanket, and canteen, settled my pack on my back, and followed the directions on my wristcomm with Forux riding on my shoulder. His little legs struggled to keep up over the untamed forest floor so I usually carried him for at least part of the walk.

The hike might be strenuous, especially with a heavy pack, but it was a beautiful one. The thick trees in this hemisphere had turned spectacularly blue-green with the arrival of autumn. The air was cool but wouldn't get cold until the suns went down. On the forest floor, the only sounds were those of birds, creaking branches, and rustling leaves. Perfection.

Trees covered ninety-eight percent of all land masses on Hyderia. The planet was a preserve protected by its sister planet, Nyvor. Three hundred years ago, the Nyvorans had nearly laid waste to the entire surface of their homeworld before they realized the error of their ways and embraced conservation. They kept Hyderia as pristine and unspoiled as their own planet had been once upon a time and left it populated solely by its indigenous wildlife.

The Nyvoran Ministry of Natural Sciences had built six research stations on Hyderia: three located throughout the northern hemisphere and three in the south. At the moment, the only active station was Nova Cal.

The Ministry didn't make it easy for anyone to come here, even scientists. It had taken me well over a standard year to obtain permission for a six-month stay and the promise I would be considered to extend that stay in six-month increments as long as I shared my findings with the Ministry as well as my university lab back home on Fyloria.

Every step on Hyderian soil was a privilege, and even now, nearly four months after my arrival, I didn't forget that. I'd already put in my application to extend my stay. With any luck, my previous discoveries and research would make it any easy decision for the head of Hyderian Natural Sciences on Nyvor. If not, surely this new order of fungi—if indeed that was what I had—would tip the scales in my favor.

I took a short break about two-thirds of the way to the tiny mountainside clearing where I had landed one of Nova Cal's two small, two-person transports. While Forux explored the undergrowth, I sat on a fallen tree to drink water and eat a nutrition bar designed to provide energy and ease the strain from the hike.

Places to land any size of aircraft were few and far between on such a heavily forested planet, so I took advantage of those I found. Usually I ended up landing where I could and then hiking hours or even days to the location I wanted to visit, carrying my equipment, shelter, and supplies on my back. I used to use an antigrav sled, but decided the safer bet was to pack light and carry what I could rather than rely on tech that left me stranded more than once on a mountainside with a full day's walk ahead of me and a pile of equipment and supplies sitting on the ground.

Little growls and rustling in the undergrowth drew my attention.

"Come on, Forux," I called, capping my canteen and stowing it in my pack before I hopped off the tree. "We need to get going."

My companion emerged from the bushes, wiggling backward and dragging a short branch.

"What do you have there?" I asked, peering at the branch.

Forux wagged his tails and grinned. I had no idea whether he understood my happiness at finding fungi or not, but maybe he wanted to get in on the foraging in his own way.

"Did you find a perfect stick?" I chuckled. "Okay, you can bring it."

With a happy yip, Forux carried the branch in his teeth and trotted ahead of me as I made my way up the mountainside. I tried not to look at my wristcomm except to check my direction because the blue dot representing me seemed to take an eternity to get close to the green one that indicated the location of the transport.

Finally, through the trees, I caught a glimpse of cobalt blue sky. I heaved a sigh of relief. "Good news, Forux. We're almost—"

A glint of bright, crackling red in my peripheral vision made me turn my head. My footing gave way under my left boot, my ankle bent with an agonizing crunch, and down I went.

Trees, rocks, and leaf-covered soil spun around me as I tumbled down the steep slope. A protective emergency force field formed a cocoon, activated automatically by the fall sensor in my wristcomm.

Finally, I hit a large rock, ending my out-of-control tumble. The force field cushioned the impact, then crackled one last time and faded.

Oh, gods—*ouch*. I whimpered.

I'd ended up lying on my side against the boulder that had stopped my fall. Before the force field activated, I'd bounced off enough rocks to feel bruised all over. At the moment, my primary concern was my ankle. I already felt it swelling inside my boot. The white-hot agony made nausea surge and I let out a cry of pain.

Whining, Forux sniffed my face, and then passed his keen nose over my body before he got to my ankle. He whined again.

"Yeah, it's broken," I grated out, trying to breathe deeply and slowly so I could think clearly. "It hurts, Forry."

All four of his ears went flat against his head. I only ever called him Forry when things were bad.

With another whimper, I unfastened the straps of my pack, set it aside, and rolled to my back, my chest heaving. Above me, the thick foliage blotted out every bit of sky. Suddenly the forest canopy felt a little less beautiful and more ominous.

My travel-sized medical kit couldn't heal a broken bone relatively quickly like the medical bay back at the research station, but I could at least stabilize my ankle and dull my pain in the meantime.

Of all the rotten, rotten luck.

No, I couldn't blame this on bad luck. My tumble was my fault for not watching where I put my feet. I knew better than to get distracted on uneven terrain. But what the hells had I glimpsed from the corner of my eye? What could possibly make that bright red glimmer?

It had sparkled or crackled like energy, but there was nothing artificial out here in the wilderness. If anything, the glint had reminded me of a tiny version of Hyderia's spectacular upper-atmospheric korae, but obviously it wasn't that. Those massive electrical discharges took place forty kilometers or more above the ground, and they covered many square kilometers. They weren't single tendrils a meter or less in length.

The agony in my ankle made it hard to think. Every movement sent sizzles of pain through my lower left leg, but I managed to sit up against the boulder and unseal my pack. Forux lay next to me and put his chin on my leg.

"Thanks, friend," I said, scratching him on the top of his head and behind all his ears. His tails wagged a little, but his furrowed brow made it clear no amount of scritches was going to make him feel better.

First things first: check the condition of the specimen containers. One by one, with trembling hands I took them out of the pack to make sure the stasis generators that preserved their contents were running normally. The containers themselves were damn near indestructible, but the generators weren't. Only when all twelve checked out—especially my prize *Basiforuximycota*—did I breathe a shaky sigh of relief.

That done, I dug out my medkit, unsealed an analgesic transdermal patch, and pulled up my left pant leg to slap it on my bare skin. Technically I could have put the patch anywhere, but it made me feel better, at least psychologically, to put it directly on or close to the source of pain.

Within just a few heartbeats, the painkiller flooded my body and swept away the agony. I leaned the back of my head against the boulder and groaned again, this time in bliss. All the gods above and below, bless the J'Norans. They'd developed some of the galaxy's deadliest weapons, but also pioneered cutting-edge medicine, especially triage care. This powerful analgesic tended to make me nauseous, but I'd take that over the agony.

The absence of pain allowed me to remove my boot and wind a bone stabilization wrap around my swollen and discolored ankle and foot. As soon as I sealed it, the wrap activated, forming a thick, padded brace with a hard exterior I would be able to walk on. A sizzle of pain made me suck in air through my teeth before it faded thanks to the analgesic.

I'd only fallen about ten meters down the mountainside, but from here, it looked like a kilometer. By the time I limped to the transport, I'd have little to no chance of making it back to the research station before the suns set. Damn it to all the hells.

My wristcomm beeped. The signal was a transmission relayed by the transport. My stomach, already unsettled by the fall and pain, lurched. Only one person would be contacting me this way.

Part of me wanted to ignore him, but there was a good chance he'd gotten some kind of alert about my fall and was responding. As much as I disliked him—hated him, in fact—he was Nova Cal's director of research. I didn't technically answer to him, but he *was* in charge of the station. And if I didn't answer, he might take it upon himself to come check on me, lest I be unconscious or deceased at the bottom of a ravine. Not that he would care except it would require him to write some reports.

The device beeped again.

I cleared my throat and tapped the band on my wrist. "This is Elena." At least my voice didn't shake.

"Dr. Regis." Ardruc's greeting was as brusque as always. Maybe I'd half expected him to at least sound slightly concerned, but I should have known better. "I received an alert that you experienced a moderate fall."

He didn't ask if I was all right, or even what happened. He simply stated a fact and then waited for me to explain my *moderate fall*. Gods, didn't he ever tire of being awful?

Forux curled his lip and growled. Which Ardruc had probably heard.

"My ankle is broken, but stabilized," I gritted out. "I'm on my way back to the transport. I'll send you my ETA once I'm in the air."

"What caused the fall?" Still brusque, still as clinical as a primitive computer. "For my notes."

For his *notes*. My fists clenched.

Should I tell him about the strange red glint and how much it resembled the phenomena he studied? Almost as quickly as I'd thought about it, I scoffed. Imagine the scorn I'd receive for suggesting some kind of upper-atmospheric electrical discharge could manifest as a tiny tendril deep in the forest.

The alternative explanation was almost as painful, though. "I lost my footing on a steep slope," I said, wishing I had the energy to come up with a convincing and less embarrassing lie. "Nothing too interesting. Loose rock, probably."

"Noted. Please keep me apprised of your flight status." The signal ended.

"Big, pompous, winged asshole," I grumbled.

With a groan, I struggled to stand using the boulder for support. "I wish you were venomous," I told Forux. "For that matter, I wish *I* was venomous. But then I'd have to get close enough to him to bite him. No thanks."

Forux yipped in what sounded like agreement.

Cursing and bracing myself on the boulder, I made it to my feet. My first order of business was to find a sturdy fallen branch for a walking stick. Luckily, I had my choice within easy limping distance.

I found one about as long as I was tall, broke off the twigs, and held it out for Forux's inspection. "My turn to find a perfect stick, I guess," I said wryly.

He sniffed my choice and wagged his tails. I took that as approval.

My pack probably weighed just under twenty kilograms. Heavy enough when I didn't have a broken ankle, but now…ugh. If only I could lessen the weight and leave everything but the specimens behind.

Nyvoran law stated that nothing could be left behind during field research. Maybe I could get away with it and come back later for the rest, but I didn't want to risk my approval status or my renewal application. Nothing to do but get the pack on my back and start climbing.

As I settled it on my shoulders and fastened the straps across my upper chest and around my waist, Forux circled my legs repeatedly. I didn't need to be empathic like him to understand how worried he was. So for his sake and mine, I took a couple of deep breaths.

"One step at a time," I told myself aloud. "Just like everything else you've done. One step at a time."

I glanced at my wristcomm's navigational screen to ensure I was headed in the right direction, planted my walking stick firmly, braced myself, and took a step.

With Forux at my side and my stick for support, I climbed the slope, following the trail of disturbed ground that showed where I'd fallen and on alert for anything I might trip on or that could cause me to lose my footing. At least the painkillers and bone-stabilization wrap did their job and no one was around to watch me cursing and limping. I kept my eyes on the ground, ensuring each step I took was a secure one.

Every few minutes I paused for a quick rest and scanned my surroundings. No sign of the red glint, whatever it had been. It hadn't been my imagination or a trick of the light, but I had no idea what it *could* be.

Ardruc was the scientist specializing in upper-atmospheric cold plasma phenomena, not me, but I'd spent many nights on the roof of the Nova Cal station watching the korae in awe. To my eyes, what I'd seen looked like a tiny kora. Or maybe a ground-level static form of electrical discharge? But I'd been exploring the forests on Hyderia for months and never seen one. Others had spent years and even decades here and never reported a sighting of such a thing. And surely if it existed, Ardruc would know.

"I know what I saw, though," I grumbled aloud.

I argued with myself—silently and out loud—all the way to the transport. If nothing else, it helped keep me from thinking about my ankle or Ardruc. What Forux thought of my muttering, I couldn't tell. He stayed in front of me carrying his prize stick.

When I finally emerged from the tree line, nothing had ever looked so beautiful as the transport and the clear sky above it— well, besides my intact specimen of *Basiforuximycota*.

The late afternoon sunlight was waning rapidly as the suns set. Even at the transport's top speed, I had more than an hour of flight time once I was airborne. Staying the night and waiting until morning was not an option. I needed to get back to the station to heal my broken ankle.

I opened the transport's door using my wristcomm. "In you go," I told Forux, and set my pack on the floor of the little two-person transport. "Let's go home."

Well, not that Nova Cal was *home*, but it was the closest to that we had. I'd never had any real emotional attachment to any place I'd lived, really. My research took me across Alliance space and I rarely stayed more than half a standard year on any planet or moon.

Hyderia was the first planet I'd lived on besides my home planet of Fyloria where I felt even an inkling of belonging. This world was wondrous and beautiful, from its korae to its fungi. I could see myself staying here for longer than anywhere else—despite the presence of Dr. Ardruc Husiorithae.

Once Forux jumped inside, I sat in the transport's open doorway to apply a new analgesic patch. I didn't want the old one to wear off during the flight. Flying was nerve-wracking enough for me as it was. The fact it was a requirement for my research and I had to pilot a transport all the time didn't lessen my anxiety.

I stuffed the empty patch packet into my pack, stowed the pack in a cargo bin, and started to get to my feet.

A glint of shimmering bright red shone through the darkness of the forest, maybe ten meters from where I sat. I stilled.

It looked like a thread of a kora, all right, or a tendril of plasma, but only about a meter or so long and hovering vertically off the ground. What. The. *Hells?*

A moment later, the little kora darted away and disappeared into the forest.

My hand went to Forux's warm, furry head. "Did you see that?" I whispered, scanning the trees for another glimpse of the red kora.

Forux chuffed quietly, his sharp gaze and alert ears fixed on the trees. We watched for nearly ten more minutes, but nothing stirred. The forest remained dark and silent.

Finally, I gave up and shut the outer door. As I started departure procedures, Forux stood on the co-pilot's seat, staring out the front window with his front paws on the instrument panel. He growled at the setting suns.

"I know, I know. We're going." I powered up the engine and engaged the liftoff thrusters.

Two minutes later, I had the transport in the air and on its way to Nova Cal. I sent my flight information to Ardruc and increased my speed, racing nightfall to get to relative safety.

During the journey, my thoughts were full, but not of my prize *Basiforuximycota*. Instead, I imagined impossible kora that despite every bit of logic in my body I thought had darted into the trees to hide from me. If that was true, what looked like kora wasn't just plasma—it was *alive*.

I glanced at Forux. He laid all his ears flat against his head, his brow furrowed.

"Me too, friend," I said, with a white-knuckled grip on the flight controls. "Me too."

CHAPTER 6
ARDRUC

Everything about Elena Regis set my teeth on edge, from how she hummed as she worked to the dreamy way she gazed at everything from fungi specimens to clouds and falling leaves and even the massive upper-atmospheric phenomena I had dedicated my life to studying.

I knew her credentials—knew every detail of them, in fact—and had read every paragraph of her published work. She was not a true scientist. Her mind did not work like mine. It was not clockwork. It was a tangled patch of forest undergrowth: wild, undisciplined, and uncontained. Personally and professionally, she was utterly incomprehensible to me.

So why the hells did my hearts race and my blood ignite whenever I caught her scent? Why did I *need* her as much as I needed air to breathe and food to eat?

And how could I get her to leave the station permanently so I could focus on my work again?

The days she spent in the field were a welcome respite and a chance to regain my equilibrium. I dreaded her returns. No, that was not quite true. I both dreaded them and yearned for them, and truly I could not determine which emotion dominated the other.

Still, I chose to be waiting on the station's rooftop landing pad when Elena returned from her foraging trip. She had reported being injured. Perhaps she needed assistance getting down to the medical bay. I might prefer to keep my distance, but the title of director of research came with responsibilities to those who lived and worked here. There was no one else to help her but me. Dr. Rg had departed a month ago, having had their fill of my foul moods.

The small transport arrived after nightfall. I stayed well clear of the landing dampers and thrusters until the engines shut off. A few moments later, the transport's side hatch raised, revealing Elena and her faithful companion. Forux spotted me first and, as usual, growled.

Elena's left ankle and foot were encased in an emergency medical wrap. Her dirty jumpsuit, a dozen cuts and bruises, and the leaves in her hair testified to the extent of her fall. The sight of her injuries and her pallor made my stomach hurt.

She slid her backpack to the doorway at the top of the ramp and looked up as I approached. Clearly exasperated, she blew hair that had come loose from her braid out of her face. Her long hair seemed entirely impractical given her love of field work.

Usually her eyes sparkled more than a true scientist's would, as if she found more joy than quantifiable knowledge in fungi. I saw no sign of that sparkle at the moment. Instead, I read profound disquiet in her eyes and the set of her jaw. Because of her injury, or her late arrival? Or for another reason?

Using a tree branch for support, Elena straightened in the doorway. "Is there a problem?" she asked, her tone icy and more than a little strained.

"Do you need assistance?" I stopped at the bottom of the ramp. "This ramp is very steep, and I am sure you are in pain."

Unlike me, Elena rarely hid her emotions under a clinician's calm façade. A myriad of reactions crossed her face: irritation, confusion, anger...and then her eyes narrowed, as if she suspected my motives for offering assistance.

"I made it halfway up a mountain," she said shortly. "I'm sure I can get down a little ramp."

I found myself caught between two polar reactions to her dismissal: the desire to return to my lab and leave her to struggle, and the need to carry her to the medical bay and tend to her injury, though she was clearly capable of walking.

With effort, I unclenched my jaw and stilled my swishing tail. "I offer to carry your pack, then. Surely that would be the logical choice."

Her glare did not diminish, but her shoulders slumped, as if she had resigned herself to agreeing.

"Fine," she said with a sigh. And then, grudgingly, she added, "Thank you."

When I picked up her pack, I estimated its weight to be nearly twenty kilograms. That was nothing to me, but twenty kilos was more than twenty percent of her body weight. She had climbed a steep slope wearing this on her back with a broken ankle? My chest rumbled. Forux growled again.

"He'll be careful with it," Elena said soothingly. Apparently she had misinterpreted Forux's snarl for concern that I might drop her pack or heave it over the edge of the roof out of spite.

Elena bit her lip and started down the ramp, steadying herself with the branch. Every time she wobbled, my fingers twitched and my feathers ruffled.

She let out a sigh when she reached the bottom of the ramp. "Back on solid ground," she murmured.

To my sensitive nose, Elena's familiar scent was tinged with the sharp, metallic notes of pain and unhappiness. My wings fluttered uneasily. I stilled them and folded them behind my back.

Slowly, we made our way from the landing pad to the lift entrance. Forux walked between Elena and I, watching me warily for reasons I did not understand. I had never posed a physical threat to her, but perhaps his concern was heightened by her injury.

"Was your trip successful?" I asked.

Elena glanced at me. Her jaw was set, and she was doing her best to disguise a wince with each step.

"I don't know what you would consider successful," she said, her tone still frosty. After a beat, she added, "I may have discovered a new order of fungi. I'll know for sure when I get it to the lab." Despite her obvious discomfort, her eyes lit up with a hint of that familiar sparkle. "It's absolutely beautiful."

Fungi were orders of magnitude less interesting to me than the korae phenomena of Hyderia, but as a scientist I understood both the importance of the find and her pride in the discovery.

Elena had applied to the Nyvoran government to extend her stay at the station. Yet another discovery on top of those she had already made would increase the likelihood of their approval. The prospect both thrilled me and filled me with despair.

"Congratulations on your find," I said, my tone carefully neutral. I activated the roof doors. As they slid aside, revealing the lift's interior, I added, "Or a conditional congratulations, pending closer examination of the specimen."

"Thank you." She hobbled into the lift. Forux followed, and I entered last, ducking through the doorway.

As the doors closed, I turned to place my palm on the scanner that would admit us into the facility. My wing brushed Elena's arm. "Pardon me," I said.

She moved to the opposite side of the lift. Forux put himself between us once more.

"This thing wasn't designed for Fortusians, was it?" Elena forced a ghost of a smile. "Or at least, not for a Fortusian plus anyone else."

"It was not," I agreed.

She blinked at me. Only when the lift began its descent did I realize that was one of the very few times we had agreed on anything.

When the doors opened, she let out another, much deeper sigh and stepped out into the corridor.

"Thank all the gods above and below, it's good to be back. I'm off to the medical bay to put myself back together." She held out her hand. "I'll take my pack now."

The most logical thing for me to do would be to hand it over and return to my own lab, where a mountain of data from last night's atmospheric events awaited my examination.

Instead, I found myself gesturing in the direction of the medical bay. "I will accompany you." At her frown, I said, "It is not too great an imposition to ensure you have everything you need."

Truly, I was not sure which of us was more bemused at my offer to help.

"Suit yourself," she said finally.

In the medical bay, Elena limped to the diagnostic bed. It lowered automatically to accommodate her height. She leaned her walking stick against the wall and sat with a sigh of relief. Forux jumped onto the bed and sat beside her. She scratched his head.

I set her pack on the counter and picked up a medical scanner. I located the osteorepair device and an analgesic patch and brought all three items to the bed.

"Thanks for your help." She gestured at the bed to her right and reached for the medical wrap on her lower left leg. "You can just put them there." Her tone was dismissive.

When I hesitated, she frowned. "I'm fine from here. You've already gone well above and beyond your duties as the DR. When my ankle's healed, I'll let you know so you can add that to your *notes*."

The bitterness in her statement and the way her jaw clenched revealed how deeply my choice of words in my earlier communication had upset her. I very nearly flinched and had to still my facial expression to hide my reaction.

I wanted to stay and ensure she recovered from her injury, but I could not tell her why without giving myself away.

I had so carefully avoided allowing my concern about her fall to show in my tone or words. I *wanted* her to remain alienated from me, did I not? I *wanted* her to be angry so perhaps she would retract her application to extend her stay and return to Fyloria or leave for some other planet to study its fungi.

I did not want to be distracted by her beauty or brilliance, or give in to the yearning in my hearts. I had work to do. But with every day that passed, my resolve fractured more. When she was within reach and her scent wrapped around me, I felt damn near helpless to stand firm against a call that went deeper than my bones.

I focused on the harshness of her tone instead of the way pain shone in her eyes because her suffering made me irrationally angry and protective.

"Please keep me informed on your status," I said. "My practice is to keep detailed and complete notes."

"So is mine." Elena picked up the medical scanner, calibrated it for a human, and passed it over her left ankle. She held up the scanner's screen for my inspection. "Simple fracture of the lateral malleolus. A half-hour's work for the osteorepair device. The medical wrap did its job."

"Noted." I took a few steps back. "I will return to my lab, then."

"Well, all that pretty korae isn't going to analyze itself." Elena hesitated, as if she wanted to add something, but then apparently changed her mind. "Enjoy your data," she said instead. She reached for the sealed seam of the medical wrap, then glared at me. "Do you mind?"

Removing the wrap would cause her pain, and apparently she did not want me to be present. I opened my mouth to remind her she could apply another analgesic patch, but she knew that—and I doubted my advice was wanted. She might not want to take another dose. For all its benefits, that particular medicine sometimes caused nausea in humans.

So I turned on my heel and left.

I was halfway to my lab when her stifled cry of pain drifted down the corridor. My entire body shuddered. I stumbled into the wall, bracing myself with one hand, then leaned against its cold surface to catch my breath. The draw of a true mate bond had been bad enough when she was not hurt. Now every part of me wanted me to run to her and provide comfort and care.

Something new burned in my chest, near my hearts: a strange, warm vibration that tried to rise into my throat and become a vocal sound. This was my coo, a song I instinctually made to comfort my mate. I had never made it before because I had not had reason to do so. Elena's injury had caused yet another change to my physiology.

I clenched my jaw to hold in the song. A bolt of pain made me grimace. The discomfort and urge faded, leaving a hollow ache. Finally, with effort, I continued my walk to Lab One. I hoped Elena could not hear my uneven gait.

I could try to isolate myself as much as possible, but I could not delude myself into believing that was a solution. I would have no peace until I gave in to what my body and soul wanted most...or Elena left Hyderia for good.

CHAPTER 7

ELENA

Ardruc had stepped foot in Lab Three only a handful of times in the four months I had lived at Nova Cal.

And given how immersed he was in his own work and the frostiness of our conversation after my return with a broken ankle, I fully expected not to see him for at least a couple of days. Judging by the relaxed way Forux had sprawled on the floor at my feet, he and I were both relieved at the prospect of quiet, uninterrupted work time.

So when the door to Lab Three *whooshed* open mid-morning the day after I got back from my ill-fated research trip, Forux raised his head, growled, and flattened his ears. If I had ears and vocal cords like his, I would have done the same.

Familiar heavy footsteps crossed the floor and stopped halfway to my desk.

"Why did you access images and data from yesterday's korae events?" Ardruc's curt voice shattered the lovely quiet of my lab.

I glanced up from my bank of seven screens. Six showed scans of samples I'd brought back from my trip. The largest one in the center showed the data he was referring to.

"Curiosity," I said.

Through the gaps between my screens, I watched his wings flutter and his tail swish.

Despite the sub-optimal temperature in my lab, with his high body temperature, he wouldn't be shivering. His species came from a tropical zone on his home planet. His natural body temperature was much higher than a human's.

Lab Three was the smallest and least-well climate controlled. As the director, Ardruc had laid claim to the facility's largest lab and given his research assistant the second-largest though they had rarely used it. Until recently, Ardruc almost always had Rg in his lab working at his side or watching over his shoulder. But then about a month ago Rg had packed up and left after one too many arguments over lab procedures.

And yet Ardruc had kept both of the largest and best-equipped labs, because, as he reminded me every chance he got, my studies didn't *require* a larger workspace or the most advanced equipment.

He'd put me in a closet or even outside sitting under a tree with a half-powered datapad if he could, but he'd have a hard time explaining that to my supervisor back at my home lab on Fyloria.

"'Curiosity' is not an adequate answer," Ardruc said, his voice colder than the air in here. "My raw data and images are not for public consumption."

Forux curled his lip.

"I am *not* the public." I kept my tone neutral as if I didn't know he'd meant that as an insult, and as if I didn't want to throw something at him. "I'm a fellow researcher. And there's nothing in the Nova Cal procedures that forbids either of us from examining the other's research if it provides insight into our own studies."

His wings fluttered again. "I see no possible way my work could overlap with yours."

There was the tone I knew so well: the one that implied my studies were so much *less* in every conceivable way.

Unfortunately for Ardruc, my mother was Dr. Hilda Disen. I'd heard nothing from her but cutting remarks about my interests and research almost every day of my life until I'd basically cut ties two years ago. If he wanted to hurt me with condescending comments, he'd have to try a lot harder.

"You got some great clear images of mesospheric phenomena last night," I said instead of telling him to go feed himself to a Hardanian bogworm. I had a three-dimensional image of a lovely red kora with long tendrils on one of my screens. "Really spectacular."

"I am aware of what my equipment recorded." The answer was clipped. "But I still want to know why you felt entitled to access data that could not possibly mean anything to you."

Maybe it was because I hadn't slept well, even as exhausted as I was last night. Maybe my rations of Bacorian coffee were running low and I was drinking less so I didn't run out before our next delivery of supplies, so I was having trouble focusing on my work. Maybe I'd just attempted to be civil and he'd thrown it back in my face once again and I was fed up.

Or maybe I really wanted to know his opinion on what I'd seen and I couldn't keep the whole strange incident to myself anymore. Whatever the reason, I decided to explain why I'd accessed his precious data.

"I saw a bolt of kora in the forest yesterday near where I landed the transport," I said. "In fact, I saw it twice. About a meter long, bright red, hovering vertically about a meter off the ground. The first time, it startled me so much I lost my footing and slipped on a loose rock. The second time I saw it, I was sitting in the transport door and I got a much better look at it. I watched it hold still for a moment, and then it disappeared back into the trees like it was trying to hide."

Ardruc stepped around the bank of monitors, his expression dark, feathers ruffling, and eyes nearly sparking with anger.

Today under his lab coat, he wore a dark blue shirt and fitted black pants designed to accommodate his wings and long tail, and boots better suited to walking through the woods than working in a lab. Maybe he planned to venture out later. He liked to go hiking and flying several times a week.

"That is not possible," Ardruc said, and even my mother had never looked down her nose at me as much as he did in that moment. "Obviously you did not see any form of korae."

Oh, *obviously*. My eyes narrowed. Forux stood up and growled, all his fluffy tails fanned out in irritation.

"Did you record an image of what you saw?" Ardruc pressed. "So it could be analyzed?"

I sighed. "No. I didn't get a chance."

"I see." He raised an eyebrow. "So you have no proof of this impossible thing you said you saw?"

Gods, I wanted to punch him.

"It must be nice to have such a clear and complete understanding of every last thing in the universe," I said, my voice as icy as the winds on Aloris. "One wonders how someone as wise and knowledgeable as yourself ended up working alone at Nova Cal. Is it maybe because no one can stand you?"

He stretched his leathery red, orange, and black wings, ruffling and settling his feathers before folding his wings neatly behind his back once again. His tail swished and then coiled lightly around his right leg.

"I have never said I know everything there is to know," he grated. "If you feel the need to insult me, at least choose one of my many *actual* faults. You do not need to resort to made-up ones."

"Apparently you feel the need to insult my intelligence *and* my eyesight," I shot back. "And you mock my field of study every chance you get. I've had enough, Ardruc. I tried to be friendly colleagues, and when that didn't work, I just tried to share the station and be courteous, but you won't even do that. I've never once disparaged your research. Why belittle mine constantly? If you're just bored or need to work through some aggression, you can find a different way to do it besides making fun of me and my life's work, you pompous asshole."

Well, I hadn't intended to blurt out that last part, but I couldn't take it back—and I didn't want to.

He studied me for a long time, his expression unreadable. He was probably used to people backing down from him or mumbling a polite "Yes, sir," like his assistants usually did right up until the day they left the station for less hostile work environments. Not many probably stared right back when he locked his sharp, unblinking, dragon-like gaze on them.

But I'd come too far and worked too hard for him to run me off. Hyderia was heavenly for mycology research. And now I had my teeth into a new mystery: these red tendrils.

They might be alive. Or possibly some state of being even astrobiologists didn't understand yet. I wanted to find out what it was I'd seen. And I planned to stick it out until I either proved it or convinced myself I was wrong.

And for whatever reason, my hypothesis bothered, offended, or downright pissed Ardruc off, for reasons that seemed personal as well as scholarly. I'd ask him bluntly why he'd reacted so strongly if I didn't think I had a better chance of growing wings than getting an honest answer.

"Has it occurred to you," Ardruc said, still in that rough voice, "that by arguing that the phenomena I have dedicated my life to studying are in fact some kind of living thing that you *are* disparaging my work? As if I cannot recognize the difference between naturally occurring upper atmospheric electrical discharges and an organism with consciousness?"

I blinked at him. Had we just accidentally had our most substantive conversation since I'd arrived at the Nova Cal facility?

"No, I *don't* think my theory disparages your work," I said. "Upper atmospheric electrical discharges are a scientific certainty. I'm suggesting I saw something *else* that might not have been observed before. I've discovered dozens of previously unknown fungi in the last four months. This planet has been so well protected that it may offer more discoveries and mysteries than any other in this sector. I believe this is one of them. That doesn't diminish anything about your work."

"You *believe*." Now his voice turned harsh. "Therein lies our key difference, Dr. Regis. Your beliefs are based on what, precisely?"

"Observations," I said. "Data."

He crossed his arms, his biceps straining the fabric of his shirt in a way that was not at all distracting. "And?" he prompted.

I knew what he was driving at, and I knew by answering that I'd be playing into his hands, but I didn't care. "Gut feeling." I raised my chin. "You know the history of scientific advancement. How many discoveries came after a researcher had a gut feeling?"

"And how many *gut feelings* are completely unfounded?" He scoffed. "I do not need any *gut feelings* to know you are wasting your time with this."

All the gods above and below, it was like talking to a Hardanian lava squid, and half their bodies and a third of their brains were made of rock.

"Well, it's my time to waste, I suppose," I said, turning back to my monitors. "In between studying Hyderia's wondrous fungi, I'll do the research *you* should be doing into what might be sentient plasma." I couldn't resist one more dig. "In the meantime, my lab on Fyloria will keep helping to fund this facility, and you can go back to your big, comfy lab and bask in the warmth of your own smug self-righteousness."

I wasn't looking at him anymore, but I sensed his glare drilling twin holes into my forehead.

"I mean it," I said, my attention on the center monitor and its display of a gorgeous red sprite with long, dangling tendrils that looked so enticingly like humongous versions of what I'd seen in the forest. "Go. I have work to do."

Finally, he turned on his heel and left. His wings and tail barely cleared the doorway before the door shut behind him. In his wake, an unfamiliar scent swirled in the air around me, peppery and sweet. Strange. Had it come from Ardruc? I'd never noticed it before.

I rubbed my face. I needed more coffee. Maybe I could have another cup today. We expected a delivery of supplies in a few weeks. I should be fine until then. I'd ordered extra this time, so I wouldn't need to ration it as much. It would help if I could get some decent sleep, though. I'd be far less tired, and much less likely to let Ardruc's bullshit get to me.

He really was the most insufferable asshole.

I sighed, drained the last drops of coffee remaining in my mug, and stretched with a groan. I'd been sitting too long again, captivated by the images and data of the korae and the specimens I'd brought back from my trip. I'd confirmed the *Basiforuximycota* was in fact a new order of fungi and excitedly written up my preliminary findings...and then gotten utterly absorbed in learning about Hyderia's upper atmospheric electrical discharges and cold plasma.

Ardruc's data showed last night's mesospheric activity was the biggest and most involved display of korae in weeks. I'd found images and data on this red sprite first and lost almost three hours learning about it. I looked forward to examining it in holographic form and learning more when I got back to the lab from making coffee.

"Who the hells does he think he is, anyway?" I asked Forux.

He made a guttural sound.

I'm going to kill that dragon man one of these days, I fumed, storming out of my lab and down the hall. *And pin him to the wall by his pretty little wings and that sexy tail.*

I scowled at myself. His tail was *not* sexy. Nothing about him was pretty or sexy.

When I passed Lab One, I caught a glimpse through the hall window of Ardruc standing at his desk, hands on his hips and gaze fixed on one of his monitors that showed the same red sprite I had on my screen in Lab Three.

He didn't look up when I went by, but with his sharp ears there was no way he didn't hear my footsteps. And I didn't exactly tread lightly going past his door. Not that I wanted another confrontation today, but I didn't want to be ignored as if I didn't even exist. *Asshole.*

I took my rage and my empty mug to the kitchen, found my stash of Bacorian coffee, and turned on the machine.

CHAPTER 8
ARDRUC

ELENA'S ANGRY FOOTSTEPS PASSED MY LAB ON HER WAY TO THE station's kitchen. Too early for a midday meal, so she was after another cup of that vile liquid stimulant she liked so much.

No matter where they were born in the galaxy, humans seemed drawn to coffee, which had originated on Earth and been perfected by the monk-gastronomists on Bacora. As it brewed, the stuff smelled wonderful, but paradoxically tasted aggressively unpleasant to my palate.

The deeply contented way Elena always sighed and closed her eyes after her first sip of the day made me smile despite my misgivings about the beverage.

I stared at the images and scrolling data on my monitors as the computer analyzed last night's spectacular display of large-scale electrical discharges, but none of it registered.

One wonders how someone as wise and knowledgeable as yourself ended up working alone at Nova Cal, Elena had said, her eyes full of anger and disdain. *Is it maybe because no one can stand you?*

Her scorn had ruffled my feathers far more than her words. I might have few friends and no family ties, and a long list of current and former colleagues who likely had little to say about me that was positive, but I had always commanded authority and respect.

Not from Elena, however. For all my achievements and knowledge, she did not consider me enough of an expert to accept my word about the impossibility of living korae.

Today was the first time she had confronted me rather than shrug me off. It was the reaction I had wanted to provoke with my dismissal of her bizarre claims about seeing small tendrils of plasma, but it did not feel like a win—very much the opposite.

I had been *cruel* to her today, condescending and dismissive, hoping to break her will to stay. The price of doing so was that my stomach churned and cramped. I had barely made it back to my lab without becoming ill.

Rather than give up and leave Nova Cal, she had dug in her heels and declared her intent not only to stay to study her precious fungi, but to engage in research within my own field—or at least adjacent to it in that astrobiology had some overlap with atmospheric science.

Damn it, could she not *just leave me in peace?*

I slammed my fist on my desk, rattling my bank of displays and the stack of datapads next to the interface, just as Elena's footsteps echoed once more in the hallway, coming back from the kitchen.

The footsteps paused. Behind me, the door to my lab slid open.

The reflection in my computer screens showed Elena and Forux. Her eyes still sparked with anger, much like those of her companion.

Today she wore her long hair tucked behind her ears. The sight of her loose hair made my hands tremble because I yearned to run my fingers through the silky strands.

"Ardruc?" she asked. "Everything okay?"

The note of concern in her voice unexpectedly pricked my conscience—and made me growl. I did not want her concern or for her feelings toward me to soften. The more distance we kept from each other, the better.

"Yes," I said without turning around, my voice brusque. "I knocked something on the floor."

I watched her reflection as she glanced around my immediate surroundings. Maybe she knew I had lied. The sound of someone punching a desk sounded nothing like an impact on the floor...and there was nothing on the floor of the lab. I kept my workspace tidy.

"I am busy," I added before she could say anything else. "Thank you for your concern."

With a sigh, Elena muttered something and left. It sounded like *Asshole*. A few moments later, from down the corridor, I heard the door to her lab slide closed.

The data from last night continued to scroll across my screens, but I found myself struggling to focus.

For the past several weeks, I could barely eat. I slept poorly. Since the subject of my studies occurred erratically throughout the day and night, my sleep schedule was irregular at best, but I had never had difficulty sleeping when I needed to until recently. I had even resorted to taking medication, hoping that would grant me six hours of uninterrupted sleep, but I woke repeatedly.

My abilities to reason, observe, and analyze were my most powerful and important strengths. At the moment, the data on my monitors might as well have been the scratchings of baby sand spiders.

Meanwhile, just now I had gone into Elena's lab and found her hard at work analyzing her own sets of data, her brow furrowed in concentration, and found myself embittered. Nothing was less like me than jealousy. Jealousy was irrational and unproductive—especially jealousy of Elena, who thought she saw living plasma.

With a snarl that puffed smoke from my nostrils, I took off my lab coat and tossed it on the desk, shut off the screens, and stalked down the hall, around the corner, and to the end of that corridor to apartment one, Nova Cal's largest.

Apartments two and three were mid-sized and very comfortable. Dr. Rg had occupied one, and I had reserved the other for potential visitors to the facility. On her arrival, I had assigned Elena the fourth apartment, the farthest from my own and the smallest and most utilitarian. After all, she had brought very little with her besides clothing, a few personal items, and Forux. Any distinguished visitors—especially ones who might provide funding—could not be expected to stay in our most humble quarters.

The fact the facility had not hosted visitors of any sort in two standard years was beside the point, or so I told myself.

I took my lat'sar case from my closet and sat on my neatly made bed to run my hands over it. The smooth surface felt as familiar as my own skin. I knew every scratch and dent in the case.

The damage in the bottom right corner of the lid had happened the night I fled my parents' compound. In my haste to get over the wall, I had banged it against the stone. I could have purchased a new case at any point in the fifteen years since, but I preferred to see the light damage. It reminded me of where I had come from. What I had endured. What I had escaped.

The dent in the case was a symbol of my freedom, and of the price I had paid to become Dr. Ardruc Husiorithae, noted atmospheric scientist and asshole.

The price was something someone like Elena Regis, who had grown up in privilege within the highest academic circles, would never understand, even if I told her. Which I would never do.

With my lat'sar case secure on my back, I locked the door to my apartment on the way out. I had no concern that Elena would try to enter my quarters and there was no one else at Nova Cal, but even so, I kept the door locked at all times. It was a matter of principle—a subtle pushback against the total lack of privacy in my early life.

I exited the building via the door closest to my apartment, which did not force me to walk past Elena's lab. I preferred to slip out unnoticed and not cause her to wonder why I had left or where I was going, or why I was bringing my lat'sar.

A wide deck encircled the facility, which was built on a platform above the rocky slope. The autumn day was cool, with a light breeze that stirred the leaves on the trees. I inhaled deeply a half-dozen times, clearing Elena's scent from my nose, even if I could not banish it from my bones.

I had come to Hyderia to lose myself in my studies of what was to me the planet's most fascinating attribute: its unique and nearly constant high-atmospheric plasma discharges. In my opinion, no better location existed for study of these phenomena. Each kora was unique in shape, size, location, color, and intensity. The data flowed endlessly and the images captivated me—scientifically speaking, of course. I could envision myself living out my life on this station, funding permitting, and even retiring here, with the permission of the Nyvoran government. All my research was geared toward those two ends.

There was no room in my plans for Elena or her theories. None at all. And yet my hearts and soul yearned for her. I puffed smoke from my nostrils in irritation.

Rather than take the stairs down to ground level, I stretched out my wings, inhaled deeply, and took flight.

I soared over the Nova Cal facility in widening circles, climbing from just over the rooftop to a a hundred meters or so above the ground. Such a pure and simple joy to fly like this, even for a short time. I spent most of my hours on my human feet or sitting in my lab. I did not begrudge that, since my research gave me as much fulfillment and satisfaction and even pleasure as flight, but it did make me treasure my time in the sky.

I could not land in the thick forest, so after about fifteen minutes of flying, I landed smoothly on the ground in the clearing next to the station. From here, I would walk to my destination.

Four paths extended beyond the immediate area of our mountainside facility. They served multiple purposes, from ways to exercise to leading to scenic points where I could observe the sky with portable equipment or even my naked eyes.

I took none of those paths.

Instead, my muscles warm and body full of adrenaline and

endorphins from my flight, I followed my own habitual way into the trees. My destination was a small natural clearing bounded on three sides by fallen trees. The boundaries appealed to me. I knew every detail of this path and that clearing. It was comfortable, and far enough from the station that I could not be overheard.

Some days I strolled, enjoying the fresh air, peace, and stillness of the forest, where only birds and quiet rustling of small mammals could be heard. No humming or quiet beeps of machinery. No alerts from a computer. Not even the smell of synthetic material except my own clothes.

Today, despite my lingering tiredness from poor sleep, I felt impatient, so I walked briskly. In twenty minutes I reached my destination.

In the clearing, I set my lat'sar case down, closed my eyes, and listened. Nothing.

Perfection.

I sat cross-legged on the ground and opened the case. My lat'sar lay snugly in the soft, shock-absorbent material that prevented it from being damaged. My mother's mother, the only member of the family to resist full immersion in the religious sect, had gifted me the lat'sar on my tenth birthday. My parents had allowed me to keep the gift as long as I solemnly vowed to never play anything but the group leader's own compositions on it. I had kept that vow until the day I fled the compound at nineteen.

From that day on, I took great satisfaction in playing every composition I fancied, including some of my own. And I could not recall a single bar of anything written by the man who had stolen my family from me. That was a pleasure too.

Inhaling and exhaling slowly, I stretched my back, arms, and shoulders until those muscles felt warm and loose. Then I focused on my wrists, hands, and fingers. Every step of this process was methodical and precise—a meditation that freed me from agitation and disquiet, at least for a while.

When I felt at peace, I picked up my bow, settled the body of the lat'sar on my shoulder, and rested my chin on the curved piece on its front. The weight and feel of the instrument was as familiar as that of my wings. I tuned all five of the upper and lower strings, then drew the bow across them, closing my eyes as the pure notes filled the air. I spent a few minutes playing a series of scales—one of them, coincidentally, developed on Elena's home planet of Fyloria—and then more complex sequences.

When I played *The Sea Winds*, my favorite composition by a Fortusian composer, all my world was in tune once more. The piece was perfect in every way: mathematically precise from beginning to end, as if a complex equation with a simple solution had been transformed into music.

Fortusian lat'sars made the most perfect music in the galaxy. No other instrument came close.

A flash of movement caught my eye. I turned my head, the song cutting off with a squeak of the bow.

For a fraction of a second, I caught sight of a meter-long tendril of shimmering red next to the trunk of a tree. And then it vanished around the side of the tree, moving as quickly as it had appeared.

Blinking, I lowered my lat'sar and bow into my lap.

My hearts thundered in my ears, and my thoughts slowed to a crawl. I did not…just see…a tendril of kora…*hide from me.*

I set my instrument gently in its case, leapt to my feet, and dashed to the tree. My sharp sense of smell caught the lingering scent of ozone. All the hairs and feathers on my body prickled, but no sign of anything remained.

In a kind of daze, I turned and froze.

A red tendril of plasma, as thin as a few hairs—either the same one I had spotted by this tree, or an identical one—danced over the strings of my lat'sar. A single, pure note filled the air.

The tendril shimmered, sparked, then darted into the shadows of the forest, vanishing from my sight as the note faded.

What in the names of all the gods above and below had just happened?

When I picked up my lat'sar, I found a scorch mark on the wood near one of the sound holes—the only mark on the otherwise pristine instrument. My gut contracted, though I could not be certain whether the damage or the tendril's appearance had caused it, or both.

I raised my face toward the sky, as if answers might be found there, but the thick foliage obscured my view. When I looked back at my lat'sar, I almost expected the mark to have disappeared. The scorch was tangible evidence that *something* had touched this instrument—not only touched it, but *played* it.

I waited several minutes, but saw no sign of the tendril again.

For the first time in many, many years, I found myself utterly at a loss. My stomach churned, as if the very planet on which I stood had betrayed me. As if *my own reason* had betrayed me.

Elena had claimed to have seen one or more of these tendrils five hundred kilometers from here. This one was half a kilometer from our facility.

It was possible Elena and I were not alone at Nova Cal.

Despite what I had seen, I clung to my scientific knowledge. There *must* be an explanation for this. A rational, scientific, quantifiable explanation. One that did not prove Elena right and me wrong. What it might be, though, I had no idea.

Infinitely more unsettled than I had been when I arrived in the clearing, I packed up my lat'sar and headed back to the station as quickly as I could run.

CHAPTER 9

ELENA

ARDRUC DIDN'T SPEAK TO ME FOR FOUR DAYS—NOT EVEN A SNIDE comment when we passed in the hall.

Whatever I'd done to earn a reprieve from his verbal torment, I wished I knew so I could duplicate this feat. Maybe pointing out that he'd been awful to me since the day I arrived had gotten him to back off. That didn't feel like the right answer, but at the moment I didn't have a better one.

Every time I passed his lab, Ardruc was scowling like a Ryoxvian drummer beetle had crawled up his ass. He stared at his screens and rapidly cycling series of holographic images of korae, either with arms crossed or fists on his hips. Sometimes I caught him leaning over with his palms on the desk and his head bowed, as if deep in thought. Some aspect of his research must not be going according to his meticulously crafted plans. Maybe a data point was outside expected parameters. He also seemed to not be sleeping very well, even by his standards.

If he were anyone else I'd ever worked with, I'd ask him what was bothering him, but the prick would probably just bite my head off, insult my research or korae theory again, or tell me to mind my own business—or all three. Besides, he wouldn't want my help talking through whatever problem had him in knots. I wasn't *scientific enough* in my methods. I might use my *gut* to find an answer instead of a chart.

So I focused on my own work and left him to stew.

My logged work hours focused on my new samples, including studying the *Basiforuximycota* specimen. I devoted my after-hours time to learning about Hyderia's korae phenomena. The more I knew about the korae, the more likely I was to spot key differences between it and these tendrils—and find proof of whether they were a life form.

When I confirmed that the *Basiforuximycota* was as big of a discovery as I'd suspected, my lab supervisor, Dr. N'Caro, wanted to schedule a symposium back at the university on Fyloria for me to present my findings in person and answer questions about my discoveries during my first six months on Hyderia. I'd requested to instead give my presentation via video transmission. I feared if I left, it might give the Nyvorans an excuse not to grant my request to extend my stay.

The thought of having to leave, even to be the keynote speaker at a symposium on Fyloria and all the accolades that would bring me, made my stomach hurt.

Loving this planet as much as I did was probably a mistake, since the odds of obtaining permission to stay here long-term were slim. But every discovery I made increased those chances.

That was another big reason for me to find out if my wild theory about the red tendrils was true. Even if the Nyvorans sent astrobiologists to research this potential new life form, the discovery would be mine.

My mother might not care what fungi I discovered or the medical benefits derived from those discoveries, but even *she* would have the acknowledge the significance of uncovering a previously unknown form of life that existed as sentient korae.

"Why do I bother thinking about her at all?" I asked Forux, who'd curled up at my feet while I sat at my desk to examine scans of the *Basiforuximycota's* spore-laden lamellae. "Why do I never learn? She wouldn't care if I discovered a portal to another universe. Why do I care what she thinks?"

Forux raised his head and laid his ears flat, his brow furrowed.

"Because she's my mother," I answered myself with a sigh. "And some dumb part of me still wants her approval. How pathetic am I?"

He whined and shook his head briskly, his ears flapping.

"You're right." With a smile, I shook my head too. "I can't keep chasing something that doesn't exist. She wanted me to be a physicist like her. As soon as I took a different path, any chance of approval blew away like a feather in Solani sandstorm." I glanced at the scans on my screen, then back at Forux, who'd raised his head. "When I look at these samples, my heart is full. What else do I need besides that joy and you? Well, and coffee."

With a quiet chuff of agreement, he rested his head on his fluffy paws and closed his eyes.

Speaking of coffee, I wanted another cup, but I'd already used up my ration for the day. The chronometer read 2150. Well, that was a full day's work done anyway. I'd reached a good stopping point. Time for a treat of another kind.

Forux, stretched, yawned, and followed me to our quarters. From the moment I'd walked through its creaking door, I'd known I was going to be *persona non grata* here for the duration of my stay. I'd also decided not to waste my time being angry about our accommodations. I'd stayed longer in far humbler places.

As such, I only rarely lay in my narrow bunk with Forux snuggled beside me and imagined Ardruc in the enormous, Fortusian-sized bed in his comparatively luxurious apartment—the layout of which I knew because it was in the facility's records. I'd certainly never seen inside it. I couldn't imagine a circumstance in which I ever would, or would want to.

Because the nighttime temperature was chilly, I changed from my lab attire into a thermal jumpsuit and stuck matching gloves and a cap in the pockets. The jumpsuit tended to keep me plenty warm, but sometimes the roof was very windy. I wanted to be able to stay up there as long as I wanted without my hands turning to icicles.

"Do you want to go to the roof with me?" I asked Forux. "Or stay here and nap?"

Forux tilted his head, glanced at my bunk, and then trotted to my side. I smiled and bent to scratch his head. "Thanks, friend."

I took my bedroll that I typically brought on multi-day research trips and headed up to the facility's roof.

The mostly single-level Nova Cal station was built on a platform five meters off the rocky sloped ground. The facility could be accessed from ground level by the lift or sets of stairs, or from the air via the landing pad on the main roof.

I took the lift up to the large square landing pad. Both of the facility's two small transports were on the pad. I crossed the roof to a ladder that led to the highest roof of the building above the imaging lab. Unlike the rest of the squat facility, the interior of the lab was ten meters tall to allow for enormous holographics, galleries of images, large amounts of displayed data, and many other uses. Its roof, which was entirely covered with native grasses, offered the best views of the mountainside, the valley below, and the sky.

Sometimes I brought a backpack stuffed with portable viewing equipment to get a close-up view of Hyderia's famed upper-atmospheric korae. Tonight, I came empty-handed. I'd spent way too many hours lately staring at screens and holograms and data. I wanted to connect with the planet—to *see* the sky, listen to all the natural rhythms, and feel the grass under my feet.

I unfurled my bedroll, which expanded to form a comfortable sleeping surface complete with adjustable headrest, and sat cross-legged on its softness. As much as I loved the station's grassy roof, at this time of year it tended to be cold and hard. Forux settled in next to me, curling up against my hip. With his thick fur, he wasn't in any danger of being cold, so his closeness was more about his love and desire to stay nearby. I ran my fingers through his fur and scratched him until he made quiet rumbly purrs.

This roof was quieter than the landing pad area, especially when the imaging lab wasn't in use. Silence reigned, except for the faint humming of the station, and with the exterior floodlights off, no light pollution ruined my view.

The night was lovely and clear. Only minimal cloud cover and little to no chance of rain. On most planets that would mean probably no lightning, but not on Hyderia. A clear night simply meant a better view of the korae.

If I was lucky, we'd get another great display of upper-atmospheric phenomena tonight. It would all be captured by the station's array of imagers, telescopes, and a myriad of scientific devices for later analysis.

Even if there was only a few korae, that was fine. Once my eyes adjusted to the dark, the nighttime view of the mountainside and valley was breathtaking, and well worth the climb up here. This mountain range, like all others on the planet, was heavily forested. Only the windswept peaks were rocky and barren.

Hyderia was paradise, or as close to it as mortals could access. I planned to work as a field researcher for a long, long time still, and the prospect of spending that time here, either at Nova Cal or as a permanent resident, was a dream. I'd demonstrated my commitment to conservation and ecologically centered research throughout my education and professional career. And if I had any good luck coming in my life, I wouldn't mind using it all to get that highly coveted approval from Nyvoran Ministry of Natural Sciences.

The air was cold enough for me to see my breath, but my jumpsuit kept me toasty warm. I put on my thermal gloves and hat and lay down, settling in with my head on the bedroll's plush headrest. With a contented sigh, Forux tucked himself between my elbow and my side. Above us, distant stars and planets glowed in the sky. A comet or asteroid was passing overhead, trailed by a streak of white.

Unbidden, an image of Ardruc lying up here staring at the sky popped into my head and made me chuckle.

Unlike me, he'd lie so awkwardly and uncomfortably. He'd probably glare at the sky, even, and say this was a waste of time. From here, with the naked eye, what could we see of the upper atmosphere but flashes of light? *What use is this*, he'd demand, and then stomp back to his lab to sit in front of a screen filled with numbers.

I sighed and shook my head at the imaginary scene.

The stars always sparkled most brightly when I looked at them from this rooftop, or so it seemed. Not a scientific observation at all, but still a true one. And yet another statement that would have earned a look of utter disdain.

"Stop thinking about Ardruc," I scolded myself aloud. Why let thoughts of him ruin my perfect night of stargazing and korae-watching? He wasn't worth it.

I shook my head more vigorously this time, as if I could banish him from my brain that way. For good measure, I inhaled deeply and exhaled slowly and repeatedly until my feeling of peace returned, pushing thoughts of my grumpy, ill-mannered colleague far away—

—Just in time for a burst of red korae to bloom soundlessly across the sky in a series of long hanging tendrils.

No matter how many times I witnessed it, the sight left me speechless. My breath caught in my chest and my heartbeat pounded in my ears.

Down in Ardruc's lab, the computer was dutifully recording, assessing, analyzing, and compiling data, from the levels of infrasound produced by the korae to the color and every other atmospheric condition associated with the burst for later assessment. He might be watching on his screens as well. The array of satellites around Hyderia provided excellent images.

Up here, in awestruck silence, I watched the korae flare, hang in space, and then slowly fade. Only when the sky went dark once more did I breathe again.

I wasn't an atmospheric scientist, but I understood the basics of the theory and science of upper-atmospheric electrical discharges. The science was clear: nothing about it was magical. And yet everything about it was pure magic.

"Beautiful," I whispered. "Thank you."

Who I might be thanking, I had no idea. The sky itself, maybe, or whatever aspects of this planet created these spectacular and unique displays.

The breeze swirled around me with a sound like a deep breath or soft gasp.

The sky blossomed into a display of a half-dozen bursts of red, orange, and blue korae, all what looked like many kilometers wide at the top with long tendrils sparkling below. It looked as if a hanging garden made of cold plasma had burst into bloom directly above the station.

Instinctively, I covered my mouth with my hand to muffle my strangled shriek of wonder and disbelief. I'd never seen such a display anywhere—not even on Hyderia. Nothing had even come *close* to this in any record I'd seen.

Ardruc's data could tell me for certain later how far above the ground the korae was. Most discharges on Hyderia were forty to fifty kilometers from the surface. It was impossible to tell with the naked eye exactly where this display occurred, but strangely I thought it was far closer than normal. It must have been a trick of my eye, though.

The korae faded, replaced by faint shimmers of green and blue before the sky went dark. I took my hand from my mouth, but my breathing still sounded ragged.

Was Ardruc working late in his lab? I hadn't bothered to check before I came up to the roof. If he'd been sitting at his computer when that display happened, all his screens probably lit up with images and data about distance, diameter, temperature, voltage, power, energy, and current. The display would be quantified in every way possible. He must have been astonished by it, at least in his own scientific, clinical way.

For a moment, I wondered if he'd wish he'd been up here to see it in person, but then just as quickly decided he wouldn't. Its beauty would have been wasted on him anyway. I'd never met any scientist with such an apparent lack of wonder.

A burst of red tendrils appeared in the sky, crackling through the darkness and undulating as if dancing in the upper atmosphere. Eyes wide and heart pounding, I watched and waited.

The second bloom of multi-colored korae was even larger and more brilliant than the first. This time, the korae took the form of red, orange, and blue light that appeared round from the ground, meaning they were likely vertical and columniform—terms I had learned during my recent headlong dive into atmospheric science. I'd know for sure when I got to examine the data and images.

If Ardruc were up here, he'd likely have already run to his computer. I, on the other hand, wanted to see the display in all its glory with my eyes, even if the images recorded by the facility's ground-level and orbiting arrays would be much clearer and arguably more useful. The wonder of it captivated me. The data would be at the computer when I got there.

I was the only person on this planet who'd just seen these displays with the naked eye. And strangely, that fact made me feel both incredibly lucky and incredibly lonely, to the point my chest actually ached. I wished I had someone with whom to share the wonder of this moment.

Instead, all I had to look forward to was climbing down the roof ladder, then taking the lift or the steep roof stairs that led to the hallway near my lab to see what data had been gathered that might help support my hypothesis. If I was lucky, I'd either avoid Ardruc or still be getting the silent treatment. If he tried to be nasty to me after this beautiful korae show, I wasn't sure I could keep myself from taking a swing at him. All the gods above and below knew he would deserve it, even if with his reflexes I wasn't likely to actually make contact.

There I went again, letting thoughts of Ardruc ruin my night. I let out a little growl that sounded very much like Forux's.

An agonizingly brilliant reddish-white flare directly above me blinded me. I threw my arm over my eyes, turned away from the light and heat, and screamed. Searing pain in my face felt like I had been flash-burned and I smelled singed hair. The agony was so intense that nausea surged. I made a choking sound.

Something punched me in the chest so hard that everything in my body went rigid and then numb. It felt like a giant fist had hit my sternum and then stayed there, crushing me. My heart stuttered. From somewhere close by, I heard a whine.

Oh, gods. Forux. Terror turned me cold.

The pain and inability to breathe made my brain feel cottony, but I got my eyes open and slid my arm down just enough to squint over it.

A blazing reddish-white tendril of glowing gas particles—of plasma, of *kora*—about a meter long hovered parallel to my body above my chest, crackling with power and heat. The sight paralyzed me in fear and awe.

Gods above, what was this?

This wasn't possible. Korae didn't *hover;* it was a discharge between two electrically charged regions of the atmosphere. Korae didn't freeze in place; science measured its appearances in terms of milliseconds. Korae wasn't a meter long; it was three to four kilometers, usually, or as much as seven hundred kilometers or more under extreme conditions.

Korae didn't do *any* of the things this bolt was doing. So what the hells was I looking at? I let out a mewl that was part pain and part fear.

A single thread of plasma flicked out from the bolt and touched my gloved right hand.

Searing pain made me scream and flinch away. Forux snarled and tried to bite the plasma, but thankfully it moved too quickly and he missed.

I curled up on my side with my hand against my stomach. When I looked back, my chest heaving with ragged breaths edged with sobs, the tendril of kora was gone.

"What the hells?" I rasped. "What in *all the hells?*"

The night remained silent and dark.

Whining, Forux sank his teeth into my sleeve and pulled, urging me to get moving toward the ladder. Despite my agony, I resisted, in case the tendril returned. But after a full minute, nothing happened. No tendrils, and no more korae.

Gasping for breath, shaking too hard to stand, and holding my burned hand to my chest, I crawled across the grass, following Forux to the ladder. My descent to the lower roof was more of a fall than a climb. The jolt of hitting the lower roof barely registered over the searing pain of my burned face, chest, and hand.

Without remembering most of the journey, I made it to the lift doors. The stairs would be closer to the medical bay, but I didn't think I could manage them. As it was, I struggled to stay on my feet and press my uninjured palm to the scanner to unlock the doors. I trembled so badly that it took two tries. Finally, they slid open and I fell into the lift. Forux paced beside me, whining and growling.

I was lightheaded and my ears were ringing so loudly that I barely heard the beep when the doors closed. The lift automatically returned to the main floor.

Fighting dizziness and nausea, I made it to my feet again just as the lift slowed and stopped. When the doors slid open, I fell through the opening into the hallway beyond—

—and landed in a heap right at Ardruc's feet.

CHAPTER 10
ARDRUC

T HE SMELL OF E LENA'S BLOOD AND BURNED FLESH HIT ME LIKE A
physical blow.

She looked as stunned to see me as I was to see her. From the
floor, she blinked up at me, her eyes unfocused, clutching one hand
to her chest. The skin on her face was bright red with first- and
second-degree burns, as was the back of her right hand where her
glove had been burned away.

And most horrifying of all, something had burned a hole
through her thermal jumpsuit directly above her single, fragile
human heart.

When our gazes met, I read mistrust in her expression, and
some anger, but mostly agony and desperation.

"Please help," she rasped, her voice little more than a wisp. "It
hurts." Her plea was a punch in my gut.

Minutes ago I had stood in my lab shaking my head at the
thought of Elena on the roof watching the korae display with
nothing but her human eyes. But as the images and data on my
screens grew stranger and stranger, my uneasiness had grown to
the point that I found myself heading for the roof. Whether my

purpose was to see the korae for myself, or to check on Elena, I did not know.

Nothing in my life had prepared me for the visceral horror that gripped me at the sight and smell of Elena's blood and pain. Fear wrapped itself around my hearts and squeezed.

Forux looked up and snarled, as if urging me to act.

I scooped Elena up as gently as I could and bolted for the medical bay. Despite the warmth inside the station, she shivered violently. Her breathing had turned rapid and shallow. Her skin appeared cool and damp. The cause was likely to be shock.

She clenched her jaw and nearly doubled over in my arms. A tiny, broken sound of pain escaped her pale lips.

As I ran, pressure built in my chest—the same discomfort that had developed when I heard her cry out as she removed the medical wrap on her ankle. My coo. That time I had held it in, but now the urge to let it emerge as a vocalization overwhelmed me. My vocal cords thrummed as if I were growling.

Gods above, why should I continue to resist the call of a true mate? Was I not simply making myself more miserable every day for reasons that seemed less clear by the minute? Every instinct promised that way lay happiness and contentment and joy, if only I could bring myself to believe it.

Tentatively, I opened my mouth. The thrumming in my throat became a deep and resonant song somewhere between a rumble and a deep bass note. With a sigh, Elena relaxed in my arms, her head against my chest. The smell of pain faded and her shivering eased.

Impossible. Impossible that a *sound* I made could have such a profound and instantaneous physical and emotional effect. As impossible, I supposed, as a tendril of kora a meter long that played a stringed instrument and hid among the trees.

In the medbay, I lay Elena carefully in the emergency medical pod. She murmured something, and then her head rolled to the side. The word sounded like *Asshole*. Not an unfair assessment, if I were to be honest with myself.

The screens above her head came to life as the pod activated with a series of beeps and red warning lights. I stepped back to let the equipment do what it was designed to do.

Like most field researchers, I had medical training, especially in triage care. That training was not required to utilize the equipment in the bay to treat burns, assuming that was the extent of her injuries. The medical bay was designed around the premise that the facility would not have any medical personnel on staff.

Forux stood up on his back feet and put his front paws on my knee. When I did not react, he bit my shin through my pants leg hard enough to draw blood. With a curse, I picked him up and tucked him against my side so he could see Elena. He vibrated with agitation. I found myself scratching his head in a vain attempt to provide comfort.

My heartsbeats pounded in my ears as Elena's lips turned blue. What was happening? I stepped closer to the screen to read the diagnostic scans.

Elena had suffered burns to her face, chest, and hand, and gone into shock, which I had already noted. The next piece of information, however, left me cold. Her heart had received significant damage. According to the readout, if left untreated, the damage would have been fatal within the hour.

Another, much stronger wash of rage swept through me. I snarled, puffing smoke from my nostrils. What the hells had happened to Elena on the roof?

The medical pod equipment went to work immediately, injecting painkillers and other drugs and elevating her legs to increase blood flow to her head. A force field crackled to life around the bed. I averted my eyes as the field disintegrated her clothing.

When the force field shut off, I looked back to find the bed had covered her to the waist with a thermal blanket. A second thermal wrap covered her shoulders to keep her warm while the medical system treated her various burns and the damage to her heart.

My gaze went from the burn on her chest to the diagnostic screen: *Cardiac damage appears to be the result of exposure to high-voltage electricity.*

I struggled to make sense of what had happened. Elena's injuries could not be the result of a korae or lightning strike. As painful and life-threatening as they were, a strike—even if it were not a direct hit—would likely have proven fatal, or at least far more catastrophically damaging. When she woke, I hoped Elena would be able to explain how she received these injuries.

Deeply unsettled, I stretched my wings and folded them behind my back. My tail swished back and forth.

I should go up to the roof and begin my own investigation by gathering evidence. Elena did not need me here now that the medical bay had taken over her care. In fact, she likely would not *want* me here, especially when she was unclothed and unconscious. She had asked for my help while disoriented by shock and severe pain, but that did not mean her feelings about me had changed—as if calling me an asshole with her last breath before passing out had not made it a certainty.

Elena remained pale, but at least she had stopped shivering and no longer appeared to be in pain. The screen above her bed showed images of her damaged heart, now under repair by the medical pod. And though her burns had begun to heal, they were still angry and red.

I had no reason to stay in the medical bay. I needed to examine the roof and get to my lab. The korae display that had taken place minutes ago had been highly unusual, even by Hyderia standards. I wanted to analyze the images and data gathered during the event.

And yet, I lingered.

Some analytical part of my mind latched onto my reluctance to leave as a mystery or problem that needed to be solved.

What did I feel when I looked at Elena? Irritation, because her injuries had disrupted my routine. Frustration, because her strange love of stargazing on the roof had somehow led to this. Sympathy, because she was hurt and had experienced terrible pain. For all my clinically dispassionate nature, I was not pitiless or cruel.

Anger, because she had been harmed.

Fear, because she might have died.

Tenderness, because my body had instinctually made a sound that had eased her pain.

A strong compulsion to stay, because she should not be alone so soon after nearly dying.

Why these feelings? Because she was my true mate. My song and its effects were proof I could not deny. I was a scientist still, though at the moment I felt very far removed from the dispassionate scholar I wanted to be.

The diagnostic screen beeped and added a new line: *Stabilized*.

"She is stabilized," I said to Forux, whose little body had quivered with agitation for the entirety of the time I had held him. For once, I did not think his distress had anything to do with me. Arvals did not understand human language per se, but the species was empathic and could comprehend simple concepts.

"I am going to leave you here and investigate the roof," I added, speaking slowly and attempting to project calm and reassurance. "The medical bay will alert me if her condition changes."

Forux growled quietly, his gaze still fixed on Elena.

I brought over a tall lab chair and placed Forux on its seat so he could keep watch on his beloved Elena. He nudged my hand with his nose, met my gaze, and then looked at Elena.

Her right hand was undergoing treatment, so I walked around the bed to her left side. Very slowly, I reached out and touched her hand. My breath caught in my chest.

As clammy as it had been when I first picked her up at the lift, her skin was wonderfully and reassuringly warm now, thanks to the care she was receiving. But more than that, this first gentle touch had the world-tilting sensation of having found something very important after a long search.

I knew in my soul this moment was a crossroads.

The voice of logic I had chosen to shape the course of my life told me to continue on my current path because it was safe and known and enough. But every other aspect of myself said to forget safety and familiarity, and to the deepest hells with *enough*.

To my surprise, I found the idea of choosing happiness—or at least, the chance for happiness—more exhilarating than frightening.

Hard on the heels of that revelation came the painful knowledge that since the moment Elena had set foot on Hyderia, I had been so unkind and even cruel to her out of my own selfishness. I was in fact the very worst of assholes. How I might even begin to earn her forgiveness, I did not know.

If only I could blame my parents or the sect leader for my predicament, that might ease my guilt and disgust at myself, but I was not a child who sought to avoid responsibility by shifting blame. I had made a hundred choices over the past four months, all of them inexcusable. And worst of all, I had known that all along. I certainly did not deserve Elena's kindness or forgiveness, much less her affection.

I had escaped a hell of my parents' making only to make my own.

Forux growled, but the sound was distinctly different than the warnings I typically heard from him. Less threatening and more like a scolding. A reminder that it was Elena who needed my attention, not myself and my regrets?

I took her much-smaller hand in mine and squeezed. Even unconscious and far removed from whatever danger she had faced, she smelled of fear.

My song rose again in my throat. This time, I did not try to hold it back.

The low note filled the medical bay. Elena exhaled with an audible sigh. The little furrow between her brows vanished. The scent of fear faded, taking with it some of my own apprehension. I might have called my song miraculous were I not still a man of science who had made the physiology of true mates my new area of expertise after Elena's arrival at Nova Cal.

With a quiet chuff, Forux relaxed his ears and tails, rested his head on his paws, and appeared to settle in for a bedside vigil.

It took an enormous effort for me to let go of her hand and leave the medical bay. With each step away from Elena, my feet seemed to weigh thirty kilograms each.

I will return soon, I thought, though I was not sure if I was reassuring Elena or myself.

I stopped at the weapons locker for a plasma gun on my way to the roof stairs. When I passed the lift, the lingering smell of Elena's blood and burned flesh made my stomach wrench and fury flare.

As the roof hatch opened, I emerged cautiously onto the landing pad. Other than faint traces of Elena's blood and burns, I neither smelled nor saw anything out of the ordinary.

The roof over the imaging lab, where Elena preferred to stargaze, was a very different story.

The air nearly crackled with the aftermath of what I would have thought was a direct strike by lightning if I did not know better. I found no damage to the grass or Elena's bedroll. And despite the size of the earlier korae, the sky showed no sign of any such activity now. The night was eerily still.

I crouched to pick up Elena's abandoned bedroll. Her scent permeated its outer fabric and inner fill. Without thinking, I pressed the bedroll's headrest to my nose and inhaled. Beneath the more recent smells of pain and fear was that pure joy of *Elena,* and I drank it in.

The scent of her cascaded through me, soothing hurts endured over years of isolation and before that, mistreatment, ostracism, and abuse. The wonder of it was nearly incomprehensible.

For a time, I lost track of where I was, what I was doing...even *who* I was in the tidal wave of comfort and peace. Finally, I let out a deep, shaky breath and rose.

The scent of ozone abruptly increased. I became suddenly aware of my own relative vulnerability on this wide expanse of roof.

Warily, I turned back toward the ladder that led to the landing pad.

A tendril of red plasma peeked over the edge of the roof.

Peeked? I scoffed at my own word choice. Plasma in any form did not *peek*.

Slowly, the tendril rose into view. It was about a meter long and very bright in the darkness. Was it the same tendril I had seen in the forest two days before, or another similar in appearance? I could not tell.

As before, the fact that what it was doing was impossible did not stop it from doing it.

It hovered a meter above the grass and about four meters from me, close enough that my skin buzzed and prickled with a sensation akin to powerful static. My feathers and wings fluttered uneasily and uncomfortably.

Slowly, the tendril dipped until it almost touched the grass, then raised again. Another slow dip, and then a third. With every movement it made, I felt as though I had lost my grip on reality. But this was no dream, and I did not think it was a hallucination. These movements seemed deliberate. A form of communication?

Even from a few meters away, the plasma's intense heat hurt my skin. If it came closer, I might be burned.

Wait—had this tendril caused Elena's injuries? I let out a low growl.

The tendril crossed the roof in less time than it took me to blink and vanished over the side of the building.

I dropped Elena's bedroll and launched myself into the air in pursuit.

The tendril darted across the clearing toward the forest, where it could easily have lost me in the trees. Instead, it turned away from the tree line and zipped under the station's platform to the other side of the facility. I gave chase, and it darted into the sky, zigzagging closer and then away from me.

I caught an updraft, soared above the tendril, and watched its movements as it zipped back and forth around Nova Cal, but not away from me as if trying to escape.

Realization dawned: by all the gods, it was *playing*.

My worry and anger over Elena's injuries collided with a much different set of emotions: wonder and amazement, with shock and disbelief mixed in.

That tendril of plasma was some form of life.

Everything I knew was against it, but my instincts told me it was true. In addition to the evidence of my own eyes, I had a *gut feeling*. My world turned upside down yet again.

For two years, I had studied every aspect of the korae—or at least, I thought I had. I had never seen this behavior, and surely neither had anyone else in the centuries visitors and scientists had come to Hyderia.

The implications were as jarring as the epiphany that the plasma was somehow sentient and, of all things, playful. The korae, or perhaps this species of korae, had chosen to reveal itself to us. But why?

What did I have to analyze? Hyderia had no imaging arrays that captured the roof or the area immediately above it. There had never been a need. All our equipment was trained on the upper atmosphere forty kilometers above and higher. Everything that had just transpired was not recorded.

If I contacted anyone with the claim the conservation world of Hyderia was home to sentient korae, I would either be mocked as I had mocked Elena, or the planet would be flooded with researchers of every kind. The latter consequence seemed far worse than the former.

This felt like a private, confidential revelation—something we had been chosen to discover, when no others had apparently been so trusted.

The tendril darted toward me several times and then away, clearly teasing or baiting me to give chase. Before I could plan my next move, my wristcomm beeped with a signal from the medical bay.

When I tapped the device, the computer's dispassionate voice said, "Patient is experiencing cardiac arrest. Please return to the medical bay."

My own hearts seemed to freeze in my chest. To hells with this tendril—Elena needed me *now*.

At full speed, I dove straight for the facility's deck and landed hard on my feet. My momentum sent me skidding forward and I nearly crashed into the exterior door. I slapped my palm to the scanner, muscled my way inside as the door slid open, and ran for the medical bay.

The fact I heard no alarms from the bay, as I would have expected given the emergency, did not process until I had already reached the doorway.

The sight inside the medical bay caused me to skid to a stop for the second time.

A meter-long tendril of green plasma hovered about three meters from Elena's bed. The smell of ozone seared my nostrils, but this tendril's power felt much more muted than the one I had just seen on the roof. Almost as startling was that Elena was sitting on the side of the bed, still naked but wrapped in a thermal blanket, and very much *not* in cardiac arrest.

Her burns remained pink, so the equipment had not completed its healing, but she appeared alert and no longer in agony. I began breathing again after a quick glance at the diagnostic screen confirmed that at least the damage to her heart had been repaired prior to the interruption.

Her hand rested on the bedside control panel. She must have sent the signal to summon me. Forux sat on the bed beside her, growling, his teeth bared at the tendril. The scene looked very much like a face-off. Anger and protectiveness as much as anything drove me to approach.

"What do you want?" I grated at the tendril.

Elena stared at me, then back at the tendril, her expression a combination of shock and confusion.

"Who are you?" I said when the plasma did not move. "Can you communicate?"

The tendril dipped slowly once, like the red plasma on the roof. Was this a form of communication? Or simply movement?

I approached the invader, putting myself between it and Elena. "Please move two times if you can understand me."

The tendril dipped twice.

For one of the few times in my life, my jaw dropped.

Elena slid from the bed and made her way unsteadily to my side, holding her thermal blanket in place with one hand. Worry and irritation made smoke puff from my nostrils.

"How can we learn to communicate with you?" she asked the plasma.

The tendril extended delicate threads as fine as Barmian spider-silk toward Elena. She flinched away from their crackling heat.

In a flash, I leapt between the plasma and Elena and spread my wings to block her from harm. My feathers ruffled with fury and protectiveness. "You will not hurt her."

The plasma retreated. Its threads moved across the floor, searing something into the metal tiles. Then the tendril zipped around us and out the open medical bay door.

I chased after the plasma, but by the time I reached the doorway it had vanished from sight, leaving only the scent of ozone in its wake.

When I returned to the medbay, Elena was standing over the scorched floor. I joined her and stared at the marks. Across the metal, the tendril had drawn a series of swooping, almost elegant symbols that could only be some form of language.

The korae of Hyderia were not only alive, but intelligent.

For only the second time in my life—the first being the moment I recognized Elena as my true mate—I stood rooted in place as disbelief, awe, shock, and wonder clashed with trepidation and the stomach-lurching sensation of being utterly at a loss.

Elena wrapped her blanket more tightly around her upper chest, turned to me, and put her free hand on her hip.

"*You*," she said, her voice tight with pain and suspicion, "have some explaining to do."

CHAPTER 11
ELENA

"Well?" I prompted when Ardruc remained silent, his gaze fixed on the symbols burned into the floor. "Why the hells are you suddenly talking to plasma like you knew it was going to respond? You said I was wasting my time and disparaging your life's work to even *suggest* such a thing was possible. Or am I misremembering your words?"

Still nothing. His thunderous scowl, the way a muscle moved in his jaw, and his twitching tail indicated he was furious, but something about the way his eyes tightened also made me think his emotions were much more complicated that that.

Well, that made two of us.

My skin felt tight where the tendril had burned me and my chest ached. While Ardruc gathered his thoughts, or whatever the hells he was doing, I stalked over to the emergency med pod and scrolled through the scans and diagnostics for information on my injuries. Burns…assorted bruises and lacerations, probably from my fall off the ladder…and most alarming of all, nearly fatal damage to my heart. What did that red tendril do to me?

I pressed my palm to my chest. A flare of pain made me suck in air and unwrap the blanket to see my skin between my breasts. I'd been too busy worrying about the sudden appearance of the plasma tendril and covering my nakedness to notice anything earlier.

Thanks to the medical bay equipment, the burn on my chest had healed somewhat. But in the center of the remaining redness was a red mark on my skin in the same shape as the first symbol the tendril had scorched into the floor.

I went cold all the way down to my core, and it had nothing to do with my lack of clothes or the temperature in the medical bay. What. The. *Hells?*

When I looked up, Ardruc was right in front of me, his gaze fixed on the mark on my chest. Despite his size, the man could move as fast as the electrical discharges he studied, and he did it silently.

"Hey." I wrapped my blanket tightly again. "Keep your eyes to yourself."

"My apologies for startling you." His eyes darkened, but not from anger like usual. Instead, he appeared very concerned and even solicitous. "For the record, I only looked at the mark," he added, his voice now so gentle that it unsettled me. "May I see it again?"

If he were almost anyone else, or this had been a different day, I might have thought he was trying to get another peep at my naked body. But for some reason, I believed him when he said he'd focused on the strange symbol. More to the point, I was struggling to hold back a rising wave of terror. Maybe if we examined the mark in a scientific and clinical way—the way Ardruc looked at every damn thing—I could keep the panic at bay.

I gripped the top of my blanket and looked up to meet Ardruc's golden gaze, hoping for the icy detachment I'd loathed for months. Instead, I saw anger, regret, and worry—the very emotions I did *not* want him to have.

Ardruc made a quiet rumbling sound in his chest I had never heard before, and I liked it.

"Elena," he said softly. "Please sit."

Trembling, I half sat, half fell onto the edge of the diagnostic bed. The blanket slipped just enough to reveal the top part of the mark, which hadn't disappeared or been a figment of my imagination. Not that I'd expected it to be, but I struggled to grapple with what had happened to me on a night when I'd planned to relax by watching korae on the roof with Forux and then go to sleep in my creaky little bunk.

I'd gotten sick or been injured before a half-dozen times during field research—most recently, during my ill-fated final trip across the ice on Aloris—but never experienced this level of fear. This wound had been made deliberately, and it was a symbol of something unknown. I still hurt from my half-healed burns too. I took a ragged breath.

That sweet-peppery scent I'd caught in my lab days ago swirled again, filling my senses even over the lingering odor of ozone. Inexplicably, my unease and pain lessened. Ardruc hadn't moved at all, but for some reason I thought he was the source of the scent.

"What's that smell?" I asked, frowning at him. "It's sweet, but with spices, like..." I tried to think of something comparable he might be familiar with. "Bacorian brandy," I said finally. Not a good analogy, but the best I could do.

He tilted his head. "I do not smell anything but you."

Suddenly, I was acutely aware of how close he stood, with one warm, pants-covered leg against my bare knee, and the way his beautiful wings blocked my view of most of the medical bay. The tip of his tail brushed my foot, almost like a caress.

He was very much in my personal space, but it didn't get my hackles up. And unlike every other interaction we'd had, he didn't look like he wished he was anywhere else but in my presence. What the hells had happened to the disdain he'd heaped on me from my first moments on Hyderia?

Well, that was a mystery for another time. I had far, far more serious concerns at the moment than Ardruc's personality change.

I moved the blanket so we could see the mark between my

breasts again. It wasn't raised like a brand, or cut into my skin—just a red swirling symbol that might have been tattooed into my flesh.

Ardruc bent to look at the mark more closely just as I took a deep breath to try to settle my nerves. Suddenly that sweet peppery scent was everywhere, filling my nose and lungs and seemingly seeping into my skin. It washed over me like a wave in the ocean, or as if I were standing under a waterfall. I had the very strange thought that if I were an arval, I might have purred, which made no sense at all.

"It's you," I whispered. "It's *you* I smell."

Why did he smell so good? I didn't even *like* Bacorian brandy. What was happening to me? Did it have something to do with the mark? Fear and confusion made my stomach clench.

Ardruc rumbled again. But this time, the rumbling didn't stop. It grew deeper and became a low note that made me shiver, but not in a bad way.

He clenched his jaw and took a step back. Then he flinched, almost to the point of doubling over.

"Ardruc?" I started to get up. But before I could move, his mouth opened, and he…sang.

The single note, deep and resonant, rolled through me and filled the room. All my pain and fear and confusion evaporated, leaving me warm, secure, and relaxed.

A little *too* relaxed, in fact. My legs turned rubbery, and I started to slide off the side of the diagnostic bed.

In a flash, Ardruc was at my side, the last of the strange, magical note still reverberating in his throat. He slid me gently back onto the bed so I was sitting rather than perched precariously and sat beside me. I couldn't help it; I rested my head against his bicep, which was far more comfortable than it had any right to be.

"What was that?" I murmured.

"It is…complicated," he said, his voice thick with emotion in a way I'd never heard before.

I might have been irritated with him for trying to dodge my

question if I weren't so relaxed. Still, I wanted an answer. "Uncomplicate it, then," I said.

His entire upper body moved as he inhaled deeply and exhaled slowly.

"I am able to ease your discomfort and negative emotions with a unique sound my body instinctually creates." His tone was a facsimile of the clinical detachment I'd wanted earlier, but not a very convincing one because his voice wasn't steady. "It would seem your presence triggered a physiological response within me."

I thought about what I knew of Fortusian biology. Their extensive use of genetic engineering was the subject of entire courses at universities on more than one planet. I hadn't taken any of those courses, but my astrobiology course had discussed their practices and physiology.

Suddenly, Ardruc's abrupt attitude change began to make sense. Through the warm haze created by his song, shock, disbelief, and alarm made my stomach churn anew.

I sat up and turned on the bed to face him. His expression was guarded, but he didn't move away.

"Are you telling me," I said slowly, "that my injury tonight caused you to recognize me as your true mate?"

"No," he said. But just as I was about to sigh in relief, he seemed to steel himself and added, "I recognized you as my true mate the moment you arrived at Nova Cal."

"*What?*" I gaped. "But you've been *so horrid—*"

The shame in his eyes and his grim expression were the clues I needed to piece it all together.

I cut myself off and stood, though I had to brace myself against the bed controls. My hands trembled in rage.

"You...self...centered...*bastard*," I ground out.

He rose too and took a step back to give me space.

"It was bad enough when I thought you were just an asshole," I fumed. "Don't tell me you've been treating me this way *for entirely selfish reasons* because you don't want a mate so you tried to drive me off the planet I've wanted to study since I was seventeen years old."

At first I thought he was going to assume that haughty pose he liked so much, with his hands clasped behind his back and chin raised. Instead he took another deep breath, fluttered his wings, and shook his head, his hands at his sides.

"You are right, Elena. Everything you say is true. I—" Whatever he was about to say, he seemed to change his mind. After a beat, he said, "I cannot offer any explanation that would excuse my behavior, or even begin to earn your forgiveness. I can only say from my…hearts…that I am truly and deeply sorry."

For a long time, I didn't know what to say, or even where to start.

At least some of the plasma bolts on Hyderia were sentient. One had damn near killed me after marking me with a symbol we didn't understand. Another had scorched what I was certain were words into the floor before vanishing as quickly as it had appeared.

And *on top of that*, Dr. Ardruc Husiorithae had just admitted he'd been an utter asshole to me for four straight months not because of anything I'd said or done, but because his blood and apparently other parts of his body sizzled in my presence.

Great gods above and below, what the hells was I supposed to do now? About *any* of these things?

I glanced at Forux to see what he thought of the situation—or maybe because I was sorely tempted to ask him to bite Ardruc. To my surprise, despite the tension in the room, he'd curled up on a chair to watch us with his head on his paws.

"I suspect your companion has known the truth for as long as I have," Ardruc said, his voice mild. "He is very sensitive to emotions. He encouraged me to hold your hand while you were undergoing emergency care."

Ardruc *held my hand?* I stared at my hand, and then at my traitorous arval companion, eyes narrowed.

"I deserve all your ire," Ardruc continued, either oblivious to my rising fury or trying to defuse it somehow by talking. "I also deserve any professional repercussions that may come from complaints you file with the Ministry or your own university—"

"Shut *up*, Ardruc." Gods, that felt good to say.

He blinked. His mouth snapped shut.

I thought back to those first moments on the landing pad the day I'd arrived, when he'd greeted me from a distance with a very neutral expression—and then physically recoiled when I came down the ramp and gave him a Fortusian-style bow of greeting. I'd replayed that moment more than once but never had a clue what the real reason had been for his reaction to my arrival.

It was no small challenge, but I tried to put myself in his shoes and imagine how I might feel if one day, out of the clear cobalt sky, a complete stranger appeared in my life my body and soul recognized as a true mate. I'd fallen in love a few times in relationships that ultimately couldn't survive the demands of my work or theirs. That feeling was nothing compared to what I imagined the draw of a true mate might be, and it hadn't involved any complete strangers.

Yes, I would have experienced a lot of emotions if our situation were reversed, and not all of them would have been good. But would I have reacted like Ardruc? Would I have been rude and cruel to force that person to abandon their dreams of working on Hyderia, especially once I knew how much being here meant to them?

Hells no, because I was many things, but I wasn't an...well, *asshole* was no longer an adequate descriptor.

I wanted to call him every name I could think of, and maybe take a swing at him too. And judging by his look of resignation, not only did he expect both, he thought he deserved them too.

Maybe his wretched expression held back my tirade, or maybe it was the gentleness he'd shown when terror overtook me. Maybe it was because while I wouldn't have made the same choices, I understood how thoroughly this had upended his world. Or maybe, just maybe, it was that song that washed away my pain and fear, and the fact it was irrefutable proof of what he'd said. Maybe it was all of the above, plus my exhaustion and a few more reasons I was too overwhelmed to process right now.

Whatever the cause, I didn't call him a Barmian wood slug, as much as I wanted to, and I didn't throw a punch…for now.

"I am too tired and in too much pain and too worried about sentient plasma tendrils and this weird mark to yell at you right now," I said instead.

His obvious astonishment very nearly made me smile despite everything. I'd seen more emotion from him in the past five minutes than in four whole months. That would be more disconcerting if my brain weren't already spinning in a dozen other directions.

"You are absolutely going to get one hundred percent of my ire as soon as I have the energy for it," I continued, and his expression turned wary again. "In the meantime, what the hells is this on my chest, and how can plasma be *alive?*"

CHAPTER 12
ARDRUC

I WANTED ANSWERS TO THOSE QUESTIONS AND MANY MORE TOO, BUT at the moment I struggled to focus on anything except Elena's obvious exhaustion and pain. To address the latter, she needed ten more minutes in the medical pod. And for the former, a good night's sleep.

Unbidden, an image appeared in my mind of Elena sleeping in my bed, with my arms around her and my wing folded over her to keep her safe and warm. I had never in my life envisioned such a peaceful moment. I yearned for it so much that I ached.

I was also acutely aware that if I suggested such a thing, I would likely see proof of her skill and training in J'Noran hand-to-hand fighting. She had earned a series of sashes throughout her childhood and adulthood, according to information in her personnel file.

What I said and did from this moment on would determine whether I had a chance to salvage something out of the mess I had created. I could not change the things I had done up until now, but I could make better decisions going forward. And perhaps one word or action at a time, I might be able to repair some of the damage I had caused.

"Ardruc," Elena said, her gaze searching my face.

Truly, I could not tell if she said my name any differently that time versus any time before this or if my own thoughts had made it sound this way, but the syllables caressed my ear altogether more like music than a spoken word.

"Given the immediate threat seems to have passed, I suggest you should first heal your burns," I said. Even to my own ears, I did not sound at all like Dr. Ardruc Husiorithae, Nova Cal Director of Research. Instead, I sounded like a man who knew he was treading on the very thinnest ice, and who must now grovel for his life. "After that, we can discuss our next steps."

"Oh, you *suggest*. No orders for me?" Elena tilted her head, a ghost of a smile on her lips that faded all too quickly. "I guess when you're right, you're right." She glanced down at herself. "I'll have to take off this blanket, though, so you're going to turn your back. And sit so you're not towering over me while I'm lying down."

I moved one of the tall medical bay chairs from the counter to near the head of the bed. I sat facing away, and positioned myself so I was not looking at anything that showed her reflection. "Is this acceptable?" I asked.

"Yes." Rustling behind me indicated Elena had settled back into the medpod. As its scanners and equipment activated, she let out a breath. "I need to be distracted," she said. "Talk to me about these plasma tendrils."

While the medical pod treated her burns, I described my encounter with the tendril on the roof that then led me on a chase through the sky around the station.

"Like a child," she murmured. "Playing a game, hiding in the forest, peeking at strangers from behind trees and then running away."

"Perhaps," I said. "Ordinarily I would dismiss the idea of a plasma 'child' as impossible, but as we witnessed a half-dozen impossible things in the last hour, I may have to redefine that term for myself."

She chuckled, then whimpered. "Ouch. Please don't make me laugh…which are words I never thought I'd say to you. *Ever.*"

"I will endeavor not to be funny," I said.

"Was that a joke, Ardruc? Surely not."

A warm sensation pooled in my chest at the sound of her saying my name in that light tone. "Of course it was not a joke," I said. "It is well known that dragons have no sense of humor."

"I must have missed that detail in my astrobiology course." She sighed. "I did try to tell you about the plasma tendrils, you know. It shouldn't have taken tonight's encounters to get you to listen to me."

"I know. I am sorry." We had enjoyed such a lovely moment of levity, but the grim reality was that I had to confess to yet another transgression. Nothing to do but say it. "I am also very sorry to say that tonight is not the first time I have seen one of these tendrils."

Rather than reply, she very audibly took several deep breaths, as if fighting to remain calm and still.

I described my brief encounter with a tendril in the forest and how it had played a note on my lat'sar.

"So it played music because it saw you playing?" she asked. "That's amazing. *Almost* as amazing as how someone as brilliant as you could have made so many terrible choices over the past few months. Really, I am mystified." Her tone turned wistful. "I wish I could have seen it and the playful kora. The one that came in here wasn't playful. But maybe they aren't korae. What do you think they are?"

"I do not know," I said. "For the past several days, I endeavored to find more evidence of similar occurrences in my records and those of scientists who studied here before me. I wanted something to analyze that could provide answers as to how what we saw was possible."

"And of course you didn't tell me." Elena sighed. "And?"

"And I found nothing. I also searched for any examples of

similar life forms elsewhere in the known galaxy. There were none. These life forms may be unique to this world."

"That's what my gut has been telling me." She exhaled. "Okay, while I'm lying here unable to move for another four or five minutes, do you have any other confessions? Let's just get it all out in the open. I have no idea how we go forward from here, but I don't want any more surprise admissions, or to find something out on my own. Whatever else you've done, you have to tell me now."

She was not offering forgiveness yet, or even the hope of it, but I would be a fool not to make a clean breast of things.

"I have only one more confession to make." I cleared my throat. "I drank some of your coffee."

She gasped. Forux raised his head and growled at me.

"I am sorry," I said earnestly. "I tried to develop a liking for it, since you enjoy it so much."

"I…" She hesitated. "Okay, I'm furious at you for being the reason I am running low and having to ration, but that is actually kind of sweet. I may not feed you feet-first to Forux after all."

Forux put his head back on his paws and snuffled. Whether his reaction was disappointment or relief, I could not tell.

"Coffee situation aside, what do we do about the tendrils?" Elena continued. "Should we contact the Ministry and report what's happened?"

I had been weighing the same question since my encounter in the forest. Everything that had happened tonight had infinitely complicated the matter—including my admissions about my behavior and Elena's reaction.

"I am unsure of the best and most correct choice," I admitted. "I would like to hear your opinion."

"Well, well. So the all-knowing director of research is having a scientific and ethical quandary and wants *my* opinion?" she said, her tone mocking. "Will wonders never cease?"

Before I could reply, the medical pod beeped and powered

down. She sighed. "Oh, thank all the gods above and below." I heard rustling behind me. "Okay, you can look at me."

When I turned, I found Elena sitting up on the bed, one bare leg hanging off the side as she held the blanket gathered around her chest.

She touched her cheek. "I feel like I'm okay now. Does it look like I am?"

I glanced at the diagnostic screen, then at her face and right hand. "It appears so. The diagnostics show all damage to your epidermis and heart has healed. How do you feel?"

Elena made a face. "Before all this happened, if you'd asked me that, I would have told you 'I'm fine' and gone back to my quarters to cry into Forux's fur in private." She puffed out a breath. "But now, I'm going to say I honestly feel like shit." She glanced at her chest, where the very tip of the mysterious mark was just visible above the edge of the blanket. "And I'm worried. And a little scared."

I reached for her hand, then hesitated. "May I?"

She studied me. "Why should I say yes?"

I considered my words carefully. "Because I would like to comfort you if I can, and I too am worried."

The corners of her mouth turned up. "Well, if you need to, you can hold my hand." She turned to dangle her legs over the side of the bed and raised her right hand, palm out.

If holding her hand earlier as she lay unconscious had felt like a crossroads, this mutual touch felt like a momentous first step down an entirely new road full of possibility and promise.

From an arm's length away, I placed my much-larger palm against hers and spread my fingers in an invitation. After a beat, she laced her fingers through mine and held on.

The evening—no, the past four months—had passed in endless avalanches of emotions, many of them conflicting. I braced myself for more of the same.

Instead, when her fingers closed on my hand, all the tumult washed away, leaving only peace in its wake. In all my years, on all the planets I had visited, I had not known such wonder as feeling utterly at peace in my soul.

Perhaps that showed on my face, because Elena tugged on my hand, urging me to move closer. I did not want to tower over her, so I used my free hand to raise the bed to bring us eye level to one another before moving to stand in front of her with one thigh pressed against her knee.

I bent my head to her shoulder and drank in her scent, noting every nuance like a Bacorian sommelier tasting the finest of wines. Everything about it soothed me, except the metallic smell of her fear and the heavier traces of weariness…and what might have been loneliness. Those scents and feelings resonated with me most of all.

I took a chance and wrapped the end of my tail very loosely around her lower leg, hoping the sensation would comfort her as it comforted me. She didn't relax, but she didn't glare or shake me off.

"This feels like meeting for the first time all over again," Elena said, then frowned. "No, that's not quite right. I don't know if the Ardruc I've known for four months was the real you, or this is, or neither, or both. Who the hells *are* you?"

That was a very good question—one of many I now had to confront.

"I would like to think the asshole I have been for the past four months is not the real me," I said, which earned me a fleeting smile. "The man I was before you arrived was not kind or hopeful or desirous of companionship either, however. I have been lost since I met you, trying to figure out who I am beneath all the façades I have chosen to use. That probably makes little sense to you."

"No, it makes sense. More than you know." She squeezed my hand. "I'm tired, though, and I can tell you are too. This isn't the time to make life-altering decisions about whatever *this* is—" she waved her hand at the air between us "—or what to do about the tendrils and the mark. We need sleep."

I wanted to be in my lab, analyzing data and searching for images of the strange tendrils, but she was right: I needed a clear head. Far more was at stake than my research into the korae. The future of Hyderia hung in the balance…and potentially Elena's life as well.

But the thought of Elena and Forux leaving my side to sleep in her little bunk in her little quarters made my feathers prickle and my stomach churn.

"Will you sleep—" I began.

"Can I sleep—" she said at the same time, then chuckled. "I guess neither of us feel like sleeping alone tonight, huh?"

"I suppose not. You are most welcome to stay with me." I reached for the bed controls to lower it so she could stand, but she caught my hand.

"I need to think," she said. "I thought I hated you. I *did* hate you. You were so incredibly unkind."

I swallowed hard. "I know."

"Even knowing now why you did it, it's not going to be easy for me to work through that." She held my gaze, unblinking. "And I'm not making any promises or offering forgiveness anytime soon. Just because you believe I'm your true mate doesn't mean I'm going to feel the same. We're not starting over. We're starting from *here*. And I am tired, and scared, and confused, and hurt, and really, really angry, though I'm too exhausted to look like it. So if you were thinking about seducing me tonight, forget it. We're going to sleep so we can wake up tomorrow and start sorting out this mess." She let go of my hands. "Okay, *now* you can lower me down."

Thoughts of seduction had not entered my brain, though she might not have believed me if I said so. That image of sleeping curled around her surfaced again, but even that was likely not what she had in mind. I would settle for having her nearby—close enough for her scent to reach me, and to comfort her if she wanted or needed that. She might, since she had asked to stay near me tonight.

A chance was more than I deserved. Anything more was as much of a miracle as sentient plasma.

CHAPTER 13
ELENA

WWE SET THE COMPUTER TO WORK ATTEMPTING TO ANALYZE OR translate the symbols on the floor, and then Ardruc followed Forux and me to our little apartment.

He stood in the doorway, watching as I collected my sleepwear and a change of clothes for the morning, with his brow furrowed as if worried I might faint, morph into living plasma, or evaporate into thin air. I might have mocked him for it if I wasn't so damn tired.

I draped my clothing over my arm. "Ready."

He glanced around the apartment's combined sleeping and living area. "Where does Forux sleep? Does he not have a bed?"

Forux fanned out his tails and showed Ardruc his teeth.

"Forux shares my bed," I said, joining him in the doorway. "We're a package deal."

"Of course," he said, though the feathers on his wings and in his hair ruffled in a way that made me think he was less than thrilled about the prospect.

I had a strange urge to smooth those feathers. What would he do if I did?

"You are swaying on your feet," Ardruc said, in that disarmingly gentle tone that caused me to forget for a moment or two how pissed off I was at him. And then he offered me his arm.

Part of me wanted to tell him not to overdo it on the gallant gestures, but the part that was exhausted and achy and freaked out—which was the majority of me, truth be told—argued that I could let him take care of me just for tonight. Tomorrow, after a good night's sleep, he'd be back at arm's length while I figured out what the hells to do with him.

I tucked my hand in the crook of his elbow for the walk to his apartment...which had never seemed so far from mine as it did now. And standing next to him in bare feet made me very aware of just how much *bigger* he was. I felt tiny by comparison. My exhaustion and hurts and worries made me feel small too.

He walked very slowly to keep pace with me. Everything about this new thoughtful and kind version of Ardruc unsettled me.

"Your door creaks," Ardruc said. A muscle moved in his jaw. "I am sorry."

I focused on putting one foot in front of the other. "It's okay. I don't really notice it anymore."

"Would you like me to help move your belongings into one of the empty apartments?"

Someone's conscience was bothering him. And to think, for four months I was absolutely certain he didn't have one.

"Ask me again when I have enough energy to think about my answer," I said wearily. "All I can think about right now is sleep." And this damn mark on my chest. A creaky door wasn't in the top one hundred things worrying me at the moment.

When we reached Ardruc's apartment, Forux ran ahead of us through the large living area and straight into the bedroom, where he jumped onto the bed and curled up in the bottom corner closest to the doorway.

"He guards me," I said at Ardruc's raised eyebrows. "But he likes to be comfortable while he does it."

He led me to the door of his bathroom. "Do you need my assistance?" he asked.

"No." Even if I did, I wouldn't tell him so. Even shreds of dignity were still something.

His quarters looked exactly like what I'd expected: very utilitarian, exceedingly neat, and sparsely decorated with a few everyday items and artworks he'd probably collected from planets he'd visited. I spotted a Tivoran water sculpture preserved in a stasis cylinder, an Engareni lava candle, and a surprisingly luxurious set of hand-forged Bacorian serving dishes stacked neatly on a table.

Not one personal item, though. No screens displaying images of family or friends. I'd almost think no one actually lived here, much less for two years.

"Elena?" Ardruc touched my arm.

"Yes. I'm moving." I went into the bathroom and waved my hand over the scanner to close the door behind me.

When I emerged in my most comfortable sleepwear—a light, long-sleeved tunic and matching pants—Ardruc was sitting on the end of the bed scratching Forux behind his ears.

My jaw dropped. "He's never let anyone touch him but me since he was a baby."

Ardruc gave Forux a last scratch and rose. "I am honored, then. Perhaps it will make you feel better to know he bit me earlier when I did not do what he wanted."

"It does, actually." I trudged to the bed. "Which side is yours?"

"You are welcome to choose which you like best."

Since Forux was already settled on the right side of the bed, I folded back the bedding and slid under the covers next to him. The bed was huge and soft and it cradled my aching body and it didn't squeak every time I moved. Oh, heavenly. I damn near moaned. No wonder Forux was purring.

In the doorway, Ardruc passed his hand over the light controls. The apartment went dark except for a faint glow from the front room, leaving him silhouetted in the bedroom doorway. His eyes shone gold in the sudden near-darkness. Beautiful.

"What is beautiful?" Ardruc asked.

I blinked, and then my stomach lurched. Oh, gods…I'd said it aloud.

"Those Bacorian dishes in the front room," I said, fighting the urge to pull the covers over my head. "Really gorgeous."

"Thank you. I think so as well." He hesitated. "I will join you in a few minutes. If you are already asleep, I will try not to disturb you."

"Take your time." With a yawn and a grimace, I curled up on my side facing the doorway with my back to his side of the bed.

Ardruc went into the bathroom. As soon as the door slid closed behind him, Forux chuffed softly.

"Traitor," I muttered. "You've never let *anyone* pet you but me. Don't get any ideas about staying here, either. This is just for tonight. There's nothing wrong with our bed."

He growled. Arvals didn't like lies. I suspected sensing dishonesty caused them discomfort of some kind.

I yawned again and closed my eyes, hoping to fall asleep quickly before Ardruc came back. I sure as hells felt tired enough.

But as minutes passed and I lay in the bed listening to Forux's throaty purr, sleep didn't come.

With an exasperated groan, I rolled to my back and pulled down the V-neck of my sleep shirt to look at my chest. The mark wasn't visible to my human eyes in the near-dark and it produced no sensations, but I *felt* it there. And there wasn't a damn thing I could do about it.

With a sigh, I let go of my shirt and curled up again, this time with my back to the doorway. I closed my eyes and turned my face into the pillow.

The bedding smelled like Ardruc—or, rather, like that Bacorian brandy scent I'd noticed earlier, plus a hint of smoke. I inhaled deeply several times.

When I opened my eyes again, Ardruc stood at the side of the bed, a faint silhouette with glowing eyes. He seemed to be shirtless and wearing sleeping pants. If only the room had a little more light, so I could see…

Stop that, Elena Regis. You don't need to see a damn thing.

To my surprise, he lay on top of the bedding rather than under the covers. Maybe with his body heat and wings he didn't require anything else.

"You are not asleep," he said, his voice very quiet. "You are troubled."

"I knew you were a genius," I said, but without rancor. I was too tired and unsettled to be angry or even come up with a good insult.

A warm hand tentatively touched mine. "May I?" Ardruc asked.

I was also too tired to figure out a reason to refuse. "Yes."

He covered my hand with his and squeezed. He felt so warm, and I was so cold. "It is unfair that this has happened to you," he said. "I would trade places with you if I could."

"I don't think I'd wish it on anyone else, even you." I sighed. "I should stop joking at your expense. I'm not rude by nature. I think it's a coping mechanism."

"You may joke at my expense as much as you need to," he said. The warm golden glow of his eyes was damn near mesmerizing. "I know you are worried. You have every reason to be. But between my scientific methods and your brilliance and intuition, I believe we will solve the mystery of the mark."

"Oh, now I'm *brilliant*, am I?" I chuckled softly. "I thought you hated everything about my intuitive methods and gut feelings."

"It is not that I hate them. I do not understand them." He hesitated. "Or at least I told myself I do not, but I am reconsidering that belief. But we can discuss that more tomorrow. Please try to sleep, Elena."

"I can't," I said, and I hated how much my voice trembled. "I'm so tired, but every time I close my eyes all I can think of is that damned mark and sleep just evaporates."

"May I try to help?"

"How so? A lullaby?"

"Of a sort." He hummed softly. "I am no expert in true mate physiology, and much of what I know is purely theoretical."

I smiled despite my tiredness. "Let me guess: once I arrived, you researched it?"

"Yes." He moved a little closer. "I did not expect to use the knowledge in practice, but I wanted to understand my condition."

I almost chuckled. "Am I a condition?"

"Scientifically speaking, yes." He squeezed my hand again. "One that has become…not disagreeable."

Not disagreeable? He really needed to work on his flirting. "So what did you find out that might be applicable in this situation?"

"You have heard my coo. That is not my only way to provide comfort. From my dragon DNA, I believe I have the ability to produce several kinds of pheromones that affect only my true mate. They serve various purposes. One of them may help you sleep peacefully."

"*May* help?"

"As I said, this is based on research. I have never put any of it into practice." Ardruc hesitated. "As I have committed to being truthful with you at all times, I will tell you I am compelled to help ease your exhaustion and worry, just as I am compelled to coo when you are hurt. If I do not act, the urge causes discomfort and even pain."

Oh. Suddenly, calling me a "condition" made a lot more sense.

Not that long ago, I might have taken some pleasure from the thought of him experiencing discomfort. In fact, I'd wished him more than just discomfort on several occasions, up to and including asphyxiation in the cold emptiness of space.

At the moment, though, I hurt too much to want anyone else to be hurting—even Ardruc.

"What do you need to do to put this into practice, then?" I asked. "Can you control the release of pheromones?"

"Yes and no. It is instinctual, but I am apparently unable to release them unless I know you would welcome them. It is a way to ensure I do not use them against your will. I can go into more detail on this if you would like, so you understand."

"Maybe tomorrow." I yawned. "I don't have enough working brain cells right now to think about molecular biology. Just for tonight, I consent to falling asleep peacefully courtesy of your pheromones."

"May I lie next to you so I may drape my wing over you?" he asked. "I believe that encourages the pheromone production."

"Go ahead," I said. "Just for tonight."

Cautiously, he slid closer and rested his wing on top of the covers. His smoky brandy-and-pepper scent filled my nose. I let out a little sigh of contentment.

Maybe taking his cue from Ardruc, or maybe because he thought I'd finally settled into a position for sleeping rather than tossing and turning, Forux curled up against the back of my legs, his purr a soothing rumble.

This new proximity meant my head was right next to Ardruc's bent arm. I nestled the crown of my head against his forearm. The weight and warmth of his wing sent a wave of comfort and… peace?…through me.

"Elena," Ardruc murmured.

Strangely, I didn't think he was talking to me—more like he just wanted to say my name aloud and savor it. A far cry from the frosty "Dr. Regis" I'd heard so many times since the day I arrived. I'd never had an inkling of what Ardruc had hidden beneath those four icy syllables.

I smelled nothing different—not that I should have, since pheromones were odorless. But the process must have gone as Ardruc's research had indicated it would.

In only a handful of breaths, my eyes drifted closed. My arms and legs went from restless to heavy and still. Thoughts of the mark on my chest were not accompanied by spikes of uneasiness or fear anymore. All my worries and aches drifted away, leaving me content and very, very sleepy.

"Ardruc?" I murmured.

"Yes?" he asked, also quietly.

"Thanks for the lullaby."

Something brushed my forehead. Maybe his lips. "You are most welcome," he said.

Soft darkness swept me away.

CHAPTER 14
ARDRUC

I woke slowly from a long, abyssal, and dreamless sleep, rising up through layers of consciousness over what felt like a long time instead of my usual abrupt, very dragon-like transition from sleep to fully awake.

I felt extremely well-rested, relaxed, content, and secure, as though I had slept soundly in a very safe place.

The second physical sensation that reached me through my semi-conscious fog was my mate's glorious scent—the balm for my soul I had craved for so long. The third, the feeling of a soft, warm body wrapped in my arms: Elena, breathing deeply and evenly, tucked against my bare chest, safe and treasured under my draped wing, as I had dreamed of holding her.

I drifted for a long, mindless time in this bliss, content not to wake just yet and feeling no urgency to do so.

Gradually, like an alarm in the far distance, something began to nag at me as *not right*. Uneasiness formed a knot in my stomach as a string of realizations crystallized in my cottony mind.

I had slept *too* deeply, *too* dreamlessly, for too long.

Even content with Elena in my arms, I should *want* to rise and begin the search for answers about her strange mark and the apparently sentient korae, but I did not.

The air in my apartment did not smell as it had for the past two years, and not only because Elena had shared my bed.

And my utter lack of reaction to these realizations was not normal. Something was terribly wrong.

It took all my willpower to force my eyes open and break the spell. For several heartsbeats, I stared blankly, my body cold with shock, fighting to process what my eyes beheld.

My apartment was gone. No, not gone—transformed. *Impossibly* transformed.

The walls and ceiling had all but disappeared behind a thick layer of vines, branches, and blue-green autumn foliage. Mushrooms in all colors, shapes, and sizes peeked through the foliage, growing in clusters. Lichen in various colors covered whole sections of branches.

The windows alone had remained uncovered. I had made them opaque before going to bed so the early morning light did not disturb Elena's sleep, but now they were clear and what appeared to be mid-morning sunshine poured in.

The sunlight glimmered on a thin layer of sweet-smelling dust, pollen, or spores that covered every surface in the room, including Elena and I. And Forux, who lay curled up against the back of Elena's pajama-clad legs, snoring quietly.

The shimmering particles disintegrated, leaving only their scent behind. Had they caused us to stay unconscious and created a state of euphoria? The prospect angered me—and intrigued me, scientifically.

I moved my head so I could see Elena's face. She slept as peacefully and deeply as I had, a thin veil of loose, golden hair over her face. Her lips were turned up at the corners. Perhaps she remained in the state of bliss I had experienced before my instincts alerted me to our circumstances.

Her body temperature was warmer than usual, likely due to my body heat. I enjoyed that sensation and the thought I had kept her warm. But I had fallen asleep with my hand on hers and my wing draped over her atop the bedding. At some point, without waking me, she had extricated herself from beneath the covers and become wrapped in my arms, her face nestled against my bare chest.

Or had *I* moved *her?* I had no memory of doing so, but I had been insensible to the transformation of my living quarters.

I would have called it impossible for me to have done such a thing in my sleep, or to have forgotten what I had done during the night. But after the events of the past week, I could call nothing impossible now, surely.

My tail was wrapped around her calf too. However it had happened, I had protected her and treasured her in my sleep.

My stomach lurched again. How long *had* we slept? And if Elena had not moved of her own accord, how might she react to finding herself in my arms? I did not want to disturb her rest, but I must.

"Elena," I murmured, smoothing her hair back from her face. The strands were every bit as silky as I had imagined. "Elena, wake, please."

She let out a contented sigh. Warmth blossomed in my chest and my unease faded. As much as her weariness, worry, and pain had disquieted me, her happiness, regardless of its cause, provided profound comfort. I had no time to relish this feeling, but it was another joy of finding a true mate—or what it might be like to have one.

Elena stretched languidly, like a sleepy Solani desert lion in the midday sun. Her eyelashes fluttered open.

We gazed at each other for a few moments as she blinked slowly, struggling to shed the weight of sleep.

What she might be thinking, I did not know. My own thoughts were of her beautiful blue gaze and how much I wished I could simply lose myself in it rather than confront our situation. Was that a lingering symptom of our long sleep and possible intoxication by the dust, or the longing for my true mate? Perhaps both.

Her gaze left my face to scan the room behind me. She stilled, her eyes wide. Shock, wonder, fear, and a half-dozen other emotions crossed her features. Watching her process the scene around us was like observing a recording of what my own expression must have looked like when I woke.

"Ardruc." She extricated one of her arms and rubbed her eyes. "What…the…*hells?*" She blinked at me a few times, as if only now realizing I held her.

Her gaze moved to my chest, where it lingered, scouring the planes of my muscles and following the scale pattern on my skin.

Finally, she blinked again and focused on my face. "I was under the covers when I fell asleep," she said, frowning. "Did I climb into your arms or did you move me?"

"I do not know." I wanted to kiss her forehead, but resisted the urge. I did not know if the gesture would be welcome, and as such I would not risk it. "I have no memory of moving or of moving you. Also, I must warn you: I believe we have slept for much longer than a single night."

"I feel like I've been asleep for a week." Elena turned her head to look behind her. "Where's Forux?"

Rumbling, eyes half-lidded, the sleepy arval clambered over Elena and wedged himself between us with a snuffly sound. He seemed oddly unconcerned about the change in our surroundings. Possibly whatever had forced us to stay asleep still affected him.

Elena scratched the top of his head and nuzzled his fur. He closed his eyes and resumed snoring.

I extricated my arm and glanced at my wristcomm. "We have slept for a full day and night. It is 0830 hours."

"Yep, it feels like a whole day and a half." She stretched again. "Ooh, I feel rested."

I glanced at her chest. "The mark?"

She pulled the neckline of her sleep shirt down and stared. "Oh, gods."

The strange symbol had turned from red to blue-green while we slept. The color matched the foliage around us. And it shimmered in the sunlight, much like the pollen or spores that I was all but certain had drugged us.

She studied the mark in the sunlight from different angles as I described the strange particles.

"I do not know if those particles caused us to stay asleep and feel euphoric," I finished. "But my instincts tell me they did."

"There you go, being intuitive again." She gave me a wan smile and covered the mark. "This is getting dangerously close to becoming a habit with you."

Despite our situation, her teasing was a joy. "It would seem so," I said.

She stunned me by pressing her nose to my chest above my hearts and inhaling deeply. She let out a long sigh, her breath warm on my skin. I took a chance and rested my chin on her head.

"At least I got the best sleep of my life," she murmured. Her palm rested on my chest, her fingertips lightly stroking my skin as I rumbled in contentment. "I'm not sure why I'm sniffing you," she added, "but it makes me less anxious, and it feels really good."

"It feels very good to me as well." I pressed my lips to her silken hair. "So you may do this whenever you want."

"Thanks." Her tone was dry. "I'll just sniff you whenever I'm unhappy. That's not weird at all."

"It is not so weird," I countered. "Scent is powerful between true mates. And besides, what would we consider 'weird' now?"

"Those are both good points." She groaned. "Gods, I slept amazingly well, but my brain feels so foggy. I need coffee. *Lots* of it. Preferably intravenously."

I grimaced, but rubbed her back reassuringly. "After such a long sleep, I can well imagine you do."

"I hate to say it," Elena said, the corner of her mouth twisted up in a wry smile. "But we're going to have to get out of bed and find out just how much of the station has changed and whether we can contact the Ministry."

Every cell in my body protested the thought of letting her go, but she was right. We needed answers and must make decisions. Both required leaving this bed.

"Yes." Reluctantly, I loosened my hold on her, unwrapped my tail from around her leg, and began to move away.

In a blink, she leaned in and pressed her lips to mine.

And just like when I had caught her scent for the first time on the roof, I lost all sense of myself and my surroundings. Everything faded away, leaving only her.

Fire rushed through my veins, igniting everything in its wake. All that I was burned for her, wanted her, *needed* her. I drank in the sweetness of her lips, the softness of her body, her heartbeat, her scents, everything that made her Elena.

My chest rumbled and my wings shivered. Gods, I wanted more of this.

Why had I held back for so long? What good had it done either of us? *What if I had gotten my wish that she would leave and I had lost her?* The thought left me cold.

To banish the chill, I cupped her face with my hand. Just that small touch, the feeling of her skin against mine, made my cock stir, my tail twitch, and my hearts pound.

When she drew back, I found myself at a loss for words. "Elena…"

"Sorry for surprising you." Her smile warmed me like the brightest sunshine. "I have a feeling we're about to be very, very busy and focused on other things, so I went for it. I wanted to know if I'd like kissing you."

Her racing heart and the scent of desire had already answered that question for me, but I brushed her lower lip with my thumb and asked, "And did you?"

"I did." Her smile turned impish. "Let's do it again soon."

With that, as abruptly as tearing off a bandage, Elena rolled out of my arms to sit on the edge of the bed, her back to me. "Went to bed in a research station, woke up in the forest," she muttered. "Ardruc, did you know the floor is grass?"

"I did not, but I smell grass, so I am not surprised." I scratched Forux's head, left him snoring, and moved to my side of the bed.

Indeed, the flooring had disappeared under a thick layer of soil and dark blue-green grass. When I set my feet on it, it was very soft and released a pleasant scent. In fact, the entire station smelled like forest now—natural and green and *alive*—and hardly at all like the odors of chemicals, metal, fuel, and wiring that had often made my sensitive nose twitch, especially when I returned to the station after spending time outdoors.

"It's like Hyderia has claimed this station as its own," Elena said, just as I opened my mouth to say the same thing. "Not taken it back, since the Nyvorans built it, but *taken* it."

"The station's basic functions seem intact," I noted. "The air circulation system appears unaffected and we have power. But I am concerned about the medical bay equipment, food preparation, sanitation, and the rest."

"Me too. At least all our data and research is secured and backed up." She stood and stretched, her arms over her head, and bent at the waist to put her palms on the floor between her feet. "We should try to find out what that dust was that you saw," she said as she straightened. "If we could bottle some, it could be the cure for insomnia. That discovery could fund this station and keep us comfortable here for the rest of our lives."

My brain skidded to a halt on the casual way she spoke of spending her life on Hyderia with me.

To cover my reaction, I rose and stretched as well, marveling at how warm and ache-free my muscles felt, even after sleeping for such a long time. I had seldom felt better rested in my life.

As I spread my wings and settled my feathers, Elena padded barefoot to the wall, where leafy vines and branches all but obscured every square centimeter of the partition between this room and the living area. Out of the corner of my eye, I watched her reach for one of the branches.

She gasped.

I half-ran, half-flew to her side, my feathers prickling with anger, protectiveness, and worry. From my fluffed hair to the tip of my tail, my body's reaction to that soft sound of surprise and alarm was unified: *My mate must not come to harm.*

Strange and freeing to find myself responding in such a way after months of burying these urges and a lifetime of never experiencing them at all.

Elena was not hurt, however.

I watched, dumbfounded, as a vine detached from the rest of the foliage and extended toward Elena, its blue-green leaves caressing her outstretched hand. It twined itself as gently and lovingly around her fingers, wrist, and forearm as I had encircled her leg with my tail. She watched it move, eyes wide with wonder. I caught the scent of her fear, but it was mild. She appeared far more in awe than afraid.

"Elena?" I touched her other hand because she seemed nearly mesmerized, and to reassure myself. "Are you well?"

"Yes." She looked up, her eyes sparkling. "It's welcoming us."

Uneasiness and suspicion made me want to rip the vine from her arm and drag her away. "How does it speak to you?" I asked.

"It's not speaking to me in words. It's a feeling." Elena's smile turned wry. "I'm aware of how weird that sounds, for the record. I can tell you're worried." She took my free hand and squeezed. "I know just as little about what's going on as you, so keep an eye on me, okay? If I start acting strangely or growing branches, you have my permission to do whatever you need to do to protect me, even if it's from myself."

"I will." I studied the foliage. "We should investigate the rest of the station and then decide what to do next."

"I know," she said with a sigh.

Gently, she extricated herself from the vine. It unwound itself readily from her arm and returned to the branch, settling in among the mushrooms and lichen. Only when I confirmed that no marks or wounds had appeared on her skin did the tension leave my shoulders.

Elena's gaze swept over me. Her tongue darted out to moisten her lips.

I was suddenly acutely aware of all my bare skin, and that my sleep pants rested low on my hips, revealing my lower abdomen and the darker red scale pattern that ran from my navel to my groin. Her gaze lingered there, and drifted a little lower.

Her sleepwear was as simple and comfortable as mine, but the way it draped her body made me want to fall to my knees and press my face to her abdomen to breathe her in. I ached for her scent, her softness, her touch.

Beneath the thin material of my sleep pants, my cock began to harden and bead with lubrication, preparing to please my mate. The tip of my tail quivered.

All the gods above and below, if I did not distract myself some-how, my desire would become very visually apparent *very* soon, but I could not tear my gaze away, much less redirect my thoughts.

"I desperately need you to put clothes on," Elena said, her voice husky. "I'm trying to remember how mad I am at you, and I need to be able to think like a scientist. This will all be much easier if I don't have to look at you with no shirt on."

She reached out with both hands. My breath hitched. Where would she touch me? Could I bear it? Could I control myself if she put her hands on me? I genuinely did not know.

Her thumbs hooked into the cinched waistband of my sleep pants. My hearts stuttered in my chest.

Her gaze locked on mine, she drew the top of my pants up over my hips and let go, allowing the fabric to snap snugly onto my waist.

"Have mercy on me, Ardruc," she said with a knowing smile, as if she heard my hearts pounding and blood rushing. "Go dress like you're the director of research. If you don't, I'll tell Forux to bite your tail. Or better yet, *I'll* bite your tail."

That threat had quite the opposite effect of what she had intended. It conjured fantasies of her mouth on me, her teeth in my flesh, the tip of my tail between her lips...and delving into other warmer, more intimate places.

I had to force myself to walk away from her, go to my closet for clothing, and hurry to the bathroom.

Like the rest of my apartment, forest foliage and fungi had taken over the bathroom. To my relief, both the water-based and sonic cleaning systems still worked, so perhaps all the station's basic life-support functions still operated.

A cold shower might have served me best, but for expedience I utilized the sonic system to clean my body before dressing quickly in a shirt, pants, and boots. Every moment I was separated from Elena rather than guarding her from potential threats caused my guts to churn.

When I emerged, I found Forux awake but dozing and Elena examining the mushrooms and lichen growing among the branches.

"Look at them," she said, without turning around. "I know you don't care that much about fungi, but just look at their colors and variety. And they're more like us than they are like plants, you know—at least, genetically speaking."

"I have heard that is true." I joined her and let my fingertips brush hers. "I know little of fungi, but I see why you call them beautiful and fascinating."

"I feel the same about your korae—both the regular ones and the living ones." Elena glanced at my attire and smiled. "Much better. Very professional, and *much* less distracting." She gathered up her own change of clothes and headed for the bathroom. "I'll only be a few minutes," she said before closing the door.

Forux rose, stretched, and made a chuffing sound as he ambled to the edge of the bed near where I stood. I scratched behind all his ears, eliciting a deep, rumbly purr.

"I adore your mistress," I confided as he yawned. "Our station has been taken over, some computer functions may no longer work, and Elena says the forest welcomes us—whatever that may mean. I do not know what lies ahead, but I *do* know I have to get this right."

Forux tilted his head.

"Good point," I said. "What do I mean, *get this right?*" I thought about the question. "I would like to know what life is like with a true mate. Is it as happy and contented as the research says? I would like to make up for my poor choices, if I can. And most of all, I want Elena to be happy. How do I ensure she is?"

Forux settled on the bed, his front paws tucked under himself, and held my gaze.

I studied his pose. The tucked paws implied he felt safe and relaxed and believed he would not have to run or escape from anything. The position also conserved body heat. For all the changes that had taken place while we slept, the temperature in my apartment was very comfortable. I had seen no indication that Elena was either too cold or too hot—no shivering, nor flushed skin or perspiration.

Perhaps I was reading too much into Forux's body language, but the little arval had demonstrated not only perceptiveness but intelligence. I believed he had understood my question and done his best to answer.

So I must keep Elena safe and warm and all that urge implied. And stay nearby as well to offer protection, care, and support when needed, but not so closely that I became a hindrance or, worse, smothering. I must respect her space.

I gave Forux a nod. All these things, I could do—I *would* do—with joy in my hearts, until Elena decided whether she found me worthy.

In the meantime, we had many mysteries to solve.

CHAPTER 15
ELENA

When I came out of Ardruc's bathroom freshly sanitized and wearing a jumpsuit and boots, he and Forux were waiting for me with nearly identical expressions of anticipation tinged with impatience.

"We are ready to explore the station," Ardruc announced, his hands folded behind his back and tail swishing. "Once you have had your coffee, of course."

He'd always kept his tail wrapped around one of his legs. Only now did I realize how much his feelings affected its movement. Before his confession about being my true mate, he'd made sure it was studiously restrained every minute I was nearby to hide his emotions. That revelation made me sad.

"Let's hope I can still make my coffee," I said. "If I can't, I may have to stand up on the roof until I get a shock from a kora to get myself fully awake."

"The medical bay has a considerable stock of stimulants," Ardruc offered helpfully as we headed for the door of his apartment. "Most are far less dangerous than strikes by korae or lightning, and more palatable than coffee."

I ignored that last bit. "Let's just see what the kitchen looks like before I move on to contingency plans."

Ardruc waved his hand over the scanner by his apartment door. It slid aside soundlessly—unlike my own door, which, as he'd noted, creaked. He must have remembered that too. We exchanged quick, knowing smiles as Forux preceded us into the hallway.

The forest had indeed taken over Nova Cal.

Thick, fragrant grass covered the floor. The walls and ceiling had all but disappeared behind leafy branches and vines. Much like the windows in Ardruc's apartment, the many skylights remained uncovered. The station's design reflected the Nyvorans' love of natural light. I'd always appreciated the skylights, which allowed us to only need artificial light in our labs and during the night, but now I marveled at the way the sunlight spilled over the foliage and grass—and how much the mushrooms and lichen seemed to flourish.

"This is incredible," I said, my voice almost a whisper. "All this grew in just forty-two hours? I keep thinking it's all impossible, but it isn't because we're looking at it."

When Ardruc didn't reply, I looked up. He appeared deeply unsettled and even bewildered, as if his world had upended itself and set him adrift.

For as long as I'd known him—and for a long time before, if rumors about him were true—he'd relied on methods and procedures based on known quantities. He'd scoffed at gut feelings and daydreams to the point of being pedantic. Why he was this way, I didn't know, but he'd definitely relied on hard science to provide a firm foundation for not just his research but his entire being.

Now we were surrounded by impossible things, and the director of research had utterly lost his footing.

I found myself taking his much-larger hand and squeezing. "Let's have coffee," I suggested. "Everything seems more possible after coffee."

Ardruc remained grim, but his lips turned up at the corners. "Let us hope that holds to be true."

The kitchen was at the opposite end of the T-shaped station from Ardruc's apartment. Our first stop on the way was the weapons locker, where we each picked up plasma guns and holsters for them.

"We do not know whether these will affect potential adversaries," Ardruc noted as I buckled the straps around my waist and thigh and slipped the gun into the holster.

"True. That's why I also have this." I withdrew a slim dagger from its sheath in my right boot.

"A very nice weapon." He studied it. "Is it J'noran? What is that on the blade?"

"Yes, I bought it on J'nora." I turned the dagger so it glinted in the light and he could see the symbols etched in the metal. "The writing is a blessing I received while living and researching on Palus. It doesn't translate directly, but basically it says, *May this blade protect its bearer, and may it never fall from her hand.*"

"That is a lovely sentiment." He secured his own weapons. "And long may it be so."

I returned the dagger to its sheath. "If we can't shoot them and we can't cut them, I suppose we'll have to outsmart them."

He chuckled. "Let us hope it does not come to that, as I feel much less knowledgeable and intelligent today than ever in my life."

"Even more so than the last time you went up for an academic review?" I teased.

"Well." His mouth turned down, but his golden eyes twinkled. "Perhaps it is a tie."

The next door past the weapons locker was Ardruc's lab. As badly as I wanted and needed coffee, our curiosity demanded we stop to see what its interior looked like.

Unsurprisingly, the walls, ceilings, and floors had filled with grass, branches, vines, and leaves, but his workspaces—computer terminals, screens, countertops, and so forth—were left clear.

Forux and I followed Ardruc inside Lab One. We found the computer compiling information from the massive korae that had taken place the night before last when I was burned. All his screens showed images and data, much as they'd done every hour I'd resided at Nova Cal.

"Normally I would hesitate to ascribe intent to flora or fungi," Ardruc said, leaning on his desk with both hands to study the screens. "But it would almost appear as if the forest would like us to continue our work."

Meanwhile, I wanted to know whether the station's computer-run systems were operating normally. "Computer, open a comm channel to Minister Ganna on Nyvor."

The computer beeped. "All interplanetary communication systems are offline."

My heart sank. "Explain the nature of the status of the interplanetary comm systems."

"The comm systems are functional," the computer reported in the same emotionless tone. "The relay satellites are not responding and may have been damaged by weather. Current status unknown."

In other words, Ardruc and I could communicate within range of the station, but the satellites that permitted us to contact anyone on Nyvor, Fyloria, or any other planet wouldn't work. The small transports on the landing pad were not capable of spaceflight—only flight within a certain radius inside the planet's atmosphere. We were cut off completely.

My other biggest concern was my own research. "Computer, what is the status of the sample labeled *Basiforuximycota Prime* in Lab Three?" I asked.

Beep. "The sample is stable," the computer reported.

From his desk, where his screens still showed images of korae and the data associated with them, Ardruc looked at me over his shoulder. "I am supremely grateful my equipment and my ability to continue my research appears intact."

"I hope the same is true for mine." I scrubbed my face. "I want to check on my lab and medbay. And then…"

"Yes, coffee." He ushered me out of Lab One and down the hall toward Lab Three.

Long before we reached it, I knew something was vastly different about my lab versus Ardruc's. At this end of the hall, foliage covered the skylights, and without artificial light the corridor was dark. The glass wall between my lab and the hallway was covered completely as well. I couldn't see inside my lab at all. My curiosity and awe gave way to trepidation.

Apparently, I was not alone in my reaction. When I reached for the scanner to unlock the door, Ardruc caught my hand.

"May I?" he asked, his tone cautious, as if he feared I might snap at him for acting protective.

I was perfectly capable of a lot of things—hiking up mountains carrying heavy packs, flying a small transport, identifying rare fungi, consuming possibly unhealthy quantities of coffee—but we had no idea what might be waiting for us in my lab. Just because we hadn't been physically attacked up to now didn't mean we were safe. That red kora had damn near killed me. Whether that had been deliberate or on accident, we had no idea, and I wasn't about to take chances.

Plus, I had nothing to prove to Ardruc, and nothing to lose by allowing a giant dragon man with lightning-fast reflexes to be the first through the door.

"I've got your back," I said, gun at the ready. "If anything rushes us, we shoot first and ask questions later."

"Agreed." He waved his hand over the scanner and braced himself.

As the door slid aside, two things happened nearly simultaneously: a blue-green glow washed over us, and Forux darted past my legs and into the lab.

"Shit!" I started to follow. Ardruc's arm blocked my path. He moved aside, though, and from the doorway I got my first look inside Lab Three.

"Oh," I breathed.

My lab was dark…and *alive.*

The room had no artificial light except the bank of computer screens. The skylights, like the floor, walls, and ceiling, were covered completely with foliage. But unlike every other room we'd seen, my lab was filled with glowing, bioluminescent fungi.

Nothing moved inside the lab except Forux, who was sniffing his way around. Strangely, the stillness wasn't eerie—it felt warm and welcoming.

In a kind of daze, I holstered my weapon and walked past Ardruc into a shimmering heaven of mushrooms and lichen in every shape and color imaginable. They grew on the branches and vines on the walls and ceiling and in the grass, though they seemed to have left pathways clear for me to move around the lab. Some I recognized from either studying them myself or the research of earlier mycologists, but many I didn't.

I had the strange feeling the subjects of my research had come to me on purpose and taken up residence in my lab as if they wanted to make my work easier. Like Ardruc, I struggled to assign intention to fungi, but everything we've seen since I woke up made me think our new environment was the result of deliberate choices made by the planet's native forest.

The wonder of it battled in my gut with uneasiness. We still had no idea why this had happened or what was expected of us.

A oddly shaped grouping of *Basiforuximycota* in the center of the lab caught my eye. I had not found them growing in any other formation than clusters in the forest.

Ardruc took my hand. "The symbol, Elena. Do you see it?"

I looked again, and then I saw what had caught Ardruc's attention: the same strange symbol that had been scorched into the floor of the medbay and had appeared between my breasts, formed in the grass by glowing *Basiforuximycota.*

Suddenly cold even in the warm lab, I pressed my palm to my chest. Up to now, the station's transformation had caused me far more awe than fear. Maybe that was a lingering effect of the strange euphoria combined with the gentle touch of the vine in Ardruc's apartment, or just my curiosity and scientist's thirst for knowledge overriding my nerves. Plus, my burns and being drugged aside, we hadn't been physically harmed in any way, so I hadn't felt especially threatened.

I was afraid now, though, and growing more so by the moment.

What did this all mean? Intelligent korae, flora that acted more like fauna, fungi growing in a distinct shape that matched the symbol on my skin that had been left, as far as we could tell, by a tendril of plasma…

What the hells was happening at Nova Cal? What was happening to *me?*

Caught between curiosity and the urge to flee—somehow—I looked up at Ardruc. He must have read my thoughts in my expression. Or maybe he shared my feelings.

"I suspect we will find the transports inoperable," he said, touching my face. "But we will look to be sure."

"Let's check the roof." I squeezed Ardruc's hand before letting go. "Come on, Forux."

With a yip, Forux followed us away from the lab and down the hall to the roof access door. We found the stairs carpeted with grass and lined with foliage, but traversable.

When Ardruc opened the roof hatch, his wings fluttered and his tail swished. A moment later, I joined him at the top of the stairs and saw what had caused that reaction.

The grass that had once grown only above the imaging lab now covered the entire roof. And the transports and landing pad had nearly disappeared under a thick canopy of tree limbs and vines.

We could try to hack our way through to reach the transports, but I had a feeling the branches and vines would simply keep growing back as fast as we could break them. And that might elicit an angry response from whatever intelligence wanted us to stay here. Who or what it was, why we were its prisoners, and what it might do if we decided to fight our way free, I didn't know.

Maybe I should have been angry, or terrified, or *something*, but mostly I felt numb. Shock, maybe, tinged with defeat.

"That's it, then." I slid down the wall and sat on the grass, my knees against my chest. "We're trapped, at least until someone realizes we've gone silent and comes to investigate. Or until the supply delivery." My stomach lurched. "Assuming the forest and korae let anyone get close to us. Nothing can land here now, with the landing pad covered. And if the forest has filled in nearby clearings too…" I let my voice trail off.

"Elena." Ardruc knelt beside me and took my hand again. He did that a lot now. Was it for my sake, or his? "Do not despair," he said softly, brushing my cheek with his fingertips. "We will solve these mysteries."

"How do you know?" My throat felt tight. "We have no idea what's going on or why."

"We have some clues." His touch on my face became a caress. "Whatever is at work has had ample opportunity to do us harm if that was the intention."

I rubbed over the mark on my chest with my fist. "Other than this, you mean? And taking us prisoner?"

"Your burns may have been caused accidentally," Ardruc pointed out. "Those injuries aside, our welfare seems to be of concern. Our extended sleep was peaceful and even euphoric and our labs and the station's life-sustaining functions remain fully online. That all leads me to believe we are welcome to stay here, and that some task has been laid before us that we do not understand yet."

"Maybe whatever the kora wrote on the floor in the medbay is a clue," I said. "I wonder if the computer has been able to translate it yet."

"We will check after breakfast." He tugged on my hand. "Come to the kitchen. I will make you coffee and food, and we will attempt to reason this out."

"I appreciate the offer, but I'm picky about how I make my coffee." I let him draw me to my feet. I tilted my head back and looked up at the empty sky. "We need to talk to that kora again, or one of its brethren. We need some answers."

"Maybe they are waiting to see how we react," he suggested. "And then they will send an emissary to speak to us again."

"Let's hope so," I grumbled. "I don't like being kept in the dark."

Ardruc escorted me to the roof hatch. Over his shoulder, he whistled for Forux. To my surprise, my arval companion bounded over from where he'd been sniffing the transports and obediently followed us.

"Unbelievable," I muttered. "First he lets you scratch his head and pet him, and now he comes when you whistle. The last person who tried that, he bit. Twice. And he used to not like you any more than I did…or at least, that's what I thought."

"He certainly disliked me strongly." Ardruc steadied me on the stairs with his hand on my elbow. The grass and vines made the steep steps treacherous. "Considering my behavior, he had every right to do so."

I harrumphed. "He sure forgave you quickly." A sudden thought made me glare at my arval's fluffy tails as he bounded ahead of us down the steps. "Was it because of the comfortable bed, Forux? He went from enemy to friend that quickly because of the bed?"

Ardruc chuckled, then rumbled and puffed smoke out his nostrils to cover the sound.

I hadn't ever been this close to him when he did that. His smoke smelled very good—even better than the hints of it I had enjoyed seeping from his pillows and bedding.

While humans could be true mates of Fortusians, we had no biological imperative like they did. And yet in this moment, I could believe there was something about Ardruc's natural scents that had a similar effect on me. I just wanted to breathe him in because when

I did, I felt...better. Safer. Comforted. But why, if as a human, I didn't feel the draw of a mate bond?

"Oh," I said aloud, pausing mid-step.

"What is it?" Ardruc asked.

"Those pheromones you mentioned last night—well, the night we fell asleep," I amended. "Are you releasing them now?"

His brows went up. "I may be. Not consciously, but it is instinctual. Why do you ask? Do you feel...not yourself?"

"I don't know," I confessed. "I'm not sure how I'm supposed to feel with all this going on. But..." I cleared my throat. "Your scent makes me feel better. Scientifically speaking, as a human, I don't know if that's psychological or biological or both."

"I could go to the medical bay and check." He tilted his head, his brow furrowed. "Does it bother you that my pheromones may influence how you feel? If so, it is likely with some research I can find a way to cease production of them."

The way his eyes tightened let me know he didn't want to. His instincts demanded he care for me, and if his pheromones eased my fears, taking them away would do the opposite.

It meant a lot to me that he'd asked what I wanted, without hesitation, despite his instincts. It was a reminder that while the draw of a true mate was powerful and innate, we both had choices to make.

Still, I was a scientist, and as usual my dominant reaction was curiosity. "I think I would like to know for sure, one way or the other, so I don't have to guess," I said. "But I don't think I want you to take anything or stop producing the pheromones. Just knowing is enough for me. I have enough mysteries in my life at the moment."

"That is true." He smiled, clearly relieved. "If you change your mind, please tell me so. I will not be offended."

At the bottom of the stairs, I preceded him into the hallway. If it weren't for the mark on my chest and our apparent captivity, I could lose myself in the station's new beauty. The forest had always been where I felt most comfortable.

Halfway to the kitchen, though, a sudden thought made me stop in my tracks. Ardruc had to almost hop to one side to avoid running into me. "Oh, gods," I whispered.

"What is it?" Ardruc was in front of me in a blink, his wings fluttering and his gaze searching my face. Forux circled our legs, his tails vibrating in alarm.

"What if the supplies can't get here in two weeks?" My lower lip quivered. "I'm almost out of coffee!"

Ardruc's mouth twitched before he schooled his features and became solemn once more. "We will endeavor to find a way to avoid that calamity. If nothing else, I am certain the station's food synthesizer can reproduce coffee."

Synthesized coffee? I very nearly gagged.

With his hand on the small of my back providing warmth and reassurance, he led me to the station's kitchen.

I expected the combined kitchen and dining area to look similar to the rest of the station, and they did...except for a key difference. All but one of the tables in the dining area had disappeared—somehow—and in their place was a small fruit orchard and vegetable garden, bathed in bright sunlight coming in from the enormous skylights and floor-to-ceiling windows.

The orchard was comprised of short, almost bushy trees laden with a variety of small, colorful fruits native to Hyderia that usually made up about a quarter of our monthly supply delivery. I also recognized the vegetables growing in the garden bed, which had been formed by living branches and filled in with rich soil.

Neither the fruits nor vegetables looked ready to harvest yet, but after all, we'd only been asleep for a day and a half.

What was I *saying?* Fruits and vegetables took weeks or months to grow and ripen, not hours or days. And yet here they were, growing right in front of my disbelieving eyes.

I leaned against the doorframe and scrubbed my face with my hands. "Ardruc."

Somehow, that single word was a full sentence to his ears. "I know," he said, urging me forward. "Sit down. You need to eat. I will make us breakfast." When Forux snuffled, Ardruc added, "And you as well, of course. Stay with your mistress and I will bring your bowl."

I dropped into a chair at the one remaining table and rested my chin on my hand as Ardruc busied himself in the kitchen, moving back and forth between the food storage units and the preparation station. Forux curled up at my feet, his chin resting on the toe of my right boot and eyes half closed.

"I would have predicted Forux would be beside himself with all this going on," I mused. "Instead, he's acting like it's just another day at Nova Cal. And he's never this relaxed while he's waiting for breakfast. Do you think he's still under the influence of that strange dust?"

"He seems perfectly alert," Ardruc pointed out, stirring something in a pot on the cooktop. "Does he usually alert you to threats?"

"Yes. He always has." I rubbed the bridge of my nose. "The other night, he tried to attack that kora that burned me, and he definitely growled at the one that communicated with us. But now look at him. Not a care in the world, though he's empathic and feeling all my worries."

"Perhaps he is remaining calm for your sake." Ardruc glanced over his shoulder at us. "Is that possible?"

"It's definitely possible." I bent and scratched Forux behind all of his ears. "Thanks, friend. You're helping."

He licked my hand and snuffled.

In less than ten minutes, Ardruc delivered Forux's bowl of warmed meat. As my little arval ate happily, Ardruc placed a mug of coffee and a plate in front of me with a bit of a flourish. The coffee smelled wonderful, and the plate contained three thin cakes, each rolled around a filling of what appeared to be diced red bano fruit and cream, topped with sliced fruits on top. His own plate had the same food, but six of them instead of three.

"What is this?" I leaned over and sniffed. "It smells good."

"A dish I learned to make on Bacora." He sat down across from me. "They are called *crepec*. I believe the dish originated on Earth. I did not ask if you preferred meat as part of your breakfast. I apologize if so."

"No, this looks good." I eyed my plate. "It's a lot of food, though. And Forux might think everything's fine, but I'm too uneasy to have much of an appetite."

"You must eat," he said earnestly, picking up his utensils. "For energy, and so we can think and reason. A few bites, at least."

I cut off a small section of one *crepec* and put it in my mouth. Oh, all the gods above and below. I closed my eyes and moaned.

Ardruc chuckled. "You approve?"

"I do." I opened my eyes to find him smiling. Really *smiling*.

I couldn't think of a single time that he'd smiled since my arrival. He'd half-smiled at me a few times this morning, but nothing like his expression now. Even his eyes seemed to sparkle with something like joy.

Was he smiling because he'd cooked for me and I liked what he'd made? Because I probably had a goofy, almost blissful expression on my face after tasting something so delicious?

I paused with my next bite halfway to my mouth.

Because I was his true mate, and that meant he needed to make sure I was safe and warm and never went hungry?

A true mate. Someone he craved with all his body, hearts, and soul, whose scent and presence had upended his life so completely. And that someone was *me*.

I'd never been that important to anyone, except maybe my parents—at least until my mother discovered I had no interest in physics and my father became so immersed in his art that we scarcely saw him more than a few times a week when he emerged from his studio, and then a few times a year when he began traveling the galaxy looking for inspiration for his increasingly enormous art installations.

I'd loved and been loved, but this was different.

The moment Ardruc had revealed the truth and let himself look at me with all the tenderness and care he really felt, I'd felt something stirring inside me. Yes, I was still angry about how he'd treated me, but I couldn't pretend that anger prevented me from recognizing how comfortable I was beside him. That comfort didn't erase the last four months, but it offered something unexpected: a kind of security. A footing, almost, or a home.

Like Forux's calm, Ardruc's presence was reassuring, even as we faced so much uncertainty and the possibility the forest and korae of Hyderia might have us trapped.

And that brought up the biggest question of all: did I feel this way about Ardruc because of the circumstances and his pheromones, or because I really felt a connection with him? I honestly couldn't tell.

What the hells was I going to do?

Well, for starters, I was going to eat these *crepec*, because they were delicious. And then we were going to try to figure out what was going on.

"Elena?" Ardruc asked, brow furrowed. "Are you all right?"

I used my fork to cut my *crepec* into smaller pieces. "I'm okay. Just lost in thought."

He leaned back in his chair. "Have I said something wrong?"

"No, not at all." I ate another mouthful of my breakfast. "What do you want to do next?"

He studied me for a few beats. "I suggest we finish evaluating the changes to the station," he said finally. "And then attempt to make contact with the korae. What are your thoughts?"

"That sounds like a good plan." I took a bite of *crepec* and chewed.

Ardruc watched me eat with a combination of concern and

unhappiness, his breakfast seemingly forgotten. Strange how after so many months of inscrutability he was letting me see his thoughts and emotions so clearly. Had he forgotten to hide them from me, or was it a conscious choice? He'd promised not to hide anything from me anymore. Maybe this was part of that vow.

I didn't want to close myself off from him just as he was opening up to me, but I'd never felt less sure of my own emotions and perceptions as I did right now. I needed something else besides Ardruc that made me feel secure so I knew I was responding to him for the right reasons and not just as the single lifeline available to me in the midst of a storm.

I had to be able to trust myself. If I didn't, I couldn't trust anything, or anyone.

"Let's eat," I said, giving him the best smile I could muster and making my tone light. "Food first, then mystery-solving and korae-contacting."

Judging by Ardruc's grim expression, I didn't fool him one bit, but he did pick up his fork again and resume eating. The only sounds in the kitchen were the low hum of the machinery and Forux's happy chewing. His appetite rarely waned for any reason.

"I made sure our last supply drop had plenty of meat for Forux," I said between bites. "But he'll need more eventually, especially if we can't get a supply drop. We can live on fruits and vegetables and synthesized foods, but arvals are carnivores. He's never wanted to eat synthesized meat, and yes he can tell the difference."

Ardruc tilted his head. "He is clearly domesticated, but is he capable of hunting for his meals?"

I made a face. "I'm reluctant to just let him out to hunt. We might not see them around much, but most of the animals of the forest are a lot bigger than him and some of them are predators. I don't know how long our isolation is going to last. It's not an immediate concern, but I have to think of him too."

Ardruc set his fork down next to his empty plate and glanced at

Forux before meeting my gaze. "In that case, if it becomes necessary, I will hunt on his behalf."

I hadn't been angling for him to offer, or even really thought about the fact Ardruc was as much a predator as he was a man, courtesy of his dragon DNA. Our interactions had all been very professional—well, with the exception of the past day or two—and to me he'd always been Ardruc the Director of Research, not Ardruc the man and even less Ardruc the hunter.

But suddenly the intensity of his vertically slit eyes pinned me in place and conjured an image of him swooping through the sky, that bright golden gaze trained on his prey. And though I would never have thought it likely, the image elicited an immediate wave of desire, even more so than the sight of him without a shirt this morning.

Oh, dear. I was turned on by the thought of Ardruc the winged predator. Pheromones? Or just my hormones?

I squeezed my thighs together and scooped up a big bite of *crepec*, hoping to hide my reaction.

Ardruc gathered up his dirty dishes and took them to the sink, opting to wash them by hand rather than use the sonic cleansing system. Maybe he wanted to conserve our resources.

I watched him cleaning up, the way his muscles moved under his tight shirt and the perfect curve of his ass and the glimmer of sunlight on the feathers of his beautiful wings. And that *tail*...

I took a long drink of cold water, closed my eyes, and exhaled.

Ardruc Husiorithae, have mercy on me.

CHAPTER 16
ARDRUC

IF I HAD THOUGHT THE SCENT OF ELENA'S HAIR AND SKIN WAS powerful, that was nothing compared to the sweetness of her arousal.

With trembling hands, I washed the last of the dishes and tried not to think about how badly I wanted to sweep everything off the table, place Elena on her back, and bury my face between her thighs so I could drink in every bit of that scent as she moaned my name. My feathers ruffled and my tail twitched until I stilled them both.

Her reaction had followed immediately on the heels of my offer to hunt on Forux's behalf. Earlier, she had responded to my lack of clothing, which was flattering but perhaps not entirely unexpected. But if the thought of me as a predator excited her even more…

A telltale warmth on my shoulders told me she was watching me as she finished her meal. I stretched my wings, flexed the muscles in my back, and ruffled my feathers before I folded my wings and let my tail sway. And I puffed smoke from my nostrils for good measure.

I continued washing up without missing a beat, as if I had not done it all deliberately to hear her sharp intake of breath and quiet rustling as she squirmed in her chair.

I was a surprisingly wicked man, and I had no intention of repenting for it.

By the time she put her fork on her empty plate and pushed it away, I had finished my cleanup work other than her dishes. I dried the pan in which I had made the *crepec*, set it on the shelf, and turned.

Elena was leaning back in her chair, legs crossed, one elbow on the table, her lips turned up at the corners.

"Oh, is the show over so soon?" she asked, raising an eyebrow. "Pity. I was just getting interested."

Of course I had not fooled her. I could not outsmart Elena Regis, who was as brilliant as she was beautiful. This was *play*.

I had no need or desire to outdo her in any way. I was content in her presence. We were compliments, not competitors or rivals. But if I allowed myself to be more the hunter with her than scientist, I might give her what she wanted and endear myself to her, and that I very much wanted to do.

And the way she was sitting, almost reclining, eyes twinkling as she smirked, felt very much like a dare.

In a single leap, I crossed the kitchen, landed astride her legs, and tipped her chair onto its back feet. I balanced her there so she lay beneath me as if we were in bed, her heaving chest only inches from my own. And I let my eyes glow.

"The show need not be over," I murmured, lowering my head so my lips were near her ear. She shivered, and a soft moan escaped her lips. The scent of her arousal grew.

Belatedly, I realized Forux had done nothing to defend his mistress against my very predatory movement. Instead, he had curled up under the table, head on his paws and eyes closed, apparently peacefully digesting his breakfast.

Elena took advantage of my distraction to raise her head and capture my lips with hers. She tasted of bano fruit, cream, and joy. I closed my eyes and raised the angle of the chair just enough that she did not have to strain to kiss me.

Her little tongue darted out to brush my lower lip until I parted my lips and gave in a little more to the hunger that built within me with every beat of my hearts. She teased my tongue with hers, then flicked its tip against my incisors and sucked in a breath.

"Yes, they are sharp," I said, raising my head to smile down at her. "I am not a carnivore like your companion, but I am a predator."

"I'm starting to see that." She nipped my lower lip with her teeth. "You figured out that I like that about you."

It was a statement, not a question, but I said, "Yes. And I like that you like that about me. Perhaps I will be a bit more more predatory in the future, for your benefit."

"It might not just benefit me." Elena brushed my chin with her fingertips. "Thank you for breakfast, and for the show."

I ducked my head again and drew in a deep, much more primal sort of breath as I ran my nose along her neck and shoulder. She chuckled, but the sound did not disguise either her little gasp or how she shivered. Gods, the scent of her. I could lose myself in it completely, if only we had nothing else demanding our attention and if she would let me.

"It was my pleasure," I murmured, my lips against her collarbone. "And yours as well, if I may consider your scent as both evidence and thanks."

"You may." Her smile turned wistful. "Mysteries to solve, Ardruc."

"Indeed." Gently, I set her chair upright and drew her to her feet. "First, to the medical bay for a scan?"

Elena's smile faded. I felt a chill as though the sun had gone behind clouds.

"A *couple* of scans," she said, with a sigh. "And then maybe up to the roof again to yell at the sky until something yells back." She crouched to scratch Forux's head. "Come on, little friend. I know you're used to doing whatever you want around here, but stay close for now, okay? Just in case."

Yawning, his belly noticeably rounded, Forux padded along behind us to the medical bay.

Much to my relief, the forest had made only minimal incursions into the medical bay, mostly in the form of vines and foliage. The scanners, computer, supplies, and machinery appeared unaffected, and the symbols scorched into the floor remained uncovered. The most critical item—the emergency medical pod—had not been touched at all, as if the forest understood the need for this life-saving equipment to remain intact.

Elena studied the room with her hands on her hips. "Just how intelligent do we think the indigenous plant life, fungi, and korae of Hyderia might be?"

"I suspect quite intelligent indeed." I went to the computer to check the status of its analysis of the marks on the floor. "Likelihood of language ninety-eight percent," I read aloud. "The language appears to be logographic, but the computer has an insufficient quantity of exemplars and contextual information for make any attempt at translation."

"I figured that would be the case." She sighed. "Disappointing, though. We need to get the korae to write answers to specific questions to have a chance to learn how to communicate."

"Or offer a way for the korae to learn a language we *can* translate." Along those lines, I asked the computer to compile a list of known logographic languages and propose ways an energy-based life form might access the information needed to learn one.

As the computer went to work on the problem, I accompanied Elena to the shelf where we kept the handheld medical scanners. "I am sure it has also occurred to you," I said, "that in all the centuries since Hyderia has had visitors, its indigenous life has not chosen to reveal its true nature in this way."

"Well, as far as we know." She finished calibrating a scanner. "There's nothing in the records, but you and I both know not everything *makes it* into the records." She raised her eyebrows and glanced up. "Like your lat'sar-playing kora, for example."

"Or the kora that followed you on your hike back to your transport," I countered. "Or the playful plasma or the one that communicated with us. Neither of us described those encounters in our official records."

"Depending on how long our isolation lasts, we may never *get* to report those encounters," Elena said, with a rueful look. "But let's say for the sake of argument the sentient korae and the forest could have chosen to reveal their true nature at any time and chose not to until now. Why now? Why us? What makes us worthy of a revelation of this magnitude? Not to diminish either of us, but I'm just a simple mycologist from Fyloria and you're a stuffy atmospheric scientist from Fortusia."

Elena was not *just* anything, but I was indeed *stuffy* and understood her point.

"All good questions. We will endeavor to answer them." I folded my hands behind my back and used my chin to indicate the scanner. "If you would…?"

Elena passed the scanner over me, her lips pursed as she watched data scroll across the screen. "No pheromones detected," she said. "Interesting. I thought you might be enticing me in some way other than just your cooking."

"If so, I would not have done so intentionally without your consent." I leaned over to get a closer look at the screen. "Does it detect any lingering effects of the dust or spores that caused us to stay asleep?"

"Let's see…" She hummed and scrolled through the scan results. "Well, you have elevated dopamine levels, which makes sense given the state of euphoria we experienced. Also traces of an unknown flurane compound the scanner suggests caused extended deep sleep. That's it. You're a healthy specimen of a Fortusian male." She handed me the scanner. "My turn."

I waved the scanner slowly over her from her head to her feet. "Similar elevated dopamine, similar traces of an unknown flurane compound," I noted. "All your hormone levels are as expected, so no discernible reaction to hypothetical pheromones in that regard. Elevated cortisol concentration and heart rate indicates increased stress."

Elena chuckled, but without humor. "I didn't need the scanner to tell me that."

When the scanner passed over the center of her chest, it beeped. A red bar appeared on the screen.

"What was that?" she craned her neck to look at the screen. "What does it say?"

"One moment." I touched the red bar and read the results.

Elena tapped her foot impatiently. "Ardruc," she warned.

Stunned, I held out the scanner so she could read the screen for herself. She nearly snatched it from my hand and scrolled through the data. The color drained from her face.

"I have *what?*" she gasped.

She unfastened the collar of her jumpsuit and pulled the seam apart to reveal the tank top she wore under it and the mark on her chest. It looked the same as earlier—blue-green, like the foliage around us.

"Chlorophyll?" She looked back and forth between her skin and the scanner. "And this symbol is formed by rigid cells that contain chloroplasts and cellulose in their walls?" She looked up at me, her eyes wide. "Those are plant cells, Ardruc! In my body!"

"These are not plants," I said gently. "Not as we would define them. If these are life forms with intelligence, with clear evidence of sensory and nervous systems, we cannot call them plants. Or if we do, we must do so knowing the plant life of Hyderia is distinctly different from anything you or I have ever encountered."

"I'm part plant." She leaned against the counter, the scanner dangling in her hand. I took it from her and set it aside. "Should we cut it out of me right now, in case it tries to spread?" she asked. "I like being human. I don't want to start growing branches."

"We can certainly have the medpod evaluate it more closely." I took her trembling hand and squeezed, hoping to reassure her. "And attempt to remove it if you wish."

"What I *wish* is that I knew what it means and whether it's dangerous." She scowled. "And whether or not it's dangerous, they had no right to do this to me without my consent."

"Absolutely, that is true." I followed her to the medpod and helped her lie down. "May I?" I asked, gesturing at her jumpsuit.

"Yes." She swallowed. "Thank you for always asking."

"Of course." Gently, I opened her jumpsuit along the seam to her navel, folded the fabric back, and pushed her tank top up to her collarbone so the pod had full access to the mark.

I could not look at her with any semblance of clinical detachment, but this was a medical procedure and at least I could be the one caring for her. To my surprise, she grabbed my left hand and held on.

I used my free hand to select the scans I wanted the pod to conduct on the mark, including a three-dimensional visualization at the microcellular level. And then I drew up the chair and sat beside her.

The pod hummed and the screens above the bed activated as the scans began.

"Talk to me." She rubbed my palm with her thumb and stared up at the ceiling, biting her lip.

"What about?"

"Anything. Tell me about Fortusia. I've never been there."

I flicked my gaze to the medpod's display screens and hoped she had not seen my flinch.

"It is a beautiful planet," I said, my tone neutral. "Like Nyvorans, Fortusians love nature. We build our cities using eco-architecture to blend the natural beauty of the planet with urban needs. The waters and sky are pink due to native minerals. Most of the planet is temperate. And of course our use of genetic engineering makes us fascinating to off-worlders. Tourism is a major part of the planet's economy, especially in the resort cities like Onat'ras."

I described the beauty and natural wonders of my home planet for the next ten minutes or so while Elena listened and the medpod completed its work. Forux, meanwhile, curled up next to my chair for a nap. His snore made me smile despite Elena's uneasiness.

When the last scan ended and the pod powered down, Elena took a deep breath and squeezed my hand. "Fortusia sounds like a wonderful planet. Do you want to move back there someday if you get the chance?"

"No, I do not think so." Stepping foot on Fortusia would bring me within reach of my parents and the sect leader, whose rage at my escape had reportedly been terrible. "For all its wonders, Fortusia does not have any korae or related phenomena," I said instead, which was true. "Even before the revelations of the past few days, studying korae was my life's work. Now, I cannot fathom leaving that behind."

"I can certainly understand that." She used the pod's controls to adjust the bed so she was sitting up and pulled down her tank top to cover herself again. "But maybe we could visit someday. I think I'd like to see what fungi are native to your world."

My hearts skipped a beat. Did she realize she had said *we* could visit? I did not think she had noted her choice of pronoun in that sentence. I doubted I would ever return to my homeworld, but her casual use of *we* filled me with warmth.

"The fungi on Fortusia are known to be spectacular," I said when she seemed to be awaiting a response.

I adjusted the array of diagnostic screens so she could see the results too. The long list of green and blue notations and lack of red and orange eased some of my worry.

"None of the scans found cause for alarm," I said after skimming the findings. "The cells are unique, as we already noted. There is no indication the mark will spread or has the ability to change your physical form, genetically or otherwise."

"Well, that's something." She scrolled through the scan results on her own screen. "As far as the computer can tell, the mark is basically an organic tattoo." She tapped the screen and read the text that appeared. "And apparently the pod could remove it fairly easily." She glanced at her chest. "Well, that does make me feel better."

"It is a relief," I agreed. "Do you want to remove the mark?"

She thought about it. "I'm still not happy about being plant-tattooed without my permission, and I want to know what its purpose is, but if it's just a tattoo and I can remove it at any time, maybe I'll leave it for now."

"It is entirely your decision." I touched her hand. "Should we go outside and look for some answers?"

"Yes." She sealed the seam of her jumpsuit and fastened the collar. As she swung her legs over the side of the bed, she added, "We should take some tiles with us in case we run into a kora who wants to talk to us. The more examples of the writing we can get, the better chance of figuring out the language." She made a face. "Or *can* we call the living ones korae? Are korae plasma discharges in the atmosphere, and the living plasma something else?"

"I do not know." I helped her rise from the bed with my hand under her elbow. "That is one of the many questions I hope to get answered. I would also like to know if they have a name for themselves."

"That will be my first question, if we figure out a way to ask it." Elena sighed. "The computer can help us to a certain extent, but we could really use an astrobiologist. As a mycologist, I'm out of my depth with anything that's not a fungus."

"And speaking of which, you have your own wealth of new subjects of study," I pointed out.

"I know." Her eyes lit up. "I'm excited to get into my lab and study the mushrooms and lichen there." She chuckled. "I thought my discovery of the *Basiforuximycota* would be the most thrilling part of my week. Now..." She waved at our surroundings, and then looked at me with something akin to exasperation. "Well, it's been a *wildly unpredictable* couple of days."

"A very accurate observation," I said, which earned me a laugh.

Given our shared concern over our circumstances, I was very glad to hear her laugh.

The computer had not yet completed its work of searching its vast stores of knowledge for languages most likely to allow translation and options for creating an interface an energy-based life form could use to exchange information. It might be a full day or more before we had workable solutions to the challenge of communication.

Elena and Forux went to her lab to pack up research equipment as I hurried to Lab One to do the same. I selected several datapads, a variety of portable scanners, and four recording devices and packed them into cases I stacked onto an antigrav sled and piloted down the grassy hallway.

Hoping to obtain more writing from the korae, I also collected metal floor tiles from the kitchen orchard area and stacked them into a fourth carrying case. And as an afterthought, I stopped by my apartment to get my lat'sar.

I found Elena and Forux waiting for me at the door that led to the roof stairs.

"I don't trust the lift," Elena said, settling what appeared to be a very heavy pack of equipment onto her back. Two more waited on the grass at her feet. "I've set all the station's doors to remain unlocked too."

"I concur with that decision. The station's operations are far from what I would deem trustworthy." I adjusted my lat'sar case on my back. "I can carry one of your packs so you have a hand free to hold the railing. The stairs are treacherous."

"That's true." Elena sighed and stared up the steep grass- and vine-covered steps. "*Or* I could make two trips so you don't have to be my pack-dragon."

My hearts fluttered very unexpectedly when Elena referred to me as *her* dragon—pack or otherwise.

"I do not mind being a pack-dragon," I said. "As I rely on your expertise to understand and explain the nature of this planet's fungi, you may rely on my ability to more easily carry heavy scientific equipment to the roof."

"Well, when you put it that way, thank you." She handed me one of her packs and started up the steps carrying the other, steadying herself on the railing.

She reached the roof hatch and activated it. As it opened, revealing a clear late-morning sky, she looked up and said, "Everything looks the same as it did earlier. No sign of any korae."

We emerged onto the overgrown landing pad. Elena headed straight for the ladder that led to the upper roof over the imaging lab. She climbed it with her equipment, then returned to scoop up Forux and took him up as well.

Rather than climb the ladder, I took flight with our packs in hand, made a circle around the station, and then landed a few meters from where Elena was now sitting cross-legged on the grass unpacking her equipment.

I made three trips between the top of the stairs and the upper roof. When I landed with my final two cases, she raised her eyebrows and smirked. "Suddenly allergic to ladders? Or showing off your wings and all those pretty feathers?"

I spread my wings so the sunlight gleamed on my bright feathers. I was not a vain man, but if she found my feathers *pretty*, I was not above showing them off.

"Just stretching," I fibbed with a smile, without caring that she could tell I had shown off for her. "It feels good to fly."

"I can well imagine." She looked around at the treetops and valley below. "Everything's been so quiet. I wonder if they're waiting to see how we react to the station transformation?"

"Possibly." I set my lat'sar case on the grass about three meters from Elena's equipment. Forux was sniffing his way around the roof, his tails fanned out. "It is difficult to guess what living plasma might think or do, if indeed that is what we are dealing with."

"Despite being very different life forms, they seem to understand at least some Alliance Standard, so they've made an effort to learn how to communicate." She activated a portable scanner and positioned it on the grass. "We're relying on their ability to communicate with *us*, though, since so far we have no idea how plasma communicates. I took several courses in biolinguistics as part of my mycology studies. They focused primarily on how fungi communicate, obviously."

"How *do* fungi communicate?" I asked as I knelt to set up my own equipment. "I confess, I know very little about that subject— far less than you now know about upper-atmospheric plasma discharges."

"For starters, the number of species of fungi on each known planet ranges from one hundred thousand to two hundred thousand," she said. "Even on planets with little other life, fungi can be found. No one knows how many species of fungi exist just on Alliance planets and moons, but it's surely in the millions. Even with all that biodiversity, most fungi share some key characteristics."

"Such as how they communicate?"

"Yes." Elena smiled. "Fungi conduct electrical impulses through filamentous structures called hyphae that form mycelial networks. Hyphae function much like how nerve cells transmit information in humans. Fungi also release chemical signals, including pheromones, to communicate with each other and other organisms. Their communication seems to focus on food sources, potential threats, and mating."

"Those are the basic needs of most organisms," I observed. "And it strongly suggests at least a basic ability to process information as well as pass it on."

"Not just pass it on. Through these networks, fungi communicate, exchanging nutrients, water, and signaling molecules. It allows them to coordinate their growth, reproduction, and defense strategies. And in symbiotic relationships with other organisms like plants, fungi help absorb nutrients and water while plants provide fungi with resources produced during photosynthesis." She spread her hands to indicate the forest around the station. "This forest is an ecosystem, but via its fungi, it's essentially a neural network."

I shook my head in amazement and crouched to adjust the settings on an imaging device. "This is all absolutely fascinating."

A pause, then: "Yes, it is."

Elena's grim tone made me swivel to face her. She set an empty specimen container in her lap and studied me. All the joy had vanished from her expression. My hearts wrenched.

"You know, I can't help but remember the number of times you disparaged my field of study without actually knowing much about fungi or what I do," she said. "I wish I could say it didn't hurt every time, but it did."

"I am sorry." Balancing on the balls of my feet, I dropped my head, my forearms on my thighs. "I make no excuses. My words and actions were reprehensible. I cannot make it right, though I desperately wish I could."

"I know you do." She took a deep breath, exhaled, and leaned back on her hands to gaze at the sky. "Well, I'm set up. Now all we need is a visitor." Her tone and body language indicated she did not want to continue our conversation.

A kind of helplessness left my gut feeling hollow.

Our undeniable mutual attraction, the complimentary way in which our minds worked, the peace we felt in each other's presence —all those were wonderfully good things about being true mates. She was everything I could have dreamed of in a partner.

But I had so thoroughly bungled everything, and hurt her so deeply, and forced her to hate me. Elena could not be expected to forgive me, much less trust me or be interested in any kind of relationship. As for a lifetime together…the very thought was ludicrous, no matter how much desire we shared in unguarded moments.

I had never wished I had fewer hearts than my creators had given me until this moment, when both ached so intensely that I felt short of breath.

In the meantime, Forux completed his thorough olfactory investigation of the roof and returned to Elena's side. He curled up with his head on her thigh. What I would give to be able to do the same.

Instead, I settled in and did my best to focus on calibrating each piece of equipment to maximize its ability to potentially record and analyze any korae that appeared—but none did, even after Elena called out greetings and invited company.

In the end, we sat in silence for more than two hours, each engrossed in our own research.

Just as I was about to cautiously inquire whether she wanted to take a break for a midday meal, Elena's voice startled me. "You could play your lat'sar," she said.

I looked up from my study of images and data recorded during the spectacular and complex korae displays from the night she had been burned.

She set her own datapad in her lap. Its screen showed an analysis in progress of a sample of lavender lichen.

"One of the tendrils came to watch you play in the forest," she said, her tone and expression neutral.

My hearts ached at her detachment, but I could not argue that I had more than earned it.

"Maybe music will earn us a visitor," she added. "That's why you brought it up here, right?"

"That is true." I slid my lat'sar case closer and opened it. "I will need to warm up before I play."

"Go ahead." She returned her attention to her datapad, one hand scratching Forux absently behind his ears. "I've never heard a lat'sar played in person, so this will be a treat."

I had not played for anyone else's ears but my own in a very long time. And very unexpectedly, the prospect of playing for Elena in particular caused a ball of nervous tension to form in my belly.

To ease my apprehension, I focused on the familiar process of preparing the instrument and warming up as Elena alternated between reading her datapad and scanning our surroundings for any hint of visitors. Once I began my scales, she seemed to relax and even smiled a little as she stroked Forux's fur.

What would I play for her first? *The Sea Winds*, my favorite and most challenging piece? Or would she interpret my choice as showing off? Perhaps I should choose something more freeform—more emotional and less technical.

Or…

The breeze swirled around us. I closed my eyes, inhaled deeply, and listened to the wind and the rustle of leaves, the music of Hyderia.

Yes, I was playing to try to draw in visitors, but more than that I was playing for Elena, who had never heard a lat'sar in person before, and whose heart I would give anything to lighten and soften.

I pictured Elena's expression of pure wonder and delight when she looked at her beloved fungi. I wanted to play not technically, not mathematically, but with that kind of joy. The joy I had felt when I opened my eyes earlier today and beheld Elena sleeping peacefully under my wing.

I fixed that image in my my mind, kept my eyes closed, and drew my bow across the lat'sar's strings. The chord that emerged was pure and floated on the wind as if it belonged there.

I left precision and mechanics behind and played instead from my aching hearts.

CHAPTER 17

ELENA

D R. A RDRUC H USIORITHAE WAS AN ARROGANT, BRILLIANT, SELFISH, beautiful bastard, and he'd made me miserable for four whole damn months.

And since I'd survived being burned, being near him had made me more content and aroused than I'd been in a long, long time.

He'd apologized for what he'd said and done, and I knew in my heart he was deeply sorry. I also felt so profoundly instinctually comfortable with him I could *almost* believe I could move past all that hurt. But all it took was a reminder, like his sudden fascination with all things fungi, to bring back that anger and pain. It doused my contentment and desire like a bucket of icy water.

As he warmed up and played scales on his lat'sar, I scoured an analysis of a sample of a lichen I'd named *farodiorma petacellatum.* I was looking for any indication of unusual hyphae or mycelial networks that might signify unexpected forms or methods of communication—and any explanation for the nearly overnight growth of fungi within the station, a process that by all rights should have taken years or decades rather than hours.

All the samples of fungi I'd examined since my arrival had shown perfectly predictable behaviors, but clearly the fungi of

Hyderia were far from what anyone would call *predictable*. What had everyone who'd studied here before me missed? What had *I* missed?

A sweet chord, followed by a beautiful, simple, lilting melody, made me look up from my datapad.

Ardruc's eyes were closed as his bow danced across the double layer of strings on his lat'sar. His warm-up and scales had been so structured and regimented and so expertly played that once he moved on to playing music, I'd expected him to choose an extremely difficult and technical piece.

Instead, he'd either chosen the airiest, most emotionally charged song he knew, or he was taking inspiration from our situation and surroundings and actually improvising.

My datapad forgotten, I coaxed Forux into my lap, ran my fingers through his thick, soft fur, and listened while my arval purred.

Gods above, Ardruc played beautifully. When the breeze picked up, he played more quickly and loudly. When it faded, the music grew so introspective and quiet I had to strain to hear it. Heartache ebbed and flowed in melodic lines in minor keys.

Unexpectedly, I recalled afternoons spent in my father's art studio during my childhood before he deemed my presence "distracting"—and long before he began traveling from planet to planet creating art installations inspired by the native cultures and natural beauty of those worlds, with no time for his daughter.

He'd let me sit in a corner or by the window with my datapad and stylus sketching fungi I'd found in the woods earlier in the day. My own artistic abilities were limited to drawing my favorite fungi from memory or a new specimen I'd brought home in my pocket, while my father created wonders seemingly out of thin air.

He'd worked in many artistic forms then, from the most modern material fusion and immersive anamorphosis to primitive forms like paint on stone and hand-worked sculpture made with manual tools. He liked to defy expectations and rules of form as much as my mother liked the rigidity of physics and its laws. That they even tolerated each other, much less *loved* each other, had mystified me even from a very young age.

Especially when I was young, the way my father created art seemed more like magic than study and practice to me. When I'd asked what inspired him, his explanation was for a child frustratingly unhelpful: "I listen and remember."

Only later did I realize I did the same thing when I ventured into the forest: I listened to the flora and fungi around me and the wind and even the sounds of animals to understand my environment. That habit had continued into adulthood and throughout my studies and travels. Sometimes I listened as Dr. Regis, a scientist, and sometimes as wide-eyed Elena.

And that was why I knew right now Ardruc was listening to Hyderia's beauty as well as his own emotions and mine to create this music.

A few days ago I would have bet any amount of money Ardruc could only look on Hyderia as data points and charts. And yet in this moment he was playing a duet with the wind—while revealing his wonder, joy, and pain in a wordless way that echoed my own conflicting feelings.

I was hurting, but so was he. And not just because he knew he'd wounded me with all his indifference and harsh words. His pain felt deeper than that.

My analytical brain pivoted from the mystery of Hyderia's lichen to the mystery of Ardruc Husiorithae.

Something made him push me away. The thought floated into my head seemingly out of nowhere. It was part logic, part intuition, and part interpretation of the music he played.

I was no expert in Fortusian biology, much less the physiology of true mates, but what I *did* know was the call of a true mate was extremely powerful. So why would Ardruc try to alienate his mate to the point of driving them off the planet? What could be stronger than the strongest need of all?

Fear. Fear of being hurt. Maybe fear of being hurt again.

Someone very well might have wounded him and made him want to take refuge in his work while rejecting a true mate and the possibility of true happiness—actions that went against every instinct in his body.

How badly had he been hurt to make him do what he'd done to me? To do what he'd done to himself?

It didn't excuse his choices and I didn't forgive him yet, but my heart softened. My anger, meanwhile, found a new target. I wanted to know who'd hurt him and why.

In the medbay earlier, Ardruc had actually recoiled when I'd mentioned the prospect of visiting his home planet, though he'd tried to hide his reaction. I could guess where the source of his pain was. Not that I felt any better about the prospect of returning to Fyloria for any length of time.

I looked up from scratching Forux's head and froze.

Six tendrils of plasma—two red, two orange, and two blue—hovered just beyond the edge of the upper roof behind Ardruc. How long they'd been there, I wasn't sure. So much for being an observant scientist, Elena Regis.

Crackling quietly, they swayed and dipped in tempo with the music. Even from this distance, my skin prickled with the force of their energy. Forux watched the korae too, but rather than try to attack them or snarl in warning, he stayed at my side and only leaned his ears toward them.

Ardruc's expression changed. Maybe he'd noted my reaction, or maybe he sensed the korae's presence. Or both. But he didn't open his eyes and he didn't stop playing.

I slid a glance over to confirm all the scanners were registering and recording the korae. They were.

As ridiculous as it might have sounded, I almost didn't care if our equipment was recording this. All the gods above and below, the plasma tendrils were *dancing* to Ardruc's music. Hyderia was home to living plasma. I was looking at a life form utterly unknown to science, at least as far as we could tell. The wonder of it made my heart race. I had to force myself to breathe slowly.

Two more korae appeared from the forest to dance: one red and one green. Then another blue. And then two more orange with a small red one between them. They swayed, bobbed, and even undulated in rhythm as Ardruc played.

Within a few minutes, a dozen more tendrils in all colors arrived, hovering around the perimeter of the roof. Ardruc's playing had become a concert, but more than that it felt like a shared experience bigger than musician and audience. Something truly sublime.

Music needed no translation. Like most art forms, it transcended language, culture, and even the vast differences between carbon-based humanoids and living plasma.

Had any scientists who'd lived on Hyderia before us encountered these korae? I wished I knew. If they had, and had kept it a secret, there must have been a reason. And if the korae hadn't shown themselves until now, why communicate with Ardruc and me? Why did the forest put us to sleep, transform our station, and prevent us from leaving? And why did I have this tattoo?

So many questions, so many worries, but I didn't want to break the spell.

Ardruc's music was truly breathtaking. Despite the proximity of so many korae, I found myself drifting on it like a leaf on the breeze, my fingers in Forux's fur.

A green tendril—either the same one who'd come into the medical bay the other night, or an identical one—moved slowly from the edge of the roof to hover between Ardruc and me. An orange tendril joined it.

I flinched, remembering the pain of being burned. But though my skin and hair prickled, their power felt muted. Maybe they'd learned we were vulnerable to burns?

Ardruc continued to play, his sharp gaze fixed on the korae and feathers ruffling with obvious unease. My own awe was definitely tempered with apprehension.

The tendrils swayed back and forth along with the music, then twirled around each other before drawing apart again. They repeated the pattern in place several times, then rose into the air above us to continue the dance.

Almost in unison, the rest of the tendrils joined them, and suddenly all the tendrils were dancing and twirling along with the wind and Ardruc's music.

"You play so beautifully," I murmured, knowing his sharp ears would hear me. "I didn't think anyone could improvise like this in a duet with the wind."

The wind picked up and swirled around us. Ardruc responded with a quick succession of chords that rose in pitch and volume. The korae in the air moved faster too, twirling and swaying, shimmering and sparkling. In happiness? Were they having fun? We knew so little about them, but their movements felt joyous, even rapturous.

My neck started to cramp from looking up, so I lay down with my head on one of my packs to listen to Ardruc play and watch the korae dance. Rumbling in contentment, Forux clambered onto my stomach and curled up.

A warm, welcoming feeling seeped into me from the grass I lay on. I pulled up my sleeves and stretched out my arms to feel more of that comfort.

Vines unwound from along the roofline and snaked their way across the grass to stroke my fingers. Leaves caressed my palms and rested lightly in my cupped hands as if they wanted to be cradled.

Ardruc's lat'sar music faded to a single sustained chord. "Are you all right?" he asked, his voice pitched low.

"Yes." I raised my left hand so he could see the leaves on my palm. "They're just resting there. And the ground is warm and welcoming."

"Incredible." His gaze moved to my hand and back to meet my eyes. "What does your gut tell you?"

I smiled wryly. "How mad does it sound if I say it feels like Hyderia is trying to take care of us and make us happy?"

"Utterly mad," he said, his eyes twinkling. He played a flurry of notes that sent the tendrils spinning in a joyful whirlwind. "Mad and marvelous."

Smiling, I turned my gaze skyward again.

Far, far above us in the mesosphere—where atmospheric discharges of electricity generally belonged—a huge display of multicolored korae bloomed silently across the sky. Its actual size was hard to discern with the naked eye, but it must have been many kilometers wide.

The tendrils abandoned their dance to emulate the korae's patterns and colors. They swayed in place for a few beats, then began dancing again in an intricate imitation of the korae. The twin displays were breathtaking. The korae faded, but the tendrils continued their dance.

A few seconds later, two sets of multicolored korae appeared in the atmosphere. The tendrils above us divided and echoed the korae's pattern and colors again, dancing and twining around each other.

Our rooftop visitors' movements seemed like more than a dance now—more like they were trying to tell us something.

"I don't think our visitors are korae," I said softly. "I think they're a plasma-based life form *imitating* the korae. It's a duet, like you playing with the wind. It's music and dance. It's *art*."

Ardruc's music faded. Out of the corner of my eye, I watched him put his lat'sar snugly into its case and close the lid. I missed his music immediately, but the tendrils around and above us continued dancing and emulating the korae display in the sky.

Slowly, as if worried about startling the tendrils, Ardruc picked up one of his own empty equipment bags, rose, and made his way across the roof to where I lay. I left my right arm extended to hold vine leaves but tucked the other against my side in a silent invitation. He put his pack down next to mine, folded his wings neatly, and lay down to my left. That wonderful sweet-peppery scent enveloped me. I inhaled deeply and sighed.

Side by side, we watched in silent awe as the tendrils alternated between dancing with each other and imitating a succession of enormous and brilliant korae displays.

When it came to the natural world, fungi would forever be my first and true love. They contained endless mysteries and wonders, and even if I spent my entire life studying them—which I planned to do—I would understand only the tiniest fraction about their essential qualities. Analyzing fungi felt like peering into the infinite. My studies were humbling and at the same time wonderfully fulfilling.

Korae and these tendrils, however they might be related—or indeed if they were at all—had a strong claim to second place now in my mind and heart. Maybe my instincts had told me there was something more to this planet's upper atmospheric electrical discharges than met the eye before that first encounter in the forest. Or maybe it was just their beauty and colors and power that had enthralled me much like they had long captivated Ardruc, though he'd hidden that wonder under his cold, distant façade.

Now that façade had cracked. I hoped it would fall and smash like a dropped vase on marble, never to be used again. Maybe I could help him smash it.

Hard to believe just a few nights ago, I'd lain almost in this exact spot and pictured what Ardruc would think about rooftop korae-watching. In my imagination, he'd scoffed and stomped back downstairs to stare at his data.

At the moment, his glowing golden gaze was nearly rapturous as the tendrils danced and korae filled the sky with color and raw power. I slid my hand over and touched Ardruc's fingertips. He curled his fingers around mine.

Warmth, comfort, and peace swelled from the ground and

through the vines wrapped around my hand. The sensation filled my body from my head to the soles of my feet, concentrating in and around the mark on my chest. Then it traveled from my chest, down my arm, and through my hand into Ardruc.

Time seemed to still.

The air turned to shimmering mist in endless iridescent colors, swirling and flowing around us in streams and layers. Silver-blue threads formed webs connecting mushrooms and lichen to roots and grass, branches and vines, twigs and leaves, and from those leaves to my hand and then Ardruc's.

As if a veil had been lifted, a vast and wondrous network of life had appeared. Its threads coursed around and through us, pulsing steady and strong and humming with sensation.

Three enormous korae bloomed across the sky, sending waves through the threads. For a moment, I felt as if my body were floating above the grass as the power and beauty of it coursed under and through me. The sensation reminded me of floating on my back in the ocean—but it was as if I were the ocean too, a consciousness without body or form.

Panic started to rise. But when I focused on moving my fingers, my physical sensations returned. Ardruc squeezed my hand as if he was my anchor, or I was his.

A gust of cool autumn wind swept down the mountainside. The trees swayed, dancing in a wave of pleasure that thrummed through the threads and resonated in my soul—and in my chest where the tendril had marked me with a symbol made of plant cells.

Great gods above and below, the planet's ecosystem was marvelously and intricately interconnected in ways I couldn't begin to fathom.

Hyderia was *alive*.

CHAPTER 18
ARDRUC

Elena's little gasp made me turn my head to look at her.

As if that movement had broken a spell, the vision around us of threads and webs connecting the flora, air, and fungi of Hyderia vanished. The tendrils above us stilled in mid-dance and hovered, though the korae display continued unabated high above.

Elena swallowed hard and turned her head to look me, her beautiful blue eyes wide in what might have been shock combined with awe and bewilderment.

My own wonder battled with a strong sense of *what now?*—combined with relief that as far as we knew, the tendrils were not korae, and Hyderia's korae were indeed upper-atmospheric plasma discharges. At least in all my many mistakes, I had not, in fact, been wrong about that.

"Well," Elena croaked. "That was quite a sight."

"It was." I squeezed her hand. "Are you all right?"

"Yes." She extracted her free hand from the vine and touched her chest where the symbol was hidden by her jumpsuit. "I felt the threads tugging on this. I think I'm part of the ecosystem." She made a face. "Yes, I'm already part of the ecosystem because I live here, but I mean I'm *really* part of the ecosystem now. I think I've been plugged into the network."

"I felt the tugs too," I said, which seemed to surprise her. "When I took your hand, I felt a connection through you. Warmth and comfort and reassurance. The feeling was very welcoming, as you said earlier today when the vine in my bedroom touched your arm."

She smiled. "It feels nice, doesn't it?"

"It does." Though not nearly as nice as holding her hand.

She looked up at the tendrils. "They stopped dancing. Are they watching us? Waiting to see what we do?"

"I do not know." I studied them. "It *does* feel like they are waiting."

Her mouth turned up at the corners. "Gut feeling?"

"Gut feeling," I admitted.

Chuckling, she sat up. I followed suit, still cradling her hand. Forux yawned, stretched, and moved to the grass to sprawl out and warm his fluffy belly in the sun.

Looking up at the tendrils, I had an idea. I did not know how Elena might respond, though, and nervousness made my stomach churn worse than when I thought about playing my lat'sar for her.

Before I changed my mind, I asked, "I want to fly up to see the tendrils. Would you like to join me?"

Her mouth fell open. She craned her neck to look up. "Yes," she breathed, returning her wide-eyed gaze to my face. "I would love that."

My hearts soared. It was only a little thing for her to agree to fly just above the rooftop to try to get a closer look at our visitors. Even so, her trust filled me with joy and contentment.

Beaming with excitement, she let me help her rise. She squeezed my hand. "Your brandy scent just got sweeter," she said, looking up at me with that wry little smile I adored. "You must be excited to fly with me."

I did not think I smelled at all like Bacorian brandy, but if she thought so and liked the scent, I would not argue. "I am very pleased to take you flying," I confessed. "And I am grateful for your trust."

Quickly, I unfastened the collar of my tunic and separated the seams above my wings and down the front. I slid my tunic off, folded it neatly, and set it on top of my equipment bag.

When I straightened, Elena's lips twitched as if she was suppressing laughter. "I've seen you fly dozens of times with a shirt on. Suddenly you need to be shirtless to fly?"

Her mirth delighted me, even if it was at my expense. "I fly alone wearing a shirt, but I think fabric will make it more difficult for you to hang on to me," I explained. "Bare skin is safer. We will both have a better grip this way."

"Well, that's logical." She glanced down at her long-sleeved jumpsuit. "I'd better take this off, then. The fabric is *literally* engineered to reduce friction."

As quickly as I had removed my shirt, she took off her boots and jumpsuit. Underneath, she wore a snug gray sleeveless undershirt and shorts. The mysterious mark was just visible over the neckline of her top.

Gods above, Elena was beautiful, especially in the sunshine. I had found her captivating from the first moment I had seen her face and heard her voice in her introductory message, though I had smothered those feelings immediately. Perhaps even then, long before I met her in person and caught her scent, my hearts and soul had seen and understood more than my eyes or brain.

"Funny how pretty it looks now," she mused, staring at the swirls of the mark on her chest. "Not scary at all and full of life, like the threads we just saw all around us."

I took a chance and tucked a loose strand of hair behind her ear. She leaned against my palm and closed her eyes.

In bare feet, she felt tiny next to me. She was never fragile, never weak, and certainly never intimidated, but I could not help but worry for her safety and health. I had never experienced such contentment and joy combined with an all-consuming need to treasure and protect someone.

"Hey." Elena rested her hand on my bare chest. Her touch instantly comforted me. "Don't get too lost in that brilliant head of yours, dragon. I want to fly."

My hearts fluttered. If she would call me *dragon*, I would do anything she wanted—anything at all.

"We will fly," I promised. "One moment."

The way her skin seemed to shimmer in the mid-afternoon suns and the sight of her bare toes in the grass inspired me to remove my own boots. The moment my feet touched the grass, a strange warmth seeped into me that was more than simply the suns' heat. My breath caught and I stared at the ground in wonder.

"You feel it now too, don't you? The warmth of belonging." She laced her fingers through mine and glanced at my pants. "Anything else you feel like taking off, by chance? For safety?"

My chest rumbled. "Is there anything else you would like me to take off? For safety?"

Her chuckle sent a thrill of desire through me. "Since my life will be in your hands, I think I'd feel safer if I didn't have all that fabric between us."

She was teasing and playful, but I brought her hand to my lips to kiss her fingers. "I swear I will not let any harm come to you—not by my hand or any other's."

"You know you can't make that promise, Ardruc." She squeezed my hand to take the edge off her words. "Sometimes things happen we can't foresee. A tumble down a mountainside, a plasma tendril on a rooftop, a piece of wreckage blown across the ice."

Before I could ask what she meant about the piece of wreckage on the ice, she added, "But I appreciate very much that you *want* to keep me safe." She hooked her index finger into my waistband and tugged. "Now, off with the pants."

My hearts racing, I took off my pants and left them on top of my discarded shirt. Underneath, I wore long black undershorts.

Elena held out her hand. "So, how do we do this?"

I drew her against my chest. "I believe the best method is for you to face the same direction as me. I will hold you with my arms and tail."

Her eyebrows went up. "You *believe* that's the best method? Have you never done this before?"

My typical body temperature was already quite warm, but my face heated. "I have not."

"Okay." Her expression gentled. "I kind of like that, actually. I've never flown with anyone either. So we're both new to this." She turned her back, then looked up over her shoulder. "A bit of help, please, dragon."

My chest rumbling, I bent and wrapped her in my arms. She nestled back against my chest as I tucked her shoulder under my chin.

"There's that brandy smell again," she murmured. "I think I'll start calling it your happy scent. And my little bit of anxiety about flying just evaporated, so I think you might be doing a pheromone thing again." She thought about it. "Or maybe I just naturally feel safe with you. Could be either."

"Or both," I pointed out. She smelled so sweet and fiery, and wonderfully like home. "Thank you for your trust."

I wrapped my tail around her legs for additional security. Holding her like this was even more exquisite than waking to find her in my arms. This time I knew she was in my embrace by her own choice.

"Ready?" I asked. My voice was not quite steady, and I was quite sure she could feel my hearts pounding.

"Almost." She craned her neck and kissed my jaw lightly. "Now I'm ready."

With joy in my hearts, I spread my wings and launched us as gently as I could into the air.

Her gasp turned into a squeal as we rose one flap of my wings at a time to circle about four meters above the station. Forux ran back and forth across the rooftop, yipping in what I hoped was excitement rather than fright or anger.

Elena trembled in my arms, her chest heaving. "Should I land?" I asked, worried.

"Oh, gods, no." She rubbed her head against my jaw. "This is wonderful. I'm just overwhelmed. It's like a dream come true."

Much relieved, I kissed the top of her head. "Shall I go higher?"

She nearly quivered with excitement. "Yes!"

The suns warmed my wings as I flew higher and in a widening circle around the station. The tendrils rose and parted to give us more space.

I had never felt lighter, and the air had never smelled sweeter, than with Elena in my arms and secured by my tail. Every care and worry melted away except the need to keep her safe—a need that would never leave me now, no matter what our choices about the future might be. She was in my blood. Just having her beside me made me the luckiest man alive.

"Gods, Ardruc, why do you ever walk?" she asked as we flew out over the forest. "I'd spend every minute of every day in the sky if I had wings."

I chuckled. "I do have a job. I am a working dragon, not a dragon of leisure."

Her laugh made warmth pool in my chest. "And my wing muscles will tire eventually," I added. "I have no trouble carrying you for a short flight, but I am not yet accustomed to bearing a passenger." Oh, but how I *wanted* to fly with her again and again and again.

She squeezed her arms around mine. "Should I have put on an emergency flight pack?"

She was teasing, but I was quick to reassure her. "I will land long before we must worry about my strength giving out."

"Good to hear." She looked up ahead at the tendrils. "Shall we see what happens if we join our visitors?"

Cautiously, I turned in a wide circle and flew toward the station and the gathering of tendrils of plasma hovering far above it. They cleared a path for us as we approached.

As we passed through the gathering, their power sizzled on our skin. They fell in behind us as if we were leading a flock of birds. Elena turned to look over her shoulder and gasped at the sight of them swirling behind us.

I flew higher and circled the station in a wide elliptical path above the forest canopy. The tendrils danced in a long trail, twining around each other and shimmering in what I might have called joy or happiness if those emotions could be attributed to living plasma.

Their twirls gave me an idea. I had never done this maneuver carrying extra weight, but I could not resist a playful move.

I squeezed Elena. "Would you like me to spin?"

"Do it," she said without hesitation. "But first turn me around to face you, if you can."

Very, very carefully, my wings spread wide so I could soar smoothly, I turned her in my arms and tail so she was facing me.

Gods, her beauty and fearlessness made my hearts sing.

Some of her long hair had come loose from its braid and her eyes were wide and wild with excitement…and with arousal. Her sweet and nearly intoxicating fragrance was unmistakable despite the strong breeze.

She wrapped her arms around my neck. She fit so perfectly to me. "Ready," she breathed.

I clasped Elena even tighter against my chest, flapped my wings to gain altitude and speed, and dove, rolling us twice. Her shriek of pure delight rang in my ears as we spun in midair and then righted ourselves.

I soared on an updraft, banked, and turned to watch as the tendrils paired off and mimicked our movements by twirling around each other in a symphony of color and sparkling power.

Panting, Elena pulled my head down to hers and kissed me.

For a heartsbeat, I lost myself in her taste and scent and the warmth and softness of her skin against mine. My wings lost their rhythm and we dropped a few feet before I regained control.

She gasped against my mouth. "Don't fall out of the sky, dragon," she murmured. "If you can't multitask, let's go back to the roof."

I had planned to fly higher, to enjoy this time in the air with Elena and the tendrils, but her scent and the way she caressed my neck banished those thoughts like leaves blown by the wind.

I took my time descending though, soaring in wide circles around the station and skimming the trees to elicit gasps and thrilling scents from my mate. She grabbed a bright blue leaf from the very top of a tree and tucked it into her shirt between her breasts. A souvenir of this first flight? My hearts swelled with joy.

By the time I made the final turn and headed for the grassy upper roof, we were both trembling with adrenaline and need.

"I will land on my feet," I said, kissing her hair. "You will not need to assist."

"All right." She tucked herself against my chest.

Landing was easier than I expected, despite being barefoot and having to balance Elena's weight. I needed a few extra steps to come to a full stop and steady myself, but we landed softly and safely.

I did not, however, stay on my feet for long. With her hand on the back of my neck, Elena wiggled free of my arms and tail and pulled me down to the grass.

Mindful of how much larger and heavier I was, I folded my wings and rolled to my back, curling my arm around her so she ended up lying on top of me. Forux sniffed us as if to make sure we were unharmed after our flight, then wandered back to his napping spot next to Elena's discarded datapad.

Elena settled in on my chest, cupped my face in her hands, and kissed me.

All the world faded away.

My every sense filled with my mate. Her earthy scent, her cool skin on mine, her sweet taste, the sound of her gasping breaths and racing heart, the way the sunlight formed a halo around her hair before I closed my eyes to lose myself in the wonder of her... nothing in my life had ever felt so good and so right. My hearts raced and waves of heat rolled through me.

Only one thing remained undone to make this moment utterly perfect.

I draped my wing over us to cradle her and to shield us from being seen. This moment belonged to us alone.

I had always considered my wings perfectly weighted and sized for flight, but their primary purpose had morphed into keeping my mate safe and warm.

Elena sighed and melted against me, her curves fitting perfectly against my chest.

"Damn it," she murmured, her lips on the corner of my jaw. "You're so annoyingly irresistible now that I hate you less."

To be called *irresistible* by my mate while still euphoric from our flight...my chest rumbled in pleasure. I coiled my tail snugly around her bare calf. She quivered and nuzzled my chest.

The fragrant grass beneath us hummed with the interconnected ecosystem's energy we had observed before our flight. Elena's heartbeat and her scent completed the sensation of being at home, secure, and perfectly content.

She kissed me again, much more fiercely this time, and flicked her tongue against my lips to demand more. I ran my fingers through her silken hair and held her close.

"What may I do so you might hate me even less?" I ventured when our kiss ended.

"Let's see..." She rested her elbow on my chest, propped her head on her hand, and pursed her pretty lips, as if daring me to kiss her again.

"You've fed me," she mused. "Carried my equipment up the stairs and to the roof without complaint, let me scan you to make sure you're not influencing me with pheromones, taken me flying and landed us safely, and covered me with your wing so I don't get chilly in these shorts. And you let me call you *dragon* instead of Dr. Husiorithae. That's quite a lot of items in the non-hate column."

I cupped her face. "And yet, by my accounting a deficit remains. I must add more."

The corners of her beautiful mouth turned up. "Let me turn the question around. What would *you* like to do so I might hate you less?"

That mental list was damn near endless and focused a great deal on actions I hoped would lead her to call me *dragon*—and not quietly. My body thrummed with desire. Her own scent revealed she shared my need.

But her scent also told me our flight had filled her with endorphins and adrenaline. I could not be certain her words and thoughts were not influenced in a way that might lead to regrets later. I had already erred catastrophically with her. I could do nothing knowingly, ever, that might cause her to have regrets, or hurt her in a way I could never undo or be forgiven for.

My search for my real self continued as I stripped away my many façades and masks so my mate could truly know me. What lay beneath all those layers, I was not sure. But above all, I wanted to be an honest, good man for Elena. She deserved nothing less.

"If once the rush from the flight wanes you still want me to answer that question, I will," I said. "Better yet, I will show you. Right now, I worry you are not clear-headed."

Her smile faded. Her sweet and fiery scent changed from contentment and desire to something more like sadness and frustration. My hearts twinged. I did not want her to be sad or angry with me.

"I am quite clear-headed," she said with a scowl. "I didn't drink a bottle of Probytian moonshine; I went flying with you. Now you're walking on eggshells. Drawing back, just when we're getting closer. I don't like it."

"I *should* be cautious," I countered. "As you pointed out, I have made many terrible choices these past few months."

"Most of your terrible choices involved ignoring or overriding your instincts, and here you are doing it again." She pressed her palms to my chest and studied me as if I were a lichen whose secrets she was determined to discover. "Stop living so much in your head. What do your instincts want? You can tell me. We're both scientists. Let's examine them together."

What did my instincts want?

Her.

Everything in my body and soul needed to feel her bare skin on mine, to claim her and be claimed, to drown myself in the wonder and perfection of my brilliant, beautiful, intuitive, wild-hearted mate. To taste her, fill her, heal her and be healed. I wanted to share all the marvels and miracles of the true mate bond, the most wondrous aspect of being Fortusian. I wanted that so much, more than I had wanted anything in my life, even escape from the cult that captured the rest of my family.

Thinking about my estranged family—and how much I had risked and sacrificed to gain my freedom—made me ache even now. But it also granted me the ability to see this moment in a new and different way.

I had flown away from the compound toward a life devoted to science and reason. But what I had wanted even more were happiness and the right to choose with whom I would build my life and perhaps one day have a family of my own full of love and trust rather than hurt and betrayal.

At last, a long-overdue realization began to dawn.

Of all the terrible decisions I had made since Elena's arrival at Nova Cal, perhaps the worst was believing finding my true mate took away my choices when in fact it was proof of the power of choice. All my choices had led me to this place, this moment, when Elena gazed into my eyes and asked what I wanted.

Gods above, she was everything I had ever wanted and more.

"Dr. Husiorithae." Frowning, Elena pinched my chin none too gently to draw my attention. "I *said*, let's examine your instincts togeth—"

I rolled us over, pinned my mate to the grass with most of my weight on one knee and elbow and my wings draped over us, and let my eyes glow.

"My instincts tell me I am your dragon," I rasped, and kissed her.

Her lips parted to welcome my hungry mouth. With a satisfied moan that ignited my blood, she arched up against me, hooked her leg over my thigh, and ran her hands through my hair, pulling hard enough to make me growl. She even sank her little teeth into my bottom lip and licked the bite. Delicious pain. My chest rumbled.

A shudder of desire rolled through me. My cock hardened, beading with lubrication and throbbing with need, ready and aching to please my mate. My tail lashed back and forth through the air like a whip, its tip quivering.

Licking blood from my lip, I rose above her, captured her hands, and pinned her wrists into the grass above her head.

A few drops of my blood landed on her mouth. Her little tongue darted out to lick them off. She moaned, her chest heaving. "You taste so good," she gasped.

"Did you bite on instinct?" I asked. Even to my own ears, my voice sounded an octave lower than normal.

"I'm a scientist." She pulled at my grip, but not as if she really wanted to be freed, so I did not release her. "I did some research earlier while you were packing to come to the roof."

I dipped my head to inhale her scent near the nape of her neck. "And what did your research indicate?"

"I didn't have much time, so I have only preliminary findings. But I did read that male equatorial dragons enjoy biting and being bitten during mating." She raised her hips to grind against the hard length of my cock, where it strained the fabric of my undershorts. Gods above. "And as it so happens," she added, "so do I."

Wonder and hunger for my mate battled for supremacy in my soul.

I nudged the strap of her top aside and closed my teeth on her shoulder. Not hard enough to draw blood—not yet. The scent of her desire intensified.

"Any other preliminary findings?" I murmured into her ear. "Regarding the mating practices of male equatorial dragons?"

She whimpered. The scent of her arousal threatened to push me beyond all reason.

"The most significant variable," she gasped as I laved the mark my teeth had made with my tongue to heal it with my saliva, "is which traits the genetic engineers preserved when they combined dragon DNA with human genetic material and other sources. I'm forced to say further research is required. This could take the form of a verbal interview with the subject in question, or empirical study."

My quivering tail traveled up the inside of her thigh and brushed the hem of her little shorts. Her sharp intake of breath matched the sudden increase in the scent of her arousal. I did not need to see it to know beneath the thin fabric, her sweet pussy dripped for me.

I kissed my way along her shoulder to her jaw, where I bit her lightly again. My bodily fluids had healing capabilities for my mate —a trait I planned to put to use thoroughly should we continue playfully biting.

"Which method for further study do you prefer, Dr. Regis?" I made my tone businesslike despite the roar in my ears and the throbbing in my cock. "Interview? I pledge to answer all questions thoroughly and honestly."

"Very admirable." Unlike mine, her voice was breathless and ragged. "But I've always preferred field research and empirical study."

She turned her head to give my teeth better access to her delicate jaw and throat. So trusting, my mate. When I bit her throat ever so carefully, she groaned. She truly did enjoy biting and being bitten, perhaps just as much as I.

The roar in my ears grew. My muscles clenched and relaxed in what felt like a full-body spasm that ran from my shoulders down my back and chest and through my legs to my feet, where my toes curled and dug into the grass. I huffed in an almost beastly way.

"Beyond the spirit of scientific inquiry, I must admit I'm extremely *and very personally* curious about the prospect of you experiencing a mating frenzy," Elena continued, moving against the hard length of my cock as my tail quivered. Gods, the fabric between us was so thin. "It's a common trait among dragons, but not one that Fortusian genetic engineers always preserve when their genetic material combines with human and other DNA."

Was that what my desperate hold on reason was holding back? A frenzy? Was that why she had brought up the topic?

Another shudder ran through my body, making my feathers ruffle and skin blaze with heat and need.

With effort, I raised my head and released one of her hands so I could cup her face. Her eyes were wild with desire. Mine must look much the same.

"I do not know if I possess that trait," I said, my voice strained. "But I believe I might. I am…holding something back."

"I can tell." Her smirk made my hearts flutter. "You feel taut, like a trigger half-pulled."

Unable to resist any longer, I slipped the tip of my tail inside the hem of her shorts. She moaned and widened her legs a little more, whimpering for me to touch her, to delve inside her, but I hesitated —still afraid of losing myself, afraid of doing anything she might regret later.

"Don't tease me, Ardruc," she said, her eyes suddenly fiery. "Pull the trigger or don't, but do *something*. I don't like to be emotionally edged. *Physically* edged…well, maybe that's something we can do later."

Visions of bringing her repeatedly to the brink of release only to draw back and let her need build to almost unbearable levels before giving her what she craved conjured the most powerful wave of heat and need yet.

I drove the madness—the *frenzy*—back once more with force of will.

"I need to know what you want," I grated. "My hearts are unshielded now. You could hurt me, break me beyond repair. I cannot bear to make a wrong decision when it comes to you."

"I understand that kind of fear." She took advantage of her freed hand to run her fingertips over my lips as she held my glowing golden gaze with her own breathtakingly and so-human blue one. "I will tell you very plainly what I want. I want to know who you are, dragon. I want to see and hear and *feel* you when you're not lost in your head, without bad memories or all these fucking masks hiding you from me. I want you to know I am the one person with whom you must drop all pretense."

Since early childhood, I had not been able to be myself with anyone, even my family. Elena was offering me a gift beyond price —no, *many* gifts beyond price. More than I could begin to count.

"I want to feel you inside me in all the ways a dragon man can take his mate," she added, and now the roar in my ears drowned out everything but her voice. Another wave built, rising more quickly and more powerfully than any before it.

"I want to know I can be myself with you," she said. "I need to know I'm right about the kind of man you are, so I know what I'm feeling is real."

"What do you feel?" I asked, my voice barely more than a growl. "That you hate me less?"

Her gentle smile nearly undid me.

"After hearing and seeing you play and thinking about what you've revealed to me, I think I understand you now." Elena stroked my cheek with her fingertips. "Honestly, I barely hate you at all," she whispered.

The wave inside me began to crest. I shuddered and bent my

head, muscles straining as I fought to hold it back. Elena startled me by grabbing my hair and yanking my head down to hers so our noses touched.

She stared directly into my eyes. "Let go, damn it," she commanded. "Break free. *Be my dragon.*"

Gods above, I would never be anything else.

Finally, *finally*, I dropped the last of my resistance to the siren call of my mate. The roaring wave swept me away.

CHAPTER 19

ELENA

ARDRUC'S EYES WENT COMPLETELY BLACK. MOVING SO FAST THEY blurred, his wings snapped wide. A cloud of thick sweet-peppery brandy scent fell from his wings and enveloped me.

My skin blazed with heat as if I had caught fire, but I felt no pain —only an intense wave of desire that made me writhe and cry out.

My wail was smothered by Ardruc's mouth, which covered mine and filled my throat and lungs with more of that wonderful, almost intoxicating scent. It soaked into my skin, entered my bloodstream, and amplified every sensation.

Every beat of my racing heart sounded as loud as plasma cannon fire. I would swear I could feel each blade of grass beneath me, every atom of air on my skin and in my lungs, and every hair on my body. And beyond that, every leaf stirred by wind in the trees around the station and the vines that had taken over the edge of the roof tingled in my awareness.

The tendrils had disappeared at some point, and Forux had apparently chosen to jump down to the landing pad area. We were alone on the roof.

The Ardruc above me looked almost nothing like the man I'd known, or thought I'd known. Like a predator studying his prey, his wild eyes scoured my body. His masks were gone. His reserve had evaporated, taking with it—I hoped—all those ghosts of his past that had made him so miserable and alone.

Was this a mating frenzy? Gods, I hoped so.

My pussy, dripping and desperate to be touched and filled, clenched hard. My toes curled and my heels dug into the grass as I bucked up against him.

"Take me," I commanded, my voice hoarse. "Ardruc, dragon, *please*. Take your mate."

With a snarl and puff of smoke from his nostrils, he ripped my top in half down the front. My taut nipples, suddenly exposed to the air, ached to be sucked and bitten.

Apparently not satisfied with baring my breasts, Ardruc raised my torso and ripped my top again down the back.

In moments, I found my arms pinned above my head. When I tugged on them, I couldn't move. A glance upward revealed he'd tied my hands to a heavy crate with the scraps of my top.

When I looked back, Ardruc's face was directly above mine. Through the wildness and need in his dark eyes, I caught sight of a question—or a fragment of one.

"Yes," I said. "Go on."

His enormous hands, so hot against my much-cooler human flesh, cupped my breasts. I groaned and writhed as he flicked my hard nipples with the tip of his tongue and then closed his lips on the little nubs. And then his teeth—

I screamed and arched up against him, yanking on my bound wrists to no avail. His teeth were so sharp, so perfect. The pain was perfect too—just a little too much, a little past my limit, absolutely exquisite. My pussy gushed with pleasure and need. My shorts must be drenched, and yet the tip of his tail hovered inside the fabric, still quivering, still just short of where I wanted it to be.

He raised his head and loomed above me, all darkness and dragon and desire.

"Elena," he growled. His hand traveled down my stomach

toward my waistband. Smoke swirling from his nostrils, he slid his hand under the fabric.

"Yes," I said again, trembling with need. "Gods, yes, please."

The first brush of his fingers on my slick, delicate skin made me writhe and cry out. His reaction was a full-body shiver. He withdrew his glistening fingers and inhaled my scent before licking them clean.

He licked and laved his way down my body, igniting little explosions of need with every swoop of his hot tongue and touch of his hands. When he sat on his heels between my knees and looked up to meet my gaze, the hunger on his face made me open my legs more.

"Please," I begged again. "Ardruc, my dragon. I need you."

He gripped my shorts in both hands and ripped them in half, baring me to his hungry gaze.

I whimpered and panted as he pushed my legs wide. I needed to be touched. My pussy clenched, desperate to be filled. My bound hands and that single earlier caress—just a tease, not nearly enough to send me over the edge—added to my sense of helplessness. If he didn't touch me, put his mouth on me, make me come…

With another snarl and puff of smoke, he ripped off his own shorts.

Oh, gods—his cock was orange and red, enormous and beautiful, with the same scale pattern as the rest of his skin. Nubs and ridges ran down its length, glistening and shimmering in the sunlight. Liquid beaded from his flesh. From its tip dripped pearlescent precum that made me lick my lips.

In an inhumanly fast movement, he all but dove between my thighs, his hands sliding under my hips to raise my dripping pussy to his face. He inhaled deeply, his chest rumbling as I trembled.

"Sweet little mate," he rasped. "You smell like you want to come for me."

His long, hot tongue delved between my folds. My cry echoed through the valley.

I wanted so badly to run my fingers through his hair and pull, to hold him there between my legs as he explored me with his tongue. I twisted and pulled at the fabric tied around my wrists until it bit into my skin but it didn't give at all. The pain and desperation felt so good and made me gush even harder for him.

Ardruc's tongue circled my clit. I cried out.

Helpless and at his mercy, I writhed as his tongue and lips fluttered on my clit, driving me with breathtaking speed toward ecstasy. After our playful moments in the kitchen this morning, the thrills of flying, and the intensity of lying on top of him—and then *under* him—after we returned to the roof, I was already teetering on a knife's edge.

It took only seconds of Ardruc's attentions to send me hurtling over the cliff.

Screaming, wailing, writhing desperately against my bonds, I flooded Ardruc's face for the first time with my orgasm.

His grip tightened on my hips to hold me against his mouth while he continued to suck my clit and lap up my release. I'd have bruises there—trophies, rather. The marks of my dragon mate. The thought sent me careening back over the edge with soft orgasm.

In the midst of that pleasure, two of Ardruc's fingers slipped inside me. He pumped them slowly, coating them with my release.

My chest heaving, I looked down at the toe-curling sight of Ardruc putting his glistening fingers in his mouth and sucking them.

"You called my name when you came, little mate," he said, flashing his sharp teeth. "You said *Ardruc.*"

His gaze on mine, he lowered his head and sucked along my slit to capture my slickness. I whimpered.

"Call me your dragon," he commanded, glowering at me from between my thighs. "Call me your mate."

"My dragon," I gasped.

He dipped his fingers back into my pussy and pumped them.

"Your dragon," he agreed. His fingertips curled up, stroking, searching, but only giving me the most gentle caress. "Your dragon what?"

I yanked on my bound hands, desperate for him to stroke me harder, but he continued to brush the very tips of his fingers over my G-spot.

"My…mate," I managed to say. "My dragon mate."

"Yes, your dragon mate," he rumbled. "Would my little mate like to taste her dragon's cock?"

Before today, before Ardruc, if anyone had called me their *little* anything, I would have knocked them flat on their ass.

But Ardruc didn't mean it condescendingly or patronizingly. He knew I was his equal. He *wanted* an equal. He wanted and needed me just as I was, and I wanted and needed him too.

"Yes," I gasped. "Please…"

More slow, delicate strokes and no release. I whimpered. "Please what, my little mate?"

Oh, you beautiful bastard. "Please make me come again. I'm so close…"

His fingertips added just a little more pressure. I moaned and my legs squeezed his broad shoulders.

"Please make me come," I pleaded. "And then please let me taste your beautiful dragon cock."

Slowly, masterfully, mercilessly, playing me as if I were his lat'sar, Ardruc coaxed me back to the precipice with slow, even strokes, letting the orgasm build and build as I wailed and begged and pulled at my bonds, desperate to come.

I might have regretted bringing up the topic of edging if I didn't love every moment of this torture.

"Beautiful little mate," he cooed as I writhed and whimpered. "Beautiful Elena with a beautiful little pussy that wants to come for her dragon. Beautiful Elena, with a beautiful little mouth and beautiful little pussy that want to be filled with her dragon's cock. Beautiful Elena—"

Whatever he said next, I didn't hear it.

With a wail and shudders, my legs shaking, I came impossibly hard, squeezing and gushing on Ardruc's fingers.

Pleasure flooded my body, graying out my vision. Each wave traveled through my skin into the grass below me, sending pulses of light and some kind of power through the humming threads of Hyderia's life force around us.

The threads hummed and pulsed, sending a wave of joy and contentment back through me—and into Ardruc, who growled and rumbled.

His glowing gaze on mine, he withdrew his fingers and licked them clean as I drifted in a haze. "Thank you," I murmured.

Running his nose over my tingling skin, he prowled up my body, his cock arching up toward his hard abdominal muscles.

When he got closer, I noticed his brandy-and-pepper scent had changed, becoming richer, deeper, infinitely more arousing. I could lose myself in that scent forever.

Finally, he straddled my chest, his weight on his knees, his beautiful, dripping cock and heavy balls just out of reach of my lips and tongue.

"Elena," he said. His voice was less gravelly now, but his raw desire and need shone in his eyes as he caressed my face. "You are radiant when you come. Your screams are the most beautiful song I have ever heard."

His long tail caressed its way up my body as he curled it around to bring its tip to my lips. He brushed hair back from my face. "Lick my tail, little mate."

Oh, that beautiful, sexy tail.

It was as long as he was tall, or nearly so, and a little rougher in texture than the rest of his skin. I loved how thick it was where it emerged from the base of his spine and how it tapered to just a few inches just above the dark red tip. And the frills than ran down its length moved like waves as the sunlight shone through them, making them appear to glow orange.

I opened my mouth and let him slip the tip of his tail between my lips. It was almost the same thickness as his beautiful cock and it thrummed. Oh, gods.

I licked the tip and swirled my tongue around it. He groaned. It tasted like him too—but smokier and richer.

Ardruc caressed my cheek with one hand and gripped his cock with the other. "Bite my tail, little mate. Do not be gentle."

Carefully, I bit him. He rumbled. "Harder."

With a moan, I sank my teeth deeper into his tough, scaly skin. A shudder ran through his body.

"Yes," he growled. His hand glided up and down his glistening, dripping cock. "You called me dragon when you came just now. Did you know?"

I shook my head, my lips tight around his tail.

"You called me your mate. Your dragon. In your release, you called for me." He inched forward until the head of his cock was right above my face. I moaned around his tail, my mouth watering.

He gripped my chin. "Little mate, your mouth is so perfect." Another slow, deliberate stroke, and precum dripped onto my chin. "Everything about you is perfect, especially your orgasms. I will live for your orgasms, I think. I will live to hear you scream my name."

I could be on board with that too.

More slow strokes, more drips down my chin and on my face. I sucked and bit his tail desperately now because I wanted to be touching myself, or for him to be touching me or inside me, and my pussy was dripping and untouched.

Gods above, these torments were as arousing as imagining his tail or cock inside me and the way he stroked himself.

When he withdrew his tail from my mouth, I whimpered and raised my hips in a desperate plea.

Instead of filling me, he leaned over and brought the tip of his cock close to my lips. "Would you like a taste, little mate?"

I wanted more than a taste, but a taste would do to start. "Yes, please."

As he stroked himself, a drop of precum gathered on the tip of his beautiful, thick cock, glistening in the sun. "Open your mouth," he commanded. "Hold out your tongue."

Whimpering with need, I squeezed my thighs together and obeyed.

"Beautiful Elena," he growled.

His precum, mixed with the lubrication that beaded from his cock, dripped onto my tongue. He tasted just as I'd imagined: salty, earthy, smoky, and almost electric.

I started to close my mouth and swallow, but he shook his head. "No, I want to give you more."

My pussy clenched desperately. I had played with other lovers, dominating some and letting others dominate me to varying degrees, but I'd never wanted someone to dominate me completely until now.

I kept my mouth open and tongue out, waiting for more.

Ardruc stroked his cock and dripped precum onto my tongue, into my mouth, onto my chin and lips and cheeks. I whimpered every time a drop didn't hit my tongue, and whimpered more when I had to fight to not disobey and give in to the growing need to close my mouth and swallow.

Ardruc smiled at me with his sharp teeth. "Little mate, you obey me so well," he said, and now his voice was deep and primal again. "Keep your mouth open and tongue out."

He spread his wings. I shivered hard with arousal.

He stroked himself faster, his abdominal muscles rippling and wings stretching as far as they would go. He was magnificent. My whimpers and gurgles turned desperate.

His tail curled around my right calf and tugged. "Open your legs."

Trembling and moaning, I did.

The quivering tip of his tail trailed up my leg, along my inner thigh, and delved along my slit until it found my clit and vibrated against it. I cried out and almost closed my mouth, but he grabbed my mouth and held it open with a gentle but firm grip on my jaw.

"No, no, little mate," he grated. "Mouth open and tongue out. You are going to taste my cum as you come."

My pussy gushed at his promise. His tail abandoned my aching clit and slid lower. I raised my hips, desperate for penetration.

His chest was heaving now. The drips from his cock became rivulets that ran over his fingers and splattered my face. His balls tightened.

"Give me your tail," I said, or tried to say. The words were indistinct because he was holding my mouth open.

His tail plunged into my pussy, quivering and vibrating, and found my G-spot perfectly on the first try. My cry was garbled.

I orgasmed impossibly quickly, desperately, and violently on Ardruc's tail.

Ardruc came moments later with bellows and roars, his head thrown back, body shuddering, and wings wide. Massive spurts of gleaming cum jetted over my tongue, down my throat, across my face, and into the air. He tasted so good: sweet and wonderfully smoky, with notes of spices and petrichor.

His chest heaving, he looked over his shoulder, where his tail was buried in my quivering, dripping pussy. Then he turned back to admire the mess he'd made with his cum—and my mouth, still open, still waiting.

"My mate," he rasped, caressing my face. He scooped up a streak of cum and placed it on my tongue. "Do I taste as good to you as you do to me?"

Unable to speak, I nodded.

"Not possible," he said, and fed me more. "You taste like the heavens, little mate." He stroked my cheek. "Would you like to swallow now?"

I nodded again.

He moved down my body enough that he could bend over and kiss my brow.

"Go ahead," he murmured into my ear as he released my jaw. "Let me see you swallow it all like a good little mate."

I swallowed. I licked my lips too, then opened my mouth to show him that I'd swallowed all the cum he'd given me.

"Good girl." He caressed my lips, his touch light as a feather, and eased his tail out of my pussy. I whimpered at the loss. "You deserve a reward. Would you like to take my cock now?"

My eyes widened. "So soon?"

Indeed, between us his cock remained hard and ready. And though I'd already come several times, I wanted it. I wanted it desperately.

"I will always be insatiable for you." He dipped his head and closed his teeth on my shoulder again—harder than before. Hard enough to hurt. I moaned.

"I need your sweet little pussy, Elena," he rasped into my ear. "I need your greedy little mouth. I need your exquisite little ass. I need to take you in all the ways a dragon man can take his mate, again and again. Every cell in my body needs you."

Well, that was the very definition of a mating frenzy, though he seemed more in control now after he'd come.

And more than that, this was Ardruc here with me, a beautiful, insatiable Fortusian male who, at the urging of his mate, had finally managed to get out of his head and let his instincts and body guide him.

Every instinct in his body wanted *me*, Elena Regis, a mycologist with a robust academic record, a host of discoveries and accolades, a long list of casual and short-term liaisons, and no experience being the center of anyone's universe.

Ardruc cupped my face. "I like having you at my mercy," he said, his gaze on mine. "It is a side of myself I did not know I had."

"I like this side of you." I turned my head to kiss his palm and then bit the fleshy part below his thumb. "I like being dominated by my dragon mate. I want more of this."

His cock leapt in eagerness.

"I want to chase you through the forest," he said, and I moaned. "I want you to run. When I catch you, I will take you in every way.

First in your mouth, then in your pussy, and then your ass. I am a predator. I want to *chase*."

Ardruc bent to sniff my throat like a beast scenting its prey. I quivered.

"How much of a head start should I give you, little mate?" he rumbled.

Gods above, I wasn't prey, but I wanted to be chased. "Fifteen minutes," I croaked.

"Fifteen minutes it is. We will go first to your apartment so you can dress, and then we will go to the forest." He glanced over his shoulder. "As much as I desire to continue to take you in full view of these recording devices, the forest calls to us both. We will keep the recordings for our own private enjoyment."

My eyes widened. I'd forgotten all about the recordings we'd made of the tendrils and that we'd left the equipment running during and after our flight.

I'd just climaxed repeatedly on the tongue, fingers, and tail of Dr. Ardruc Husiorithae, Nova Cal's highly esteemed director of research, and then quite happily let him come all over my face, and it was all recorded. And much to my astonishment, I liked that. A *lot*.

Hmm...I might be a bit of an exhibitionist as well as happily submissive to my dragon mate.

Well, the life of a scientist was a life of discovery—even about oneself.

CHAPTER 20
ARDRUC

M Y HEARTS SINGING AND NOSTRILS FLARING, I PLUNGED THROUGH the forest following the siren call of my little mate's scent.

I had no idea where the phrase *my little mate* came from. The words had popped into my head in the midst of the first rush of the mating frenzy, when my thoughts were jumbled and hazy and my need for Elena swallowed up everything I was and had ever been.

The first time it came out of my mouth, part of me worried my brilliant and strong mate might take offense. Instead, my Elena's sweet pussy gushed at the words. She liked my nickname for her as much as I liked to be called *her dragon*.

She did not simply let me dominate her; she craved it. I knew from the way she had twisted her hands in her bonds to emphasize how helpless she was to be tied up, and she obeyed me even when it caused her discomfort or pain. She wanted me to come on her face and feed her my cum. She got off beautifully being submissive and wanted recordings of our lovemaking to watch later.

My mate was perfect. We were a *perfect match*.

This should not have surprised me. To be true mates, we must resonate in every way. But with every new experience, we found a new aspect in which we complimented each other, and the wonder of it was almost enough to distract from my need to find her and take her.

I huffed. *Almost.*

The grass under my feet, the trees around and above me, the fungi and leaves and vines all thrummed with what seemed to me like joy and excitement as I passed by, as if the planet was part of our courtship.

I did not know why Hyderia had chosen to reveal its wonders to us or what might come next, but for the first time in my life I cared only about this perfect present. My mate was running and hiding somewhere in this forest, waiting and *wanting* to be caught and taken. Nothing else mattered.

Skin tingling and cock throbbing with need, I hunted.

All my senses narrowed to her scent and the little signs she had left of her passage through the woods: bent twigs, footprints in bare earth, a spot on a fallen tree where she had clearly scraped her arm or leg climbing over it. My hearts twinged at the smear of blood on the bark. When I found her, I would heal her wound and give her such endless pleasure that she forgot the injury entirely.

My mate's well-being and safety were now the center of my existence. Nothing in the universe could make me more content than making her happy.

My hearts raced faster the closer I came to finding her. Her scent was now so fresh that it made my blood hum and sizzle. I must be only moments behind her.

To my left, a flash of movement: blonde hair and green clothing. The softest sound of footsteps in the grass, barely audible even to my sharp ears.

A low growl escaped my lips and a puff of smoke swirled from my nostrils. *Little mate, little mate…*

Silently, I slipped through the trees and undergrowth, circling around that thrilling glimpse of Elena until I found her.

She was whimpering and gasping for air as she ran, though she tried to muffle the sounds. Her excitement and anticipation buzzed on my skin like static. She knew I was closing in and her run was about to come to an end.

So I let her keep running, just to let her anticipation build a little more. The more desperate she became, the more she would enjoy what I planned to do.

She passed right by the tree I hid behind, her head swiveling as she scanned her surroundings. Her gaze slid past my place of concealment and focused on a little clearing up ahead where some fallen trees had formed a kind of barrier. She smiled to herself and changed direction.

My crafty little mate thought she had found a hiding place.

Silently, I slipped from tree to tree as Elena made her way toward the little shelter on her tiptoes, trying not to make a sound.

To be able to play with a lover, to embrace my predatory soul, to feel so free to be myself…how glorious.

Three meters from the clearing, just as she reached a lovely patch of soft grass ringed with brightly colored mushrooms, I leapt out from behind a tree and wrapped my arms around her from behind.

She shrieked as I took her to the ground, turning in midair so I took the force of the impact and she was unharmed.

The moment our skin touched, my mating frenzy changed form from the need to hunt to the need to *take*.

I rolled us, flipped her over onto her back, and pinned her wrists above her head with one hand.

Wild-eyed and chest heaving, she squirmed in my grip until I squeezed tighter. "There is no escape, little mate," I grated.

She whimpered. Gods, the scent of her arousal was maddening.

I lowered my head to capture her mouth with my own as my free hand pushed her top up to bare her breasts. Her pretty pink nipples had already formed hard peaks.

"I'll take off my clothes," she gasped. "You don't have to rip them off."

"I do not *have* to," I agreed, my lips moving along her jaw. "But I *want* to."

I sucked her right nipple into my mouth and used my tongue and teeth to make her wail and writhe. The red marks I had left earlier had already healed thanks to the healing power of my cum, so I made new ones. Every time my teeth closed on her delicate skin, she cried out and her arousal grew.

I rose to my hands and knees to loom over her. "Stay where you are," I commanded. "Do not move."

"Yes, dragon," she gasped.

My cock, already hard as stone, twitched and spurted precum in my pants at her obedience.

Impatient to have her mouth on me, I wanted to rip my pants off. Instead, I stood and unfastened them as Elena watched, her hands still over her head.

When I freed my dripping cock and slid my pants down my legs, she licked her lips and opened her legs.

"I told you not to move," I reminded her.

With a moan, she returned to her earlier pose. "Please," she gasped. "Please let me suck your cock, my dragon."

I draped my pants over a fallen tree and knelt. "Crawl to me, then, little mate."

Breathing hard, she rolled to her hands and knees and prowled toward me, taunting me by how slowly and sinuously she moved.

I wanted very much to tear her clothes from her body, but she had brought few clothing items with her to Nova Cal and we must conserve resources. Perhaps I could make do by stripping her naked.

"I want to see your beautiful body. Raise your hands." I pulled her top off over her head and tossed it onto the tree next to my pants. "Turn around," I commanded.

Still on her knees, she turned her back to me. I pulled her very utilitarian pants down to bare her perfect ass. My cock twitched again and splattered precum over her skin. She moaned.

With her legs trapped in her pants, I took advantage of her pose to stroke my fingertips along the cleft of her lovely ass and over her dripping pussy. She cried out, her pleas for my fingers and tongue tumbling over each other in her desperation for release.

"Not yet, little mate," I said, and circled her asshole with a wet fingertip to see it flutter and hear her wail. "Such a pretty, perfect ass. I cannot wait to stretch it."

Her moan made my balls draw up. Finally, I pulled her pants the rest of the way off and threw them aside. "Turn," I said.

When she faced me again, her eyes were wild and her face had flushed with need.

"Hmm." I cupped her chin with my hand and studied her mouth as if I had not already long since memorized every detail about it. "I am not sure my little mate can fit my big dragon cock in her mouth."

"I can," she promised. "I will."

"Show me." With one hand on my cock and the other on her chin, I guided her forward. "Open your mouth and stick out your tongue, little mate."

With a moan, she obeyed.

The moment the dripping head of my cock reached her little pink tongue, she licked me hungrily. Stars exploded across my vision, my balls clenched, and I very nearly came. My mate's tongue could elevate me to the heavens with a single touch.

"Clean it," I grated, my voice little more than a growl.

She licked up my precum one mind-bending caress of her tongue at a time.

"Good, little mate," I said when she finished. "Now you may suck my cock."

With a throaty sound, she gripped my cock in her shaking hand, opened her mouth as far as she could, and slid her lips over the head. This time, the starbursts in my vision all but blinded me.

Gods, she was perfect.

Stroking and circling my slick length with her hand, she took my cock into her mouth as much as she could and sucked, flicking her tongue over the opening. Each little teasing caress drew a burst of precum and made me quake.

I rumbled and growled, my thumb on her lower lip to hold her head at the perfect angle for me to thrust gently and carefully into her mouth. Her throat could not accommodate me, but I brushed against it because the ragged sounds she made sent shivers through my entire body to the tip of my tail.

"Is it good, my dragon?" she rasped when I withdrew.

"It is more than good, my little mate." I kissed her forehead. "It is heaven itself."

"Will you come in my mouth?" Her tongue darted out and swirled around the head of my cock. "Please, my dragon?"

"No, little mate." I caressed her cheek and took her jaw in my hand again to hold her steady as I thrust back into her sweet mouth. "I will come in your throat."

Her muffled moan and the way her eyes almost rolled up from the force of her need caused my balls to tighten even further.

She took me as deeply into her mouth as she could and hummed around my cock. Three thrusts were all it took for me to break.

Growling, shaking, head thrown back and body wracked with shudders, I came in great spurts. Choking and gagging, she fought to swallow my cum, but its abundance ran down her chin.

When her nails dug into the flesh of my thighs, I withdrew from her mouth so she could gasp in air, her chest heaving. I cupped her breasts and rubbed my thumbs over her nipples.

"You are so beautiful," I rasped. "So perfect."

She smiled, almost preening at my praise, and licked her lips. "Thank you, my dragon. May I clean your cock?"

Gods above. My hand trembling, I held it out for her. "You may."

On her hands and knees, she set to work immediately, licking up every drip as I quaked. When she finished, I wiped the cum from her face and fed it to her.

"What a good little mate you are," I cooed as she sucked my

fingers and then bit them. "You deserve another reward. Does your sweet pussy need attention?"

"Yes," she said with a whimper. "Please, dragon. I need you to fill my pussy."

"Lie down, then, little mate," I said, caressing her lower lip with my thumb. "Spread your legs and show me your pretty pussy."

With another whimper, she obeyed, her arms extended over her head without being told. Her slickness had dripped down her thighs until they gleamed, and her clit peeked from her folds, begging for my attentions.

"Your sweet pussy is very needful," I observed, on my hands and knees between her thighs. "But how well will it take my cock, little mate?"

She moaned. "I'll take your cock so well, my dragon." Her hand moved toward her swollen clit. "Please…"

"No, you cannot touch yourself," I said sharply, and she whimpered. "Today, your pleasure is mine to give."

Slowly, savoring every sensation, I ran my hands up her thighs, sliding my palms over the silky liquid that had dripped from her pussy. Making her wait so long for her own release had gifted me an abundance of slickness.

She trembled almost violently as I pushed her thighs up and even more open until every detail of her beautiful, glistening pink folds were bared to my sight.

"I think you will take my cock very well," I said. "But first, you must come on my fingers a few times so you can take me."

"Please," she begged. "Please, dragon, make me come."

I rubbed two fingertips over her folds, spreading her open, admiring how beautifully she whimpered and dripped for me. She was so desperately aroused, she would come quickly the first two times.

I was right. The moment I dipped my fingertips inside her and circled my thumb over her clit, she came.

Beautiful and perfect, she wailed and gushed, drenching my hand in a release that smelled as sweet and pure as the heavens.

I wanted nothing more than to sheath myself in my mate and make her come again and again on my cock before I filled her pussy with my cum. But she was tight around my fingers and not ready for me yet.

As her first orgasm waned, I pumped my fingers into her, spreading them steadily until she began to ride my hand.

"Yes, like that, little mate," I coaxed. "Take your pleasure."

I curled my fingertips inside her, seeking that soft place that wrenched a guttural sound from her throat. Then I added a third finger and stroked her deliberately until she began to scream.

"Come on my hand again, beautiful Elena," I said. "Come for me."

This orgasm was even more powerful than the first. She was nearly sobbing as she broke, and I caught the words *Ardruc* and *dragon* in the torrent of sounds she made as she came.

I had thought my lat'sar made the finest music in the galaxy, but I had been wrong. My Elena's cries were the most beautiful music in existence.

She was still tight around my fingers, but my patience was at an end. On my knees, I scooped her shuddering body up in my arms and held her to my chest.

"It is time to take your dragon's cock," I said, my lips on her hair as she gasped into the side of my neck. "Show me how well you can take me, little mate."

"Yes," she breathed, reaching between us to wrap her hand around my cock and position herself over its head. "It's so big. Gods, Ardruc."

She lowered herself onto me as I marveled at her beauty, her scents, at the way she bit her lip and gasped for air and focused on aligning the head of my cock with her pussy, so perfectly wet and dripping with her own releases and her need. I wanted to remember every detail of this moment for all my days and take it with me into eternity.

When my little mate took the head of my cock into herself, my bellow and her cry blended and filled the forest.

"Ardruc," she whispered, her hand on the back of my neck and her nails digging into my flesh.

I was beginning to understand the difference between when she called me *Ardruc* and when I was *Dragon*.

"Elena." I ran my fingers through her hair and held her so I could gaze into her eyes. For all my desire to command and take her, she needed me to be patient and gentle now. "Take me as you will, my lovely mate. My body was made to fit into yours."

She rested her forehead against my shoulder and panted.

Keeping still took every ounce of my willpower, but I would not hurt my mate for all the world.

I held her steady and let her roll her hips to take me an inch at a time. She cried out with every little movement, with every ridge, nub, and vein of my cock that stroked into her. She even fell against me, the words *too big, Ardruc,* and *please* muffled by my chest.

When she had taken me halfway, I held her to my chest and rolled gently forward to place her on her back in the grass.

She wrapped her legs around my waist and squeezed my forearms. "Yes," she breathed. "I'm ready."

I covered her body with mine and thrust, taking inches more of her each time. She was so tight, so wet, so wonderful, so perfect. Her screams of pleasure rang in my ears.

She dug her nails into my shoulders and down my arms, blending pain with pleasure. I wanted her to draw blood—to mark me all over, to stake her claim on me for all to see. I wanted to be *Elena's dragon* from now until my last breath.

When I reached her body's limit and she could take no more of my cock, I withdrew completely and plunged into her again, and again, and again, bellowing and roaring as smoke poured from my nostrils and my tail whipped through the air.

She threw her head back and screamed, the sound guttural and pure ecstasy. Her orgasm ripped through her with such force that she bucked against me, her back arching. Her pussy squeezed and fluttered around my cock, and nothing had ever, *ever* felt so good.

With a snarl, I withdrew, flipped her over, moved her to her knees, and thrust into her from behind as she clawed into the ground. Her cries and pleading for more were endless.

This time when my mate came, her release rolled powerfully through her entire body, through the soil, through me, and through the forest as a kind of shockwave. The ground, the trees, the leaves, the mosses, the mushrooms and lichen…everything around us seemed to heave and thrum.

The wave swept back through us and carried me over the edge.

With a bellow, I wrapped my arm around my mate's waist to hold her to me and came in spurts that wracked my body more forcefully than any ever before in my life. The world around us pulsed along with us.

"Dragon," Elena wailed. "Dragon, I'm coming."

I filled my mate's beautiful pussy as she orgasmed around me. Streams of hot cum overflowed from her and ran down our thighs.

I dipped the tip of my tail into the cum, swirled it around my mate's fluttering asshole, and slipped it inside. Her wail sent a pulse through me and out into the forest.

"Yes," she gasped, her back arching. "Yes, take me in every way, dragon. Take me *now*."

My vibrating tail tip delved deeper inside her. With guttural cries, she pleasured herself on my tail and my half-hard cock. I could not discern between her ecstasy and my own, or the movement of our own bodies and the planet's heaving and pulsing around us.

My mate, my mate. My body sang of her. The soil, the forest, the air, even the *planet* sang of her. My beautiful, brilliant, perfect mate.

My tail sank deeper into her, stretching her, pleasuring her, driving her to absolute wildness.

A ripple of something powerful and intensely erotic ran through my body, down the length of my tail, and pulsed in its tip. Elena moaned and thrashed beneath me.

Then another ripple, more powerful than the first. And another. Then more, one after the other, pulsing through me in waves, every one of them making me quake and drawing spasms and screams of ecstasy from my mate that felt and sounded for all the world like she was experiencing back-to-back orgasms.

Nearly convulsing with the force of these pulses, I bent almost double, helpless as my body hurtled us toward something new—some aspect of my physiology I somehow knew had been unlocked by making love to my mate.

"Elena," I rasped. "Elena. *Elena.*"

I shuddered violently, pitching us forward. We landed face-down in the rich forest soil.

I rolled us to our side immediately, afraid of crushing Elena beneath my weight, and wrapped my arms around her to hold her tightly as the pulse rose to an impossible crescendo—and broke.

Together, with a hoarse bellow and a beautiful scream, we plunged headlong into a shared orgasm so powerful that everything faded.

I lost all sense of self and place. Ecstasy and the joy of my mate was all I knew for a very long time. Nothing else mattered except that I was her home, her anchor, her partner, her mate, and she was all of those things to me and infinitely more.

When awareness returned, the afternoon light was waning. I found myself curled around my mate on thick, fragrant moss that had grown from the forest floor to provide us with a soft bed. My cock and tail still nestled comfortably inside her, and my wing covered us to keep her warm and safe. The crown of her head was tucked under my chin. Her long hair was full of leaves and bits of moss and she smelled of forest and me. Her breathing, like mine, was slow and even.

We might have lain like this for a very long time, but I felt no discomfort—only satisfaction. And my mating frenzy seemed to have eased, at least for now. My head was clear and my desire for her was very present but not all-consuming.

"Elena," I murmured.

She stretched languidly. The sensation of my cock and tail moving inside her sent a wave of pleasure and contentment through me.

"Mmm…Ardruc." Her voice was drowsy. She laced her fingers through mine where my hand rested on her abdomen. "Did you just fuck me insensible?"

I kissed her hair. "I believe I did."

"Oh, the dragon is so smug." She chuckled. "I take it you didn't know about that special talent of yours?"

"Which one?" I asked, feigning innocence.

"Oh, dear—now he's smug *and* playful too." She *tsk*'d. "You lied to me about not having a sense of humor. Naughty dragon."

Heat stirred in my groin. Being called *naughty dragon* was quite arousing. I might explore more ways to be her naughty dragon.

She craned her neck to look at me. In the muted light, her blue eyes seemed as fathomless as the deep ocean. "The planet made love with us," she said. "Did you feel it?"

"Yes, and I saw it too." I rested my forehead on hers. "To my knowledge, this is the first time the world has truly moved when I came."

"Mmm." She sighed contentedly. "It definitely moved for me, in all kinds of ways."

"I do not know how it is possible that we have this connection to Hyderia," I said. "But we have become part of this world…and this world has become part of us."

"And I've become part of you, and you've become part of me." She ran her thumb over my lower lip. "Do you like the feeling of your cock and tail inside me, dragon?"

"Very much." I gently nipped the tip of her thumb. "Do you like the feeling of my cock and tail inside you, little mate?"

"Very much." Elena smiled. "I feel very claimed."

Everything about her—her scent, her relaxed body, the way she caressed me—indicated this pleased her. Still, I was relieved when she added, "I'm rather surprised to discover I like being claimed, though not as surprised as I was to find out I enjoy being dominated…but only by you. If anyone else had tried it, I would have pushed them out an airlock."

She did not ask and I saw no sign of any jealousy, but I felt compelled to say, "I have never once thought of claiming anyone, nor of dominating anyone. Not until you."

"Strange, for a male dragon." She pursed her lips in the way that made me long to put some part of my body between them. "They are usually very territorial and dominant," she mused. "This is an interesting insight. I'll have to add it to my notes, along with my firsthand observations about your mating frenzy and related practices."

The scent of her arousal swirled around us.

"Little mate." I pressed my lips to her ear and delved the tip of my tongue along its interior curves to make her shiver. "You smell very enticing suddenly. Does talk of research make you needful?"

"Well, not *all* research," she breathed. "But your cock and tail are inside me as I'm thinking about being dominated by a dragon and I suppose that *might* make me needful. And there is one way in which you have not yet claimed your mate fully."

Her lovely ass, which I had yet to fill. I lost my ability to breathe and think for a moment.

"Ardruc," she said quietly before I could regain my power of speech. "Before we do anything else, I want us to talk face to face."

My body rebelled at the prospect of separating from her, but she was my world. I might like to dominate her when we made love, and she might like to be submissive, but in all ways and at all times her wishes would forever be my commands.

Carefully, slowly, I withdrew my cock and tail, watching for any sign of discomfort or pain. She sighed and seemed disappointed as I slipped from her, but she did not flinch. I missed her tight warmth immediately.

Then she turned in my arms and nestled herself in my embrace. My fleeting sense of feeling bereft after our separation vanished immediately when she kissed my chest.

She looked for all the world like a goddess of the forest, bathed in the muted colors of suns-set, in our bed of moss with leaves in her hair. But I did not feel like a god beside her—more like a simple man who had inexplicably found himself favored by the loveliest, more perfect woman he could imagine.

"I feel incredibly good with you," she said, rubbing her nose on my hot skin over my breastbone. "Treasured and protected and respected. I understand some of the physiology of true mates and how that has affected you. I look forward to learning more as we spend more time together and I do my research."

She took my hand and brought it to her mouth to kiss and nibble my fingertips. I rumbled for my bitey little mate.

"You said earlier I could break your hearts." She took a deep breath. "The truth is, true mates or not, I'm afraid you'll break mine. I've never let anyone get close enough to me to risk that kind of hurt."

"Neither have I." I leaned my forehead against hers. "Which I am sure does not surprise you. I have had lovers, but none touched my hearts until you."

"I want to know why that is, dragon." She squeezed my hand. "I want to know why you've needed all these masks and façades and walls around you for so long. You've already let me in. Now I want to help you tear them all down so you can heal, and so I'm less afraid to entrust my heart to you."

Gods above, I wanted so much to heal in her arms. I had not decided to give in to my need for my true mate for that reason, but the bond was not just for pleasure, physical comfort, and procreation, though those were some of its more celebrated features.

At its core, the true mate bond was meant to heal. My lack of nightmares since Elena's arrival and the way my soul had quieted were irrefutable proof of that even without all the research that showed it to be true. I would be the greatest of fools to eschew that aspect of mating.

As a human, Elena's experience would be different from mine. She would still benefit in many ways from our bond—not all of them the same, and not all to the same extent. My purpose was to care for and support her and give her everything it was in my power to give. Nothing would make me happier.

If by telling her the truth about my history, a story I had told no one else—not one single, solitary soul—I could both heal myself and help her believe her heart was safe with me, then I must do it. But I feared reopening my deepest, most painful wounds. I feared it more than anything I had faced in my life.

"You don't have to tell me now," Elena said, cupping my face. "You can wait until you're ready." She kissed me lightly. "In the meantime, we can keep doing whatever feels right and good between a dragon and his little mate." Her lips turned up. "I have some thoughts on that subject."

"So do I." Suns-set had arrived, bringing with it the chill of evening, so I wrapped her in my arms, rolled to my back so she lay on my chest, and draped my wing over us. "It is difficult to believe after we fucked each other into insensibility, but I have not finished claiming you, little mate."

"A tragic situation we must address immediately." She crawled up my body to kiss me and gently bite my lower lip. "I need you to finish claiming me, dragon—body, heart, and soul."

"I know how to claim your body." I cradled the round swell of her ass with both hands. "You have offered some insight into how to claim your heart. But to claim your soul as you have claimed mine, what must I do?"

"I'm not sure." She pressed a kiss to my chest. "But when I figure that out, you'll be the first to know."

My wristcomm trilled. Reluctantly, I let go of Elena's ass and scrolled through the message on the screen.

"The computer has created a method by which we may learn to communicate with the tendrils," I reported. "It is synthesizing tiles the tendrils can use to inscribe answers to a series of specific questions. The linguistics system composed the questions to elicit responses that should give it enough to attempt translations. The tiles should be ready by morning."

"Good. The sooner we can talk to the tendrils, the sooner we can solve at least a couple of these mysteries—or at least I hope we can." Elena nuzzled my chest. "In the meantime, do you remember I said I had some ideas about what we might do together so you can claim me thoroughly?"

"I remember every word you have ever spoken to me. A dragon has a long memory." I picked leaves and bits of twigs from her hair. "What are these ideas, little mate?"

"I have a bit of a fantasy." Her cheeks turned an absolutely delightful shade of pink. "But it's getting late, and it's probably not anything you'd be interested in…" Her voice trailed off.

What could my little mate be thinking about that would make her flush after all we had already shared together?

"I am intrigued." I cupped her face with my hand to enjoy the warmth of her blush. "Tell me about your fantasy, Elena. I feel quite certain I will be *very* interested."

CHAPTER 21

ELENA

THE SCARLET ALGAL COMPONENT OF HYDERIA'S BOCORAL LICHEN WAS absolutely gorgeous, especially in extreme magnification on my largest computer screen—and even more so now that my lab had transformed into a living, breathing environment that embraced both me and my work.

The bocoral lichen was unique in many ways. It was one of only a handful I had discovered since my arrival that contained not the typical two algal partners but three, as well as one species of fungus and various microbes. The bocoral was its own tiny ecosystem.

And like all lichen, it was an indicator of the health of the environment. I didn't need it to tell me Hyderia was thriving because that was clear enough, but studying these robust specimens was a welcome change from other, more urbanized planets I'd visited where the lichen was in sharp decline due to pollution and loss of habitat.

The door to Lab Three opened. An enormous winged shadow framed by artificial light spilling in from the corridor loomed across the foliage, grassy floor, and fungi that surrounded me.

"Dr. Regis." Ardruc's brusque voice made me look up from my screen and its bright display of scarlet algae. "A word?"

"Of course." I swiveled my chair to face him as he crossed the lab and came around my bank of screens.

He'd donned a lab coat over a dark blue shirt and black pants. His expression was thunderous as he towered over me, his feathers bristling and tail twitching.

"I expected your weekly report today," he said curtly. "This is the third time you have ignored a direct request for a complete accounting of your lab hours."

He took a step forward, crowding me. I tried to scoot my chair back, but its feet had settled into the grassy floor and it didn't budge.

"You clearly have no respect for my authority," he continued, staring down with glowing eyes that pinned me in place like a tiny rodent under the gaze of a raptor. "I am the director of research. I am in charge of this station. When I tell you to do something, you do it."

"I'm sorry," I said, biting my lip. "I have all these new samples to study and I forgot about the report."

"So you said last time. And the time before that." Ardruc's glower sent a thrill of fear and desire through me. His stare raked me from head to toe. "What are you wearing?"

I swallowed. "My standard lab attire, Dr. Husiorithae."

He rumbled. "And what have I told you about what you call your standard lab attire?"

His gaze was so fierce. Gods above. "That I have to wear something under my lab coat," I whispered. "But—"

"And yet you have paid as little attention to that demand as anything else I have said," he snapped. "I have reached the limit of my patience with you, Dr. Regis. Get up."

When I didn't move, he leaned down until his nose was inches from my own. Smoke puffed from his nostrils and his eyes blazed. "Get. *Up.*"

With a little whimper, I rose. In my bare feet, he towered over me. And when he spread his wings to further emphasize our size difference, I moaned.

"Turn around," he grated. "Put your hands flat on your desk and do not move them."

My knees shaking, I obeyed.

Clothing rustled behind me, but I couldn't see what he was doing. His hot breath caressed the nape of my neck just before his hand closed around it. My legs nearly went out from under me.

"You think because you report to your university on Fyloria and the Ministry on Nyvor that you do not need to follow my policies," he said, his mouth next to my ear. "I think I must teach you a lesson, Dr. Regis."

Gods above, he was *entirely* too good at this.

I'd never thought I'd get to indulge this secret fantasy. Until Ardruc, I'd never found the right partner to make it good enough to measure up to my imagination.

His hand tightened just enough to make me squirm. "Do you agree? You need a lesson?"

"Yes," I breathed.

Another little squeeze. "Yes, what?"

"Yes, Dr. Husiorithae," I whimpered. "I need a lesson."

His dominance was everything I wanted and more. This moment was so much better than I'd even dreamed of. I was dripping so much now that I felt my slickness running down my thighs.

His teeth closed on my earlobe in a flash of pain that made me quiver. "I am glad you agree."

His free hand reached around and pulled the front of my lab coat aside so he could cup my breast and pinch my nipple. I moaned.

My lab was not cold, but my skin pebbled when he exposed it to the air. My nipples were already painfully hard—and had been from the moment he'd first towered over me in feigned anger.

With one hand on the back of my neck, he pinched and stroked my nipples until I whimpered for mercy—and then he pinched them more.

"You are brilliant," Ardruc growled. He abandoned my sensitive nipples and slid his hand down my stomach to brush over my slit, as if to see how wet I was for him. I gasped.

"Intuitive. Insightful. Beautiful." His fingertips traveled around my hip to delve along the cleft of my ass, teasing and tormenting. "And so desperately in need of a hard lesson in who is in charge," he finished. "Bend over."

When I resisted, he pushed my head down until I was bent over my desk. And then he rolled my lab coat up to bare my ass and dripping pussy. I sensed his intense gaze raking over me, taking in every detail. I mewled.

"I like that sound." His fingers stroked the back of my neck, digging in lightly as his clothing rustled again. He tightened his grip. "Make it again, and do not stop until I tell you."

As I whimpered for him, I caught the unmistakable sound of him stroking his cock. Gods, I wanted to see him. My pussy clenched and gushed.

I moaned and tried to turn my head. "Please…"

"No." His hand closed on the back of my neck, pinning me firmly to the desk. "Spread your legs, Dr. Regis."

Aroused beyond all reason, I obeyed. "Wider," he said. I whimpered again.

Two hot, wet fingers rubbed over my slit and brushed my clit much too gently to give me what I wanted. I made a desperate sound. "Please…" I begged.

"Please what, Dr. Regis?" More feather-light touches. I wanted to scream.

"Please rub my clit," I gasped. I tried to move, to take pleasure for myself, but he moved his hand away and held me in place by the back of my neck. "Please put your fingers in my pussy and make me come," I pleaded.

"I am not here to do what *you* want, Dr. Regis," he growled into my ear. "I am here to teach you a lesson."

His wet fingertips trailed over my dripping pussy and up to my asshole. "So pretty," he mused, tracing its edges with a wet fingertip to make me flutter. "So perfect. You have such a lovely and disobedient little ass, Doctor."

His fingertip moved away so he could stroke himself and then returned slick with his lubrication. With steady, unyielding pressure, he slipped it into my asshole. I wailed in pleasure.

"Yes," he rumbled, pinning me in place by the back of my neck. "Such a shame I must resort to these measures to get you to obey my policies."

"I'm sorry I forgot the report and about my attire," I gasped. "I'm sorry. It won't happen again."

He added another well-lubricated finger and began to stretch me. I whimpered.

"I think you are only saying what you think I want to hear, Dr. Regis," he growled. "I do not think you mean what you say."

"I do," I wailed. "I will do whatever you want, whenever you want me to do it."

He added a third finger, and now the pain and pleasure and my need to come was overwhelming to the point I was nearly sobbing. Still, he left my dripping pussy untouched.

When his fingers slid from me, I arched my back, hoping he would turn his attention to my clit.

Instead, his enormous cock—bigger still than three of his fingers—pressed against my asshole. It was so big. Too big. I cried out and squirmed, caught between the most powerful need and arousal I had ever experienced and a thrill of fear.

His hand tightened on the back of my neck. "You asked for a lesson, little mate."

Finally, *finally*, the tip of his tail flicked repeatedly against my aching clit. I wailed. Gods, I was so close...so close...

"You asked to be claimed and filled in every way," he reminded me, his voice still wonderfully deep and brusque and in character for the benefit of my fantasy.

But then he bent over and kissed my ear and murmured, "Do you still want this?"

Even now, even after I had made it clear what I wanted and why, he wanted confirmation. He wanted to know I hadn't changed my mind and that he wasn't doing something I didn't want. My dragon treasured me above all else. That alone nearly sent me careening over the edge.

"Yes," I screamed. "Take me now. Take my ass, dragon."

Growling, rumbling, one hand on my neck and the other steadying himself, he rubbed my clit with the tip of his tail as he pushed the head of his huge, beautiful, dripping cock into my ass.

I screamed and screamed, and I came.

I came hard around his cock—so hard that my hearing and sight faded to ringing in my ears and swirls of colors mixed with stars.

Every sensation of his intrusion was amplified. I felt every detail, every ridge and bump and vein of his cock as he thrust inside me further each time, stretching me in a symphony of pain and pleasure and filling me so perfectly that I couldn't stop screaming.

"Take my cock, little mate," Ardruc cooed. "Now you are mine."

His vibrating tail tip traveled along my slit to where my dripping pussy clenched desperately on its own emptiness.

"Yes," I pleaded. "Please, *please*."

When he filled my pussy with his tail and thrust his cock into my ass in the same rhythm, I convulsed with pleasure.

"You are beautiful when you take my tail in your sweet pussy and my cock in your ass, little mate," Ardruc rumbled. He let go of my neck and stroked my back as he rocked inside me. "You needed me to claim you this way."

"Yes." I was holding on to my desk now as he thrust into me, deeper and better each time. "Please, Ardruc. Please, dragon."

I had no idea what it was I was begging for now. What more could he do that was better than this? But still, I wanted more.

His arm wrapped around my waist, and suddenly I found myself yanked away from my desk.

He braced himself with his hips against the tall counter behind my desk, wrapped his hands under my thighs, and held me as if I weighed nothing at all.

Ardruc pressed his mouth to my ear. "I am going to truly fill you with my cock and tail now," he growled, smoke swirling from his nostrils. "And I want you to see. Look at the screen. Look at yourself, little mate."

He must have switched off my largest desk screen because instead of the scarlet algae specimen I'd been studying when he came in, I saw our reflection on the dark glass.

Still in his lab coat but wearing nothing else, Ardruc held my legs wide to show his tail buried in my pussy and his cock in my ass. His eyes glowed golden and he'd spread his magnificent wings until they spanned almost the entire length of the counter. His feathers gleamed in the bioluminescent glow of the fungi in my lab.

"Look how beautiful you are full of my cock," he said into my ear. "My mate is the most beautiful woman in the galaxy."

I had no idea what he was talking about. When I looked at our reflection, all I saw was him.

My dragon was gorgeous and powerful. I wished I could save the reflection just so I could look at him like this whenever I wanted.

"Keep your eyes on the glass." He bit my earlobe. "Watch me fuck your sweet pussy and your beautiful ass."

I whimpered. "Ardruc..."

He lifted me easily, then moved his hips and arms in tandem to plunge his cock into my ass as his tail rubbed and vibrated inside my pussy. In this position, the pleasure of taking him doubled. *Tripled.* I wailed and sobbed and trembled violently, hurtling toward release with terrifying speed.

"Come for your dragon, little mate," he ordered, his mouth on my ear and his gaze locked on mine in our reflection. "Squeeze my cock and cover my tail in your sweet cum."

He bounced me twice on his cock and tail and I came with a scream, my head thrown back against his chest. As my ass clenched around him, he bellowed, his body shaking as he fought to stay in control.

But I didn't want him to hold back now. I never wanted him to hold back ever again. Not with me.

"Ardruc," I gasped. "Dragon. Gods, please come."

With a groan, he thrust into me a few more times, and then he did.

In the reflection on the screen, I watched him orgasm. He was magnificent as his head went back, his muscular body convulsed, and his hips jerked uncontrollably with every jet of beautiful, gleaming cum that filled me and then spilled over his lap and thighs. His bellows and groans were like a song.

Ever the predator and dominant dragon, he took me to the floor on my hands and knees and pumped into me from behind, releasing the final spurts of his hot cum and thrusting deep to push it inside me.

"Take it," he growled. "Take it all, little mate. I want you filled to the brim."

That demand and his vibrating tail sent me careening over the cliff one final time. My arms and legs gave out. With a cry, I sagged into the grass, lost in a haze and held up only by his arm around my middle.

No secret workplace fantasy—no matter how long I had harbored it—could ever compare to the reality of being taken by a dragon.

"Elena," he rasped in my ear. He supported all of his own weight and mine on his knees and one hand braced into the grassy floor. His arm tightened around me as we trembled. "Now I am yours completely."

I'd wanted to be claimed, and I *had* been, but I'd claimed him too when I'd persuaded him to break free, get out of his head, and take me in every way. He was mine now.

The sensations of having him buried doubly inside me were the best and most satisfying of my life. No one else could satisfy me like this—I knew that as surely as I knew he felt the same about me.

"There's no getting away from me now," I said breathlessly as he panted against my shoulder. His smoky, sweet-peppery scent swirled around us, blending with the smells of the forest and sex.

I would never be able to look at my desk again without thinking of this, and that was perfectly fine with me.

When he spoke again, his voice was brusque. "Well, did you learn your lesson, Dr. Regis?"

I quivered around his cock, still buried nearly to the hilt in my ass. "Mmm, very thoroughly. Thank you for indulging my fantasy."

"Little mate, it was very much my pleasure." He nuzzled the back of my neck. "I think we will indulge in many fantasies together. I have some of my own I would like to pursue."

What kind of fantasies might a dragon man have? I could only imagine.

"It is time for me to feed my mate and take her to bed." Ardruc kissed my shoulder. "We must go to my quarters and clean ourselves. Will you join me in the shower, Elena?"

"Happily." I squeezed his hand. "When you move, do it slowly."

He wrapped his arms around me and slipped his tail from my pussy. "I would never hurt you," he said, tucking my shoulder under his chin. "You know a Fortusian's bodily fluids have healing properties for our mates?"

"I did see that information during my research." I breathed deeply, bracing for him to withdraw his cock. "And I noticed all the bumps and bruises and scrapes I got from running in the forest are gone. That is a very nice side effect."

"It is one of many ways in which I am made to care for you." He squeezed me. "If you are sore, you will not be for long. I will coo for you as well, little mate. You will not feel pain, only pleasure."

Just as he'd promised, the deep note of his song for me swept through my body like a wave of warm honey, taking with it every last bit of trepidation and discomfort. And he stayed still while I eased myself free of his cock with a gasp and a sigh. No pain at all—only comfort and bliss and a deep yearning to be held.

Exhausted and sated, I closed my eyes and let him cradle me for a while. He cooed and stroked my hair.

"Beautiful Elena." He kissed my temple. "This was not too much for you?"

"No. It was everything I wanted." My voice was little more than a wisp. "But I wouldn't mind if you wanted to carry me to your quarters."

"It would be my privilege, little mate." He rose smoothly. "I will happily be your chariot whenever you wish, in the sky or on the ground. Or anywhere else you please."

I chuckled and rested my head against his chest.

Ardruc pressed his lips to my hair. "While we wash, you must tell me about your other fantasies." He rumbled. "Perhaps one of them involves...a shower?"

How could he *possibly* be thinking about more sex? Oh, right—mating frenzy. And his shower *did* have a lovely bench because it could also be used as a sauna.

But I was utterly and thoroughly exhausted. The only purpose for this trip to Ardruc's shower was to get clean before making some kind of meal and collapsing into bed.

"Ardruc Husiorithae," I groaned. "If any of them do, I am *not* telling you."

CHAPTER 22
ARDRUC

I woke from a dream of making love to Elena bathed in sweat and lost in a haze of heat and need.

We lay as we had fallen asleep after our shower and a quick evening meal: naked on my bed with me curled around my little mate with her back against my chest and my wing draped over us as a blanket.

My entire body thrummed with desire as it had in the throes of my mating frenzy, but this cresting wave of wildness had changed from the need to claim my mate to something else entirely.

My cock—already hard as stone and dripping with both lubrication and precum—ached in a way I had never felt before, not even since Elena had arrived on Hyderia and altered the workings of my hearts, body, and soul. The discomfort bordered on pain.

"Elena," I rasped, my chest heaving and my ragged voice somewhere between pure predator and pure desperation. *"Elena."*

She stirred in my arms. "Ardruc?" she asked sleepily. After a beat, she stilled. "What's wrong?" She sounded much more awake now.

I was panting, the sound edged with a growl. "El...*Elena.*" I could not form a full sentence.

She turned to face me immediately, her eyes wide and straining to see me in the faint light in the bedroom. Gods, she was beautiful. Radiant. I shuddered hard.

"Oh, gods, Ardruc. Are you hurting?" She cupped my face and stared into my eyes. "Is it the mating frenzy?"

Her touch sent a bolt of need straight to my core. The ache in my cock grew, concentrated near its base, becoming a strain.

With a growl, I rolled her to her back and went to my hands and knees above her, smoke puffing from my nostrils as my wings stretched wide. "*Mate,*" I grated.

Her scent filled my lungs. I did not smell or see fear, but worry creased her brow and tightened her eyes.

Her gaze swept over me, scouring my face, my shoulders and chest, and moving down past my waist. She gasped. "Ardruc—"

Every fiber of my being demanded I take my mate, but her reaction and use of my name reached whatever shreds of reason I still had. I followed her wide-eyed gaze to my heavy, throbbing cock where it rested against her thigh.

"You have a knot," she whispered.

In my muddled state, I could not process what I saw, or what she had said.

She grabbed my chin and raised my head so she could look into my eyes. "You're all right, Ardruc." Her tone was quiet now—not clinical like a scientist or physician, but soft and composed. I clung to the reassuring sound of her voice like an island of calm in the midst of a hurricane.

"You've claimed your mate, and now you've developed a knot," she said, caressing my face. "Sometimes a male Fortusian develops a knot after reaching sexual maturity, and sometimes it happens once they find a true mate. It's in the research I read."

A knot. *A knot.*

Developing a knot in my adult life was technically possible, but I had never considered it likely to happen. Male equatorial dragons did not have knots. But Elena was right that it was common among

Fortusians with external genitalia because of our genetic engineering. My body had changed form and developed a new kind of want and need: not just to mate, but to breed. Gods above, what would we do? What would *Elena* do?

A new terror chilled me to the bone. Would she reject me? We had not discussed the matter of procreation. I had no idea what her thoughts were on the subject, and my own were, to say the least, very complex.

Beneath me, her scent changed, becoming richer, sweeter, and even more intoxicating. My condition had caused some kind of emotional response—but thank all the gods above and below, I did not think it was the one I feared.

She cupped my face, her tender touch almost jarring against the need building to a crescendo inside me. I shoved the wave back with brute force and a puff of smoke. I must know what Elena wanted.

"I am not capable of conceiving right now," she said, caressing my lower lip with her thumb. "To become pregnant, I would need to undergo the appropriate treatment to begin ovulating again. That is not something I'm ready to do now or anytime soon, but I am open to talking about the future."

I was more grateful for her candid words than I could have said even if speech was within my capability.

I am open to talking about the future...

A future with Elena would be paradise, no matter what form it took.

She pulled me down until my torso rested on her abdomen and my head rested on her breast. Trembling and breathing raggedly, I let her hold me.

"My beautiful dragon." She kissed the top of my head and smoothed my hair and feathers. I shivered at her gentle touches. "I want you to give me your knot. It will feel very good for both of us —or at least I *think* it will. I've never taken anyone's knot before, but I've heard it's quite good."

"Elena." I closed my eyes and breathed her in. The more her scent enveloped me, and the more she tenderly caressed me, the ferocity of my need became more manageable. "Thank you," I rasped.

I slid my hand down her abdomen, past the little patch of silky hair at the apex of her thighs, and found she was already slick. When I circled her clit with my thumb and slipped two fingers inside her, she moaned and ground against my hand.

"Dragon," she murmured, her lips pressed to my hair as her hips moved. "I think if you coo…it will be easier for me…to take you."

I would coo, but she must come for me before I gave her my knot. Her pleasure and needs would always be more important to me than my own, regardless of circumstances.

I curled my fingers inside her and stroked over the soft place that made her shudder hard and gush. Her arm around my neck pulled me tighter against her heaving chest. I sucked and laved her nipples in turn, biting lightly until her gasping cries rose in pitch in a way I had already learned to recognize.

Her cries turned into one long wail. The ache in my cock and balls became nearly all-consuming, and my growls blended with my mate's cry.

She threw back her head and climaxed with a scream, her nails digging into the back of my neck and her pussy and thighs squeezing my hand as she flooded my fingers with her release. Beautiful. She was beautiful and perfect beyond belief.

I rolled her to her stomach and drew her hips up so she was on her knees, bent over with her cheek pressed to the bed. Whimpering and trembling, she spread her legs wide, ready and dripping for me.

I licked her sweet pussy to drink up her release, and then as she wailed, I stopped fighting the wave of need and let it take over.

My first thrust into her fluttering, tight pussy was so intensely pleasurable that my eyes nearly rolled up into my head.

She was wonderfully wet for me. I buried myself in my beautiful mate in three thrusts. Her screams of ecstasy grew in volume each time I rocked inside her. When my knot bumped against her, the pleasure made me bellow. Gods. Gods above.

There was nothing I wanted more than to bury myself completely inside her and feel her come on my cock while I pumped her full of my cum. Craving her screams and the way she fluttered around me, I rocked on my knees, working myself deeper.

Caught up in a frenzy of need and feeling almost drunk on my mate's cries of ecstasy, my thoughts spun out of control and went utterly wild in a fantasy of a future I had never ventured to consider.

I wanted to breed her. I wanted to make love to her knowing she was fertile and she wanted our child. I wanted to put a half-dragon, half-human child into my mate and see her belly become round. I wanted to hold her and coo as she brought our child into the world, and cradle them both as she held our child to her breast. I saw the scene as clearly as I had seen anything else today.

In the midst of the need, my hearts filled with warmth and contentment. I would not be making a child with her today or anytime soon, but it was enough to be with her and think someday I might.

She was crying out now, her fists twisted in the bedding to hold on as I thrust into her. "Dragon," she wailed, shuddering hard. "Dragon, give me your knot."

Gods, I wanted to, but my knot was enormous and her sweet pussy was so small. It stretched to take just my cock.

Unbidden, my song rose in my chest. My body had known what to do even if Elena had not already instructed me.

I cooed for my beautiful mate. With a moan, she seemed to melt in my grip, her scent a heady blend of arousal, her own sweet cum, and that unique kind of contentment only I could create for her with my song.

I thrust until my knot pressed against her, and then in a series of careful thrusts I pushed it inside her lovely, dripping, welcoming pussy.

"*Dragon*," Elena screamed.

All my senses faded to the echo of that word and a single sensation: a roaring rush that swept through all my limbs and built to a crescendo in my balls. My knot swelled inside my mate and I was helpless to hold back any longer.

Wracked with convulsions, groaning and calling Elena's name, I emptied myself into my mate. Again and again I released, filling her and filling her more, as she came for me one final time. Her pussy squeezed and fluttered around my cock and my knot, and gods above I would feel that sensation in my dreams.

The wrenching power of this orgasm left me feeling both hollowed out and more complete and alive than at any moment of my thirty-four years.

The scent of my mate's tears reached me even through my haze and dragged me back to my senses.

Shaking and spent, my cock still locked snugly inside her, I gathered her in my arms and lay us on our sides on the bed. I stroked her hair and held her tightly as she trembled.

"Sweet Elena," I murmured in her ear. "Sweet, perfect Elena. My love. Beautiful little mate."

My only answer was a quiet sob. Gods above, my Elena was crying. My body still sang of her and what we were sharing, but my hearts seemed to rend into pieces.

I wrapped her more tightly in my arms and folded my wing over us. "My love, what is wrong?"

"Ardruc." She took a ragged breath. "What do you mean, *my love?*"

I had said it twice now without thinking, but I had meant it and all the gods above and below knew it was true.

Whether this was the right moment to tell her this I was not sure, but I had sworn to myself that above all else I would be a good, honest man for my mate.

"I have loved you almost from the moment you arrived," I said. "I was simply too much of an idiot and an asshole to admit it to either of us."

She laughed, and then it turned into a sob. I cradled her and stroked her hair and cooed while she cried.

Why did my song not comfort her if she was sad or hurting? I did not smell or sense physical pain, which eased some of my fear and worry, but I could not bear for her to weep. She was trembling so hard that she shook us both.

"Elena, please," I pleaded.

"I wasn't ready," she rasped, and I thought she meant I had given her my knot before she was ready for it and I had hurt her. My guts felt as if I had been sliced clean through. I whined. I had never made that sound before.

"I wanted your knot, but I wasn't ready to feel so much," she choked out, and I started breathing again. "It was like I *felt* how much you need and want me...and love me." She sniffled. "No one's ever felt that way about me. You big, dumb, lovesick dragon."

My brain, still reeling from the abject terror caused by thinking I had hurt her, skipped completely over *big, dumb, lovesick dragon* and focused on the fact our knotted coupling had overwhelmed her.

While I had lost myself in need and desire and pleasure—and the fantasy of having a child with her—my beautiful Elena had been swept away by emotions that left her raw and hurting. I had not caused this pain, but I must find a way to ease it. My coo was not enough. She needed something else from me.

She had requested that I explain my need to hide behind masks and erect walls between myself and others, but I felt quite certain I was not the only one in this bed who built walls and kept old hurts hidden away.

"Elena." I nestled her in my arms and tucked her head under my chin so she would feel as safe and warm as I could make her. "You deserve all my love and devotion, and that is what I intend to give you. Whoever offered you less when you wanted and deserved more, I would like to know." I nuzzled her shoulder. "Let me help you heal, my love."

"Oh, you…you…*dragon*," she huffed, sniffling and indignant. "I asked you first."

"I will trade a story for a story, then." I smoothed damp, sweaty hair back from her lovely face and gently wiped away her tears. "If you are not too uncomfortable, and if you are willing to tell me what weighs heavily on your heart."

"Given the size of your cock and knot, I probably *should* be uncomfortable, but I am actually incredibly, *unbelievably* comfortable." Her mouth quirked and she managed a wobbly smile. "I suspect pheromones, hormones, and endorphins are playing a role in how good I feel right now."

"Regardless of the cause, I am very glad to know you feel good. I have never felt anything better than being inside you." I kissed her temple. "Are you willing to share a story?" I asked, my lips pressed to her sex-warmed skin.

"I am." Her smile faded as she laced her fingers through mine. "But don't worry; it's not a long one. My mother stopped liking me and started mocking my interests when I was seven and I told her I wanted to study fungi instead of being a physicist. I often think she never really loved me—just tolerated me until I decided I didn't want to grow up to be her. We haven't spoken in two years. I haven't seen my father in person in five years. He *does* love me, which is something, but he's very busy being a distinguished and celebrated artist. Last I heard, he was creating an art installation on Tivor, but that was before I arrived on Hyderia, so he might be anywhere by now. And that's the whole story."

She'd spoken so matter-of-factly and so quickly, as if she wanted to not only get the words out as fast as possible but distance herself from them. Now she was quiet again, her head resting on my arm, lips pressed tightly together and eyes closed. She did not weep, but she trembled.

My hearts ached and my anger simmered toward these people who had dared treat Elena so callously. But I did not believe grief and rage would ease her hurt, so I set those emotions aside—no easy task—to focus on comforting her.

I held her quietly, my lips on her temple, and waited for her to continue, enjoying all the little movements her body made around me and listening to her heartbeat.

"It was hard growing up as the daughter of Dr. Hilda Disen," she said finally. She sounded more like herself now, but the hollowness in her voice made me ache anew. "I had a lot of privileges, but I also dealt with a lot of very high expectations. That's rough on a child. I thought excelling in my studies would make things better, but instead the kinds of stress and pain just changed. I quickly learned a lot of people assumed every opportunity or award I earned was somehow influenced by my mother."

Did she suspect I had believed that too? I thought back to when I had first been notified about her impending arrival and discovered her familial connection to Dr. Disen. I did not recall thinking her mother had somehow helped Elena obtain approval from the Ministry.

"I did everything I could to separate my life from hers," Elena continued. "I used my father's surname. I attended universities on different planets. I never mentioned her and never worked with anyone with professional or personal connections to the university on Fyloria where my mother is chair of the heliophysics department. In fact, I avoided connections to my home planet completely until I needed a research position with a reliable source of funding. All the best opportunities were on Fyloria and I felt I had no choice. So I applied for a position in the xenobotany department at a university that's on the opposite side of the planet from my mother's university. But no matter what I did, the specter of nepotism hung over me."

My own experiences differed mightily from hers, but I understood the insidiousness of specters. I cooed very softly and stroked her hair.

"You know what's worse than being suspected of nepotism?" she asked. "I could never be certain I *was* accomplishing things entirely through my own hard work. I doubt my mother ever lifted a finger to help me in my career. But it wasn't as if I could keep her identity a secret, so it was always possible committees took it into consideration whether I wanted them to or not."

She swallowed audibly. "That insecurity is so deeply ingrained in me that when I got the message from Minister Ganna saying the Ministry had approved my application to work here, a little voice in the back of my head said my mother *must* have pulled some strings because it's damn near impossible to get permission to live and work on Hyderia. And try as I might, I can't talk myself into believing otherwise."

Elena took a deep, shaky breath and met my gaze with red-rimmed eyes. Her expression looked bruised. "This isn't a *woe-is-me* speech, Ardruc. I know I benefited from where I come from and my life is good…and now it's getting even better." She caressed my face. "But I would have given a lot, once upon a time, for my mother to love me and be proud of me regardless of what career path I took. Once I figured out love wasn't really her thing and even how much she *liked* me was conditional, and that my father's obsession with his art outweighed his love for me, I had to start trying to let go of those needs. It's taken me this long to mostly find peace, but it still stings." She took a deep breath and let it out. "I've never said any of that to anyone."

I tucked her head under my chin once again. "Thank you for trusting me with this, Elena. I am sorry you carried this burden alone for so long."

"Thank you for listening." She snuggled deeper into my embrace. The sharp, metallic scent of her pain and grief faded. "I feel so much better."

"I am glad." I kissed her hair. "It matters little, I am sure, but I never thought your arrival here was due to anything other than your own hard work."

"It actually *does* matter. It matters a lot. You believed in me even before you met me. Not many people give me that chance." She moved to look at me, her brow furrowed. "Wait…do you think your instincts played a role in that? Did you get insights into who I am because I'm your true mate?"

I could not help but chuckle. "Ever the inquisitive scientist." I rested my forehead on hers. "I do not know. I am tempted to say it would be impossible for me to know anything instinctively about you until we met in person, but I recall very clearly standing in my lab and watching your message and feeling quite uncharacteristically…interested…in everything you had to say."

"Feeling *quite interested*." She chuckled. "What an Ardruc way of describing—"

My cock slipped a bit. Startled, I twitched. A rivulet of hot cum trickled between us. She gasped.

"My knot is easing," I said, pulling her tightly to my chest. "Does it hurt?"

"No, not at all." Her fingers tightened on my arm. "But I'm not ready to let you go."

"Little mate, I am going nowhere." I rested my head on hers. "I do not need a knot to remain inside you. As long as you want me to keep you filled, I will stay right here."

"Keep me filled, then." She wrapped her arms over mine. "I feel so good when you're inside me. And I don't care if it's dragon pheromones or true mate magic or just plain old human hormones and sensory receptors."

I started to object that there was no magic to being true mates, but closed my mouth. There was indeed magic in everything we had together. To claim otherwise would be untrue.

"I just want to feel like I belong with you," she said softly.

"You do," I said, equally quietly. "And I belong with you."

As my knot eased, I held my sweet mate and told her how beautiful and perfect she was, how much I loved her, and how much I needed and wanted her. And when I pressed my lips to her ear to tell her all those things again and again while circling her clit, she whimpered and moaned and came in my arms in a soft orgasm that rippled along my sensitive cock and made me rumble.

"Perfect," I murmured into her ear as she trembled and panted. My knot was gone now, but my cock remained comfortably sheathed in her sweet, fluttering pussy. "You come perfectly every time, little mate." Unwilling to waste a drop of her release, I licked my fingers. "I know you enjoyed being taught a lesson in your lab, but I think my little mate likes to be praised most of all."

"Yes, I do." She bit my arm lightly. "Gods above, Ardruc. I had no idea *how much* I liked it until today."

I kissed the tip of her ear. "It is lucky, then, that there is so much about you that is worthy of praise."

Her chuckle turned into a yawn. "No, I'm not tired," she said paradoxically. "I'm completely awake and ready to hear your story." She yawned again.

"Little mate, you are exhausted," I scolded. "My story will keep." I rubbed the crown of her head with my chin and settled my wing over us. "You need your sleep. In the morning—in just a few hours, in fact—we must learn to talk to plasma tendrils. I need my Elena at her best and most brilliant, not half-asleep and unable to tell lichen from…from…" I floundered.

She chuckled sleepily. "Empiriosporium," she murmured. "Stick to atmospheric science, dragon. Leave the fungi to me."

CHAPTER 23
ELENA

My dragon mate woke me just after dawn with his face between my thighs, my legs on his shoulders, and my wrists tied to the bed with soft but strong cords he'd found somewhere. I'd been so exhausted and slept so soundly that I hadn't felt him unwrap himself from around me and rise, much less tie me up. Sneaky dragon.

Still, as wake-ups went, this was a new favorite.

"Good morning, dragon," I murmured, my eyes half-lidded in the morning sunlight spilling through the windows. "Having break-fast in bed?"

He rumbled and circled my clit with the tip of his tongue. Mmm. My toes curled.

"I am feasting on my mate," he said, his golden eyes glowing between my thighs.

"I'm a scientist, not dragon food," I protested with feigned indignation. I made a show of pulling at my restraints. "But oh no—I'm helpless to stop you."

With a low chuckle, he kissed my inner thigh and reached for something sitting on the bed beside him: a cup from the station's kitchen.

Only then did a familiar scent reach my nose. I blinked at him. "What the—what are you doing with that?"

Grinning to show his sharp teeth, he tipped the cup and let its warm contents trickle down my slit…before bending his head to lick up every drop and then swirl his tongue around my clit until I wailed.

"Oh, yes," he murmured, dripping more onto me as I gasped and trembled. "Now I see the appeal. It simply needed to be sweetened."

Given I came on his face three times by the time he made it through half the cup and he put the rest on the bedside table for me to drink later before covering my body with his, I couldn't bring myself to be mad that he'd used up some of my precious remaining coffee.

Some hazy time later, I lay gasping on his chest with his spent cock still inside me and his tail wrapped possessively over my ass. The room smelled like sex and coffee and Ardruc's smoky-sweet-peppery brandy scent. My wrists had red lines from the cords and I had teeth marks in all my favorite places plus a few new ones.

Gods, I could get used to this. Maybe I already had.

Ardruc's wristcomm trilled. He rumbled but didn't look at it.

"Are the tiles ready?" I murmured. "It's almost 0800 hours. We need to go talk to plasma, remember?"

"I know." He kissed the top of my head and caressed my back, trailing his fingertips along my spine until I quivered. "I am not used to preferring lying in bed over rushing to my lab to begin the day's work. Whenever I try to think about what we must do today, my attention returns to you." He rumbled again. "How do people survive dividing their time between their mates and their work?"

"Willpower and necessity, I suppose." I chuckled. "Most bosses won't accept 'My mate is lying on top of me and I don't want to get up' as an excuse for not showing up at work."

He raised his eyebrows. "But what if I am the boss, and it is my mate who is on top of me? May I not give myself permission to spend the day with my love?"

Being called *my love* jolted me, though not as much as it had last night. The first time, I was upset and thought I'd heard him wrong, but the second time he kissed my ear and murmured the words, I knew I hadn't misheard.

The easy way he said it just now, in a tone that sounded like *well, of course I love you, little mate*, made warmth pool in my chest.

I didn't love him yet—or at least I didn't *think* I did. My emotions remained as tangled as the vines that had taken over the station. I liked him very much, and I cared about him deeply, and I'd enjoyed the hells out of being claimed and taking his knot. And I'd actually thought about a future with him to the point I'd discussed my reproductive choices with an ease and level of openness I wouldn't have predicted.

Strangely, he didn't seem to be waiting for me to say *I love you* back. There wasn't a question hanging in the air in the wake of his words like I'd heard before from one or two previous partners. He simply offered his love without demanding anything in return.

I needed a few moments to process that.

He caressed my bottom with his tail, which was a sensation I liked very, very much—almost as much as the heat and gentle reassurance of his cock nestled inside me.

"We *are* going to spend the day together, just not in this bed," I said finally and kissed his chest so he'd rumble in the way that made him vibrate underneath and inside me. "Most mated pairs and polycules don't get to work together, you know. They have separate duties in separate places, often on opposite sides of the city or even off-planet on a satellite or moon."

"What an unpleasant thought." His brows drew together. "I cannot fathom it."

"Me either." I sighed. "Come on, lover. I want breakfast, a full, hot cup of coffee, and to learn how to communicate with the tendrils so we know what's going on and why I have this tattoo."

He grew serious. "You are right, of course," he said and cupped my face. "We have important tasks to accomplish. Unless the mating frenzy becomes unbearable, we will focus on work today and save our pleasures for tonight."

He *sounded* very convincing, but his tail remained firmly curled over my ass and resisted when I started to move.

"Ardruc Husiorithae." I glared at him. "If you don't let me get up, I will shower without you."

Grumbling, he moved his tail.

By 0900 hours, we were clean and dressed and finished with our breakfast. Ardruc and I packed up some necessities and collected the tiles the station's computer had synthesized. Accompanied by a sleepy Forux, his belly full of his own morning meal, we returned to the roof.

Another beautiful autumn day on Hyderia, with clear sky, bright sunshine, a light breeze, and clean, fragrant forest air. We'd left our equipment running since yesterday in case the plasma tendrils returned, but according to the computer, they had not.

Ardruc had transferred the recordings of our rooftop activities to his private, secured data storage. Thinking about watching those recordings made me warm and fidgety, which in turn made Ardruc's tail quiver and nostrils flare. So I distracted myself by laying out the new tiles across the grassy rooftop in the spacing and arrangement suggested by the linguistics system.

All but two tiles were marked with questions in Alliance Standard and four known logographic languages. The other two tiles bore images of Ardruc and me, along with our names, species, planets of origin, ages, and other basic information.

Ardruc had made another tile himself, this one marked with a copy of the symbol on my chest and a request for translation and explanation.

After establishing communication with the tendrils, getting that explanation topped our priority list—so much so that I'd tied the sleeves of my jumpsuit around my waist and worn an undershirt with a low neckline so the tattoo was plainly visible. It remained unchanged according to the scanner in the medical bay, which was reassuring. I liked how its colors matched the leaves of the forest and shimmered in the sunlight. But even so, I needed to know why I had it and what it meant.

As I positioned the last tile, Ardruc suddenly staggered and caught himself on the crate we'd used to bring the tiles to the roof.

"Ardruc?" I stood. "Are you all right?"

"Yes." His voice was strained. "It is…an urge. It will pass."

My heart twinged. There was a lot for both of us to like about a mating frenzy, but if we couldn't just indulge in satisfying our desires until it waned, there were definite downsides too. And most of all, I didn't want him to be uncomfortable or in pain.

"Are you sure?" Hesitantly, I took a step forward. I was afraid to get too close if it would make the situation worse, but I wanted to be supportive. "We can take a break if we need to. We aren't on a set schedule." My mouth quirked. "You wouldn't have to do much persuading."

"I would love to say yes, but I must learn to master this." With obvious difficulty, he straightened, though he braced himself with his leg against the crate. "I did some research myself, Elena. The frenzy does not mean I must give in every time my body demands you, especially—"

He cut himself off. "Even in the early days," he continued after a beat, "I can control myself with focus and self-discipline." He forced a smile. "Doing so will make our time together tonight even more pleasurable."

Despite his attempt to lighten the mood, uneasiness roiled in my stomach. Was he trying to hide something from me?

"*Especially* what?" I asked. "What were you going to say?"

"Especially if we are not trying to conceive," he said, his voice quiet. "It is a factor in how strong the urges are. As you are not currently fertile, I am more easily able to stay in control."

"Well, that makes sense." I frowned. "Why did you not want to say that?"

"I am sorry," he said earnestly. "I did not want to insult you by implying you were more or less captivating to me depending on your fertility. I desire you *immensely*. The only reason I am not deep inside you right now is that we agreed to focus on our work during the day."

His words and fervent expression made me smile. The uneasiness in my stomach evaporated.

"Oh, is that all?" I laughed. "I promise I wouldn't have assumed you found me less appealing. I remember all the things you and I did yesterday before the subject of fertility even came up. I think it's pretty clear you want to be deep inside your mate every chance you get—oh, hells." I scowled and pointed at the recording devices. "Make sure this conversation disappears from these records. If this experiment with the tendrils ends up in an archive or being reviewed by masses of scientists and the public because we've discovered a new life form, I don't want the whole damn galaxy to know about..." I waved my hand at the air between us "...*any* of this."

"I will take care of it." He took a deep breath, exhaled, and crossed the roof to my side, his spine straight and wings folded. The urge must have passed.

Tension I hadn't realized I'd been holding left my shoulders. His well-being had become essential to my own. I supposed the same was true for him but to a much greater extent. He didn't seem to mind, though—very much the opposite.

"I am still your dragon, little mate," he murmured, kissing the top of my head. "Even when I am not deep inside you. And yes, I will delete this part too."

"Thank you." I touched his hand. "Back to work, Dr. Husiorithae."

He gave me a perfect Fortusian bow—the kind I had given him when I arrived at Nova Cal, when I received no response because unbeknownst to me, his life had been changed forever in that moment.

"Of course, Dr. Regis," he intoned.

Damn it, now I associated my title and name in his voice with my *lesson*.

He smiled like he knew what I was thinking and went back to his recording devices. I scowled at his broad back and those big, pretty wings that gleamed so brilliantly orange and red in the morning sunlight.

No tendrils came during setup or after we placed the tiles and recording equipment, and no korae appeared in the atmosphere. The morning was peaceful and quiet.

As we waited for visitors to arrive, we sat in the grass just close enough to reach out and touch each other every so often. Ardruc reviewed recordings and data from last night's korae displays and I resumed my study of my lichen specimens, searching for anomalies. We worked in comfortable silence listening to the wind in the forest.

Forux, for his part, dozed on his back between us, his tummy skyward to soak in the suns' warmth. Whenever he snuffled and wiggled for attention, we took turns scratching his head and belly. I tried not to be offended that Forux purred louder when Ardruc rubbed his belly than for me.

The fact Forux had accepted Ardruc meant a lot. In addition to their empathic abilities, arvals possessed a strong intuition for deception and ill intent. In a way, I trusted his instincts more than my own. I didn't suspect Ardruc of being untrustworthy or duplicitous, but it was good to know he had Forux's trust too.

That thought made me recall Forux's endless growls and snarls every time we'd interacted with Ardruc before he admitted the truth. Arvals didn't like lies, and Ardruc had been living a lie from the moment we'd met. What I'd interpreted as simple dislike on Forux's part had been a much more complicated response.

If only arvals could talk, the last four months might have gone very differently. Whether that would have been for better or worse, I wasn't sure. Maybe events had played out exactly as they were supposed to.

What a strangely unscientific thought. I harrumphed at myself and gave Forux extra ear scratches by way of apology for my lack of understanding.

After nearly two hours of waiting for the tendrils to appear, Ardruc set his korae data aside, methodically stretched and warmed up his fingers and hands, and opened his lat'sar case.

As soon as he began playing scales, I set my datapad in my lap and started watching for visitors, my heart racing in both anticipation and nervousness.

We wanted and needed answers, but part of me was just as afraid of what they might be as the possibility of not being able to find a way to communicate. Mixed feelings about getting answers to scientific questions wasn't like me at all, but rarely if ever did those questions have such a personal importance.

Ardruc paused mid-scale and leaned over to kiss my temple. "All will be well," he murmured.

Why was he so sure? Instinct? Or had finding his true mate given him so much comfort that our situation didn't trouble him as much as it troubled me?

I heard and sensed him starting to coo. "No," I said, raising my hand. "Not right now. I want to feel what I'm feeling. I need my instincts." I managed a fleeting smile, hoping to take the edge off declining his offer in case suppressing his coo gave him a painful twinge. "But thank you."

His low song faded. With a gentle smile, he drew his bow over the lat'sar's strings. "As you wish."

Though he didn't coo, when he began playing, his music had a similar soothing effect. Unlike yesterday, he played what was unmistakably a composition rather than improvising. The song was light and airy and made me think of a gentle waterfall or a light rain.

He played the entire song, and then another longer, much more complex and difficult piece, and then another, but the tendrils didn't appear.

Despite how beautifully and masterfully Ardruc played, my initial sense of comfort gave way to stomach-churning anxiety. I caught myself rubbing the mark on my chest without realizing it and dropped my hand back to my lap.

When the third song ended, Ardruc closed his eyes and breathed deeply. I thought he was experiencing another spike of the mating frenzy until he drew the bow across the strings in a beautiful chord that somehow seemed in harmony with the wind in the trees.

The compositions might have been a masterpiece by most listeners' standards, and he played them masterfully, but I found them a pale facsimile of his improvised duets with the world around us.

Maybe I wasn't the only listener who thought so.

One by one, and then in pairs, brightly colored tendrils appeared, rising from below our line of sight to hover just beyond the roof's meter-tall, vine-covered perimeter wall. They swayed and bobbed along with Ardruc's music.

Were the tendrils uninterested in the compositions Ardruc had played? They hadn't responded to Ardruc's scales either. Maybe they thought the compositions were like scales—some kind of warm-up or practice rather than music. I tapped my lower tip with my index finger. Maybe to them, improvisation was true music. True *art*.

What evidence did I have to support my theory? We'd witnessed the tendrils emulate and dance along with korae, the size and shape of which were determined by a host of factors that changed with each occurrence. An argument could be made that was nature's version of improvisation.

So I could see an analogy between the korae and Ardruc's improvisation and by extension why the tendrils found both to be art by their reckoning, while more structured forms—scales, compositions, and the station's humming power conduits—didn't register with them as such.

It was just a half-baked theory right now, but my gut told me I was onto something.

My heart wanted me to ask Ardruc to take me flying with the tendrils. Our flight yesterday was one of the most wonderful experiences of my life and had led to many very pleasurable and satisfying hours. And I had a new fantasy I wanted to ask Ardruc about—one that involved yet another kind of claiming. Something told me he would be interested in this one too.

I loved watching the tendrils dance to Ardruc's beautiful music too, but we needed to get them to respond to the tiles. Everything else would have to wait.

For nearly an hour, Ardruc played and I waited and watched and listened. If the tendrils noticed or were interested by the tiles, I saw no sign of it.

Research and scientific inquiry required a lot of traits and skills, especially patience. Ardruc seemed content to play and let the tendrils dance, but even his music and their shimmering movements couldn't soothe my restlessness.

Watching the tendrils, I had a sudden, wildly ridiculous idea. Maybe my theory about improvisation and art forms could help persuade the tendrils to respond to the tiles. But it would require me to risk embarrassing myself in front of Ardruc, whoever might watch these recordings later, and what might be several dozen sentient tendrils of plasma.

I sighed. Oh, well. It would be worth it if we got the answers we needed. And it wouldn't be the first time I had to take a risk in the name of science. At least I didn't have to worry about injuries caused by sub-zero temperatures or flying debris—just wounds to my pride.

I'd already removed my boots so I could better enjoy the warmth and hum of the grass. I rose, untied the sleeves of my jumpsuit from around my waist, and slid the garment down my legs and the rest of the way off, leaving me once again in a tank top and shorts.

Ardruc raised his eyebrows and played a little surprised trill of notes that made me chuckle despite my nervousness.

I closed my eyes, rocked back and forth to lose myself in the music and the cool breeze, and took deep, cleansing breaths.

I raised my hands over my head, arched my back, and twirled on the ball of my right foot. I hadn't done this in a very, very long time, but in a way that made it easier. I didn't want to dance with technical perfection and precise movements, in the way I'd been taught by instructors growing up on Fyloria. In fact, according to my theory, I needed *not* to dance like that if I wanted to find a way to connect and hopefully communicate with the tendrils.

So I followed Ardruc's lead and just…improvised.

In tempo with his music, I twirled, leapt, spun, swayed, and moved my arms and legs in whatever way felt right. Afraid I'd become self-conscious if I saw Ardruc watching me, I avoided looking in his direction and instead focused on the grass, sky, trees, and tendrils. Forux joined in by running around the roof in happy, albeit confused circles.

Ardruc played joyfully, with no hint of the melancholy tones he'd favored yesterday. Maybe he liked watching me dance. The wind swirled, the trees swayed, and the tendrils twirled and danced as well.

A green tendril drifted onto the roof and began to mimic my movements. My heart was already racing with exertion, but it sped up as the tendril moved back and forth. A small red tendril—possibly the one that had burned me, since it was the only small red tendril I'd seen so far—joined the green one.

We danced for a while, and then I took my chance.

I picked up the tile with my image and information and held it in front of my chest. "Elena," I said, pointing to the image and then to my face. "My name is Elena. I am a human."

The tendrils swayed back and forth but didn't react in any way I could see.

I put down my tile and picked up the one with the first question composed by the linguistics system, inscribed in five languages: *What is your name?*

I set the tile on the grass and moved back, swaying to the music.

The tendril closed the distance between us, moving so close that my skin tingled. Ardruc continued to play, but he stood and watched the green tendril with undisguised concern.

The tendril hovered for several seconds, and then extended a single thread of itself to the tile's surface. I took a deep breath and held it. *Please let this work.*

The tendril inscribed something on the tile.

Moving slowly, I circled to my left until I could see the inscription. The markings resembled but did not match my tattoo.

The light around the edge of the tile blinked, indicating the linguistics system was working to translate.

The tendril moved to the next tile, paused, and then inscribed a series of marks before going to tile number three. My heartbeat pounded in my ears. Was it working?

The lights on the first tile stopped blinking and turned solid. Words in Alliance Standard glowed across the surface.

I made a choked sound. Ardruc's lat'sar fell silent.

I am Ka, the tile read.

And beneath that:

We are the Vorsa.

CHAPTER 24
ARDRUC

With a gasp, Elena went to her knees in the grass, her wide eyes fixed on the words glowing on the surface of the first tile.

I put my lat'sar in its case, closed the lid, and joined my mate to watch the green tendril of plasma move slowly from tile to tile inscribing its answers to the questions the linguistics system had devised.

Only the first tile had completed its translation so far. Seven words glowed on its surface above the swirling inscription left by the tendril.

I am Ka. We are the Vorsa.

Elena's hand found mine. She was shaking. "The Vorsa," she whispered, her expression a blend of elation, awe, and disbelief.

I went to one knee beside my mate and squeezed her hand. Beneath her excitement about our communication with the Vorsa, her worry sizzled on my skin. I wanted so much to coo and wrap her in my arms and let her inhale my scent and calming pheromones, but she had asked me not to alter her emotions. I must always respect her wishes even when it made my hearts ache to let her suffer.

How did other Fortusians who had found their true mates withstand the constant desire and need to protect and treasure them? I had no one to ask—no close friends and no family. No one who could offer me wisdom and counsel. I had never felt as much on an island as I did at this moment.

Perhaps it would get easier with time. I would learn. After all, I had once known little about upper-atmospheric electrical discharges and now I was an authority on the subject. What better focus of study and learning could I have than Elena and our bond?

I caressed her hand with my thumb. When her lips turned up at the corners, I found I could breathe a little easier.

I wanted Ka's answers to all the linguistic system's questions, but most of all I wanted it to explain the tattoo on Elena's chest. Elena had put the tiles in the sequence the computer had recommended, meaning the tile bearing the tattoo's shape and my request for a translation and explanation was at the end.

It felt like an eternity before Ka reached that final, all-important tile. The linguistics system was still working to translate all the other tiles except the first one.

Ka hovered over the final tile for a very long time without responding. Was it unable to understand the question? Reluctant to reply? Struggling with how to answer? With whether to answer honestly?

My uneasiness and impatience gave way to rising anger. My wings shivered and smoke curled from my nostrils.

"Ardruc," Elena murmured, her hand tightening around mine. I squeezed back and focused on her scent until my anger and frustration eased.

Finally, Ka extended a thread and inscribed something on the tile before drifting back to hover motionless and crackling in the middle of the roof.

The tile's lights blinked, and blinked, and blinked…and then went solid blue.

We rose and moved to see the words glowing on the tile's

surface under the question regarding the meaning of the symbol on her chest: *Elena is caretaker-listener.*

A second set of translated words appeared: *Mark given too soon by young one. We apologize for injuries to Elena.*

The blinking lights on a few of the other tiles turned solid as more answers appeared, but my gaze remained fixed on the words *Elena is caretaker-listener.* What did that mean?

My wristcomm trilled with a notification that the linguistics system was ready to attempt live translation, with the caveat to keep my questions simple and try to use as many words already shown on the tiles as possible.

With shaking hands and a grunt of effort, I took two larger tiles from the crate and laid them side-by-side on the grass between Ka and us.

"Why did the young one give the mark to Elena?" I asked.

The lights on tile on the left blinked rapidly, then four lines of text appeared. The linguistic system presented my question written four ways: in Alliance Standard, in symbols that looked like the original writing of the Vorsa, and in two known logographic languages. The other tile blinked, awaiting a reply.

Ka swayed back and forth, then extended a thread to the blank tile. It inscribed a lengthy series of symbols, then retreated.

The tile's lights blinked for a long time. Rather than wait at my side, Elena walked past the other tiles, reading the translated responses. Perhaps I would be better served to do the same rather than stand and stare impatiently, but I stayed. I wanted the tendril to know how much this answer meant to me—how much *Elena* meant to me.

In fact, I could think of no reason not to make it abundantly clear.

"I love Elena," I said, and watched my words appear on the left tile in three languages while the linguistic system attempted to translate them into the Vorsa's language. "She is my mate. I treasure and honor her above all else."

The right tile first displayed its translation of Ka's earlier response.

The Vorsa feel fear and anger, it read. *Vorsa World <word not translated> requires caretaker-listener and protector. The Vorsa believe Elena is caretaker-listener and protector. Young one acted before elder Vorsa contacted Elena. The Vorsa apologize.*

Elena returned to my side to take my hand and read the translation. Her emotions, like mine, seemed almost incomprehensibly tangled, but most of all she appeared hopeful. Because we might be about to finally get answers?

"Why are the Vorsa afraid and angry?" Elena asked. Her words appeared below mine on the left tile, now in only Alliance Standard and the Vorsa language.

I wanted more explanation of the mark and its significance, as well as clarification about *caretaker-listener*. Elena seemed more concerned about the Vorsa. I supposed one explanation might lead to the other, but Elena was my first concern.

The right tile's surface cleared for Ka to respond. Again, it wrote a lengthy reply that took the computer a full two minutes to translate.

When the translation finally appeared, Elena stiffened.

We honor Ardruc for his love and devotion. And below that:

Not-Vorsa steal from Vorsa World <word not translated>. The Not-Vorsa cut deeply and remove parts of Vorsa World <word not translated>. Vorsa World suffers. Elena and Ardruc must protect Vorsa World <word not translated>.

"Someone is stealing from Hyderia?" Elena demanded, then winced. "I'm sorry, Ka. Hyderia is not what you call your world—that's what the Nyvorans named it. Our computer doesn't yet understand what you call your world. We can call it Vorsa World for now."

"Are the Not-Vorsa removing resources from this world?" I asked Ka, then wondered if the term *resources* translated. "They are taking parts of this world to use themselves?"

Ka wrote on the tile. A translation appeared within a few seconds. The linguistics system was getting faster.

The Not-Vorsa take parts of Vorsa World <word not translated> away. The Not-Vorsa take without permission.

Trembling, Elena squeezed my hand. "Somewhere on this planet, someone is stealing resources. But who is doing it? Who are the 'Not-Vorsa'? And how does the Ministry not know so they can put a stop to it?"

I opened my mouth and then closed it again.

Where the thought came from, I was not sure. Many ruthless profiteers preyed on both Alliance and non-Alliance worlds, stealing resources, people, and anything else of value. And yet…

And yet, I had a gut feeling what the answer was.

My stomach filled with foreboding. "Elena, why does Nyvor only have one research station operating now when all six used to be occupied?"

As if her knees had given out, she dropped onto the lid of a closed crate and stared up at me, her expression a mirror of my own anger and disbelief. "No. They wouldn't. They *wouldn't*."

I did not want to believe it either. I had worked under the auspices of the Ministry for more than two years and considered Minister Ganna a like-minded colleague who valued this planet and its wonders as much as I. But the odds of outsiders being able to elude Nyvor's detection well enough to conduct ongoing thefts of resources seemed slim, if not impossible.

With dread in my gut, I tapped on my wristcomm and activated its small holographic projector. The projector showed an image of Nyvor and this planet, Nyvor itself, a series of different Nyvoran interplanetary vessels, and finally an image of Minister Ganna and several other members of the Ministry of Natural Sciences.

"Ka, does this look like the not-Vorsa who are stealing parts of your world?" I asked.

Ka and the other Vorsa erupted in blindingly bright light and searing heat.

I picked Elena up and leapt into the sky, moving so fast I barely registered what I had done until we had risen far out of range of the Vorsa's enraged reactions.

"Are you hurt?" I asked, cupping Elena's face so I could look into her eyes. I inhaled deeply to catch any hint of burned hair or flesh.

"No, I'm all right." Elena wrenched in my arms to turn and look over her shoulder. She exhaled in relief when she saw Forux had jumped down to the lower roof and was unharmed.

Below us, the Vorsa vibrated, crackled, and pulsed with light and heat that rolled through the air in nearly visible waves. The forest thrummed, the trees swayed, and bursts of korae spread across the sky. Even the wind turned hot, as if the cool autumn morning had suddenly become a summer afternoon on the desert world of Solan.

It was not just the Vorsa who were enraged by the plundering of their planet—the entire world raged too.

Elena gasped and rubbed her fist against the tattoo. It shimmered along with the pulsing of the threads around us. "So much anger and hurt," she said, looking up at me. "How dare the Nyvorans do this?"

My entire body went from blazing hot with fury to ice-cold. Each of her beautiful blue irises had a bright blue-green ring the same color as her tattoo.

"Elena," I rasped. "Your eyes are glowing."

Eyes wide with awe, she craned her neck to look all around us. "Oh," she breathed. "I can see *everything* now. This world is so beautifully interconnected and alive."

Fighting to stay calm, I cradled her against my chest with my tail wrapped around her legs. I wanted so much to fly my mate away from this place—away from the dangers of living plasma, duplicitous Nyvorans, and all the unknowns that surrounded us.

When we woke to find the station transformed and discovered the tendrils were alive, I had felt as if the ground had fallen away from under my feet. What little foundation remained had just vanished with the revelations that we could not trust the Nyvorans and the planet Elena and I loved was being secretly plundered for its resources.

The sole comfort and source of security I had left was my love for Elena, and she had been changed in ways we still did not understand by the Vorsa and their mysterious tattoo. Anger and fear for her filled my gut as heavy as stones.

Elena's gaze returned to me. "The threads are all around you, touching you, but not going through you," she said. She looked down at herself. "But they go through me."

"Because of the tattoo?" My voice was rough.

"I think so." She blinked a few times and shook her head. When she looked up again, the glowing rings had faded and her eyes were lovely blue and human once more. "Back to normal sight," she said with a sigh. "So I can control that, then. Kind of."

With my attention on Elena, I had not noticed the Vorsa had returned to their muted, less dangerous forms. Ka rose slowly to join us in midair, keeping a careful distance. It dipped three times, then returned to the roof. An apology? Elena deserved more than an apology.

Below us, Ka inscribed something on the tile. I brought us low enough to see the translation: *We apologize. We will not repeat the action.*

Warily, I took Elena back to the upper roof and set her feet on the grass well away from Ka.

"You cannot expose us to extreme heat," I told Ka as my mate climbed down the ladder to retrieve a very angry and worried Forux. "We can be hurt and killed. Your young one nearly killed Elena that way and now you have done it again."

Sincere apologies, Ka wrote on the tile. *We are angry at Not-Vorsa, not at Elena and Ardruc. We become like young ones when Vorsa World suffers harm.*

Elena returned to the upper roof with Forux in her arms and put him on the grass near her pack.

She joined me, read Ka's words, and took a deep breath. "You said Ardruc and I must protect your world. Is that why you gave me this tattoo?" She pointed to her chest.

The tattoo is a symbol of great honor to us, Ka replied. *It is our name for our world. Your language does not translate the name.*

Elena touched the tattoo. "Thank you for the honor," she said. "But I don't like that you've changed me without my permission."

We apologize that the young one placed the mark without permission. You can remove it if you prefer.

Elena studied the words on the tile and then looked back at Ka. "I will think about whether I want to remove it, then."

I wanted very much for Elena to remove the tattoo, but I also trusted her to make the decision for herself. I had pledged not to interfere with her autonomy—but had not anticipated that pledge would be tested so soon, and so mightily.

"Ardruc and I don't understand what you want us to do," Elena said to Ka.

Once the translations appeared on the tiles, we could read Ka's response.

We request Elena and Ardruc to act as our caretaker-listeners. The Not-Vorsa must stop stealing from Vorsa World. We value and honor Elena and Ardruc. We will allow no harm to come to Elena and Ardruc.

Just days ago, I had wanted few things more than to live out the rest of my life on this planet—as long as Elena remained also. My feelings about staying had become much more complicated, to put it mildly.

"If you mean us no harm, why drug us in order to transform the station and then trap us here with no way to contact anyone?" I demanded.

Ka dipped three times and wrote its reply.

We apologize. We feared Elena and Ardruc would contact Not-Vorsa before we communicated.

"That is a fair concern," Elena said wryly. She put her hands on her hips. "But what about drugging us to put us to sleep for a whole day? And the changes to the station?"

We apologize for forcing sleep. Elena and Ardruc required rest to recuperate from injuries and stress. We will never repeat the action. We transformed the station to provide a better home for Elena and Ardruc. The ways of Vorsa World are better than the ways of Not-Vorsa.

"You can say that again," Elena muttered. "Ka, do the Not-Vorsa know the Vorsa exist?"

The Not-Vorsa do not know about the Vorsa. No one knows about the Vorsa but Ardruc and Elena. We have never trusted any Not-Vorsa until Ardruc and Elena came.

Elena shook her head. "The Not-Vorsa believe they own this planet because they don't know you live here. They have kept it protected for three centuries as what's called a conservation planet —or so they claimed."

Ka shimmered. I tensed, but it did not blaze. Finally, it replied, *The Not-Vorsa speak not-truths.*

"Apparently." Elena took another deep breath. "Ka, if we show you an image of Vorsa World, can you show us where the Not-Vorsa are stealing from Vorsa World?"

Yes.

With my wristcomm, I called up an image of the planet on the writing tile. The planet rotated on the surface with a notation of the location of Nova Cal, then transformed into a two-dimensional depiction of the planet's surface.

Ka hovered over the tile for a full minute. Finally, it extended a thread and touched the image in an area on the other side of the planet from Nova Cal—well beyond the range of the small transports the Ministry had given us to use. I had never considered their limitations a deliberate choice before now.

"How could we not know about this?" Elena demanded, turning to me. "The planet has a massive array of imaging and recording equipment in orbit. You study those images and data every day."

My clenched jaw ached. The Nyvorans' apparent duplicity filled me with rage.

"It is very possible they have technology that hides the site and their ships from our view," I grated. "The Ministry provided all the station's imaging equipment. I have never noted blind spots or data I suspected was falsified or altered, but that does not mean there are none."

"What do we do?" Elena asked me. "The Nyvorans are violating Alliance law by plundering the planet's natural resources after designating it a conservation world. And they have no right to govern it at all if there are sentient indigenous life forms."

"We have to contact the Alliance," I said.

"But how, without the Nyvorans finding out?" She scrubbed her face with her hands. "They must be monitoring all our off-world communication."

Ka wrote on the tile.

We request Elena and Ardruc to be caretaker-listeners of Vorsa World and speak for the Vorsa to all Not-Vorsa. We ask Elena and Ardruc to protect Vorsa World. We do not trust other Not-Vorsa. No other Not-Vorsa may come to Vorsa World unless Elena and Ardruc believe we may trust them.

So much remained uncertain—most especially Elena's tattoo and what we would do after this first communication with the Vorsa—but at least that was a plain directive. I puffed smoke from my nostrils.

"Will you give us a clear description of what you would ask of us as caretaker-listeners?" Elena asked.

Yes. A pause, and then Ka wrote, *Will Ardruc permit us to give him a mark of honor so he may sense Vorsa World in fullness and be known to the Not-Vorsa as our caretaker-listener?*

I stiffened. Our medbay scanners had deemed Elena's tattoo not harmful and made up of only plant cells—as much as cells from plants on this planet could be called *plants*. Elena had experienced no ill effects from its presence either, though that was far from enough to convince me it was harmless.

"We don't know enough about the mark to believe it won't harm us, Ka," Elena said. Her mouth compressed into a thin line.

"Right now I'm tempted to go to the medical bay and remove mine."

The mark causes no harm, Ka wrote. *The Vorsa speak only truth. The mark is one of honor and permits full sensation of the Vorsa World. It has no other use or purpose. It can be removed at any time and the Vorsa will not take offense. Elena and Ardruc can confirm this is truth with medical bay.*

My instincts told me Ka spoke the truth. And judging by Elena's expression, she thought so too. But even so, my worry remained.

"If I receive a mark, can we remove Elena's?" I asked.

Yes, Ka wrote. *Your marks may be removed at any time. The Vorsa will not take offense.*

"Why would you want me to remove my mark?" Elena asked me, eyes narrowed. "If you trust them enough to get one, surely mine is no more dangerous."

The grassy roof beneath my feet suddenly felt very fragile.

"Up to now, one of us has had the mark and the other not," I said. "You were unsure what effects the mark might have and asked me to monitor your condition in case your behavior changed. If we both have marks, how will we know whether we have been affected in a way we do not want?"

Her eyebrows rose. "Then I should keep mine and you should decline. Easy enough decision."

My wings vibrated with uneasiness. "Elena…"

"I know why you want me to remove the mark." She touched my hand. "It's the same reason I'm nervous about you getting one."

She turned to Ka. "Is there another way for us to be designated as caretaker-listeners for Vorsa World? One that allows us to sense it fully, but without the mark?"

Ka hovered for a long time, then wrote its answer on the tile.

We can provide a mark on another material, but we do not know another way to show Vorsa World in fullness without the mark. We will study and learn and experiment.

"That's what we do as scientists, Ka," Elena said with a smile.

"We study, learn, and experiment. I would like us to be able to sense Vorsa World in fullness without needing tattoos." Her smile faded. "Our bodies belong to us, Ka. No one may make changes to them without our permission."

Ka dipped three times. *We understand. The young one was afraid of the Not-Vorsa and acted wrongly. When the Not-Vorsa steal from Vorsa World, the Vorsa suffer. The Vorsa World suffers.*

"We understand. I accept your apology." Elena's hand found mine. "Ardruc and I will think about how to help the Vorsa, Ka. Thank you for your trust." She sighed. "I don't want to ask you this, but can you return the station to its previous form? We don't want the Nyvorans—the Not-Vorsa—to know what's been happening here. If they see the station transformed, they'll realize something very strange is going on."

We will return the station to its original form, Ka wrote. *We hope Elena and Ardruc will ask us to give them a better home once the Not-Vorsa depart. The ways of the Not-Vorsa are wrong.*

"I would like a Vorsa home very much," Elena said softly. "Thank you. We will do everything we can to help you be rid of the Not-Vorsa."

Ka dipped once and retreated to the edge of the roof to join the rest of the Vorsa. Together, they vanished into the trees.

"I wonder how—" Elena began.

The ground rumbled and the air hummed. We ran to the edge of the roof and gaped.

Vines and trees, soil and grass, and even Elena's beloved fungi flowed from the station like an outgoing tide. Slowly at first, and then more quickly, the forest retreated from Nova Cal.

When the vines unwound from the short wall along the roof's edge, Elena sat to watch the Vorsa World give Nova Cal back. She was trembling and smelled of anger, grief, and unshed tears.

I rested my hands on her shoulders and offered her warmth and comfort until the station had emptied of forest life, the rumbles stopped, and everything was still once more. For now, that was all I could do.

CHAPTER 25
ELENA

WE HAD A STACK OF TILES TO ANALYZE, SEVERAL VERY SERIOUS problems to solve, and mountains of our own research awaiting our attention. But I didn't have the heart to think about any of it.

Nova Cal's bare walls and floors and humming machinery were cold and alien to me now. My lab had never been more devoid of life. I didn't even want to be in it.

"Take me to the forest, Ardruc," I said once we'd hauled our equipment back inside the station and left it all stacked in one of the empty, echoing hallways. "Get me out of here."

He kissed me and took my hand.

We walked out the main door and down the stairs to ground level with Forux trotting along behind. Halfway across the little clearing, Ardruc scooped me up and buried his face in my hair. I closed my eyes and rested my head on his chest, trying to drink in his scent through my nose, my mouth, my skin—every way I could. My body ached with both my own heartache and what I thought was the planet's own anger and grief.

Ardruc stopped. "Elena," he murmured. "Look."

A soft mossy path lined with bioluminescent mushrooms and lichen led from the tree line deep into the forest. It had not been here yesterday. I was willing to bet it had only appeared after the forest had retreated from Nova Cal.

Ardruc toed off his boots, took mine off too, and left them at the edge of the clearing. He carried me down the path, his bare feet almost soundless on the soft moss.

Forux followed us for a while, then found a mossy spot in a patch of sunlight and settled in.

"He will be fine," Ardruc said when I made a little sound of protest. "He will know where to find us."

About fifty meters later, the mossy path ended at the threshold of a shelter with a tall, peaked roof. Vines woven between trees and branches formed the walls and roof. Warm welcome thrummed through the soil and air as we approached.

"A gift for us." Ardruc nuzzled my hair. Chest rumbling, he carried me inside. A loose curtain of vines fell over the doorway. Narrow openings covered with leafy vines in the roof and walls allowed only slivers of daylight.

In the middle of the hut was a mound of thick blue-green moss —the same kind that had formed our little bed yesterday in the forest.

"If I did not know better," Ardruc mused, his eyes glowing in the dim light, "I would think this planet wanted me to comfort and worship my mate on this bed."

I didn't even have the energy to reply. I felt completely gutted.

I expected him to coo, and I might have welcomed it this time. Instead, he placed me gently on the moss. It was so thick and plush that it felt wonderfully close to the bed in Ardruc's quarters at the station, and its fragrance was light and sweet. I wished I had the heart to enjoy it more.

Ardruc took off his shirt and pants and left them draped on a branch. He stripped me down to my undershirt and shorts, added my jumpsuit to the branch, and lay down next to me.

He drew me into his arms, tucked me against his chest with my head under his chin, and draped his wing over us.

"Elena," he said into my hair. "Let it out."

I let out a guttural scream against his chest.

Fists clenched and hot tears sliding down my face, I raged for a long time. Every choked sob and curse coursed through me into the mossy bed and pulsed through the forest. The leaves shivered, the soil hummed, and a strong wind swept around and through our little refuge.

The betrayal. The lies. The hypocrisy. How dare the Nyvorans do this to beautiful Vorsa World? A planet full of wonders and beauty beyond all understanding, sliced into and plundered by the very people who had promised to protect and guard it. The Nyvorans had made it difficult for scientists to study here *not* because they wanted to keep it pristine, but to keep their secret.

Ardruc didn't become impatient or restless or ask me anything. He simply held me quietly and let me process everything.

Somehow, he knew when it was time to coo. His song began to resonate in his chest just as I took a deep, shaky breath—the first deep breath I'd taken since the forest retreated from Nova Cal. My chest had hurt too much and been too tight until that very moment.

Warm comfort washed through me and out into the forest, taking with it my rage and grief just when I was ready to let them go. Maybe he gifted me peace via pheromones too, or maybe it was just the gentle way he held me. I no longer cared to distinguish between the ways he soothed me. The forest quieted until not even a leaf stirred.

We lay together for a long time. Ardruc stroked my hair and my back, cooing and letting me breathe until it didn't hurt to do so anymore.

When I raised my head and kissed him, he was ready for that too. His kiss was so gentle I barely felt it—a far cry from the more ferocious kisses he'd lavished on me before.

I rested my forehead on his. "Tell me we'll figure out how to make this right." My voice was rough.

"I cannot promise that," he said, with kindness in his eyes. "But I *can* promise we will do everything in our power to make this right."

"That's good enough." I took a deep breath. "I feel like I ran away from Nova Cal like a child. I'm too old to run away."

"Not true." He caressed my cheek. "You were hurting and wanted away from the pain. You sought comfort. There is nothing childish about that." He smiled slightly. "And I left with you, if you did not notice. Dragons are very much not childish."

"Hmm…debatable," I said, which earned me a chuckle.

He kissed me again. "Elena," he murmured. "Beautiful Elena. Did you know *ele'ana* means 'time away' in my local dialect of Forusian?"

"No," I said, surprised that he'd brought up his first language. I'd never heard him speak anything but Alliance Standard. "I don't know any Fortusian."

"It is what we say when we go away to the beach or the mountains or a secret, secluded romantic place." He tucked loose hair behind my ear. "*Epet mar ele'ana* means 'I am taking time away with my mate.' If you say that, it is understood that you are not to be bothered because you will be devoted to caring for your mate." He kissed the tip of my nose, which tickled and I loved it. "*Epet mar ele'ana*, Elena. We are taking time away."

It made sense that Fortusians had a specific phrase for a romantic getaway with their mates. And I liked the way the words sounded when Ardruc said them.

"*Epet mar ele'ana*," I said, or tried to say. I failed catastrophically.

To his credit, Ardruc didn't laugh, though his lips twitched. "Fortusian vowels are notoriously difficult for human vocal cords. I am sure your pronunciation would improve with a bit of practice."

"Probably so. *Or…*" I moved to my hands and knees to look down into his beautiful glowing eyes. "Rather than having Fortusian coming out of my mouth, I'd rather have one coming in it."

He picked me up with his hands on my waist and put me on top of him with my thighs astride his hips. His cock, already half-hard and growing harder by the moment, pressed against my ass through the thin fabric of our undershorts.

"Little mate." He pushed my top up to bare my breasts and cupped them gently, stroking my nipples with the pads of his thumbs. "That is a very enticing offer, but I have already laid claim to this bed in the name of worshiping you. If anyone's mouth will be filled on it, it will be mine."

"You *laid claim* to this bed?" I scoffed. "Since when—"

"Since we first discovered it," he said easily, and pinched my nipples. I gasped at the little twin bursts of pain and pleasure. His thumbs resumed their caresses over the hard peaks. "Do you not remember me saying the forest had made it for me to worship you upon it?"

"I'm not at all sure that's the reason the forest made it." My eyes narrowed. "But fine, I'll make you a bet. If I can pronounce that romantic getaway phrase correctly in Fortusian, I get to fill my mouth. And if I can't—"

"—You will sit on my face until I drink my fill," Ardruc said. His eyes gleamed. "I accept this wager."

Three minutes later, I was naked and on my knees above Ardruc's face, my arms extended out to the sides and my wrists and forearms wrapped in vines that had obligingly unwound them-selves from the walls of the little hut for Ardruc to use. And I was fuming.

Between my thighs, Ardruc chuckled. His hot breath against my delicate skin made me quiver. "I have never been so pleased to win a bet, little mate. And I have never seen a better view."

"If anyone else had been judging, they would have said I pronounced it well enough to have won the bet and you know it." I scowled. "You weren't going to let me win whatever I said. I'll get even for this."

"No, you will not, little mate. I will keep you coming until you have no strength to seek vengeance." His arms curled around my thighs and pulled me down to his mouth.

I expected a lick or a swirl of his tongue on my clit. Instead, his long, hot tongue speared straight into my pussy.

The invasion was so abrupt and felt so good that I wailed and yanked on my bound wrists. All I got for my trouble was a satisfied rumble from Ardruc and tighter restraints.

Ardruc, on the other hand, got his first taste of what he wanted most when I gushed hard for him. His tongue swirled around inside me as if he wanted to capture every drop.

"Dragon," I gasped, eyes closed and head falling back.

"Little mate," he murmured, his lips tickling my delicate skin. "How good you taste. I want more."

His arms tightened on my thighs. A thrill of anticipation ran through me and made me quiver.

His tongue traveled along my slit up to my clit and swirled languidly. My gasp and shudder made his fingertips dig into my thighs. The pain was exquisite.

"Yes," I breathed. "Harder. Make me hurt for you, my dragon. Make it good."

He squeezed with his fingertips just as his lips closed on my clit. Pain blended with pleasure in the best way and I wailed.

With his tongue and lips, Ardruc drove me toward ecstasy with single-minded focus.

In his iron grip, I couldn't move, couldn't get away, couldn't take any pleasure for myself that wasn't given. Couldn't stop myself from screaming his name or from dripping and gushing into his mouth, even if he'd rigged the bet and didn't deserve—didn't deserve—

I broke with a cry, flooding his face as his fingers dug into my hips and held me right where he wanted me to wring every drop and wail out of me. And he sucked and slurped noisily at my pussy for every moment of my release, because he wanted me to know he was drinking from me like a man who'd wandered in a desert for days and found a spring.

Oh, I'd get him back. I'd find a way. But for now, I let the dragon have his victory—plus two more.

As I whimpered and trembled and dripped from coming a third time, Ardruc indulged in a final long, slow lick of my pussy and raised me just enough to slide out from under me and out of sight behind my back—leaving me with my outstretched arms still wrapped in vines.

"Dragon," I gasped. I tried to turn my head to see him, but our shelter was almost completely dark. He was nothing more than a shadow behind me.

"Little mate," he murmured from the darkness. "I can see you. Delicious, dripping, helplessly bound little mate."

Fabric tore.

"That had better not have been my jumpsuit," I warned.

Another rip. "Worry not, little mate," Ardruc said, his voice still soft. Was he directly behind me? "I will not force you to return to the station in the state of undress I prefer you in."

I didn't hear him moving, but suddenly soft fabric covered my eyes. I yelped and tried to pull away, but something circled my waist and held me still: Ardruc's long tail.

The fabric went tight around my head as he tied it snugly. Now I really couldn't see anything. My breathing sped up and my heart raced. "Ardruc—"

Something hot and wet swirled around my left nipple. His tongue. I gasped.

"Yes, little mate?" His voice, still soft but now edged with a growl, came from somewhere to my left. "Mmm. Such a tasty little morsel for a dragon."

I moaned and squeezed my thighs together.

Another delicate lick—this time, my right nipple. I jerked and whimpered.

"You sound so delectable when you whimper," he said, his lips near my ear. "It makes my cock drip, little mate. It makes my balls tight."

Straining to figure out where he was and what he might be doing had all my senses and nerves taut and tingling. So when his hand gripped my ass, I almost screamed.

"You might make me come when you scream," he said, caressing the curve of my ass so lightly that my skin pebbled. "I think I will have to keep you from screaming, at least for a while. Open your mouth, little mate."

I opened my mouth, ready for his delicious cock. Instead, a piece of knotted fabric that tasted like Ardruc's scent filled my mouth. Oh, gods. I moaned.

His fingertips stroked my pussy, slipping over the slickness that dripped there. I gasped, the sound muffled by the fabric.

"Would you prefer to be able to scream?" he asked, stroking gently. "Or should I tie this fabric around your pretty mouth?"

"Tie it," I said, or tried to say. The words were indistinct.

With a chuckle and a puff of smoke that smelled so good I moaned, he did.

"Now this is a beautiful sight," he said. He bit my shoulder lightly and then laved it with his tongue. "You are trembling, little mate. But you are not afraid, are you?"

I shook my head. I wasn't afraid in the least—not with my dragon.

His fingers returned to my pussy. I moaned into the fabric as he caressed me and then dipped his fingertips into me.

"You are so aroused, little mate." His fingers slid from me and I heard him licking them. "You taste even more delicious now."

He pleasured me with his fingers, murmuring in my ear as I rode his hand. I gasped and groaned into my improvised gag.

"Come for me, beautiful Elena," he commanded, his other hand gripping my hair and pulling my head back just enough to hurt. "Come on my hand like a good little mate."

I screamed into the cloth and climaxed, shaking and crying out. He was right beside me the entire time, but I couldn't see him, couldn't see anything at all. Being so helpless and at his mercy made the orgasm even better somehow.

"Little mate, I wish you could see how beautiful you are when you come like that," Ardruc said, stroking my hair as I trembled. "I will see it every time I close my eyes."

His hand slipped from my pussy. I whimpered at the loss.

The shelter fell silent.

I turned my head to the right and left, trying to catch any hint of where Ardruc was or what he was doing, but I heard nothing. My muffled sound of protest earned a soft chuckle, but I couldn't tell where it came from.

"I am going to release your arms," Ardruc said into my left ear. "Do not move."

I nodded.

The vines loosened. I winced as I lowered my arms to my sides. They'd been stretched out just long enough to ache.

Ardruc's hot fingers massaged my right arm and then my left, banishing the twinges. I moaned in bliss.

"On your hands and knees now, little mate," he murmured in my ear when all the aches were gone. "And spread those beautiful legs for me."

Quivering and dripping, I did as I was told.

With vines, he tied my wrists and then my ankles in place. I imagined how I might look and wished I could see—wished we had something to record this for later. Hmm. Something to think about in the future.

"I am admiring the view, little mate," Ardruc said from behind me. "How lovely and wet you are."

A single fingertip delved along the cleft of my ass and traveled slowly until it reached my slit. I moaned into the cloth.

"Such a beautiful pussy," Ardruc said. "I need to fill it with my cum, little mate. I need to see my cum running down your legs. Do you want me to fill your little pussy until the cum drips down your thighs?"

I nodded.

"What about your pretty little ass, little mate?" The finger traveled back up and teased my asshole. "Do you want me to fill you here too until you overflow?"

I nodded even more vigorously, already panting with anticipation.

"Good." He rumbled, and I heard him stroking himself. The slick, heavy sound made me moan and gush. "What a good little mate you are, Elena."

I sensed him right behind me just before the thick head of his cock rubbed over my pussy. "Can you take me like this, little mate?" he asked. "Can this sweet little pussy take a big dragon cock?"

The thought of being stretched by his cock made me shiver hard. I nodded. "Yes," I tried to say around my gag. "I can take you."

Somehow he understood. "You *will* take me," he said, and the way he said it—as a statement of fact—made me moan louder. My slickness dripped down my thighs.

His cock head rubbed along my slit again and again, and then pushed against my pussy. It felt enormous—bigger than before, though that wasn't possible. Did my blindfold and restraints make him feel larger? I cried out.

"Little mate, little mate," he crooned. "Take your dragon."

His cock head pushed inside me. Oh, gods—it felt so good to be stretched. I wailed.

Slowly and steadily he thrust, pushing deeper and deeper and stretching me so impossibly that I was screaming into my gag and shaking. I wanted more. I wanted all of him. I wanted him to fill me until I was shaped around him.

Something much larger nudged against my pussy. He rumbled and dug his fingertips into my hips. "Do you feel my knot, little mate?"

Breathing hard through my nose, I nodded.

"Do you know what that knot is for?" He withdrew and thrust deeply into me again so his knot bumped against my pussy. I wailed. "It is for you, little mate. My body made it for you and you alone to take." He bent over me and wrapped his hand gently around my throat. "But you will not get it until I fill your pussy and your ass on this bed. Do you understand?"

I nodded again emphatically and arched my back so I could take him better.

"My body changed form for you, Elena, just as your sweet pussy is learning to take my cock." He rumbled. "You are a dragon's true mate, my love. A dragon's most precious treasure."

He returned his hands to my hips and thrust shallowly until the ridges on his cock found my G-spot. I cried out.

"Ah, yes, that is what my little mate likes," he murmured, and rocked back and forth right in that spot. "Come on my cock, my love."

I came for my dragon, screaming into the gag and nearly falling over. Only his grip on my hips kept me up on my knees.

As I orgasmed, he thrust deeper and harder, drawing out every wonderful wave of pleasure and forcing me to dig my fingers into the moss and twigs of our bed for purchase.

"Elena," he groaned. I whimpered, desperate to be filled. "Little mate, little mate…" The words were like a song.

Growling, he wrapped his hand in my hair and his grip hurt so perfectly that I wailed into my gag.

One hot pulse at a time, his cum filled me and spilled over to run down my thighs just as he'd promised. I wanted to see it. I wanted to see *him*. I hated that I couldn't, and I loved it too.

I loved the way my dragon had held me while I raged and cried. I loved the way he tied me up with vines and his ripped shirt. I loved the way he gave me everything I wanted and needed when he filled me. I loved…

My dragon.

CHAPTER 26
ARDRUC

I FELT IT IN MY BONES WHEN SOMETHING CHANGED IN ELENA.

My hand was wrapped in her beautiful, silken hair. My cock was buried in her sweet pussy and my cum streamed down her legs, just as I had envisioned. Her pretty ass begged for me to stretch and fill it, and her orgasms had been as powerful and perfect as I had wanted them to be.

It was a tiny thing—a tension, or a little frisson that traveled through her body—but it rang in my soul like a bell. My hunger for her became softer. I had no other words for it than that.

I withdrew from her. Her gasp and exhale were sweet sounds.

My cock dripping and still heavy with need, I spread her ass with my hands, bent my head, and slipped the tip of my tongue into her perfect little asshole. Her moan was soft too.

Yes, something had changed, and whatever it was, it made me feel whole.

I stretched her gently and slowly, one worshipful press of my tongue at a time. Her little cries and moans ran over my body like caresses. I no longer wanted them muffled. I untied the torn piece of my shirt from around her mouth and let it fall to the ground.

"Dragon," she whispered, leaning back onto my tongue. "Please."

"You do not need to ask or beg, little mate," I said, replacing my tongue with my slick fingertips. "Everything you want, you will get."

She bowed her head and murmured *my dragon* in a tone I had not heard before.

I stretched her until she was ready for me. Then I eased her wrists and ankles out of the vines. Even freed, she stayed in place, waiting and beautiful and perfect.

I wrapped my arm around her waist and sat back on my heels, drawing her with me as I moved. "Sit on my tail, little mate."

The quiet, happy sound she made was perfect too.

I held my thrumming tail steady for her as she lowered herself onto its glistening tip. I had covered it with my lubrication and cum while I stretched her.

The sight of her ready to take me—the cum still dripping from her sweet pussy, her lovely stretched ass, her tousled hair hanging loose from its braid—made me ache with how much I loved her.

She slipped herself onto my tail with a gasp and a sigh. This was not at all how I had planned to take her, but it was more perfect than I could have imagined.

She took my tail slowly and gently, squeezing me as she slid up and down, easing it deeper into herself each time. I held her hips, taking her weight so she did not tire or go too far too fast.

Once she found her rhythm, she wrapped her hand around my cock and stroked as she moved. When she cupped and caressed my knot, our groans blended.

I held her still with one hand and used the other to pull off her blindfold.

She turned to look at me, her hair coming loose over her shoulders, face flushed, and eyes as blue as the sky. I had never in my life beheld anything or anyone as beautiful as my Elena.

I cupped her face and kissed her. "Is this good for you, little mate?"

"It's perfect, dragon," she said, her voice soft and expression dreamy. "Exactly what I want."

My chest rumbling and heaving, I kissed her again as her fingers stroked my cock, squeezing and turning, sliding up and down through the rivulets that dripped from its head. Every sensation was a divine symphony of unending pleasures.

She rode me like that for a long time—slowly, perfectly, rolling her hips and taking her pleasure while giving me my own. I admired everything about her, captivated by the way her muscles moved under her skin, the gleam of her perspiration, her little gasps and whimpers.

"You feel so good inside me," she said with a moan as she slid down again, taking my tail almost to its first frill and pausing there to rest. "A perfect fit. Like this is where I'm supposed to be."

"Yes." I cradled her hips where the bruises I had made earlier were already fading thanks to my healing saliva and cum. As much as I had loved making them at her request, I caressed them with my thumbs and willed them away. "And this is where I am supposed to be."

She arched her back and rolled forward to her knees. I moved with her, keeping my tail inside her. "I'd like you to come on my ass, now, dragon. I want to feel your cum run down my legs. It feels so good."

"Everything you want, you will get," I promised. "Come on my tail, little mate. Let me hear you call for your dragon."

Moaning my name again and again, she pleasured herself on my tail as I stroked myself in rhythm with her movements. Her voice rose in pitch as she neared her release. When I rubbed her clit and vibrated my tail, she came with a wonderful, almost operatic cry that took me over the edge with her.

With groans and growls, I covered her beautiful back, ass, and thighs with my cum. She gasped and trembled every time a hot stream of it splashed over her and dripped down her skin.

"Yes, dragon," she said, grinding on my tail to draw out her own orgasm. "Mark me as your little mate."

What could I do but obey?

When I was spent, we collapsed onto our sides on the mossy bed. I kissed her forehead and eased my tail from her still-fluttering ass. "Little mate," I murmured. "Perfect little mate."

She grabbed my hand and brought it to her mouth. "So delicious," she breathed. Her tongue swirled over my fingers. "Thank you."

"You do not need to thank me, my love. Everything I give you, I give with joy." I smoothed hair back from her face and tucked it behind her ear. "You are satisfied?"

"For now." She snuggled against my chest. "But not completely. Not until I get your knot."

"I am ready to share it with you." I tucked her head under my chin and draped my wing over her so she did not feel a chill. "You may have it whenever you wish."

"Give me a minute." She pressed her nose against my skin and inhaled. "I'm in recovery."

Knowing my scent was as much a comfort and a source of healing for her as hers was for me warmed my hearts and soul.

"There is no rush, Elena," I murmured into her ear. *"Epet mar ele'ana."*

She chuckled and kissed my chest, so perhaps I was forgiven for unfairly claiming victory in our bet.

I admired her as she rested…and wondered what had happened between us that had shifted the essence of our growing bond. Other than *softer* and *more powerful,* I could not quite identify the nature of the change, but it was undeniably even better and more comforting than before. I could not think of the right words to ask her what had changed, so I was forced to speculate.

Her scent seemed richer and more deeply content now, and my gut told me pleasure alone had not caused it. Perhaps she had accepted my love a little more. Maybe she felt more at home and treasured in my arms. Maybe she believed she was safe with me.

Having my true mate at my side was a source of endless comforts and wonders. What more could I do to ensure she felt the same?

My gut twinged. For all Elena had given me, she had asked only one thing in return: the truth about my painful past. She had shared her own without hesitation and shown me complete trust.

I trusted her with my hearts, body, and soul. So what held my tongue?

Fear of reopening old wounds? Perhaps. But what weighed heaviest in my gut were worse worries. She might think I had acted wrongly in leaving, and encourage or even expect me to contact my family to try and make peace.

I closed my eyes and drank in my mate's sweet scent.

No, that was not true. I did not fear she would think or say those things. Elena had made the difficult choice to break contact with her own parents. She would understand my struggles, perhaps more than anyone else.

The truth was much harder to swallow: that despite everything I had endured and my parents' demands that I return to Fortusia and the compound, *I* feared I had done wrong to flee and leave my brother behind.

Something within me cracked open and began to bleed guilt, grief, pain, and regret.

A sound escaped my clenched jaw: a whine like I had made last night when I had thought I had hurt Elena. It was brief and almost soundless, but it cut through the quiet of our shelter like a blade.

Elena raised her head, her eyes full of worry and brow furrowed. "Ardruc?"

My chest ached like I had been speared, and everything I wanted and needed to say stuck in my throat until I thought I might choke.

She took my face in her hands. "It's all right. I'm here." She kissed me gently. "I'm *here*," she repeated, more firmly. "Talk to me."

When I said nothing, she tucked my head against her chest over her own heart, wrapped her arms around me, and stroked my hair and feathers until the worst of the pain eased and I could breathe again…and find the courage to speak.

"When I was eight years old and my younger brother Nors was six," I rasped, "my parents sold all our possessions and moved us into a compound on Fortusia. It was owned by a man named…"

I swallowed hard. For eleven years, I had been forbidden to say the name of the sect leader, who considered his followers unworthy to speak it aloud. Even now doing so caused nausea, and not just because it conjured the darkest memories of my life. The indoctrination had proven far more difficult to shed than my chains.

"Pyru Harnda," I grated out finally. "My parents told us the enclave was a school and cooperative living community, but it was…a closed sect. A cult."

Elena pressed her lips to the top of my head. "Take your time," she murmured. "*Epet mar ele'ana.*"

For all my earlier teasing, I loved the softer way the vowels sounded in her mouth and the gentleness of her consonants versus the harsher plosives and affricates of Fortusian pronunciation. A simple phrase I had never thought I would use was poetry and music and a balm when she said it.

"One by one, almost my entire family fell under his influence," I said. "My father's parents, my father's brother and sister and their mates and children, and my mother's sister and her mate all followed my parents into the compound. Pyru and his inner circle were masters of manipulation and brainwashing. The only members of the family who saw him for who he was were my mother's mother, Luvia Husiorithae, and my brother and me."

Out of fear of how much pain they would cause, I had never spoken these words aloud before. And there *was* pain—a deep, profound ache that filled my chest and resonated through my entire body. But paradoxically there was relief too, and comfort that grew with every word as if I was relieving pressure or draining a wound.

"My parents, Olme and Earra, believed completely in Pyru's anti-science and anti-technology teachings," I said. "I was already interested in science, especially atmospheric science, by the time we moved to the compound. My brother wanted to captain a cargo ship or cruiser. He loved the technology of interplanetary flight. All that ended when we moved—or at least it was supposed to."

I took a deep, fortifying breath. "We had extremely limited technology in the compound and very little contact with the anything beyond its walls. All learning materials and communication with the outside world had to be approved by Pyru. The isolation was supposed to ensure we did not lose our way and become 'obsessed' with science and tech. For Pyru, what he called 'obsession with science and technology' was the source of all evil and suffering and misery." My mouth twisted. "It was rather an open secret that in his private home he had full access to anything he wanted. My parents saw nothing wrong with that hypocrisy. They never saw *anything* wrong with anything Pyru did or said. And if my brother or I did object, we were punished for it. Very severely."

With one hand, Elena cradled my head to her breast. And with the other she caressed my wing, gentle and soothing.

"Nors was better at feigning obedience and belief than me," I continued. "Or maybe I should say I was more openly defiant. I wanted everyone to see how manipulative and wrong Pyru was, so I rarely held my tongue. For the first three or four years, I still had hope my parents would see the truth about Pyru and our whole family would leave. I thought if I pointed out the inconsistencies and all the ways he mistreated everyone, especially Nors and me, our parents would realize they loved us too much to let the abuse continue. But eventually I had to accept Pyru's hold was too strong. It was a bitter and difficult realization."

"I cannot imagine." Elena stroked her fingers through my hair, working out tangles. The sensation was heavenly. "How did your brother handle it?"

I sighed. "Nors did not want to hurt our parents by resisting, so he stopped rebelling and even accepted some of what Pyru taught. After that, I could no longer trust him to keep anything I said between us. I had no one to confide in and no support."

"What about your mother's mother?" she asked. "Did you say her name was Luvia?"

My hearts twinged. "Yes. She was not part of the sect, so we only saw her rarely. And only with one of Pyru's inner circle present to watch and listen." The memory of those meetings—of my desperate need for her to hug me and bring me little gifts I could treasure, all under the watchful eyes of Pyru's hand-picked minders—burned in my gut like coals.

"Luvia gave me my lat'sar for my tenth birthday," I said with a fleeting smile. "I was surprised I was allowed to keep it, but Pyru granted permission as long as I only played music he composed, and played for him whenever he asked."

"Gods above," Elena muttered. She stroked my cheek with her thumb. "I'm very glad you received that lat'sar, Ardruc. I can well imagine it was one of the few comforts you had."

"It was. When I played, it felt like Luvia was with me. I did not feel so alone."

I went quiet for a while, drinking in Elena's scent and the softness of her skin. As bad as those early memories were, the most difficult part of the story was yet to come.

"The years passed," I said finally. "Nors and I grew from children to adolescents. For us, it was a long, unending nightmare. My parents were so happy there, or at least they seemed to be, and that made it worse. Nors was very quiet and I was miserable. As is often the case in such environments, Pyru's views became more and more extreme, and his punishments more severe. He began disciplining our entire family when I did not obey him without question. By then, I cared less about my parents because they had brought this on us, but I did not want my brother to suffer. I finally began to pretend to accept some of Pyru's teachings and followed the rules, at least outwardly, for Nors's sake. I did not break, but I feared I might if I did not find a way to escape, even if it meant leaving my parents behind."

Elena settled my head on her breast again. "And Nors?"

"I hoped Nors would leave too, but I could not discuss it with him. He would have told my parents, and they would have alerted Pyru. Any chance of being able to escape would be gone then. I would be caged. It had happened before to others who had wings."

Elena's anger had grown steadily as I recounted my time at the compound, but she seemed to be able to set it aside to focus on comfort and gentle caresses. I was more grateful for that than I could have said.

I took a breath that nearly rattled in my chest. "There was, as you might have guessed, a breaking point. Just before my nineteenth birthday, Pyru announced I would be wed to another young person within the group named Aora. I barely knew her, other than she and her family were true believers in Pyru's teachings. I was expected to marry her and have children—as many as Pyru decided we should have. The marriage was to take place when we both reached nineteen years of age, which he considered to be the ideal age for marriage and for the first of our children to be born."

Elena's embrace tightened. "No," she breathed. "Oh, Ardruc. Gods, that is horrific. Forced to marry and father children against your will. What did Aora think?"

I smiled, but without mirth. "Initially, neither she nor her parents were pleased. My longtime resistance to Pyru's teachings was no secret. But my parents and others insisted I would accept my role once we were wed and Pyru's word was law, so she accepted it without question. The night of the announcement, I made plans to get away, with or without my brother. I could only hope he would see my escape as an inspiration and leave as well."

She brought my hand to her mouth and kissed it. She could probably tell from my tone that was not what happened.

"I knew I would only get one chance, so I had to wait until the right time and I could not fail," I said. "A few weeks later, my opportunity came. A severe storm occurred during a late evening meeting of the inner circle and senior adherents. A power fluctuation lowered the intensity of the perimeter forcefield. I stuffed a few things in a bag and grabbed my lat'sar and slipped out of our house. Someone must have seen me and hit the alarm. As I flew over the wall and made it through the forcefield, someone fired a plasma gun several times." I raised my wing to show her a spot where the feathers grew at an odd angle. "Luckily, my only injury was a mild burn and some scorched feathers. Whoever fired was a poor shot."

I did not say so because my mate already trembled so badly, but getting through the forcefield had given me a severe shock and left burns and numbness on my hands, feet, and face. I would not have made it through at all if it had been at full power.

Elena's hand shook as she caressed my face. "What did you do once you made it over the wall?"

"I wanted to put as much distance between myself and that place as I could, so I flew almost nonstop for four nights and slept in parks or preserves during the day." I breathed in her scent to settle my churning stomach. "It may seem strange because I was very afraid of being caught and dragged back, but those were good days. I was breathing free air and every choice I made was my own." I put my hand on hers where it rested on my cheek. "It was sweet freedom."

"You know, I wish I could coo," Elena said suddenly with a scowl. "It's not fair that I can't."

Her almost petulant tone made me chuckle and lightened my heavy hearts. "Little mate, you do not need to coo. Just being near you, basking in your scent, touching your skin, hearing your voice, is all I need."

She gathered me to her chest again and pressed little kisses into my hair. "So you flew for four nights…?"

"Yes. Once I reached a port city in another province, I found someone who could arrange to get me off-planet. I left Fortusia a week later as a laborer on a cargo carrier bound for Valodia. I have not returned to Fortusia in fifteen years."

"And your brother?" she asked.

"Nors did not leave." I squeezed her hand. "I found out later that after my departure Pyru betrothed him to Aora. They wed when he was twenty, according to public record. They had three children." I took a deep breath that hurt. "My father, Olme, sent a message four months ago to tell me Nors had died. That was the first I had heard from him in more than a decade."

Elena's sharp intake of breath made me raise my head. Her eyes blazed with fury and shimmered with unshed tears. She cupped my face in both hands. "Ardruc."

Her voice, like her scent and the tender way she embraced me, held all her care for me, and all her grief and anger and sympathy too.

Her warmth gave me the courage to say, "Olme told me Pyru wants me to return and wed Aora in place of my brother, as if I would ever let that man make the most important choice of my life for me. The message was forwarded several times between my former employers and labs until it arrived at the Ministry on Nyvor. It just happened to reach me the day you came to Nova Cal."

"Oh, gods." Her tears spilled over. "I couldn't have timed my arrival worse if I'd tried."

"No, no." I pressed my forehead to hers. "That day I thought the same, but I have come to understand what made me think so was my pain and all these memories I buried. In my hearts I know you arrived at precisely the right moment. I am deeply sorry I took so long to understand that and accept the miracle of you."

Despite her tears, her expression turned wry. She sniffled. "I'm no miracle, dragon. Don't be ridiculous."

With her thumbs, she wiped away the wetness under my eyes. "You would have no way to know this, but I was originally supposed to arrive at Nova Cal two days earlier," she said. "There was an accident on Aloris that ended up delaying my departure due to medical reasons." Her mouth quirked. "So was I late getting here, or on time?"

"I still say you were on time." I frowned, recalling her offhand comment from yesterday about a piece of wreckage blown across the ice. "An accident? What kind of accident?"

Elena waved my words away with a casualness that did not match her flinch. "Another time, dragon. We're talking about you."

She rested her forehead on mine, took a deep breath, and clasped my hand in of both her much-smaller ones. "You made the right choice leaving the compound, Ardruc. I can't imagine how hard that was for you, or how much you suffered there, or how much you've suffered since. But what I *do* know is you knew then what was right and I am so, so glad you followed that instinct and didn't let those people take any more from you than they already had."

The conviction in her voice and the fierceness of the way she gazed into my eyes told me she meant every word. Elena was brilliant and wise and intuitive, and when I did not trust my own gut, I knew I could trust hers.

"I am so deeply sorry for the loss of your brother." She reached up to smooth hair out of my eyes and tuck it behind my ear before taking my hand again. "I know this is something you'll struggle to accept because I would feel the same, but he made the decision to stay just as you made the choice to leave. There are *many* people at fault for his death, but none of them are you."

She squeezed my hand again. "You need to let yourself grieve for him and for your parents too. And you are allowed to be angry at them even while you grieve. It's not one emotion or the other. That's not how brains work." She managed a little smile. "Even dragon brains."

My beautiful, brilliant Elena.

I bowed my head. "I can bear to think about all this now because you are here. You cannot imagine how much that means to me."

She tilted my chin up with her fingertips so she could look into my eyes. "You said you know in your hearts I came to Nova Cal at the right time. Well, I believe that too, and not just because I'm your true mate. I needed to find you too." Tears welled again in her beautiful blue eyes. "And we are the right people to help protect this world. The Vorsa know it. So do I, and so do you. That's why you've known all along we would be all right. You had a *gut feeling.*"

My hearts seemed to swell until they pressed against my ribcage. "Elena…" I tried to pull my hand out of her grasp to touch her face, but she held on with startling strength.

Another frisson passed between us, stronger and more profound than before. Quiet and peace filled my hearts.

"You already claimed my body and my heart," she said, her voice trembling. "Now you have my soul too. Take care of it, dragon."

Oh, my Elena. I had no words worthy of such trust.

The few inches between us suddenly felt like too much distance. I sat up and pulled her onto my lap so she was in my arms with her legs around my waist and her chest pressed to mine. I buried my face against the side of her neck and lost myself in the wonder of her.

We stayed like that for a long time. In her arms, in this place, minutes and hours meant little or nothing to me. I was taking time away with my mate.

At Pyru's bidding, my parents would have denied me this joy. They would have forced me to wed a woman I did not know, did not love and would never love, who was not my true mate. And they would have done so happily, secure in their belief they had done the right thing, and ignored my misery—while their leader basked in the power he had over his followers and those he had trapped.

Elena was right; I had made the correct choice to flee. Leaving had been my first step on my long journey to her. That knowledge began to heal hurts that had festered for a very long time.

When Elena stirred, the sun was no longer overhead. "You feel quieter," she murmured, her lips against my chest. "More at peace.

And you smell even more like smoky Bacorian brandy." She chuckled and rubbed her nose above my hearts. "I may even start to like the stuff."

"I do not doubt you, but I still do not smell brandy," I confessed. "All I smell is you."

"What do I smell like?" she asked curiously.

"From the moment we met, you have smelled of rich soil and lush plants and growing things." I caressed her silky hair. "That scent has only become stronger during your time here. But now you also smell of contentment…and me."

"Which makes perfect sense. I'm full of both, and I like it that way." She kissed my chest. "In fact, I want to be filled some more."

Her head resting on my shoulder, she found my cock and stroked it gently and evenly. In moments, it swelled, hardened, and beaded with lubrication. My entire body thrummed and rumbled with need.

The straining sensation at the base of my cock and the urge that accompanied it were still new feelings, but unlike last night and earlier today, they were a quiet needs. *Patient* needs. Needs only Elena could sate.

My hearts, body, and soul belonged to her, and hers to me. And whether we stayed on Vorsa World or left for some other planet or moon, we would be home.

"Dragon," Elena said softly, still caressing, still gentle. "You said everything I want from you, I can have."

"Yes, my love." I puffed smoke against her ear and enjoyed her little shiver. "Anything you want is yours. Tell me what you desire."

"I want your knot," she said. She raised her head and met my gaze with her own equally hungry one. "And I want to be claimed like a dragon's mate—in the sky."

CHAPTER 27
ELENA

I expected Ardruc to refuse—to tell me it wasn't safe, he wasn't used to flying with me yet, I was too precious to him to risk it. And I was prepared to argue until I got my way.

Instead, he scooped me up, rose from our mossy bed, and took me outside the shelter. The curtain of vines over the doorway drew aside for us.

When we looked skyward, the canopy of leaves parted with a shiver and a sigh to reveal a breathtakingly beautiful late afternoon sky.

"Arms around my neck and legs around my waist," Ardruc said, his lips pressed to my ear. "And whatever you do, do not let go."

My heart pounded so loudly he could have heard it all the way back at the station. "Never," I promised.

He spread his beautiful wings, wrapped his tail around my left thigh and his arms around my back, and leapt into the air.

We rose above the forest canopy in just a few flaps of his powerful wings. Instead of flying toward Nova Cal, he flew away from the station along the mountain's slope, staying a few meters above the treetops. I tilted my head back, closed my eyes, and breathed deeply to let the fresh, clean air fill my lungs and soul.

When we were around the mountain and out of sight of the station, Ardruc banked, turned, and flew out over the valley. The treetops fell away, and suddenly I found myself soaring through nothingness, surrounded by only fresh mountain air and Ardruc's arms.

My cry of wonder and amazement ended abruptly when he kissed me. "Ardruc. My dragon." I gasped the words into his mouth.

As he rumbled, I wrapped one hand around his dripping cock between us and stroked. His beautiful wings didn't miss a beat, but a shiver ran through his body.

"Take my cock, little mate," he said into my ear, his arms and tail so strong around me. "Claim your dragon in the sky."

Whimpering and gasping, I rubbed the head of his cock against my clit and my slit, coating it in my slickness and driving myself closer to a climax. Smoke swirled from his nose and his eyes glowed.

I positioned his cock at my entrance just as his teeth closed on the side of my neck near my shoulder. I moaned. "Dragon…"

He gripped me tightly with his arms and tail and thrust, burying himself halfway in a single movement. My wail echoed through the valley.

"Yes," he breathed. "Yes, take my cock, Elena. Take it all."

I moved against his grip, crying out as I worked to take him deeper. At this angle, the ridges of his cock stroked over my G-spot each time he thrust. And his knot bumped against me, a promise of the pleasures still awaiting me.

We were terrifyingly far above the treetops, and yet I trusted Ardruc with my life. The rush was beyond anything I could have imagined, and it drove me toward bliss as much as his cock. I gasped against Ardruc's shoulder and sank my teeth into his bicep.

Ardruc groaned into my ear. "Come for me, little mate. Squeeze my cock."

He changed his angle just slightly, pulling out farther and driving deeper once, twice…

I climaxed with a scream. He held me against his chest, rumbling and puffing smoke from his nostrils as I shook and wailed and gushed on his thick dragon cock.

"Yes, like that," he murmured. "Just like that."

An enormous korae burst across the sky in a dozen colors. A coincidence? Or did was the planet joining in with our lovemaking again?

More bursts of color and power blossomed far above us in the atmosphere, but Ardruc the atmospheric scientist had eyes only for me.

"You come so beautifully for your dragon, little mate," he said in my ear. "You have claimed me in the sky. And now it is my turn."

His knot pushed against me—so big, so impossibly big. I wailed.

"I am going to give this to you now," he said, his hand twisted into my hair in the way that made me gush for him. "I am going to knot my beautiful little Elena and pump her full of cum. And you will keep every drop of it inside you until we are back on the ground and I can watch it drip from you."

"Yes." Gasping, I held him more tightly. "Please give me your knot, dragon. I need it so badly."

"Yes, you do." His teeth grazed my ear. "You need to take your dragon into your sweet pussy all the way to his balls."

He cooed. Even in the sky, he had to for me to take his knot. And that meant my body went soft and pliant.

I managed to lace my fingers together to keep my arms around his neck, but my strength was a fraction of what it had been moments ago. If it were not for his iron grip and my trust in him, I would have been afraid of falling.

Even after his coo, his knot was so big that every thrust stole my breath away. But I took it all, because he was my dragon and his body was made to fit to mine. And nothing felt as good as when he was fully inside me and he was *mine*.

His knot swelled, locking us together. His breathing turned heavy and fast, and his eyes glowed as he looked deeply into mine.

And just like the first time I'd taken his knot, I felt the full, over-whelming force of his love and devotion.

Growling and rumbling, he came powerfully but not as roughly as he had in bed last night. With his arms wrapped around me and his hips jerking and thrusting, he drove me back over the edge with him. His shouts and my cries rolled through the valley.

"My mate," he rasped into my ear as he shuddered with the last of his releases. "My beautiful mate. My Elena."

Gasping and trembling and so wonderfully full of him, I rested my head against his chest.

He banked and soared over the treetops, following the course of a narrow river that wound through the mountains before plunging over a waterfall about six kilometers from Nova Cal.

I had traveled this route in a transport coming and going from foraging trips and hiked to the waterfall with Forux a half-dozen times, and never once imagined flying it with Ardruc—much less with his cock and knot inside me.

I couldn't help it; I laughed.

He kissed my temple. "Share the joke, my love?"

When I explained, he chuckled and nuzzled my windblown hair. "If you see any fungi you feel you must collect, tell your dragon and I will land."

"I'm facing the wrong direction, and I can't see much from up here," I pointed out. "We'll have to do this again when I'm facing the ground."

He chuckled again, this time in a much lower register. "Yes, we will, little mate." He kissed me. "I will take you quite happily from behind."

I quivered at the thought. Oh, yes—I wanted that too. Repeatedly.

We had a lot to think about: how to approach the Alliance about the Vorsa and the Nyvorans' illegal removal of natural resources, whether to accept the Vorsa's request for us to become caretaker-listeners for their world, whether to accept and keep their tattoos that granted full sensation of this miraculous world…and so much more. The future of this world and our role in it was not at all certain. I wasn't even sure yet what our first step should be.

But whatever we did, we would do it together.

Ardruc banked one last time in a wide circle and headed in the direction of Nova Cal—or rather in the direction of our forest shelter. I still wasn't ready to walk back into the station and face the grim reality of the decisions before us, but I might be once Ardruc and I enjoyed a bit more *time away*.

In the meantime, I held on to my dragon and let him fly us home.

Home. I wanted this world to be our home more than ever, if only we could figure out how to protect it.

As we rounded the last mountain slope and the station and clearing came into view, I peered up over Ardruc's shoulder, hoping to catch a glimpse of another korae.

Instead, I spotted a small, dark gray ship slicing through the sky directly at us. A Nyvoran transport? No, the shape and markings were all wrong.

Fear turned me cold. "Ship!" I shouted. "Ardruc, a ship!"

Hissing, he whipped his head around to look.

Then he crushed me against his body, folded his wings, and dove toward the forest canopy. I screamed, the sound muffled by his chest and the wind.

With a high-pitched engine sound, the ship pursued. Weapons fired behind us—a strange, dull noise that sounded nothing like any plasma cannon or ballistic weapon I knew. Something whizzed past that looked like a black cloud full of blue sparks. What the hells was that?

Ardruc twisted in midair and dove to his right, away from the cloud. This time I was too breathless to scream.

The treetops approached at a horrifying speed, but Ardruc didn't slow down at all. If he didn't pull up, we were going to crash right into the branches.

A second blast came from behind us. I watched over Ardruc's shoulder as another black cloud—this one on a long tether—came right at us. And this time, they didn't miss.

A crackling net closed around us and cinched tight.

The give in the tether was so minimal that when it went taut, we hit the webbing almost as hard as if we'd hit the ground.

My right elbow and knee gave with a nauseating crunch. Agony whited out my vision right before my body went numb. I felt a wrench and dull pain as if the force of the impact had yanked Ardruc free of my body, but everything was gray and hazy so I couldn't tell what had happened.

Something jolted through me—a sizzle of power that stole the breath out of my lungs and made my body seize. The heavy weight next to me must be Ardruc. I tried to reach for him but couldn't open my eyes or get my arms to move.

I only knew we were swaying in midair because my stomach lurched in a way I recognized. I moaned.

Another sickening lurch, and now I felt pressure against the webbing beneath me. We were being hoisted.

My eyelids weighed a thousand kilograms each, but I got them open.

Far above us, a dark shape—the ship—was silhouetted against the sky. The black netting we lay in sparked and pulsed every few seconds. A stun net. That explained the shocks and partial paralysis.

Ardruc's face appeared above mine. It was swollen and discolored on one side and violet blood dripped from his nose. Oh, my dragon.

"Elena," he rasped. The sound of his voice was barely audible over the ringing in my ears, but it was enough to help clear my head.

I had no idea who was trying to capture us or why, but whatever was happening, I was not going to let them get away with this any more than I was going to give up and die on the ice of Aloris when everything went to shit.

I just had to give myself a chance. I had to give *us* a chance. And we did not have to fight alone.

I closed my eyes and reached for the threads that had shared warmth and welcome, anger and grief, and even pleasure and need with us. And I *pulled* with all my might.

My senses widened, and even with my eyes closed I saw all of the living, breathing Vorsa World and the beautiful silver-blue threads pulsing around and through us.

Help us, I willed into the web of threads.

A blast of icy wind rolled over us from above. The ship's engine raised in pitch. We lurched and swayed violently. My stomach threatened to rebel.

When I opened my eyes, it was just in time to see a dozen Vorsa converging on the tether and net from all directions.

Ardruc followed my gaze and stared in amazement. And then horror. With a guttural sound, he wrapped me in his arms. It hurt, but I had no time and no energy to gasp, much less scream.

A green Vorsa—maybe Ka, but I couldn't say for sure—blazed brightly and sliced through the net where it dangled from the tether.

The net opened, and we fell.

CHAPTER 28
ARDRUC

ELENA'S SCREAM RANG IN MY EARS AS WE PLUMMETED TOWARD THE trees.

I was dazed by the stun net and still so numb in my arms and legs that I could barely hold on to my mate. But every fiber of my being narrowed to a single thought: *Elena.*

With a bellow of agony, I clutched her to my chest and spread my aching wings, desperate to slow our fall. To give us even a *chance* to survive.

This much pain and weakness meant our impact with the net had sprained muscles and torn ligaments in my back and shoulders. At least the partial numbness made the agony bearable.

I was in no shape to fly, especially while carrying the weight of another person—even a small one. But the fact I could not fly like this did not stop me from trying.

I set my jaw, tucked Elena's head under my chin and wrapped my tail around her legs, and sort-of glided, sort-of flew, but mostly fell toward the forest canopy.

All around us, the air hummed. As we approached the treetops, the ground rolled and the trees rustled and swayed, webbing together vines and slim branches thick with leaves to form a cradle.

I had no time to wonder if Elena was doing this or if the Vorsa and their world knew we needed to be saved.

A few meters above the trees, I turned in the air to take the impact, folded my wings, and dropped us into the waiting branches.

The web of vines bowed and bounced to absorb most of the force of the impact, but gods above, did it hurt. I grunted and Elena cried out in pain.

That web gave way, dropping us a meter or so to another. We fell from one leafy cradle to the next, slowing more with each short drop.

Finally, I landed on my back on a tall, thick bed of moss with Elena huddled on my chest. The final impact was far more gentle than the first, but it knocked what little air I still had from my lungs. The trees shivered one last time, and then everything went still.

The next sound I heard was Elena's rough gasp. "Ardruc." Trembling and whimpering in pain, she rolled from my chest to the moss and leaned over me. "Dragon. Say something."

She was bruised and bloody and her right elbow was bent in an unnatural direction. The stun net had left its pattern seared into her skin. But I had never seen a lovelier or more miraculous sight than my Elena alive after falling from the sky.

Tears streaked her face and her eyes with their new, beautiful, bright blue-green rings were wild with anger and fear.

She raised my hand to her swollen cheek. "Ardruc, *please.*"

I caressed her cheek, careful not to touch her wounds. "You have not lost your dragon." My voice was hoarse. "And I did not lose my little mate."

She sagged in relief and kissed my forehead. "All the gods above and below, I'm going to kill whoever is in that ship."

I caught a flash of purple out of the corner of my eye just before Forux launched himself onto our mossy bed and into Elena's lap. She winced but wrapped her good arm around him and buried her face in his fur.

I wanted to cradle them both but I hurt too badly to move yet. Instead, I focused on breathing and figuring out if I had any broken bones.

"What is going on?" Elena asked finally. When she raised her head, the glowing rings in her eyes had faded. "Who would do this to us? The ship isn't Nyvoran, I don't think, but are they behind it?"

With a groan, I blocked out the pain as best I could and sat up. My vision grew hazy for a moment, then cleared.

"It is not the Nyvorans," I grated. "That ship is from Fortusia."

Her expression went cold as she came to the same conclusion I had the moment I spotted the markings on the ship's hull. Forux growled, all four of his ears flat against his head.

"They sent someone after you." Elena's voice was quiet, even, and supremely dangerous. And were the circumstances different, I might have found it extremely arousing. "Mercenaries, maybe. But why?"

"To take me back, perhaps," I said. "If they had intended to kill me, they could have shot us out of the sky."

"Instead, they netted us and damn near killed us both doing it." Her eyes narrowed. "If they came just for you, why net me too? I wonder what they planned to do with me."

I did not want to imagine what might have befallen her if we had not been able to escape the net. Those thoughts led to a black hole of rage that made my skin buzz.

Elena squeezed my hand. "They didn't get us, and they *won't*." Blinking rapidly, she shook herself and scanned the woods. "Which direction is the station? I'm disoriented."

I tilted my head and pointed. "I believe it is that way."

"Good. Let's go get weapons and clothes. I want to get dressed before I go shoot these bastards." She yawned. "No, on second thought, I'll just wound them. We'll need them to find out who sent them."

My Elena. Woe to anyone who crossed her.

When we started to rise from our mossy bed, Elena flinched and doubled over, her hand pressed to her lower abdomen. "Oh, that hurts," she gasped.

I stilled. "What hurts?"

"Here." Her hand moved between her thighs. It came away smeared with blood. She swallowed hard and met my gaze. "From when your knot was pulled from me."

Horror, guilt, and rage turned me cold.

The numbing effect of the mercenaries' stun net had masked most of the pain when the impact caused our bodies to abruptly separate before my knot eased. I had been unable to provide the comforts and physical effects of my coo. My cock ached as a result, but no more than the rest of my battered body. I scarcely noticed that discomfort over the agony radiating from my back and shoulders.

With a moan, she slumped against me. Caught between fury and panic, I cradled her in my arms as she blinked up at me, her eyes half-lidded.

"Suddenly, I'm so sleepy," she breathed. "Am I concussed? What…what's happening to me?"

Terror made my heartsbeats thunder in my ears, but whatever part of my brain was still capable of rational thought supplied the answer.

"You are injured," I said, cupping her face. "My cum is healing you. The need to sleep as you heal is a known side effect, designed to conserve energy while you recover."

"Oh." The word was barely audible. Her eyes drifted closed. "I'm…sorry I can't stay…awake and…shoot them."

"Please do not apologize." I pressed my lips to her forehead. "Sleep. I will keep you safe while you recover. And I will not leave your side for one moment."

A fleeting smile turned up the corners of her lips. "I know."

In her next breath, she was fast asleep. Forux whined and pawed at her arm.

"She will be all right," I promised, my voice confident though my hearts were sick with worry and guilt. "I will protect her with my life."

I struggled to rise from the mossy bed with Elena in my arms. My back and shoulders protested every movement and my left knee was swollen and discolored.

As I got to my feet, the trees rustled and closed overhead to block every sliver of daylight. A moment later, the sound of a ship's engine reached us. It sounded like the mercenaries were flying low and slow over the forest.

The trees could hide us from view, but the ship was sure to have scanners. I must get Elena and Forux to Nova Cal and arm myself.

With a sprained knee, I could not run. The damage to my back and shoulders meant I would not be able to fly carrying my mate and her arval. Very briefly, I considered hiding them in the forest shelter while I tried to reach Nova Cal, but my stomach rebelled at the thought of leaving them unguarded.

So I made my way unsteadily through the forest toward the station with Forux ahead of me, all his ears on alert and fur bristling.

I walked as quietly as possible, moving parallel to the clearing and listening for anything out of place. The forest was eerily silent without even a hint of a breeze to rustle leaves, as if it knew I needed to be able to hear danger. And it very well might know. Even now, consumed with anger and worry, I was astounded by how miraculous and wondrous of a world this was.

Just as I glimpsed the clearing and Nova Cal through the trees, the ground rumbled, throwing me off-balance. I staggered and nearly fell until I braced myself against a sturdy tree.

The rumbling grew. The forest hummed and swayed. Plasma weapons fired, and then the sounds cut off abruptly.

One by one, bright, shimmering Vorsa emerged from the trees and lined up along a path that led directly to the clearing. Slowly, I made my way past them. My fury and worry about Elena's injuries made my skin blaze and hands shake.

I did not care about my own nakedness other than I wished I had a weapon, but I did not want anyone to see Elena without clothes. I had nothing to cover her and that made my hearts sick.

And it was surely the least of our concerns at the moment, but these attackers had brought an abrupt and terrible end to our first knotted coupling in the sky and I hated them for that too.

When I emerged from the trees, I was astonished to find the clearing around Nova Cal was much larger than before. A dozen Vorsa had gathered and more emerged from the forest.

The small interplanetary ship was too large for the station's landing pad and had landed instead in the newly expanded clearing, which had not been large enough to accommodate it before. It had been a trap set by the Vorsa and their world.

Apparently, the planet had waited until the ship's heavily armed pilot and copilot—two Fortusian males as tall as me, one with reptilian features and the other covered with thick, shaggy fur—had disembarked to begin their hunt for us, and then the ground had swallowed the ship entirely.

The forest had strung up the trespassers, wrapping them in vines and branches and leaving them suspended two meters off the ground. The remains of two plasma guns and several nasty-looking daggers lay in the grass beneath them, melted by the Vorsa into almost unrecognizable lumps.

The Vorsa encircled the ship and its pilots, hovering in place and shimmering with pulses of what might have been carefully controlled rage. A green tendril I believed was Ka floated directly between us and the intruders.

"What the fuck is going on?" the reptilian male bellowed in Fortusian. Like his companion, he wore a stained coverall and several empty weapons holsters. "Release us!"

Forux bared his teeth and growled. He was perhaps the least deadly being in this clearing, but I could not fault him for his courage.

"Who sent you?" I asked in Fortusian. The language felt and sounded strange in my mouth.

The reptilian male spat in my direction. "Our clients pay for confidentiality." So someone *had* hired them.

I shrugged, though it hurt. "Suit yourself." I turned to Ka. "Guard them, please," I said in Alliance Standard, since I did not know if the Vorsa understood Fortusian. "If they attempt to free themselves or attack, you may remove one of their limbs each time they try."

Ka dipped once.

The intruders shouted curses in several languages as I carried Elena to the lift doors.

Just before I placed my hand on the scanner, the furry male shouted, "Your father sent us."

Stunned, I turned. "My *father* sent you? Why?"

The pilot hissed at his companion, but the furry male ignored him. "Rich man wants his asshole runaway son back, we don't ask why. We take the contract and go get him."

My back and shoulders radiated agony, but I did not want to put Elena down. I clenched my jaw and returned to confront the captives.

"My father is not wealthy," I said, my voice strained. "You have been misled."

He shrugged and winced when the branches squeezed tighter. "He paid our asking price without haggling. Premium rate to get it done fast and quietly." He scoffed and glared at the pilot. "This shit planet seemed quiet enough until we landed in a sinkhole."

"I didn't land in a gods-damned sinkhole," the pilot snarled. "The scanners would have detected it."

The other male snorted. "Looks like a sinkhole to me, asshole."

I had no patience for their squabbling. "Did you meet my alleged father in person?" I demanded.

"Of course not," the furry male snapped. "You think we got an office? We hear about a job through a friend of a friend, we get offered a contract, we take half the money now and the other half on delivery."

"Delivery to where?"

He spat at me. "Some place near Bar'uto. Said we would get the coordinates when we had the target."

Pyru's compound was twenty kilometers from Bar'uto. And I had a very strong suspicion who my supposed "wealthy father" really was.

"My *father* is destined to be disappointed," I told the mercenaries. "This is one contract you will not be fulfilling."

The pilot hissed and struggled against the branches, to no avail.

"You have two choices," I said. "One, I let this planet bury you *and* your ship so far underground no one will ever find you or know you were here."

The pilot hissed again. His companion snarled and displayed a mouth full of serrated teeth.

"Option two," I continued, "you board your ship, leave this planet, and do not come back. If you persist in trying to kidnap me, I guarantee you will die. This entire planet guards us."

"We are businessmen," the pilot rasped. "We don't like taking losses."

"Keep the money my *wealthy* father gave you as compensation, then," I said. "If your lives are not enough profit."

"We don't skip out on clients and take their money," he ground out. "In our business, that gets you a bad reputation. Or dead."

"You have a better chance of surviving taking your client's money than if you come back here." My back hurt so badly that it was difficult to think clearly. "I will leave you to discuss it. Should I check back in the morning?"

The pilot cursed again—this time in Hardanian. "Your father was right," he snarled. "You *are* an asshole."

I ignored him and carried Elena into the lift with Forux at my side. The doors closed, cutting off the pilot's tirade. Blessed silence.

I buried my face in Elena's hair, as desperate for her rich, earthy scent as I was to get her to the medbay. The smell of her blood and burns would haunt me all my life.

The only reasons I did not go back to the clearing and ask Ka to bury those heartless mercenaries alive were my need to tend to my mate's injuries and the knowledge she would not want them to suffer that fate, if only because they were our only link to the person who had hired them.

In the medical bay, I placed Elena into the emergency medpod. My own fluids would heal her, but more slowly than the medpod could. As much as it meant to me that I was made to heal her, I wanted her well again as quickly as possible. I also needed to know the extent of her injuries.

The broken arm, sprained knee, bruises, lacerations, and burns she had received from falling into the stun net turned my stomach, but scans revealed our abrupt separation had caused deep bruising and tears. None were very serious, but the intimate nature of those injuries and the knowledge I had caused them, albeit inadvertently, left me gutted.

As the medpod healed Elena's wounds, I wrapped a thermal blanket around my waist, brought a chair to her bedside, and sat.

Forux immediately jumped into my lap and curled up. I rested my hand on his thick fur. His rumbly purrs eased the churning in my stomach.

Once we were healed, I would take Elena to our apartment, wash away all the blood and dirt and grime on our bodies, and cradle her in bed while she rested. Until then, I would stay at her side as I had promised, cooing to comfort her and so she would know I was nearby.

But every time I closed my eyes, I saw her face at the moment the net gave way beneath us: the bright blue-green rings in her eyes that told me she was seeing all of Vorsa World and had likely reached out for help when we were captured, and her expression of pure terror when we fell. And every time that image flashed across my mind, I flinched and my stomach heaved.

Yes, I had gotten us down to the treetops safely, but I had not been able to spare her from utter terror. And I would not be able to banish her memories either, no matter how much I wanted to. I would not blame her if she never again wanted to fly with me.

But even as I thought that, I knew she would ask me to fly as soon as I was healed and able to carry her. Fierce Elena did not let fear keep her from doing what she wanted. She would want to replace these bad memories with better ones. I knew that as certainly as I knew my body, hearts, and soul belonged to her.

So despite today's horrors, I would count the hours until we could return to the sky.

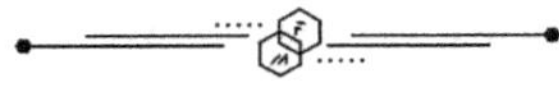

THE EQUIPMENT IN THE MEDICAL BAY HEALED MOST OF OUR PHYSICAL injuries in less than four hours.

Elena's broken arm and sprained knee and all our cuts, bruises, and burns healed most easily. The damage to muscles, tendons, and ligaments in my wings, back, and shoulders would require up to a month of recovery. I would likely not be able to fly with a passenger for at least two weeks. My hearts ached at the prognosis. Flying with Elena had become my greatest joy.

The pod also healed the injuries Elena suffered when we were forcibly separated. Even so, when she woke late that night from her healing sleep, she still ached and felt extremely tender. After another set of scans, the medbay's prognosis was that time and rest —and a break from physical activity and intimacy—would be required for a full recovery.

I made dinner in the kitchen and brought it to our quarters so we could eat in bed. Then I left the dishes stacked on the table in the living area, confirmed with a glance that the Vorsa still guarded our prisoners and nothing was amiss, and made the window opaque to block the view and tomorrow morning's early sunlight. My mate must get plenty of rest.

With Forux curled up at the foot of the bed, I held Elena against my chest with my wing draped over her and my tail coiled loosely around her calf.

"Elena—" I began.

At my tone, she raised her head and glared. "If you apologize one more time, I am going to own a pair of dragon-hide boots."

I closed my mouth.

Her expression softened. She cupped my face and stroked my jaw gently. I closed my eyes and focused on her touch and scent.

"This is not your fault for giving me your knot," she said for the third or fourth time. "It is also not your fault that you weren't able to hold on to me or coo when we hit the net. That was impossible. If it's anyone's fault, it's those men outside and whoever sent them."

She tapped my nose with her index finger as if I were an errant young dragon. "Don't take blame that doesn't belong to you. I won't let you."

Given the fierce way she stared me down, it was beyond my ability at the moment to defy her. I stroked her hair. "What can I do to help?"

Elena rested her head on my arm. "Well, the medbay has done what it can and now I just need time to heal. If that's what I have to do, so be it. But..." She raised her eyebrows. "Willing to try an experiment, Doctor? For science?"

"Not for science, but I am willing to do anything for you." I kissed her temple. "I am very much not a doctor of anything right now, Elena. I am just your dragon, and my hearts hurt for you." I stroked her soft cheek. "What would you like me to do?"

"I'm not quite healed yet, but maybe you can help with that." She laced our fingers together. "There are three basic options if you are willing to provide one of them."

I would do anything for Elena; there was no question about my willingness. She needed and wanted me to heal her. But as for the method...I felt at a loss.

Regardless of her assurances that she did not blame me, I could not bring myself to pleasure myself or to ask her to do so after what she had endured. And it was her body, not mine, so I did not think it should be up to me.

"I will let it be your choice," I said.

She studied me. "It's not that simple, though, is it?" she asked finally. "You're traumatized too by what happened to us. We both need to heal, just in different ways. So which choice would make your hearts hurt less?"

I was more grateful than I could articulate that she understood my indecision. "Saliva," I said. "Or blood."

"All right." She squeezed my hand. "I'm fine with either of those. And I'm grateful that you're willing."

"With all my hearts, I am more than willing." I pressed a kiss to her temple. "Let me care for you, Elena. It is what I am meant to do."

The pain in my chest eased now that I had a way to help. That was my purpose as Elena's mate. She healed me, and I healed her.

I moved down the bed, caressing her legs as I spread them. She did not wince, but I was careful not to strain any of her muscles or move too abruptly.

I settled in on my stomach, slid a pillow beneath her hips, and nuzzled her thigh. "Are you comfortable?"

"Yes." Her fingers twisted in the bedding. "I need you to be gentle."

"Always, my love," I promised. "Except when you ask me not to be."

She smiled. That smile was everything to me.

I studied my index finger, debating whether to bite and draw blood, and finally decided against it. Instead, I kissed her little patch of silky hair and opted to give her my tongue.

Very gently, I licked inside her, delving a little deeper with each press of my tongue.

"Ardruc," she breathed. "Thank you."

I was right, then. This was what she had wanted most of all.

She did not ride my face or moan and her hands stayed on the bedding rather than twist into my hair, just as I cradled her thighs and did not squeeze or growl. This was a different kind of worship, one my body was also made to do.

I laved her slowly, deeply, and thoroughly, listening for her sighs and sensing by her scent and little tremors where she ached most. Whenever she stroked my hair to wordlessly request a break, I rested my head on her thigh and focused on her heartbeat.

One loving touch at a time, I healed my mate and thanked every lucky star in the universe that I had the chance to do so.

I was not a violent man. I never had been. And yet I would have been capable of truly terrible acts if Elena had suffered a worse fate. Even now my gut churned and my hearts blazed with the need to make someone suffer for this.

I had come so very, very close to never holding this beautiful, brilliant, and breathtakingly perfect woman again. I knew who was responsible—or at least I believed I did—but not what I needed to do about it.

"Ardruc," Elena murmured, drawing my attention with a touch on the crown of my head. "I'm sleepy again. Is it pheromones or am I healing because of your saliva?"

"I suspect it is both." I kissed her inner thigh, marveling at its softness and how pliant her muscles were now. The sharp, metallic scent of her pain had faded. And with that, my stomach finally ceased churning. "And it is long past nightfall. Time for a dragon and his little mate to sleep."

She smiled, but it was fleeting. "Please hold me while we sleep. I'm afraid I'll dream about falling."

I feared she might too. "I promise I will hold you." I helped move her so she lay on her side facing my side of the bed, then drew her against my chest so I could tuck her head under my chin. "My love, feel my arms and tail around you. You are safe. I will make sure you do not fall."

She murmured something I did not catch, but it sounded like *thank you.*

Cooing, I draped my wing over us and settled in next to my sleeping mate. My pheromones would help grant her peaceful rest while she healed. Her presence would do the same for me.

As I listened to her soft, even breathing and Forux's little snores, I tried to focus on the miracle of my mate.

Instead, my mind conjured unwelcome memories of Pyru as I remembered him from fifteen years ago…and visions of him in his elegant house now, surrounded by sycophants, seething and plotting. Offering a contract to mercenaries and paying them a small fortune to drag me back to Fortusia in chains.

Why now, though, nearly five months after Nors died, and fifteen years after I left?

Perhaps sensing my uneasiness, Elena murmured against my chest. I cooed and stroked her hair until she quieted.

Moving slowly so I did not disturb her rest, I used my wrist-comm to do something I had not done since leaving my homeworld: I searched for information on Pyru Harnda.

The results arrived two minutes later via data relay from Fortusia. I stared at the screen for a long time.

The file contained a half-dozen images of Pyru taken by public scanners in cities near where we lived. He and some members of his inner circle had enjoyed complete freedom while the rest of us were trapped within the compound's walls. A familiar bitterness filled my mouth seeing him on the street, seemingly without a care.

In one image, he was laughing with a Fortusian man I did not recognize, but he might have joined after I left. I had never seen Pyru laugh a single time in the decade I had lived in the compound. If he had ever smiled, I did not recall that either. The image was jarring—but not nearly as jarring as the rest of the information.

Below the images, I found a brief biography culled from provincial records. As well as Pyru's educational and occupational background prior to founding the sect, it included a birth date... and a death date. The latter was a month ago.

The ground was kicked out from under my feet yet again.

Numbly, I searched for information on Nors. When the data arrived, it confirmed his death as having taken place nearly five months ago, around the time Olme had sent his message demanding my return.

If Pyru was dead, who the hells had sent these mercenaries? Surely my father did not have the means to do so, but I had no other possibilities in mind. And an inquiry into current leadership at the compound yielded no information.

My search for answers had led to more troubling questions. It was likely the only source of answers was Fortusia, the very place I did not want to go.

Nothing could be done now, so I switched off my wristcomm, closed my eyes, and nuzzled Elena's hair, drinking in her scent and willing my dreams to be of her and nothing else.

Even with my mate in my arms, it took a very long time for sleep to find me.

CHAPTER 29

ELENA

ARDRUC BROKE THE NEWS ABOUT PYRU'S DEATH TO ME JUST AFTER dawn, over breakfast in bed—the kind made in the kitchen, not the sort that involved restraints.

He made us bano fruit *crepec* and coffee and served the meal on his hand-carved Bacorian dishes. Forux got his meal in his regular bowl, but my little arval didn't seem slighted by not receiving an almost priceless serving dish.

I was very happy to wake pain-free and well rested, but Ardruc was noticeably antsy and even with his red-orange skin, he had shadows under his eyes.

Thankfully, his tension didn't seem to affect his appetite; his entire plate of food disappeared before I'd finished my first *crepec*. Then he set his dish aside and wrapped his arms loosely around my middle while I savored my meal.

"Elena," he said, his lips on my hair. "Whoever sent these mercenaries may send someone else if these men do not return."

I stabbed a piece of *crepec* with my fork with more force than was necessary. "Then we need to make it clear doing so would be a very bad idea."

He sighed. "I offered the mercenaries the choice to leave us alone, but I want to let the planet take them. You were so badly hurt. I almost lost you and they would not have cared."

"They tried to take you from me. I want revenge too." I made a face. "Or justice. The line between the two gets blurry, doesn't it?"

"Yes." He kissed the top of my head. "What should we do? I need your wisdom."

"Wisdom?" I sputtered. "I haven't even finished my coffee."

"My apologies." He put my mug into my hand. "Your scent changes when you drink coffee. It is a particular kind of contentment with a hint of coffee fragrance blended in. It is very pleasant." He nuzzled my tousled hair. "I will make it one of my priorities to see you never go without."

"Oh, that is just *shameless* bribery, dragon." I took a long, appreciative drink of the beverage in question. He'd mastered my preferred method of preparation already. "Food, coffee, forehead kisses, *and* orgasms...you must really want me to be your little mate."

"I do." He took my hand and kissed it. "I am not above bribery to ensure you are happy at my side...or at the very least, happy in a lab just down the hall from mine." He gently bit my fingertips. "I would like to marry you, Elena."

My coffee went down my windpipe. He took my mug and steadied my plate on my lap as I coughed.

"I am sorry," he said earnestly. "I should have waited until you finished your meal, but I realized during the night I have asked you to adopt the customs of my homeworld without offering you the same. I have been selfish. I am anxious to remedy the situation."

Gods above. I wheezed. He rubbed my back.

"How much sleep did you actually get last night?" I croaked finally. "You said you sleep well when we're together, but instead of resting, you stayed up thinking about our guests outside, the situation on Fortusia, and..." I waved my hand and coughed again. "Proposing marriage over breakfast?"

"I had a much more restless night than I expected." Ardruc

kissed my hair. His eyes glowed so beautifully in the early morning light. "But I did sleep well after I researched mating rituals on Fyloria and discovered a way to make myself even more *Elena's dragon*. That is the title and role I treasure most."

Oh, hells. I hadn't even finished my coffee and he wanted wisdom *and* to marry me.

Rumbling in what seemed like a mix of contentment and anticipation, he tucked my head under his chin. "Finish your meal and your coffee," he murmured. "I will wait."

Forux gobbled the last of his breakfast, stretched, and lay down next to my leg so he could rest his chin on my shin. He stared at me expectantly, all his ears tipped forward and tails fanned out on the bed.

I ate my *crepec*, drank my coffee, and thought.

My parents, for all their unusual attitudes, had married in the traditional Fylorian way. On the rare occasions when they spoke about the experience, my father beamed and my usually reserved mother had softened and smiled in a way I rarely saw otherwise. I knew about the ritual, of course, but since it was always done privately and I'd never been married, I'd never seen it performed.

The kind of long-distance marriage my parents had was not what I wanted, but I had nothing against the practice. I'd simply never considered it a likely outcome for myself. I didn't live on Fyloria and never planned to settle there, so finding a Fylorian partner didn't seem probable. Most other forms of marriage didn't interest me.

And until Ardruc, I'd never been with anyone I could envision wanting to marry. For Fylorians, marriage was about love, trust, and unwavering support above all. In other words, very much like what Ardruc and I were building together.

I had no doubts whatsoever that Ardruc loved me and I could trust him. His support would never waver. My only hesitations came from nagging feelings that I didn't deserve so much devotion, but I understood myself well enough to know those were primarily a result of my complicated relationship with my parents.

No matter which way I analyzed the question, I kept coming back to a simple truth: I wanted Ardruc to be my dragon. That wasn't an inference, a theory, or a hypothesis—it was a fact. It was the ground beneath my feet.

Once I'd eaten every crumb and drained my mug, I handed my dishes to Ardruc, who set them on the bedside table. And then I sat sideways on his lap and rested my head on his shoulder. He wrapped his arms around me.

"Item one," I said briskly. "We need to contact the Alliance about the Nyvorans and the Vorsa. I'm not sure exactly who at the Alliance to alert to the situation, but I know someone who *would* know. I can reach this person via a secure personal communication the Nyvorans can't access, and they have the clout to get immediate results."

Ardruc tilted his head. "Who is this contact?"

I smiled wryly. "Let me come back to that."

"All right." He kissed my hair. "Item two?"

"Item two is our guests," I said. "After spending the night hanging from branches and vines, they're probably ready to make a deal. I suggest we offer them a third option in addition to the two you said you gave them last night."

His brow furrowed. "What is this third option?"

"If my plan for addressing item number one goes as planned, I suggest we buy passage from our guests to take us to Fortusia and deliver us to the rendezvous with their client. That may be the only way to know for sure who nearly got us killed."

Ardruc tucked my head under his chin. "I have never wanted to go back," he said, his voice quiet. "I have few good memories of my life on my homeworld, and I did not want to give Pyru an opportunity to retaliate for my escape. But now...now he is gone, and I want answers. I want to put it all behind me for good. If you are with me, I would have the courage to go."

"You have plenty of courage," I countered. "But if you need to borrow some, I'm happy to provide it. Whoever sent these mercenaries needs to understand you are not coming back—not now, not ever. And most importantly, you are already claimed by someone who has traveled halfway across Alliance space with you to tell them so. And *that* brings me to item number three."

I cupped Ardruc's face as he stared at me in a mix of surprise and wonder. He was so beautiful.

The way he'd looked burned and bruised and the damage to his back and shoulders from landing in the stun net haunted me. I would never forgive the mercenaries for hurting my dragon, but the fault lay with whoever sent them. I looked forward to meeting that person.

"Yes?" Ardruc prompted when the silence stretched out. "Item three?"

"Item three." I smiled. "I will marry you."

His pupils blew wide, and his entire body vibrated just as it had on the roof after our first flight when he'd given in to his need for me.

Forux jumped up and ran in circles on the bed, his tails fanned out. I chuckled at my little arval's excitement.

Before Ardruc could speak, I touched his lips with my fingertip. "I'll marry you, but I also want you to know I don't consider it necessary. We don't have to balance Fylorian customs with Fortusian ones. You are my dragon. You could not be *more* my dragon than you are. And I don't need anything else to tell me so but what's in my heart." I drew his head down for a kiss. "If you are my dragon and I'm your little mate, that's enough for me."

He kissed me hard and for a long time, until my lips felt swollen and I wished we had nothing else to do today but stay in this bed or go back to our forest shelter for more *epet mar ele'ana.*

"I *want* to marry you," he said when the kiss ended. His all-black eyes gleamed. "I read about the ritual as it is practiced on Fyloria and it is a beautiful way to affirm the strength and protection love provides. I have already imagined you in my arms, in the water, and now I must make that vision a reality."

And now I pictured Ardruc in the water with me and discovered I wanted that vision to come true too.

"All right, if it will make you happy," I teased. "We'll get married."

"I am already happy," he said, very seriously. "I will be happy all my days with you at my side."

I kissed the tip of his nose as he'd done to me yesterday. And it must have tickled because his nose twitched—just enough for him to look ridiculously cute in addition to ridiculously beautiful and sexy.

Ardruc Husiorithae, have mercy on me.

I rested my head on his shoulder. "Should we shower and start the day by addressing item number one?"

"Yes." He stroked my hair. "Who do you plan to contact to help us with the Nyvorans, little mate? Am I allowed to know?"

"Of course." I kissed his chest. "In fact, I want you to get all dressed up as the Nova Cal director of research and sit next to me while I record the message. Be sure to look extra stuffy and serious and dragon-y. I'll be introducing my mate the atmospheric scientist to my mother the heliophysicist."

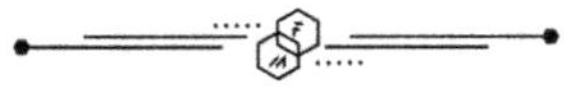

OUR SECURE TRANSMISSION TO FYLORIA RECEIVED A RESPONSE IN JUST under three hours, which in itself was irrefutable proof of how much influence Dr. Hilda Disen could wield when she wanted to.

Ardruc and I spent the intervening time working in our own labs, analyzing samples and data and ensuring all our work was safely stored in caches off-planet.

In my heart, I believed we had to travel to Fortusia, both to confront whoever was behind Ardruc's attempted kidnapping and so he could put his past behind him. But the prospect of leaving Vorsa World made my stomach churn with worry—especially since its future and thus ours was so uncertain. Ardruc and I loved this planet with all our hearts. I wanted to be its caretaker-listener and spend my life here studying its wonders with my mate.

And we needed my mother, who I hadn't spoken to in two years, and who had scoffed at my interests since I was little, to help us. I honestly didn't know if she would come to our aid. But if she didn't, I would never forgive her.

When her reply to my message arrived, I joined Ardruc in his lab to view it. Once we confirmed our identities via biometrics, the screen showed the seal of the university on Fyloria where my mother chaired the heliophysics department. And below that:

Sealed Communication for Dr. Elena Regis from Dr. Hilda Disen— Top Priority Delivery.

My heartbeat pounded in my ears. Ardruc squeezed my hand. I squeezed back and tried to breathe slowly and deeply.

My mother appeared on the screen, sitting in her university office with her hands folded on her desk. I had received numerous messages recorded in this same setting.

Two years had passed since the last time we'd spoken in any format. The office looked the same, but my mother didn't. Her blonde hair—so like my own, except she kept hers shoulder length rather than long—was loose instead of held in a tight clasp at the nape of her neck like she'd always worn it, even at home. She'd tucked it almost casually behind her ears. It made her appear softer.

Her furrowed brow and tightened eyes told me she was worried. About me?

"Elena." Despite her obvious disquiet, she smiled. The expression was fleeting, but it seemed real and not forced. "And I assume Dr. Husiorithae—Ardruc—is with you." She cleared her throat. "Hello. Hello to you both."

I blinked. Was Dr. Hilda Disen...*flustered?*

My mother leaned forward. "First, thank you for reaching out to me about the situation on Hyderia—or Vorsa World, as you call it. The news about its native plasma-based life forms is astounding."

Her eyes lit up with excitement—an expression I'd never seen directed toward anything I'd studied or shown interest in. "This discovery may change biology forever. Absolutely *incredible*. But clearly there are more troubling issues that need to be addressed."

She took a deep breath. "At your request, I have spoken with a close friend at the Division of Planetary Governance under condition of extreme secrecy. They have convened a carefully selected group to begin the process of establishing the sovereignty of Vorsa World. As you said in your message, if the planet has intelligent life, it must be independent and no longer a possession of its sister planet, Nyvor."

My stomach churned anew. Out of necessity, we had put something in motion that couldn't be undone, and so much was out of our hands.

Just a week ago, I'd felt so secure here, other than worry the Ministry might not approve my request to extend my stay. Now I was afraid of so many things: afraid for Vorsa World and its indigenous life forms, afraid this wondrous planet would be overrun, and afraid Ardruc and I might not be up to the mighty task the Vorsa had asked of us. I was a mycologist, not a diplomat. Whether I could be the caretaker-listener the Vorsa wanted me to be, I wasn't sure, but I was willing to give it my all.

Ardruc wrapped his arms around me from behind. He might have released some pheromones because my stomach settled almost immediately.

"While that process is underway," my mother continued, "an Alliance diplomatic envoy is traveling to Vorsa World to meet with a representative of the Vorsa and should arrive at Nova Cal at around 2200 hours your time. That envoy is a very close friend of mine—someone I trust completely to handle the situation and protect the Vorsa's interests. She will work with you and the Vorsa to determine what steps should be taken next—most particularly whether the Vorsa wish to join the Alliance or exclude themselves from it. I am including her dossier with this communication."

Between my mother's confident expression and businesslike tone and Ardruc's reassuring strength at my back, my anxiety lessened significantly. So far, my mother had accomplished everything I could have hoped when I sent my message, or at least found the right people to help.

"As for the Nyvorans' alleged violations of Alliance law and illegal removal of resources…" Now my mother's expression turned almost ferocious, which startled me. "I've been assured this will be investigated *immediately* by a team dispatched from Engaren. They will arrive at the coordinates you provided within ten hours, around 2100 hours your time, just before the envoy reaches you. If they find the allegations to be true, the consequences will be dire. The Alliance division responsible for overseeing the protection of conservation planets will ensure the damage to Vorsa World is repaired as well as it can be, and that those responsible are held accountable."

She took a deep breath and bowed her head for a moment. When she raised it again, I was shocked to see tears shimmering in her eyes.

"Ell," she said, and I nearly sagged into Ardruc's arms at the sound of her trembling voice saying the nickname I hadn't heard her use since I was little. "I'm thrilled by your discoveries on Vorsa World and deeply troubled by the news of the Nyvorans' theft of resources. I want you to know I'm honored you asked me for help and I'm doing everything I can to make sure you and Vorsa World are protected." She blinked rapidly. "But what I really want to talk about is that you've fallen in love and chosen a mate and plan to marry. That is *wonderful*. I'm so happy for you both."

And she *was* happy. Despite the tears in her eyes, she was beaming. I would have dropped into a chair if there had been one behind me and if Ardruc wasn't holding me up.

"I hope I get the chance to meet you in person soon, Ardruc," she continued. Her smile faded. "If you've heard anything about me from Elena, I'm sure you don't think much of me. And you would be right to do so. I have a lot of regrets. I have no right to ask for a chance to make things right, but it's long past time for me to do exactly that."

It wasn't an apology, and even if it *had* been I was a long way from feeling ready to accept one. All those years of disapproval and disdain had created a mountain of pain in my soul.

She might have done all this to try to earn my forgiveness. On one hand, as long as we got the help we needed to protect Vorsa World, I didn't care about her motivation. But seeing rare unguarded emotion from my mother kindled a little flame of hope in my heart.

I had been prepared to hear a lot of things in this communication, from a refusal to help to more disdain, or even for my message to go unanswered. The one thing I hadn't anticipated was an attempt at repairing the tattered mess of our relationship.

"If possible, I would like a chance to talk face-to-face," my mother said. "I can take a leave of absence from the university. I'm willing to meet you anywhere you would like…including coming to Vorsa World. It would be a great honor to see its wonders for myself. But I also understand if you would prefer I didn't come."

She cleared her throat and seemed to gather herself. "Please stay in contact, and I will pass along any news I receive from my contacts at Alliance Headquarters."

My mother raised her hand in a little wave. "I love you, Ell. I always have, even though I've done a poor job of showing it. I should have said that a long time ago. When I got your message today, I thought maybe you might give me a chance." She took a deep breath. "Regardless of what you choose to do, I wish you and Ardruc every happiness. We'll talk soon, I hope. Be safe." The transmission ended.

I stared at the dark screen, utterly speechless.

"Trust a heliophysicist to move the heavens to help us." Ardruc rested his hands on my shoulders and turned me to face him. "Are you all right?"

I blinked up at him. "I don't know," I said helplessly. "I'm happy she's able to help, but...I'm stunned. And I don't know how to react."

"I am sure you do not." He tucked loose hair behind my ear. "Even the people we think we know can surprise us. And I find it comforting to see people *can* change for the better."

My surprise and gratitude for her help gave way to anger. I rested my forehead on his chest. He stroked my hair and held me.

"She should have said something," I said into his shirt. "She could have reached out. I was always right here, just a message or a few days' travel away. She could have told me she loved me instead of leaving me all alone."

I expected him to coo. Instead, he continued to stroke my hair. "She could have," he agreed. "She *should* have. Instead, she was afraid and ashamed, and you were left hurting. She made a lot of bad decisions and mistakes. Parents can be flawed—sometimes terribly flawed."

And didn't he know that the hard way.

"I don't know if I can forgive her," I said softly. "Or whether I should."

"I understand." He kissed the top of my head. "You do not need to decide now or even anytime soon. Your mother has come to our aid as you hoped she would and wished us well. I am supremely grateful for that, regardless of what happens next...*Ell*."

"I haven't been *Ell* for a long, long time." I sniffled and looked up. "But I don't mind it."

With his thumbs, he gently wiped away my tears. "Elena suits you better, I think." He cupped my face in his hands. "*Little mate* is of course my preferred name for you. Or..." He bent his head. "*Doctor Regis*," he rumbled into my ear. "Who likes to be taught *hard* lessons."

A shiver ran through my entire body. Maybe he was trying to distract me from all my tangled emotions about my mother. I didn't mind, and I looked forward to my next lesson very much, but we had so much to do and no time for distractions, no matter how satisfying they would be.

"None of that now," I said sternly. When his expression turned tragic, I remembered he was still experiencing the mating frenzy and relented. "Later," I promised. "We need to talk to Ka and our guests and make plans for a trip to Fortusia first."

"And then I need to be deep inside my little mate," he said, his chest rumbling. "Where her dragon most likes to be."

CHAPTER 30
ARDRUC

THE REPTILIAN PILOT'S NAME WAS BEJO, HIS COPILOT WAS KARFF, AND after a night dangling in cages made from vines and branches, they disliked us a great deal.

Our money, on the other hand, they liked well enough.

After a brief, profanity-laden negotiation and my assurance their ship would be returned relatively unscathed from its underground storage, they accepted our terms and agreed to deliver us to their client on Fortusia once we had facilitated a first meeting between the Alliance envoy and the Vorsa, represented by Ka.

Once the deal was struck, Vorsa World released our guests at my request. We allowed them to use the vacant apartment recently occupied by Dr. Rg and provided a meal. I chose to ignore their complaints about the synthesized food, especially since they ate everything set before them.

We deactivated all computer interfaces in the apartment to prevent them from contacting anyone, and prepared to secure them inside to await the arrival of the envoy and our planned departure.

"We made a deal," Bejo snarled from where he was sprawled on the sofa. "We can't leave the planet without a ship. Why lock us in here with these..." He gestured at the two Vorsa hovering near the door. "Things?"

"For your own safety," I said. "They do not trust you, and you may do or say something they misinterpret as a threat to us." I growled. "You nearly killed my mate and I, so I would be well within my right to leave you imprisoned outside."

"Shut up, Bejo. It's a big improvement over a fucking cage." Karff headed for the bedroom. "They let us use an actual water shower instead of a sanitizer," he said over his shoulder. "And I haven't slept in a real bed for months. You can complain about the accommodations if you want. I'm going to get some sleep."

"Wise choice," I said, and backed into the corridor. "We will return when we are ready to leave. If you require anything in the meantime, inform your guards."

"Asshole," Bejo said. He propped his boots on the sofa's armrest and pointedly ignored me.

I puffed smoke out my nostrils. At least they had sanitized their clothing and washed themselves and no longer smelled of body odor and engine grime.

Oddly, I sensed grudging respect from Bejo despite his combativeness. Because we were now paying clients? Or because despite what they had done to us, we had shown them courtesy they likely rarely received? I was not sure, but I felt less uneasiness about their presence than I had earlier—especially once I secured the apartment.

Elena's familiar footsteps echoed in the corridor. I turned just as she came around the corner from the direction of her lab, accompanied by Forux. My hearts lightened immediately.

"Your tail is swishing all over the place," she said with a smile as she rose up on her tiptoes to give me a kiss. She smelled strongly of one of her lichen samples, a rich fragrance I enjoyed very much. "I never knew it moved so much until these last few days."

I sighed in feigned displeasure. "It is very unbecoming for a director of research to have a tail that *swishes all over the place.*"

"That depends on who you ask." She raised an eyebrow. "I personally think it's quite becoming for my dragon's tail to swish when he sees me. If *ever* it didn't, I would be very concerned that he no longer considered me his little mate."

Her teasing was such a joy. "In serious academic or diplomatic settings, I may be forced to ensure my tail maintains a more formal disposition." I slid my hand down her hip to cup the perfect curve of her ass. "I would hate to think my little mate might misinterpret my decorum as a lack of desire to be deep inside her."

Elena's smile turned impish. "In that case, I would simply invite my dragon to excuse himself from the serious setting to find a nice, private spot where he could thoroughly reassure me that he did indeed desire to be deep inside me."

I scooped her up so she could wrap her legs around my hips and I could kiss her thoroughly. "My playful little mate." I rested my forehead on hers. "I am the luckiest man in the cosmos."

"In this solar system, at least." Her smile faded. "I'm so worried."

"I know." I kissed her again, very lightly. "We have much to worry about. But my hearts tell me we will prevail, and so will the Vorsa and their world."

Her mouth quirked. "A gut feeling, Dr. Data Points?"

"My confidence in you," I countered very seriously, while inwardly chuckling over this new nickname—or perhaps an old nickname now used fondly rather than in exasperation. "It is easier to believe in good outcomes when I know you are committed to achieving them."

"Shameless flattery." She tapped my nose with the tip of her finger and the rested it there. "Don't think for one moment I'm susceptible to such obvious manipulation."

Lightning fast, I caught her finger in my teeth. She yelped and then giggled.

Dr. Elena Regis *giggled.*

She took advantage of my astonishment to escape my teeth. "Are you going to put me down?" she asked, still chuckling as she inspected the little marks I had left on her fingertip.

"Only if I must." I gave her one last kiss and put her back on her feet. "We have a full day's work ahead of us, which is unfair when I want so much to whisk you back to our quarters or out to our forest shelter for an hour's worship on my bed."

"Oh, it's *your* bed, is it?" she huffed. "And here I was thinking it was my bed too."

She spun on her heel to leave, but I grabbed her around the waist and pulled her back snugly against my chest. We fit together so well despite our different heights and body types. It was another reminder of how perfect she was.

"It is always our bed," I murmured in her ear, and she shivered. "But when I share it with my mate, it is an altar and I must worship her upon it."

I slipped my hand into the front of her pants and over her silky underwear. Through the fabric, I felt her heat and the little nub of her clit as I curled my hand around her pussy.

Elena gasped and squeezed her thighs to trap my fingers. My cock throbbed and my tail quivered.

"I am counting the minutes until I can be inside you here," I said softly. "Think about that while you work in your lab today, little mate. I am counting each and every minute."

She whimpered. Gods, I loved that sound. It emptied my head of nearly everything but visions of trapping her beneath me and making her scream my name.

I withdrew my hand and released her. "Time for work, Doctor."

"Yes it is, *Doctor.*" She sauntered back toward her lab with extra sway in her step as if daring me to catch her and wrap my hands around those perfect hips. But I wanted her to anticipate what I might do to her tonight, so I watched her until she rounded the corner out of sight.

We must find time for another hunt in the woods before we left for Fortusia. My eyes and skin warmed with the desire to track her, and my nostrils flared to drink in her lingering scent.

Little mate, little mate...

With a chuckle, I headed for my own lab with a song in my hearts.

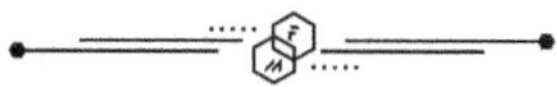

ELENA AND I FINISHED OUR WORKDAY JUST AFTER 1900 HOURS.

The Alliance diplomatic envoy was due to arrive at Nova Cal at 2200 hours, about an hour after we had been told the team of Engaren-based investigators would reach the location where Ka claimed the Nyvorans were stealing resources from the planet they had sworn to keep pristine in return for trade concessions and other benefits, as well as the good of this world.

I had envisioned spending the hours between leaving my lab for the evening and the envoy's arrival hunting my mate in the forest and then worshiping her until she was sated and the omnipresent desires of my mating frenzy eased.

But the moment we met in the hall and I saw her anguished expression, that plan changed.

"I'm so worried," she said and wrapped her arms around me. She was trembling. "I want to be there to see the evidence for myself when the investigators arrive. It's driving me crazy that I can't."

So instead of hunting her in the forest, I cradled my Elena on our bed, wrapped her in my wings and pheromones, and cooed until she dozed against my chest. That my hearts were quiet and my body had adapted so quickly from what I had wanted to what she needed astounded me.

"I'm sorry," she murmured. "I know this wasn't what you'd planned for the evening."

"There is no need to apologize. I planned to spend the evening with you." I rested my chin lightly on top of her head. "I am not suffering any hardship by comforting my mate when she needs me."

"Even with the frenzy? We haven't made love since…" Her voice trailed off. "Since we flew together yesterday."

"Even so." I kissed her hair. "My body adapts to your needs. And even if it did not, my hearts would never let me demand sex when you need quiet comfort."

She still seemed troubled, so I cooed until she sighed and snuggled closer.

"Have you ever met this Violet Storey, the Alliance envoy?" I asked, my voice quiet. "The file says she is a human born and raised on Fyloria."

"No." She kissed my chest. "My mother's note on the dossier said they've known each other pretty much all their lives, but Violet had already moved to Engaren before I was born. She's apparently one of the most senior and highly decorated members of the Diplomatic Corps." She snorted softly. "Of course my mother knows someone like that."

"If she can help us ensure the Vorsa and their world are protected and freed from Nyvor's custodial care, then I will be forever grateful to both your mother and to you for choosing to ask for her help." I laced our fingers together. "It is 2100 hours, little mate. The investigators should be arriving at their destination now."

"I know." She sighed. "Thank you for comforting me. I would have worn a path into the tile with my pacing without you." She moved so she could see my face. "If everything goes like we want it to, what do you think will happen to Nova Cal and the other research stations? The Nyvorans built them. The Vorsa don't like them, so I wouldn't feel right asking them to keep them. And they just remind me how the Nyvorans betrayed this world and lied to everyone."

My chest ached. "I do not know what will happen to the station," I said. "Everything you say is true, and I agree the decision belongs to the Vorsa. My own hearts are torn. I have called Nova Cal home for more than two years. You and I met here and first made love on its roof. I will be sorry to see it go, or to leave it."

"Me too." She swallowed hard. "If we *are* able to stay, though, we will make a new home for ourselves—one that blends the ways of Vorsa World with our research needs. And I would like to see similar stations elsewhere on the planet, staffed with researchers we choose, who are as dedicated to learning about and protecting this wondrous world as we are. That's my dream."

"Mine as well." I breathed in her scent and settled her against my chest once more.

My dreams were all of Elena and a home here studying korae while my mate researched its fungi. When I pictured it, my soul was still and peaceful. But many things stood between us and realizing that dream.

Some time later, my sharp ears caught the faint hum of the landing beacons activating.

"The envoy is arriving," I murmured to Elena, who had welcomed Forux into her lap when the sleepy arval demanded snuggles.

"Right on time." She stretched and relocated Forux to the bed, where he resumed his nap. "The waiting was the worst part. I think I'm ready to facilitate the initial meeting between the first known plasma-based life forms and one of the Diplomatic Corps's most decorated envoys."

For all her earlier nerves, rather than appearing anxious, she seemed to have regained her confidence. That did not surprise me at all.

Dr. Elena Regis was brilliant and indomitable. She had simply needed to remember that—no small feat after the whirlwind of the past week. And in the future, whenever she forgot how wonderful she was, it would be my privilege to remind her.

She rose from the bed and smoothed her jumpsuit. "Ready?" she asked.

I kissed her hand. "Ready."

CHAPTER 31

ELENA

Surveying her surroundings with a mixture of curiosity and professional assessment, Envoy Violet Storey descended from her transport onto Nova Cal's roof followed by a solemn Engareni assistant and two guards in Alliance Diplomatic Corps uniforms. Her sharp green gaze seemed to scour every detail and penetrate every secret.

The guards positioned themselves at the bottom of the ramp to watch for possible threats while Violet and her assistant joined Ardruc and me near the edge of the landing platform.

"Dr. Elena Regis," she said, in a voice that might have carried through the entire valley. "Just as lovely as your mother, I see. And as far as I can tell, every bit as brilliant."

"Thank you," I said with a small bow. With my stomach roiling with worry about what the investigators might have found, I couldn't feign my usual confidence, but hopefully I didn't look as nervous and worried as I felt. "Welcome to Vorsa World, Envoy. It's an honor to meet you."

"Oh, hardly." She waved her hand. "And call me Violet, dear. I feel like I'm your aunt. Your mother and I have been the best of friends for…well, never mind how long. Our first meeting would be a grand occasion even if I wasn't here so you could introduce me to the inhabitants of this gorgeous planet."

She turned to Ardruc, who kept a respectful distance. He was nearly twice her height and I figured he didn't want to tower over her—not that his size appeared to faze her at all. I could easily picture her staring down a charging Hardanian war-pig and then riding it into battle.

"And the very esteemed Dr. Husiorithae," Violet said, and gave him a perfect Fortusian-style bow. "I read your latest contribution to the Science Division's archives on the trip here from Engaren. Very fine work. I even understood parts of it."

His lips twitched. "Thank you, Envoy," he said with a very deep bow.

Bursts of korae in all colors spread across the sky. I didn't open my senses because I didn't want to alarm Violet with the rings that appeared in my eyes when I did so, but my Vorsa mark thrummed as if all the threads around us were reacting to Violet's presence. But was that reaction positive or negative? I couldn't tell, and that added to my uneasiness.

Violet gasped and craned her neck to watch the korae. "Great gods above and below," she breathed. "Now *that* is impressive. I've seen holos of the korae, of course, but recordings and reports just don't do them justice at all, do they?"

"No, they do not," Ardruc rumbled. "Everything about this world defies quantification."

And to think, not that long ago I would never have imagined he'd say such a thing, much less believe it.

"So it would seem." Violet tore her gaze away from the korae and turned back to me. "Well, I'm sure you're both curious about what the investigators found when they arrived at the coordinates you provided."

"I am *very* curious," I said. To put it mildly. "And very concerned."

Her mouth compressed into a thin line. "I'm sorry to say they found clear evidence of extensive, ongoing removal of natural resources by multiple private companies working under contracts negotiated by the Nyvoran Ministry of Trade and Exports. The investigation has just begun, but the team has informed me they suspect the illegal removal has been going on for at least a year. Possibly as much as two years."

Ardruc growled. I'd expected confirmation of what Ka had told us, but it still hurt. The churning in my stomach turned to unbridled rage and my fists clenched.

"I am disgusted, frankly," Violet said with a shake of her head. "The amount of duplicity and corruption required at the highest levels of government on Nyvor for an operation of this nature to take place is astounding. And as a duly sworn representative of the Alliance, I'm horrified that their operation has been going on under the noses of the Division of Conservation and Environment." Her eyes narrowed. "Whatever changes need to be made to ensure this never happens again, I will see it done. I plan to make that promise to the Vorsa and apologize on behalf of the DCE."

My chest still felt tight, but Violet's fierce determination and apparent sincerity made breathing a lot easier.

"Thank you very much for those assurances," I said fervently.

"You are most welcome." She glanced around the otherwise empty rooftop. "And speaking of the Vorsa, when might I make their acquaintance? Not to rush you, but given the circumstances I'm anxious to reassure them as best I can, as soon as I can, that the situation is being addressed quickly."

Ardruc gestured at his lat'sar case, which lay at his feet. "If I may, Envoy? As I am sure you noted from our brief, the Vorsa cherish improvisational art forms and consider them an essential component of all interactions. Ka, our primary contact among the Vorsa, requested we convene the meeting according to their ways."

"Of course." Violet clasped her hands at her waist—a habit she'd apparently picked up from the Engareni. Her silent assistant had stood in the same pose for the entirety of the conversation so far. "I would be honored to participate in Vorsa tradition."

Ardruc gave me a smile and took his lat'sar to an open area between the landing pad and the ladder that led to the upper roof. He warmed up quickly, then began to play a light but introspective melody.

Korae burst across the sky, the breeze swirled around us, the trees rustled, and the music swelled. Violet smiled and joined me in swaying in time with Ardruc's playing. Her assistant and even the guards followed suit.

As an envoy, Violet had probably been called upon to participate in a wide variety of customs on countless worlds. Doing so would be a key component of her duties. But judging by the way she smiled and her eyes sparkled, this experience meant more than simply fulfilling her duties as an envoy.

Just five minutes or so after Ardruc began improvising, the Vorsa began to arrive.

One by one, sparking, shimmering, and swaying, they appeared around the edge of the station's roof in a rainbow of bright colors. Violet watched them dance, her expression full of awe.

After a few minutes of dancing, the Vorsa rose into the air above us and began their duet with the korae. Ardruc played more quietly until he finally ended with a long, beautiful note. Then he returned the instrument to its case and came to stand next to me. I said to hells with formality and slipped my hand into his. His smile made my heart flutter.

Together, we watched the Vorsa dance and emulate the bursts of korae with what seemed to me like joy and exuberance.

I still felt sick at what the Nyvorans had done, but as I watched Violet gaze at the Vorsa and their wondrous world in awe, hope began to replace the gut-churning worry that had consumed me since Ka first revealed the planet was under threat.

Ka floated down to the roof near the ladder, where Ardruc had set up new, larger translation tiles. Violet took a few steps forward, bowed in greeting, and continued swaying.

Ka extended a thread to the inscription tile and wrote a long message. The second tile provided a translation within moments.

The Vorsa honor caretaker-listener Elena and caretaker-listener Ardruc. The Vorsa honor and welcome the Envoy Violet from the Alliance. I am Ka.

Violet inclined her head. "Ka, thank you for your welcome," she said in Alliance Standard. "I honor the Vorsa and Vorsa World. I honor caretaker-listener Elena and caretaker-listener Ardruc, and I thank them for the opportunity to greet the Vorsa on behalf of the Alliance. The Alliance honors the Vorsa and Vorsa World."

Ka dipped once, then extended a thread to the inscription tile.

The Envoy Violet knows the Not-Vorsa called Nyvorans have stolen from Vorsa World?

"Yes, I am aware." She inclined her head again. "I apologize to the Vorsa and Vorsa World that the Alliance was not aware of this crime. The Nyvorans will never again steal from Vorsa World. I honor the Vorsa for informing Elena and Ardruc of the harm the Nyvorans have caused."

Ka shimmered. *The Vorsa honor Envoy Violet for this promise. The Vorsa honor the Alliance and accept the apology.*

Relieved, I let out a breath. Ardruc squeezed my hand. I squeezed back.

"The Nyvoran contractors have agreed leave Vorsa World immediately," Violet told Ka. "The Alliance honors Vorsa World, and offers the Vorsa the choice to join the Alliance as a sovereign world. If the Vorsa do not want to join the Alliance at this time, they may do so in the future at any time. Whether the Vorsa decide to remain independent or join the Alliance, the Alliance honors Vorsa World and will ensure no Not-Vorsa violate its sovereign space or steal resources."

Ka dipped twice. *The Vorsa honor the Alliance for the invitation. The Vorsa have learned about the Alliance from the data held in the computer system at Nova Cal. The Vorsa are willing to discuss the invitation to join the Alliance with Envoy Violet.*

My heart leapt. As an Alliance planet, Vorsa World would have protection and ongoing diplomatic connections with other worlds.

But just as quickly as my happiness bubbled up, Ka's next words stunned me.

The Alliance will not need to guard Vorsa World. The Vorsa have given warning now. The Vorsa will ensure no Not-Vorsa violate the sovereign space of Vorsa World or steal resources.

My stomach lurched. Ardruc's hand tightened on mine.

The Vorsa had allowed the Nyvorans a chance to leave this world unharmed, but Ka's statement sounded very much like a warning that next time any outsiders attempted to visit or steal from this planet, the Vorsa would respond far differently. They would have every right to protect themselves and their homeworld, but what did Ka mean by *the Vorsa will ensure no Not-Vorsa violate the sovereign space of Vorsa World?* Did that include Ardruc and me?

Violet glanced at me, and then turned back to Ka. "The Alliance honors the Vorsa and will welcome Vorsa World with full recognition should the Vorsa choose to join. You stated no Not-Vorsa may ever again violate the sovereign space of Vorsa World. Is it the decision of the Vorsa that all not-Vorsa must leave Vorsa World and not return?"

Ka's threads flew across the inscription tile.

All not-Vorsa must leave immediately except Violet, Elena, and Ardruc. The Vorsa and Vorsa World honor Elena and Ardruc and welcome them to make their home on Vorsa World for as long as they choose to stay.

Oh, gods. I let out a ragged gasp. Ardruc wrapped his arms around me and kissed my hair.

The entire sky filled with bursts of korae. The Vorsa in the air above the lab twirled in pairs that reminded me of the first time Ardruc and I had flown together and he spun us in midair. I'd give just about anything to be able to fly with him now among the dancing, twirling Vorsa under a sky filled from horizon to horizon with the breathtaking korae that had brought Ardruc to this world in the first place. But we were grounded until his back and shoulders healed.

So instead I turned, jumped into his arms, wrapped my legs around his waist, and kissed him like he wasn't the director of research and we weren't in full view of a highly decorated Alliance diplomatic envoy, her assistant, two guards, three dozen sentient plasma tendrils, and an entire planet that had just welcomed us home.

"Elena," Ardruc murmured. "Look."

He turned so I could see what else Ka had written on the tile.

The Vorsa invite Elena and Ardruc to construct a new laboratory and home built in the Vorsa way. Elena and Ardruc may oversee construction of additional laboratories and homes for other scientists they believe the Vorsa may trust.

The Vorsa were offering everything we had asked for. Everything we had dreamed.

It might have been a trick of the light, but I thought Violet's eyes were shimmering with unshed tears. Even her dour assistant's feathers ruffled as she squawked quietly.

I buried my face into the side of Ardruc's neck and cried.

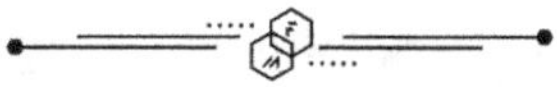

Back at Nova Cal, Violet Storey and Ka were deep in diplomatic negotiations.

But out here in the moonlit darkness, the forest thrummed happily as I slipped through the trees.

The mosses shimmered, leaves shivered and danced, the grass and vines swayed, and the bioluminescent mushrooms and lichen pulsed with light. Even the air hummed. The threads of Vorsa World sang.

And somewhere in these woods, a dragon was hunting his little mate.

He wanted to catch me. I wanted to be caught. But this time, he was going to have to work harder.

I smiled to myself, imagining Ardruc trying in vain to find my trail. He'd be mystified by how my scent led him straight to our forest shelter and then vanished right where I'd left a pile of clothes and a note scrawled on a stone outside the shelter's vine-covered doorway: *Come find me, Dragon.*

Poor dragon. Such a big forest to search at night with no scent trail to follow.

After nearly an hour, I found a pretty little clearing framed by mossy fallen trees and glowing mushrooms and lichen. Yes, this would do nicely.

When I knelt in the clearing and caressed the ground, thick moss grew across the soil, creating a velvety and fragrant bed. The bioluminescent fungi spread up the trees from the ground, forming a softly glowing ring with the mossy bed in the center.

When I reached out toward the undergrowth, leafy vines snaked across the ground to curl around my fingers and feet. I smiled at their gentle caresses.

Vorsa World was our home now. A new, deeper, and more secure kind of peace warmed my body and soul.

I'd set foot on more than a dozen planets, all wondrous and beautiful in their own ways. And lovely Fyloria, my homeworld, would always have a claim to a core part of my heart.

But the air that filled my lungs now was the air I wanted to breathe forever. This soil was the soil I wanted under my nails and in my hair and under my bare feet. Whenever I looked up, I wanted to see korae and the Vorsa dancing in the sky.

If Ardruc and I chose to have children, this was the world where I wanted them to grow up, steeped in science and wonder and surrounded by the beautiful and miraculous. It would be the best life I could give them, at least until they were old enough to chase their own dreams, and even then it would welcome them back whenever their paths turned this way.

The thrumming of the forest changed tone. I felt it in my tattoo and through the air and soil, and in the way the leaves quivered in anticipation. I smiled.

A moment later, the moss, trees, mushrooms, and sky whirled and I found myself on my back staring up into familiar golden eyes, with my hands trapped above my head with one hand around my wrists.

"Little mate," Ardruc rasped, and crushed his mouth to mine.

He was magnificent with his wings outstretched and his naked body covering mine with all its hard lines and hot skin and beautiful feathers that caught the soft glow of the fungi around and above us.

This dragon was *mine*.

When he pinned me into the moss with more of his weight, the sound I made was part gasp, part whimper, and part sob.

"I will always be able to find you, Elena," he said against my lips, his free hand cupping my breast. "Even if you cover yourself in a synthesized compound that is supposed to hide your sweet scent."

Vines coiled around my crossed wrists and up my arms as he kissed his way along my jaw to my throat. I gasped and pulled against the vines, but they held fast.

"Pick any fragrance you like," he murmured into my neck and stroked my nipple with his thumb before flicking it with his tongue. "Run as far and as fast as you can."

His hand slid down my right thigh to my knee and pulled my leg to the side. A vine encircled my ankle and coiled up my calf.

"Hide in the deepest parts of the forest if you want, little mate," Ardruc said, his mouth on my ear as he pushed my left leg to the side. "It will not matter."

Another vine coiled up my left leg. I was splayed out now, tied hand and foot, and utterly unable to move. My chest heaved and a rush of wetness traveled down my slit.

He rose to his hands and knees, his eyes glowing golden. "I will always find my way to you."

"Ardruc," I whispered. "My dragon."

He smiled and bent to kiss me so gently I barely felt it. "Yes, your dragon has caught you well this time." He rose to his hands and knees, his beautiful, thick cock gleaming and dripping onto my thigh. "I am hungry, little mate. Nothing but a feast will satisfy me tonight."

He took his time running his hands over my entire body, stroking my bare skin and testing the vines around my wrists, arms, legs, and ankles. Every touch of his fingers and brush of a leaf made me whimper and moan and gush for him.

I wanted so badly to touch myself, to squeeze my thighs together, to do anything at all to ease my desperate need, but I couldn't move—not even a little bit.

"Are you helpless and at my mercy, little mate?" he asked, prowling up my body to kiss and then bite my jaw.

"Yes," I gasped, turning my head so I could kiss his face. "Please…"

His wicked smile made me quiver. "Yes, what, little mate?"

I whimpered. "Yes, I'm helpless."

The pads of his thumbs ghosted slowly back and forth over my nipples. "You are helpless, and?" he prompted.

"I'm helpless and at your mercy, dragon," I gasped.

He rewarded me by pinching my nipples and then sucking each until I was writhing beneath him.

"Does my little mate like to be so helpless and at my mercy?" he asked, peering up at me with his lips on my right breast.

"I like it very much," I breathed.

His teeth closed on my delicate skin. Delicious, perfect pain. My cry rolled through the forest.

The breeze swirled and the ground thrummed with every sound I made as he licked and kissed and bit me. And finally when he came close enough that I was able to sink my teeth into his shoulder, he bellowed and the forest heaved.

"What did I do to deserve such a perfect mate?" he rasped into my ear. "You are beautiful, Elena Regis. So mercilessly beautiful." His gaze swept over me, from my vine-wrapped hands to my legs, spread wide for him. "I say you are at my mercy, but you should know I am forever at yours."

His hand slid down my abdomen, tracing lazy circles and patterns on my skin and moving closer to where I wanted his fingers as I quivered and moaned.

"I will fill your sweet little mouth first tonight," he promised, his fingertips caressing my dripping slit but not quite touching my clit. I mewled and tried to move, but the vines tightened around my legs.

"I will bend you over that tree and make you scream with my tongue and my tail in your sweet little ass," he continued, and I almost convulsed with the force of the gush those words created. "And then I will give you my knot and fill your sweet little pussy with cum. And then I will do all those things again."

He kissed me and bit my lower lip not quite hard enough to break the skin, but just perfectly enough to sting. I groaned.

"That is a dragon's feast, little mate," he said, peppering my face with kisses. "No less than six courses. I will fill you in every way until you can take no more."

I let out a desperate sound. "Please," I whispered. "Touch my clit. Just one touch."

"I will do much more than that for my sweet little mate. I will give you my mouth and tongue." He caressed my lips. "And you will give me yours. We will both drink our fill."

He slid his hand down my stomach and cupped my dripping pussy. The light brush of his palm against my clit made me yowl in need.

"Will you swallow every drop of my cum, little mate?" he asked.

"Yes." I moaned. "Every drop, my dragon. I promise."

He kissed me. "Good," he murmured, his lips on mine. "Open your sweet mouth for your mate. Let me see your tongue."

I obeyed, almost shivering with need.

"Beautiful," he said. "Stay just like that."

He turned, straddled my chest, and went to his hands and knees above me, moving until his beautiful cock was right above my waiting mouth.

And then without warning, he bent and closed his lips on my throbbing clit. With a scream, I bucked against all my restraints. The vines tightened.

Pleasure and the sensation of being utterly at his mercy sent me careening over the edge in moments. I climaxed with a wail that turned into a muffled gurgle as his cock filled my mouth. The soil and moss beneath me thrummed, sending pulses rolling through the forest with every wave of pleasure he gave me. And far, far above, beyond the leafy canopy, korae bloomed across the sky.

I closed my lips around him and sucked desperately, tears trickling from my eyes.

My dragon. My beautiful, delicious dragon.

With his lips, tongue, and fingers, he drove me back toward ecstasy as he thrust into my mouth, then withdrew just long enough for me to gasp in a breath. He tasted so good, so perfect, so much like smoky brandy and the earth and petrichor and everything good.

When I came a second time and screamed around his cock, his entire body vibrated with a low rumble that blended with the rhythms of the forest around us.

"Yes, little mate," he growled against my pussy as he stroked me with his fingers. "I love how you come. Let me hear you call for your dragon."

He withdrew from my mouth so I could wail and sob his name. He kissed my slit. "Yes, just like that, little mate."

Ardruc returned his mouth to my pussy with a single-minded focus on bringing me back to the peak of pleasure while I licked and sucked his dripping cock, gasping in breaths when he raised his hips.

"Are you thirsty for your mate?" he asked as I panted. He swirled his tongue around my clit. "Sweet Elena, I want to come for you."

"Please," I begged. "Fill my mouth."

He lowered his hips and I closed my lips around his cock. He groaned and thrust gently. I wanted to sink my nails into his hot dragon skin and moaned because I couldn't.

He took me over the edge with his mouth and tongue. And as I screamed around his cock, he was coming too, with bellows and growls, in hot, thick spurts that filled my throat and mouth and ran down my chin while the ground heaved beneath us. I choked and gagged and fought to swallow every drop of what he gave me because he was my dragon, and because I needed him so much it made my body hum.

He freed himself from my mouth and kissed my quivering pussy before turning on his knees to face me. "Look at you," he murmured, caressing my face and running his thumb over my lips. "Sweet Elena. You are so beautiful, it hurts."

"Ardruc," I gasped, my chest heaving. "I want to hold you."

He reached over my head and tugged at the vines around my wrists and arms. They slipped away, freeing me to pull him close so he could bury his face against the side of my neck.

"My dragon," I said, stroking his hair and feathers. "My mate."

He raised his head, his eyes glowing and expression full of wonder. "My hearts are full, my love."

I sank my nails into his biceps. He growled and bit my shoulder. "Deeper," he rumbled into my ear. "I will tattoo those marks, Elena. There will be no doubt who I belong to."

He freed my legs one at a time, kissing the little criss-crossing lines left by the vines. And then he knelt above me, his eyes glowing.

"You tried to trick me, little mate," he growled. "Hiding your scent was wicked. I believe my little mate needs some punishment."

I widened my eyes in feigned fear. "Punishment?"

"Punishment." He leaned close and bit my chin lightly. "How else may I teach her not to be so nefarious in the future? On your hands and knees, little mate."

Trembling with arousal and anticipation, I did as he demanded.

When my back was turned, he slipped a blindfold over my eyes and tied it snugly. I whimpered, and felt a trickle of slickness run down my thigh.

"Yes, little mate," he rumbled in my ear. "You should not try to trick your dragon. Punishment is required."

His hand closed on the back of my neck and pushed gently but insistently until I was leaning on my elbows with my ass and dripping pussy in the air.

"Yes, like that," he said with satisfaction. He nipped my earlobe with his teeth. "Do not move."

"Yes, dragon," I whispered. What was he going to do? I quivered with need.

I sensed him moving around me and heard little rustles, but I couldn't see anything. The ground hummed beneath me, with little pulses very like the throbbing in my clit.

When his large, hot hand suddenly came to rest on my ass, I jumped and mewled.

"Ah, that is the sound I like so much." He chuckled, and I shivered. "Can I make you do that more, I wonder?"

His hand came down on my ass with a crack and a flash of perfect pain. I shrieked and moaned as my pussy gushed.

"Such a wicked trick, little mate," he murmured. "Hiding from your dragon."

I whimpered, arching my back. "Again, please. Please, dragon."

His hand came down again, and I mewled again because he liked that sound so much. He caressed the spot he'd spanked, drawing out the sting.

"Do you like this, little mate?" His tongue suddenly dragged up my dripping slit and I cried out. "You taste like you like this sort of punishment."

"I do," I gasped. "I love it."

"Good, because I love doing this for you." He caressed my ass, and then spanked me again. I yowled and dug my fingers into the moss.

Again and again he spanked me until tears ran down my face and I was pleading to come, but he refused to give me a climax.

"Not yet, little mate," he said, caressing my hips. "I want you to remember what happens when you do such wicked things."

I wasn't likely to forget…but I *was* likely to do them again if this was the result.

Finally, he scooped me up and took me to a large, moss-covered fallen tree at the edge of the little clearing. "Bend over, lovely Elena," he said, urging me to lay with my stomach on the soft moss. "It is time for me to stretch that lovely little ass."

Whimpering, I obeyed. Vines coiled up and around my arms and legs, holding me in place with my legs spread for Ardruc's admiring gaze.

When he cupped my ass and ran his tongue along my cleft, I cried out.

"Sweet Elena," he murmured, prodding my asshole with his tongue.

The tip of his tail flicked along my slit and vibrated against my clit for just a moment—not long enough to send me over the edge, but driving me ever closer to it. I wailed.

He chuckled, his breath hot against my ass. "Yes, you will take my tail, little mate."

He tongued me as he stroked himself, and it was such sweet torture to be so close to coming and not be able to climax, to hear him pleasuring himself and not be able to see, to be so helplessly tied up while my dragon took his time stretching my ass and teasing my dripping slit with the tip of his tail.

Without warning, his tongue pushed inside my ass at the same moment his tail thrust into my pussy.

"Dragon," I wailed, writhing against the tree, fighting to escape pleasure that crested higher and higher because he'd made me wait so long. "Ardruc…"

He withdrew his tongue and replaced it with his slick fingers. "Come on my tail, my love. Come on your dragon's tail."

Deeper and deeper his tail thrust inside me, vibrating and sending waves of ecstasy through my entire body until I was screaming and coming so hard I sobbed.

He'd wanted to give me his tail in my ass, but there was something I wanted right now so desperately I would have done anything to get it.

"Give me your knot," I pleaded. "Ardruc, *please*. Please give me your knot while I'm tied up like this."

His tail withdrew from my fluttering pussy. I felt him move, and then his enormous cock head pressed against me.

His lips brushed my ear. "Whatever my Elena wants, she will get."

Slowly, he thrust into me, stretching me as I wailed and clawed at the tree. Gods, he felt so good.

"Your sweet little pussy takes me so well, Elena," he groaned, wrapping his hand in my hair. "You love this dragon cock."

"I love this dragon cock," I sobbed. "I love how you fill me."

He rocked back and forth until his ridges found my G-spot, and then he moved slowly right there so I shuddered and wailed his name.

"I think my little mate wants to come on my cock," he said, tightening his grip on my hair. "Tell me how much you want to come."

"I want to come so badly," I gasped. "Please, dragon. Please make me come."

His strokes remained slow and even. "You always come so perfectly for me, little mate. You squeeze my cock and drench me in your sweet cum. You call for your dragon. I hear you come in my dreams, Elena. That is how much I love the way you come for me."

His every movement drove me a little closer to the edge. I sobbed. "Ardruc…"

"Yes, little mate?" He pulled my hair until I raised my head. "Tell me how you feel."

"I feel so good. I feel so stretched, so full. So wet and ready for your knot." I whimpered. "Do this to me forever, dragon. Please."

"I will." He kissed my back. "I promise I will, little mate. I love you."

I came on that promise, with the words *I love you* in my ears and his wonderful dragon cock inside me. And as I cried out again and again, he cooed. Three deep thrusts later, his knot filled me and swelled, locking him inside me.

My dragon came with beautiful growls and rumbles, his hips thrusting and giving me a soft orgasm. I pictured him behind and above me with his wings outstretched, head back, one hand in my hair and the other on my hip, holding me as if he feared I might somehow slip from his grasp. A magnificent dragon claiming his mate in the forest and giving himself to her, body, hearts, and soul.

When the last of his releases ended, he freed me from the vines and carefully laid us down on the mossy ground, holding me tight to his chest with his arms around my middle so his knot didn't so much as tug at me. My sweet, thoughtful Ardruc.

He pulled my blindfold off, tossed it aside, and tucked my head under his chin as we panted and trembled together. His chest rumbled with contentment.

Big, dumb, lovesick dragon. He really was at my mercy forever and ever.

"I love you," I said.

He kissed my hair. "Of course you do, little mate."

Offended, I gasped. "What do you mean, 'of course you do'? You *conceited*—"

His chest shook. Was the winged jerk *laughing* at me after I said I loved him? I scowled.

"A dragon knows these things, Elena. Our senses are quite keen.

Also…" He nuzzled my ear. "You said so already twice tonight when you came."

I pressed my lips together. "Oh."

"Please do not pout, my love." He chuckled. "I am happy to hear you say it. You may say it as many as ten to twenty times a day if you wish. I doubt I will tire of hearing it."

With a wry smile, I turned so I could see his glowing eyes. "I may go back to hating you."

He kissed my brow. "I am told I am annoyingly irresistible, even when I am mildly to moderately hated."

"I take it back," I huffed. "You are a very unlikeable dragon."

His hand slid down my abdomen and his fingertip rubbed my clit. I whimpered.

"I must dedicate myself to finding a way back into your good graces, then," he murmured into my ear as he guided my leg back to hook over his to give him better access—and give us both a better view of my pussy stretched around the base of his cock. "A few more orgasms should do the trick, I think," he mused.

"A sound hypothesis," I gasped as he circled my clit. "But further research is definitely required to test its plausibility."

"Good." He bit my earlobe. "I will measure the success of my research by the number of times you scream my name and how frequently the ground moves beneath us. Shall we begin?"

CHAPTER 32
ARDRUC

Bejo and Karff's client had instructed them to bring me to Fortusia and leave me, preferably unconscious, in a rented storage facility at a small cargo port just outside the city of Bar'uto, about fifteen kilometers from the compound.

Instead, the mercenaries expressed concern about the security systems in place at the facility and told their client to claim his prize in a disused shipping office on the other side of the port, where security was much more lax. The client agreed readily.

Bejo and Karff had long since collected their final payment from us and departed when the door of the office opened and Olme Fornuth walked in.

He stopped on the threshold and stared at me. I folded my hands behind my back and returned his gaze without blinking.

In the message I had received nearly five months ago, Olme's feathers had appeared patchy and his skin sallow. But the man who stood before me in a long caftan and trousers designed to accommodate his tail and wings appeared healthy and in fine physical condition. So either he had manipulated his image or he had regained his health in the interim. I suspected the former.

"What is this?" he demanded as the door slid closed behind him.

"There has been a change of plans," I said, my tone dry. "The problem with hiring mercenaries to kidnap someone is their loyalty is up for bid, and their target may be in a position to make them a better offer."

Olme's sharp gaze went to Elena at my side. His nostrils flared and his eyes narrowed. "This human smells of...you."

"This human's name is Dr. Elena Regis," Elena said, with a smile so cold I felt a distinct chill. "And I smell like Ardruc because I'm his true mate."

Olme's expression darkened. His fists clenched with rage. "Impossible."

"I assure you it's true." She studied him, utterly unfazed by either his growing fury or how much he towered over her. "Well, you went to a lot of trouble and expense to have a word with Ardruc. Go on, then."

Everyone present knew Olme had not wanted *a word*, but to imprison me in the compound. She wanted him to say that aloud, to admit to what he had done and explain why.

Instead, very predictably, Olme went on the offensive. "No son of mine will have a *human female* as a mate," he spat.

I laughed.

If I had struck him, Olme would not have been staggered half as much. Elena arched a brow and chuckled, clearly savoring Olme's gobsmacked expression.

"You have no say in the matter," I said. "And I am not your son. You may have sired me, but you were no father. You and Earra were cruel jailers and tormentors, nothing more. I suffered every hour of my life with you, and you either did not see it or knew and did not care. I am not sure which is worse."

"Everything your mother and I did was for your benefit and your brother's," Olme argued. "If you had not been so stubborn and willing to be led astray by the outside world, you would have seen that. You cannot possibly be this remorseless about deserting your family."

There was less point arguing with him or prevailing upon him to listen to my perspective than trying to empty an ocean with a bucket. He would never be willing to acknowledge any viewpoint but his own. I had not come here for that purpose anyway.

"I made my choice to leave fifteen years ago and I have not had a single moment of regret since," I said. "My only lament is that Nors did not also leave."

"Your brother understood he had duties as a son, spouse, and father," Olme said, his voice harsh. "Once he wed Aora, he saw our ways were better than those outside. He chose to stay with his family until his death."

My gut roiled. Elena slipped her hand into mine and squeezed. Olme hissed at the sight.

While I was outwardly calm, Elena nearly vibrated with rage. I could well imagine what she longed to do in retaliation for Olme's many crimes, but she remained quietly supportive as I said what I needed to say.

"Why seek me out now?" I asked. "Nors has been gone for nearly half a standard year. Because Pyru died?"

After discussing Pyru openly with Elena, I no longer felt hesitant to say his name. In fact, I had all but forgotten the edict against it until Olme stiffened.

"You will call him *our beloved leader*," he told me icily. "You could not be *less* worthy to speak his name."

"He was never my leader, and he was certainly never beloved to me," I countered, my voice even. "Answer my question. Why come after me now?"

He folded his hands behind his back and assumed a posture of very obvious false modesty. "In recognition of my tireless work to benefit our community and my longstanding adherence to the teachings of its beloved founder, the inner circle selected me to ascend to the position of leadership after the untimely loss of our beloved leader. After lengthy contemplation, I have humbly accepted."

My stomach, already churning in renewed grief over my brother, lurched again at the thought of Olme as leader of the sect. He would now not only be in a position to inflict suffering on so many, but his eyes gleamed as if he relished the idea.

I had never wanted to be farther away from him than I did now. He was a sadistic, power-hungry monster, like Pyru before him, and the thought we were in any way related made me feel ill.

"This new role does not explain why you sent mercenaries to kidnap me and bring me here against my will," I said, my voice strained.

He glared at me. "It is very unbecoming for a man in my position to not have his *entire* family at his side as he takes on the mantle of leadership. My elder son's lack of respect and betrayal is still a subject of gossip in our community. I invited you back after your brother's passing as a gesture of goodwill. But since you have no compassion for his widow and children in their time of need, I had to use more assertive measures to bring you back to your family where you belong, so I am not forced to hear whispers about it anymore."

I already knew he did not want me back because he cared for me, but to be told outright that his primary concerns were his need for control and to save face...my stomach threatened to rebel.

Only now did I notice that while he persisted in referring to me as his son, Olme avoided using Nors's name, referring to him only as "your brother." Was that a conscious choice? It must be.

Nors deserved better than to be erased from both speech and memory.

Meanwhile, Elena had apparently reached the limit of her temper.

"*More assertive measures?* Those mercenaries nearly killed both of us trying to capture Ardruc," she snapped. "Did you not realize hiring people like that might lead to him getting killed?"

Olme barely spared her a glance. "Better dead than lost to the false gods of science and technology." His mouth compressed into a tight line. "Your place is with your family."

"I agree," I said. "*Elena* is my family. I have a good life and I have found my true mate. Elena and I plan to marry in the Fylorian tradition and live together on the planet formerly known as Hyderia. And you should know the planet is sentient and protects us, so any further attempts to kidnap me will be met with failure."

"And more to the point," Elena cut in, "Ardruc doesn't belong to you. He's not your possession. He had no choice but to live with you when he was a child, but as an adult, he has both the moral and legal right to choose his own path. You have no right whatsoever to interfere with that, for him or anyone else. If people opt to live within your community, that is their choice. But you have no right to keep anyone against their will."

"Some people do not understand what is right and best for them," Olme snarled. "My own son does not know. Some others are similarly misguided and I am forced to choose for them. Is it not the role of a parent and leader to save people from danger, even if it means I must save them from themselves?"

He appeared smug as if he believed he had made an important and indisputable point. And he had, though it was not the one he thought he had made.

"I am not returning to the compound with you," I said, and his self-satisfied smile vanished. "Not today, and not ever. I came here to get answers and to say what I needed to say to make a clean break. I plan to spend the rest of my days with Elena living in the present and looking ahead to our future, and never looking back at my life with you." I took a deep breath and let it out. "Goodbye."

With that, even the stale air in this disused office located in a busy cargo port tasted as sweet and free as the day I got through the compound's forcefield and flew away into the night.

Elena tugged me by my hand toward the door. "Move aside," she said to Olme.

Instead, his hand emerged from where it was hidden at his side. He aimed a small plasma gun directly at Elena's chest.

I threw myself between my mate and the weapon just as Olme pulled the trigger.

Searing pain sliced across my side. Elena's scream filled my ears. Oh, gods...*Elena*. Had the bolt of plasma hit her as well? The odor of burned flesh and feathers stung my nose.

I staggered against the wall, my hand pressed to my bloody side, and turned.

As Olme raised the gun to aim at my chest, Elena snatched up a long metal rod from a stack of abandoned cargo crates.

With a J'noran battle cry, she spun with the rod over her head, bringing it down in a perfect arc onto Olme's forearm. The shot went into the metal floor at my feet. Olme bellowed in rage and pain but did not drop the gun.

Elena changed her grip on the rod and swung its end up, catching Olme under the chin with a solid sound of metal on bone. Dazed, he slumped to the floor. She kicked the gun out of his hand and it skidded across the room into a corner.

The exterior office door slid open, revealing three uniformed provincial law enforcement officers with weapons drawn.

As they descended on Olme, Elena dropped her improvised weapon and ran to me, her eyes full of fury and worry. "Ardruc. Oh, gods."

"Elena." I cupped the back of her head. My ears rang and my legs threatened to go out from under me, but I looked her over from head to toe. "You are not hurt?"

"No. He missed me." She kissed the corner of my mouth and slipped her arm around my waist to steady me. "You were supposed to get him to admit to trying to kidnap you. You weren't supposed to let him *shoot* you."

"The wound is not serious." I kissed the top of her head. "A small price to pay to keep you safe."

"It doesn't *look* like such a small price, dragon," she grumbled.

In truth, my side and wing hurt terribly. Blood ran down my leg, and the stink of burned feathers conjured unwelcome memories of falling into the mercenaries' stun net. But as long as Elena was unhurt, I would take this injury without complaint.

And I would be lying if I claimed it was not very satisfying to see Olme Fornuth sprawled on his stomach on the dirty floor and restrained in stun cuffs, his jaw swelling where Elena had used her J'Noran hand-to-hand combat training to save our lives.

"Mission accomplished, Dr. Husiorithae," the senior constable, Klorath, said to me. "We have the recording of his confessions."

Olme hissed. We all ignored him.

Klorath clearly had genetic material taken from the Solani desert lion. His bronze skin shimmered in the overhead lights, and his mane was a dark burnished gold.

His emerald gaze raked over us, assessing our conditions. "Medical assistance is on its way. Are you hurt, Dr. Regis?"

"No." Elena squeezed me. "My mate very heroically jumped in front of me when Olme tried to kill me. You can add two counts of attempted murder to the other charges, I think."

"I believe our lieutenant will agree." Klorath glowered down at Olme, who struggled in the grip of the other constables despite the stun cuffs. "It will be a pleasure to take this...*person*...to the justice center while another team of investigators visit his compound."

"By what right do you enter our community?" Olme demanded, his voice strained.

"You gave us the right." Klorath squatted so he could pin Olme with his rather fearsome lion stare. "In full view of our recording equipment, you admitted to holding people against their will and attempting to kidnap a resident of the sovereign planet Vorsa World and bring him to the compound. Every violation of law we find, we will put at your feet and those of your 'inner circle.'"

He rose to his full height again, which even I had to admit was rather intimidating. "I suggest you make contact with a trial advocate soon, Fornuth. Even with the best representation, I am sure a lengthy prison sentence awaits you."

I expected mixed emotions at that pronouncement, but instead all I felt was relief. I held Elena's head to my chest and pressed my lips into her hair. She kissed my chest very audibly—I suspected for Olme's benefit. How I loved her.

As Olme cursed and struggled, the sound of an approaching transport drifted through the open doorway.

"Medical aid is arriving," Klorath said to me. "Come, Dr. Husiorithae, Dr. Regis. This man is no longer your problem." He bared his long canines at Olme. "He is mine."

"Ardruc Fornuth," Olme rasped as I walked past. Somehow, he managed to sound imperious despite being face down on the floor and manacled. "Do not turn your back on me. I am your *father*."

Ardruc *Fornuth*, not Husiorithae. I had not been called that for so long that it took a moment to register.

With her arm around my waist, Elena urged me to ignore him and keep walking, but I paused.

Blood dripped from my fingers where I pressed my hand to the wound in my side. The blood splattered on the floor next to Olme's head. He flinched as little droplets hit his face.

"Forget my name," I told him. "I have already forgotten yours."

And then I turned my back on him for the last time and let my mate guide me outside into the sweet Fortusian air.

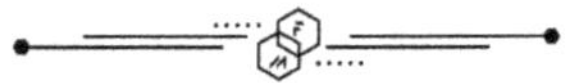

Even on a planet populated by genetically engineered wonders, I did not worry that my mate's affections might be drawn to any other person…

…but I knew I had lost her attention the moment she laid eyes on the pink and lavender lichen on the trees near Lake Lor'ima.

It was my fault for bringing her here, I thought morosely from the hammock as Elena made little *ooh* and *ahh* sounds and wandered through the trees around our rented cottage with Forux at her side.

With matters on Vorsa World in the capable hands of Violet Storey and her team, Elena had asked if we could remain for a week on Fortusia. I had expected her to say the purpose of our extended visit was so she could study Fortusian fungi, but instead she said she wanted to experience "a real Fortusian *epet mar ele'ana.*" I did not need much persuading.

So as soon as my wounds healed and I was discharged from the emergency medical center in Bar'uto, we traveled to Lake Lor'ima, a wilderness area in the northern part of the province popular with mates looking for peace and quiet and privacy.

From our rented cottage, we had a lovely view of the water. A path from our front porch led down the hill to the dock for swimming and sunbathing. The air was fresh, the water was pink and crystal clear, and the breeze was cool. The bed inside was large and comfortable, the kitchen was fully stocked with food so we would could prepare our own meals, and the large hammock on the porch easily accommodated both of us—not that Elena or her arval had sat still for five minutes since our arrival earlier today.

I might have preferred to be lying in this hammock with my mate beside me or curled up on my chest, but watching her run through the forest with almost childlike glee, marveling at the mushrooms and other fungi, made me smile and warmed my hearts. I missed the connection we shared with Vorsa World, but even here on Fortusia I could share my mate's happiness.

Before Elena arrived at Nova Cal, I had never once considered the possibility of taking time away with a mate, much less returning to Fortusia. But with her at my side, I had found the courage to not only talk about my past but to start healing from it. That path had brought me to my homeworld, to a dingy cargo shipping office near Bar'uto, and eventually to this cottage at Lake Lor'ima, where I lay in a hammock gently swaying while my beautiful mate marveled at fungi she had never seen before.

When she eventually left Forux curled up in a patch of sunshine on the porch and crawled into the hammock beside me, the pink sky was streaked with the colors of suns-set. She smelled of Fortusian soil and plants, and she cradled fragrant purple oth'canto leaves in her hands.

"Can we—" she began.

"I think—" I said at the same time.

She smiled and kissed my jaw. "You go first."

"I think we should visit Fortusia regularly," I said, tucking her hair behind her ear. "I never allowed myself to miss my homeworld before, but now I realize how much I have longed for its beauty. And you are so lovely surrounded by these colors—as lovely as you are on Vorsa World."

"So much flattery, dragon." She kissed me, her lips soft and sweet. "I was going to ask if we could visit Fortusia again soon," she chuckled. "I might have known you'd have the same thought."

"Then it is settled." I tucked her head under my chin and wrapped her in my arms. "We will happily make our home on Vorsa World, and visit Fortusia when our work permits."

We lay quietly as the suns dipped below the treetops. I dangled one leg over the side of the hammock and swayed us from time to time. Elena played with the oth'canto leaves on my chest, arranging them into patterns and stirring them with her finger.

"I've never taken time away like this," she mused. "I've had short breaks and vacations, but I always brought work with me or spent most of the time thinking about the work waiting for me back in my lab. But right now there's nothing in my head but this beautiful lake and you. And Forux, of course. I don't think I've ever felt quite this much in the present."

"I feel the same way." I kissed her hair. "It is remarkable to feel so quiet inside."

She rested her chin on my chest and smiled at me. "And we have an entire week here before we travel home."

"Home." I moved her so she lay on my chest so I could kiss her. "You are my home, Elena."

"You know what I mean." She tapped my nose in what was swiftly becoming one of my favorite habits. "Our home on Vorsa World, where we'll have a place to live and laboratories built in the Vorsa way, full of our own research equipment *and* beautiful, miraculous, sentient living things. I can't wait."

Her excitement buzzed on my skin. "Neither can I," I said. "But in the meantime, I can rediscover Fortusia and see my mate in entirely new ways."

"You know…" She trailed her fingertips over my lips. "We could get married here."

"Here?" Startled, I blinked at her. "Not on Fyloria?"

"Just look at that lake," she said, nodding down the path at the shimmering pink water. "It's beautiful, Ardruc. This is your home-world. Why not get married in that lake?"

My hearts began to race in anticipation. "I planned to ask if you wanted to marry me in the river near Nova Cal when we returned."

Her playful smile nearly undid me. "We could do both. And then get married a third time whenever we make it to Fyloria." Her mouth quirked. "That might be a while, given everything we need to take care of on Vorsa World."

She did not say so, but our timeline to visit Fyloria might also be subject to her mother's request to try to mend their relationship. She had not yet decided how to proceed in that regard.

"You would marry me more than once?" I asked in feigned surprise.

She chuckled. "You are *shameless.* But yes, I would. I will." She kissed me lightly. "Especially if means more than one wedding night."

"More than one wedding night?" My chest rumbled, and I took advantage of her nearness to graze her shoulder with my teeth. "In that case, we could marry more than three times. Once a week, even."

"Oh, *dragon,*" she said, exasperated. "As if you need any excuse like a wedding night to be deep inside your little mate."

I cupped her face in my hands. "I thought so thoroughly about marrying you, but I neglected to think about the wedding night."

She laughed, the sound like the pealing of bells. "Funny—I did the same until just now, when I realized if you carried me down to the lake and we got married right now that tonight would be our wedding night. I haven't done anything to get ready. I don't have anything special to wear. I can't decide if I like the idea of a spontaneous wedding night or not."

"I think I like the idea *very* much." I kissed her. "You do not need anything special to wear. And I am so grateful you would like to marry me on my homeworld."

"I think I'm staking a claim on you by marrying you here," she mused. "You know, I wonder—"

I silenced her with a kiss.

"For once, we should not let our scientist brains run away with questions," I said when our kiss ended and she rested her head back on my chest. "My hearts, soul, body, and instincts have no questions. They want me to take you down to the lake right now."

"Mine too." She tucked an oth'canto leaf behind her ear. "Marriage decoration," she explained at my puzzlement, and tucked another behind my ear. "And one for you."

I must look utterly ridiculous with a large purple leaf stuck behind my ear, but I could not bring myself to care.

Very carefully, I moved to the side of the hammock, scooped Elena up in my arms, and rose.

"To the lake, dragon," she said, and kissed my jaw.

My hands trembling, I carried the love of my life down the path to the lake.

Rather than walk out on the dock, I veered off the path and made my way to the edge of the lake, stepping carefully over the rocky edge and into the shallow water. I carried her until the water was waist deep, past the rocks to the soft sandy bottom, and then put her on her feet beside me.

Elena slipped her hand into mine. "Oh, you're shaking," she said with a frown. "If you don't want to do this now—"

"I do," I promised. "I have no doubts at all. I just feel…a lot of things."

"Me too. I think we're supposed to." She squeezed my hand. "I'll go first, if you want."

My hearts racing, I squeezed back. "I am ready."

With a smile that made my hearts sing, she closed her eyes, spread her arms, and tipped over backward, vanishing beneath the surface of the water with a splash.

I followed the shadow of her hand with my eyes, counted to three, and reached into the water. Her hand found mine and grabbed tight.

I hauled her from the water, set her back on her feet, and helped her wipe the water from her eyes. And then I cradled her to my chest.

"Elena, little mate," I said into her hair. "I will always care for you and love you. I will find you when you are lost and support you when you need strength. Anything you need, I will do my best to provide it. I will do everything in my power to keep you safe and warm and sheltered. You are my hearts. Please be my wife."

Sniffling, she looked up at me with wide eyes and wet lashes. "That was not the script I read," she said. "I think you made some of that up on the spot."

"I did." I cupped her head. "My research indicated improvisation is encouraged."

Her laugh was edged with a little sob. "You and your research." She managed a smile. "Yes, I will be your wife."

My hearts soared. I fell back into the water still smiling, and swallowed a bellyful of lake water as a result.

Elena's hand found mine four seconds after I went under. She did her best to pull me upright, but I had to do most of the work to get on my feet since I outweighed her a great deal. I came up coughing.

The moment I was upright, she leapt into my arms.

"Ardruc Husiorithae," she said, her expression so fierce and earnest I wanted to kiss her and never stop. "I will always care for you and love you. I will find you when you are lost and support you when you need strength. Anything you need, I will do my best to provide it. I will do everything in my power to keep you safe and warm and sheltered. You are my heart." Her beautiful blue eyes shimmered. "Please be my dragon *and* my husband."

That was the easiest question of my life to answer.

I rested my forehead against hers. "I will very happily be your dragon *and* your husband."

It was not the traditional wording—far from it, in fact. We were standing in a peaceful pink Fortusian lake rather than a fast-moving Fylorian river, neither of us had worn the customary yellow clothing, and I was still coughing up water, but ours was the most perfect marriage ritual I could have imagined.

I kissed my wife for the first time, and that was perfect too.

My wife. And I was *husband*. Dr. Elena Regis's husband. I felt radiant with pride—so much so that I expected to glow as brightly as the setting suns.

When our kiss ended, I asked, "Tell me, *wife*...do we really have to wait for nightfall to celebrate our wedding night?"

She pursed her lips and pretended to consider the question very seriously. "Probably so, *husband*, if we want to be traditional about it."

"Traditional?" I raised my eyebrows. "I do not think any aspect of our courtship has been traditional. Why start now?"

She chuckled. "I was hoping you'd say that."

I squeezed her ass in both hands. With a moan, Elena kissed me and wrapped her fingers in my wet hair. She pulled hard enough to make my eyes water, my balls tight, and my cock drip. When her little teeth closed on my lower lip, I rumbled.

My mate's fierce desire told me she might like to play a little differently today. Perhaps even dominate her dragon for a while. The restraints I had brought could accommodate my body as easily as hers.

Hmm. Perhaps I would like to try some…new things on our first wedding night.

I carried Elena up the hill to our cottage. We left a trail of wet clothing all the way to the door.

CHAPTER 33
ELENA

GIVEN THE UNDISGUISED HUNGER IN HIS GAZE AND HIS NONSTOP rumbling, I expected Ardruc to throw me on the bed and cover my body with his or put me on my hands and knees right inside the door the moment we entered the cottage. And either would have made me very happy.

Instead, he carried me to the bedroom, sat me on the foot of the bed, and went to his knees in front of me.

He was so gorgeous and perfect, my dragon man. My dragon mate. From the tips of the feathers in his hair to his toes, he was everything I wanted and needed. But it wasn't just his body I loved. I loved his sharp, analytical mind and all the ways it complimented my dreamier, non-linear thinking. What had seemed like insurmountable differences for so long had in fact turned out to be the very best of partnerships.

I leaned over, drew him closer between my thighs, and kissed him. He returned my gentle kiss.

"Little mate," he said, his hands on my knees as he gazed up at me. "I am your dragon to command tonight. Whatever you want, whatever you need, and however you want it, you may take it."

A thrill of desire ran through my entire body. With a shaky gasp, I cupped his face. "Really?"

Ardruc's eyes smoldered like molten gold in the low light. "Yes. I want to be claimed by my wife. *Very* thoroughly." His lips turned up at the corners as he slid a gray case out from under the bed. "And if she wishes, she may use anything in this case to ensure my total cooperation."

"What is that?" I breathed.

He chuckled. "We have no vines here, and though I do not mind tearing my clothing or yours to make restraints—or other such necessary items—I thought it would be prudent to obtain a small collection of things my little mate might enjoy." His smile turned predatory. "And I find myself wanting to know how she might use them on me, given the chance."

Indeed, his cock leapt and dripped as he ran his hand over the case and then trailed his fingers up my legs. I quivered and a rush of wetness trickled along my slit.

"I place myself entirely in your hands, my love," he rumbled. "What is my little mate's first demand?"

I'd never imagined taking control. Ardruc loved being dominant and I loved being submissive so much that it hadn't even occurred to me to wonder what I might do if he wanted to swap roles.

But now I *was* thinking about the possibilities, and if he wanted to be at my mercy, then that was what I wanted too.

I moved closer to the edge of the bed, ran my fingers through his hair and gripped it tightly, and drew his face between my thighs. "Put your tongue in my pussy, dragon," I ordered him.

His cock leapt again and leaked onto his thighs. "Yes, my little mate," he grated. "Command me."

I tightened my grip in his hair. "Make me come on your face."

With a growl, he wrapped his arms under my thighs, pulled me closer until I was only partially sitting on the bed with most of my weight on him, and delved his tongue into my dripping slit.

I cried out and twisted my hands in his hair. The sound he made

—a low, satisfied rumble that traveled through his entire body—made me gush again.

Oh, yes…I could get used to this. And maybe he could too.

He tongued and sucked my clit masterfully, his hands gripping my hips tightly so I couldn't move and he could drive me toward bliss with single-minded focus. And though I knew he would have done this happily regardless, the knowledge I'd *commanded* him made it better and even more pleasurable.

I wailed and pulled his hair, riding against his mouth. "Dragon, yes. Ardruc. *Mate.*"

Rumbling, he tightened his grip, took me right up to the edge, and then carried me over it. With a wail, I fell back onto my elbows, thrashing in his arms and crying out for him.

He didn't stop until I went limp, my legs dangling bonelessly over his arms. Then he licked my slit delicately again and again, drinking every last drop of my release just as I loved to do for him when my mouth was on his delicious cock.

"Good dragon," I said, hooking one of my legs over his shoulder to keep him there. "Clean me up."

"Yes, little mate," he murmured, and gods above my back arched with how much his obedience sent a sizzle of desire right to my core. Did he feel the same when I obeyed him? If so, no wonder he liked dominating me so much.

He urged me to spread my legs wide so he could lick me thoroughly. I kept one hand twisted in his hair so I could enjoy the way he moved.

But when his tongue returned to my clit and swirled, I pulled his head up. "I didn't tell you to do that," I scolded. "I told you to clean me up."

His golden gaze looking at me from between my legs made me shiver. "I am sorry, little mate," he said. "You taste so good that I forgot myself."

"Apology accepted." I tugged his hair. "Up on the bed, dragon. On your stomach."

Eyebrows raised, he climbed onto the bed and settled in on his stomach with his head turned facing me. The bed was enormous, designed to accommodate Fortusian proportions, but even so his toes nearly reached the bottom edge.

I rolled to my knees and studied my dragon's wings, back, ass, and legs. It was a view I'd only gotten to enjoy a few times since I was usually below or in front of him, and I intended to make the most of it.

I straddled his lower back with my ass resting against the thick base of his tail and hands braced just below his wings. He rumbled beneath me and spread his wings wide.

I bent over to press my lips to his ear. "Can you keep still while I explore your body, dragon?"

"No," he rasped. "I cannot. I want you too badly."

I *tsk*'d. "That's a shame. I'll have to take steps to keep you where I want you. Don't move."

When I slid off his back, he groaned.

On my hands and knees, I turned and moved to the end of the bed, giving him a tantalizing view of my ass and pussy. He groaned again. "Elena…"

"Quiet, dragon." I leaned over the end of the bed and opened the case.

Oh my. My mate had brought a treasure trove with us to the cottage. Restraints, cuffs, something that looked like a soft whip, blindfolds, gags, various items in all shapes and sizes clearly designed for insertion…there were so many possibilities to explore.

I brought out a set of restraints first. When I turned and Ardruc saw what I had, he closed his eyes and twisted his hands in the bedding.

"I am beginning to regret this decision," he muttered, but the way he quivered told me he didn't regret it at all. Not yet, anyway.

With a low chuckle, I set to work putting his wrists and ankles into the restraints and attaching them to the underside of the bed. When I finished arranging him how I wanted, his arms were outstretched and his legs slightly parted. His growls made the entire bed vibrate.

I climbed onto his back again and delved my tongue into his ear. He shivered and moaned.

"How do you feel, dragon?" I murmured.

"You do not want to know," he rumbled. "I need you so much, Elena. This is torture."

I sank my nails into his shoulders. "Good torture or bad?"

"Good." He groaned. "Gods above, Elena. You will make me come doing that."

"You can't come until I say." I twisted my hand in his hair and made my voice sharp when I added, "Do you understand?"

"Yes, little mate." He shuddered hard. "I understand."

I braced myself with my hands on his back, moved until I straddled the thick, curved base of his tail, and rubbed my slick pussy against it.

He roared and nearly levitated off the bed. The restraints snapped tight.

"Naughty dragon," I said and dug my nails into his back. He trembled so hard that he shook us both. "Stay still while I give myself an orgasm on your tail."

His moan made me gush. "Elena, gods. Please."

"Your tail is so perfect for this," I murmured as I ground myself against him. My slickness started to drip down his hot, scaly flesh. "Perfect shape, perfect size. Perfect texture."

I loved it when he talked to me like this during sex. It made me absolutely wild and almost brought me orgasms alone. But doing the talking myself…gods above, it was even better.

I bent over and licked along his spine as I rode him. "Was this tail made for your little mate to use?" I gasped.

"Yes." His back arched. "Elena…gods…" It sounded like a prayer.

He felt so good. *So good*. The texture of his skin at the base of his tail provided perfect friction for my clit. I moaned and whimpered, which made him groan. The sounds he made as he struggled not to come while he felt me riding him drove me toward a climax with breathtaking speed.

"Dragon," I gasped, grinding faster. "I'm going to come."

"Come all over me, little mate," he pleaded, his hands clenched in the bedding. "Come on your husband's tail, my love."

My husband. I was *riding my husband's tail*.

On that thought, I climaxed with a scream and near-sobs, my nails digging into Ardruc's back as I called for my dragon. He moaned under me, trembling violently, every muscle hard as stone.

I slumped forward to lie on his back, feeling my release dripping down his hot skin between us. "Dragon," I rasped. "Gods. I've wanted to do that for so long."

"I did not know," he grated. "That felt so good, little mate. You can come like that on my tail any time you wish."

I kissed the edge of his wing. "I will remember that."

I wrapped my arm around his waist and slid my hand under him to find his cock. The bed underneath was soaked with his lubrication and precum. He groaned and shuddered hard when I stroked him.

"Did you come, dragon?" I asked, knowing full well he hadn't. "Did you disobey your little mate?"

"No," he ground out. "I am waiting for permission."

"What a good, obedient dragon you are." I kissed his back in all the places I'd left marks with my nails. "I think you've earned a reward."

As he groaned, I knelt at his side and caressed his tail from its base down its length.

"Raise your tail," I said, gently lifting it out of my way. "Show me what's under it."

The guttural sound he made was very satisfying. And he looked so incredibly sexy with his tail raised and quivering.

I trailed my fingertips around the base of his tail, exploring the hot, delicate skin between it and the cleft of his firm ass. He quaked at every touch.

And when I straddled his thighs and sank my teeth into one of his thick ass cheeks, he bellowed, his hips and tail raising instinctively to beg for more.

"Good dragon," I crooned, caressing his ass before biting him on the other side and then licking the marks I'd made. "Perfect dragon. Do you like it when your little mate marks you as her own?"

"Yes," he rasped. "I am Elena's dragon. Always."

I swirled my tongue over the curve of his ass and then dipped it along the cleft. He made that guttural sound again. "Elena, I cannot…please…"

"You've been such a good dragon," I murmured. "Letting me taste you and come on your tail." I delved my tongue along the cleft of his ass again so he would make that rough pleading sound for me. "I'd like to play more with your beautiful ass, dragon. Would you like that?"

He groaned and raised his hips. "Yes."

I licked him more deeply, teasing and tormenting and driving him right up to the edge…and kept him there until he was snarling and shaking and fighting not to come.

I slid my hand under his raised hips to grip his cock. His groan made me gush hard. And when I slipped my wet fingertip just inside his ass, he roared.

"Come for me, dragon," I commanded.

And he did, with bellows and growls and my name falling from his lips, thrusting into my hand. His tail whipped wildly through the air off to the side so it didn't hit me.

"Elena," he groaned, shuddering hard. "Little mate."

I withdrew my fingertip, gave him one final gentle bite right on the best, firmest, most perfectly curved part of his ass, and crawled up his body to lie with my chest on his back so I could enjoy the feeling of him shuddering beneath me.

"What have you done to me?" he gasped. "I cannot feel my legs or tail."

With a chuckle, I brushed his hair aside and kissed the back of his neck. His smoky brandy scent was so strong there that I had to lick him too just so I could drink it in. "You came so perfectly for me, dragon."

He groaned. "You like this change of roles, little mate. I think you may like it a little *too* much."

Careful not to tug on his healing wings, I pulled myself farther up his back so I could rest my chin on his shoulder. He was smiling almost blissfully. I couldn't help but feel a bit smug.

"I'm just getting started, dragon," I warned. "You can't cry mercy yet."

"I am not asking for mercy." His eyes gleamed. "There is *nothing* you can do that will make me do that."

"That is definitely a challenge," I said, raising my eyebrows. "And I choose to accept it."

His toothy smile made me quiver. "Please do, little mate."

"I am going to let you out of these restraints." I made my tone as brusque and commanding as I could, though I wasn't nearly as good at sounding intimidating as he was. "You will lie still and not move until I tell you to."

"Yes, little mate," he said, and his meek tone almost undid me. "I will be good."

I let him out of his restraints. When he turned onto his back, the sight of his hard, dripping cock and the soaked bedding made my lick my lips.

Despite his promise to obey, I'd fully expected him to take control the moment he was free. Instead, he stretched out his arms and legs again and waited to be tied up.

Well, he *had* told me more than once that a dragon keeps his promises. I bent and kissed him.

"I love you," he murmured against my lips. "Wife."

"I love you." I touched the tip of my nose to his. "Husband."

This time I restrained him with his legs spread more. When I crawled back up the bed between his thighs, he gazed down his body at me. "Beautiful Elena, what delicious torments do you have planned for me now?"

"Only the best ones." I bent my head and dragged my tongue over his balls. His hips bucked and he groaned.

I licked his balls again to feel them tighten. "You want to come again, don't you, dragon?"

"Yes, little mate," he ground out, his voice rough. "I want to come all over you."

I moved further up and flicked my tongue on the dripping tip of his cock. He fisted his hands into the bedding.

"You want to come in my pussy, don't you, dragon?" I asked. "You want to fill me up."

"Yes," he breathed. "Yes, I want to come in your pussy, little mate. I want to fill you with my cum and make you scream my name."

I wrapped my hand around the base of his cock but didn't stroke him yet. "You want your tail in my ass, don't you, dragon?"

"Yes," he gasped. "I want to put my tail into your perfect ass, little mate."

My clit throbbed. I loved this. I loved dominating my dragon every bit as much as I loved being dominated by him.

"You want to give me your knot," I said, and stroked him with both hands. He was so slick, so perfect, so desperate. "Don't you, dragon?"

"Yes," he nearly roared. "I need you to take my knot, little mate."

I straddled his hips and rubbed my slit over his cock. He shuddered and tipped his head back, eyes closed and fists twisting in the bedding.

"No," I said sharply, and he raised his head to look at me. "Watch," I commanded.

He groaned and dripped as I rubbed my clit against his cock. The friction of his ridges and bumps made me moan.

By the time I crouched over him and positioned myself above his cock, he was panting.

"You are too beautiful," he groaned. "Elena…"

I sank onto him with a cry, feeling myself stretch in that perfect combination of pleasure and pain that only Ardruc could give me. I'd never taken his cock like this, and it felt impossibly large.

Slowly, carefully, I took the thick head into myself and let it slip free, and every movement I made drew guttural sounds from my dragon.

"Take my cock, little mate," he rasped, his golden eyes blazing with need. "I have never seen anything as beautiful and perfect as you taking my cock like this."

Whimpering, I braced myself on his chest and took him a little deeper, letting him stretch me inches at a time, filling every space as I shaped myself around him. Our cries blended and filled the room.

I took him as far as I could, and then I began to ride him right where his ridges rubbed against that perfect place just inside me. He felt so good, so perfect. So thick and hot and slick.

I was already so aroused by giving him pleasure that I came almost immediately with screams and wails, collapsing on his chest as I ground on his cock to draw out my climax.

As I whimpered and trembled, he snarled and pulled on his restraints until the bed creaked alarmingly. "Elena. I want to hold you. I need to…" He took a deep, shuddering breath. "I need to make love to you. *Mercy.*"

He'd reached his limit with this reversal of roles, at least for tonight. And I found I'd reached mine too.

Gasping, I freed myself from his cock, crawled to where his right wrist was trapped in the restraint, and let him out. In a flash, he'd released his other wrist and his ankles and then he was cradling me against his wonderfully hot chest.

"Elena," he murmured into my hair, stroking my back. "Beautiful little mate. You commanded your dragon so perfectly."

I kissed him deeply. "Thank you," I murmured against his lips. "I really enjoyed trading roles."

"I think we both enjoyed it very much." He nuzzled the side of my neck and then bit me gently. "We will do this again soon," he promised, his breath hot against my delicate skin. "Now, may I indulge one of my own fantasies?"

After revealing my secret workplace fantasy to him, I'd wondered what playful scenarios a dragon man might have besides tying me up with vines in the forest.

"What do you have in mind?" I asked.

He cupped my face. "I want to give my wife so many orgasms that she is thoroughly exhausted and forced to spend the entire following day in bed with me recovering her strength."

I gasped in mock horror even as my pussy clenched in anticipation. "Oh, that sounds terrible for your wife." I raised my eyebrows. "Not to mention I don't think it's possible to give her that many orgasms."

In a single fluid movement, he rolled me onto my hands and knees. He wrapped his arm around me from behind to hold me still and guided his cock inside me.

I moaned and arched my back. Oh, yes. This was what I wanted most of all: to be taken by my dragon.

"My love, as we have seen for ourselves, nothing is impossible," he murmured into my ear. "And a dragon never backs down from a challenge."

He thrust further, filling and stretching every bit of me as only my Ardruc could. When he was fully inside me, I gasped and wailed.

Rather than withdraw and thrust again, he held me tightly and kissed my shoulder. "And now I am finally deep inside my wife," he rumbled, sounding very satisfied. "Where her dragon husband most likes to be."

CHAPTER 34

ELENA

THREE YEARS LATER

Very unsurprisingly, I found my husband on the roof.

Hands on hips, I surveyed the grassy, vine-covered rooftop above Lyra One's imaging lab and the surrounding forest as it hummed and swayed.

All eight research stations on Vorsa World, including this one, were beautifully designed to blend the natural beauty of the planet with Fortusian eco-architecture, which the Vorsa honored and accepted for its similarity to their own preferences.

Happily, no traces remained of the Nyvorans' occupation of the planet. The terrible damage they'd caused while illegally ripping out rare metals and other resources was in the process of healing naturally as the planet slowly knitted its wounds back together.

With a smile, I studied the dragon man lying in the center of the roof, his wings outstretched and gaze fixed on the korae-filled night sky.

"Stargazing *again*, Dr. Husiorithae?" I *tsk*'d. "Don't you have data to analyze?"

"Mountains of it, Dr. Regis," he rumbled. "But it will all still be there tomorrow."

With a yawn, I padded barefoot across the roof to his side, enjoying the warm thrumming of the grass beneath my feet.

Three years after the Alliance Division of Conservation and Environment built our new laboratories in collaboration with the Vorsa, every beat of the planet's living heart still thrilled and comforted me as much as my first day on its soil.

"It's nearly 2300 hours," I said when his golden gaze moved from the korae to me. "Are you coming to bed anytime soon? You know the girls will be awake at 0600 whether we're ready or not."

"I have already asked your mother to make them breakfast so we can sleep late," Ardruc said, surprising me. "She was only too happy to say yes since she will be returning to Fyloria in a week. I think we will have to check her luggage to ensure she does not try to take our daughters with her."

I shook my head in disbelief. "I never thought I'd see my mother the distinguished heliophysicist crawling on the floor playing with my children, much less laughing and chasing them as they fly around the nursery, but I'll be damned if that hasn't been how she's spent the last two weeks. And I haven't heard a single mention of her wanting to get back to work."

"Hilda is a very happy grandmother. And I am very happy the girls will grow up knowing and loving her and their Aunt Violet." He reached out with both hands. "Come here, little mate."

Tired or not, I was powerless to resist either that nickname or the way his eyes glowed only for me.

On my hands and knees, I crawled up his body as the grass beneath us pulsed and hummed. "Tell me, lover…is all the rooftop recording equipment shut off?"

"All of it," he said, his voice edged with a growl. "Except our personal one."

"Good." I lay on his chest and kissed him. "So why are you still wearing clothes?" I murmured against his lips.

He chuckled. "Because I want my wife to take them off...*after* she takes hers off and sits on my face like a good little mate."

"Oh." I pouted. "I can't have a taste of my dragon first?"

Ardruc caressed my lower lip with his thumb. "Just a taste," he warned. "I am impatient to hear you call my name for the first of many times tonight."

After another kiss, I moved down his body to straddle his thighs and attacked the fastener and seam on the waist of his pants until I freed his beautiful cock.

"Such an eager little mate." He chuckled again, the sound a rich, deep rumble that made my pussy quiver and gush in anticipation.

Eager didn't even come close to describing how much I wanted and needed my dragon tonight.

Between the twins, my mother's latest extended visit, our research and field work, and administrative duties as co-directors of research for all the fully-staffed stations located on Vorsa World, our once-robust sex life had become...well, significantly less robust than either of us liked.

I planned to make up for that as much as possible tonight.

I pulled my top off over my head along with my undershirt. Even if it wasn't a lovely summer night, my dragon would keep me warm.

With an appreciative rumble, Ardruc cupped my right breast in his hand and stroked my nipple. "Lovely Elena. Gods, how does my wife grow more beautiful by the day?"

After giving birth to half-Fortusian twins—beautiful dragon girls we'd named Luvia and Adrea—a year ago, my body had changed a great deal. I loved most of the changes and had learned to like the rest, or at least not sigh too much when I saw myself in the mirror or in the recordings my mate and I liked to make and watch together during our rare time alone.

Ardruc, however, was obsessed with every single change in my body, and liked to kiss, lick, and bite them one by one at every opportunity—especially my breasts, which filled his hands and mouth far more now than before the girls were born.

"Keep up the flattery, dragon," I said with a wink. "You might get to give me your knot later if you do."

His eyes took on that dark golden hue that I loved so much. "And you might get to take my knot in the sky if you ask nicely, little mate."

We both knew I'd be getting his knot in the sky tonight, but it was so much fun to tease and play.

I wrapped my hand around the base of his beautiful cock, gave him a few slow, almost languid strokes, and bent my head to caress the tip with the tiniest of licks. His cock leapt and splattered my tongue. Mmm, delicious.

His back arched and a shudder ran through his body. "Elena," he groaned.

"Well, that was my one permitted taste, I suppose," I said with an exaggerated sigh. I dragged my fingers over his cock as I let go and reached for the waistband of my pants.

Suddenly, his hand was wrapped in my hair. "I think you may have another taste," he growled, and urged me to bend again.

By the time he let go of my hair, I ended up getting much, much more than a few tastes, and that was very much fine with me.

As his chest heaved and he trembled from the force of his release, I licked my lips, left the rest of my clothes scattered across the grass, and settled in on my knees astride his face.

He kissed my inner thighs thoroughly first, biting gently and then not so gently and laving the marks he left with his tongue. I shivered and quivered and dripped with need, but I let him take his time. No point trying to rush him. A dragon could never get enough of worshiping his little mate.

When he finally wrapped his arms around my thighs and drew me down to his mouth, I was so ready and desperate for him that his tongue took me over the edge in less than a minute.

"Dragon," I wailed, riding his face with my hand in his hair. I let my head fall back and let the pleasure roll through me. "Yes, gods, yes."

The planet thrummed and pulsed along with my pleasure and the trees around the station swayed. Korae filled the sky from horizon to horizon in every color.

He held me right there for a long time, his chest rumbling as he gave me two more perfect orgasms—one hard, so I would scream his name, and the other soft so I would sink my nails into his arms and moan it.

"Up on your knees, my love," he breathed, and gave me a final slow lick.

Trembling and gasping, I obeyed. He moved from beneath me, rose, and came around to stand in front of me.

Slowly, he unfastened his shirt collar and separated it down the front along the seam to reveal his chest. His Vorsa World mark, a larger version of my own, shimmered on his skin over his sternum. And his pants rested low on his hips, open in front where his cock was already hard and dripping again.

"Take off my pants, little mate," he said. When I reached up to grab them, he caught my hand and kissed my fingers. "No. With your teeth."

Quivering, I did as I was told.

I bit the fabric on his right leg and pulled until his pants slid down on that side, then repeated the movement on the left. Slowly, I worked them down his thick legs until they puddled at his bare feet and I could look up at his cock and his smile.

He caressed my hair. "Perfect, little mate. Now the rest."

I held the fabric of his pants in my mouth while he stepped out of each leg. And then he knelt so I could remove his shirt the same way.

Three years later, and he could still find new ways to drive me absolutely wild.

He cupped my face and kissed me deeply. "On your elbows and

knees, little mate," he murmured against my lips. "And spread those lovely legs for me."

I turned my back to him and bent down with my forearms on the grass and my ass and pussy in the air.

"Gods above," he breathed, his hands on my hips. "My Elena. Every time I try to stay in control, you turn me back into a big, dumb, lovesick dragon."

"I love my big, dumb, lovesick dragon," I said. "Please, may I have your cock now?"

"No, not yet." He spread my ass with his hands and chuckled when I whimpered. "But you may have my tail, little mate."

He took his time with this too, using his tongue and circling my clit until I came on his hand and tongue with desperate cries, my fingers digging into the grass. My pussy clenched on its own emptiness and I was reduced to begging, but he didn't give in.

Instead, he stretched me gently until I was ready, and then he wrapped his arm around my waist from behind to guide me back onto his well-lubricated and thrumming tail.

I loved doing this, taking my pleasure and whimpering and moaning while he watched and listened and stroked himself. And when I brushed his hand aside to stroke his cock, he began to growl. I loved that growl even more than his tail.

"Make yourself come on my tail, little mate," he said, his hand wrapped in my hair. "Show me how you like to come with my tail in your sweet little ass."

"Oh," I groaned, and took his thrumming tail deeper, searching for that perfect depth and angle that would send me careening over the cliff. "My dragon. Pull my hair."

He twisted his hand deeper into my hair, forcing me to arch my back. I ground on his tail and—oh, gods, *there.* I cried out.

"Yes, little mate," he growled. "Come for your dragon."

With wails and guttural cries, I climaxed with my hand wrapped around his dripping cock and his tail in my ass. It was torment that my pussy was empty. I wanted his cock. I wanted his knot. I wanted him to fill me like only a dragon could, and he was holding that back from me until he saw me come on just his tail.

Gods, he was a merciless, gorgeous man, and I loved him so much I ached.

My ass was still fluttering around his tail when he put me back on my hands and knees, withdrew his tail, pressed his thick cock against my pussy, and buried himself in me all the way to his knot in a half-dozen absolutely perfect thrusts.

I came so hard on the final thrust that my scream would have traveled through the entire valley and beyond if we hadn't installed sonic dampers on the roof. My dragon liked to make his little mate scream up here.

"Elena," Ardruc rasped, his arm tight around my waist. He stayed buried deep inside me, his knot pressed against my pussy. "Little mate. I love you."

"I love you," I gasped. "So much. And not just because you just made me see actual stars."

He chuckled, the sound strained. "Fly with me, my love. I need you take my knot. I want to be in the sky and as deep inside my beautiful, brilliant wife as I can be."

Gods, he did have it bad for me tonight.

"Eager dragon," I teased breathlessly. "You can't wait?"

"No." He slipped his hand between my thighs to circle my clit. I moaned. "Sweet little Elena." He kissed my shoulder. "I want to fill you and feel you come on my knot. What can I do to persuade you to agree?"

I looked over my shoulder and started to make up some ridiculous demand just to see how much I could get him to promise—and spotted an astonishing sight that emptied my head of all those thoughts.

"Ardruc," I said slowly. "Are those...*pink clouds* floating above the station?"

"They are." He kissed my shoulder again and nuzzled my damp skin. "A gift from the Vorsa and your hopelessly devoted husband."

Fortusia's beautiful pink clouds were one of my favorite things about Ardruc's home planet. For a variety of reasons, we hadn't been able to visit since the twins were born. A few nights ago, I'd mentioned in an offhand way how much I missed the pink clouds.

Ardruc inhaled sharply and stilled. "Elena, are you—"

"No, I am not crying," I said, with the tiniest of sniffles. "I got something in my eye." I sniffled again. "And nose."

To my surprise, he eased himself from me. When I whimpered in protest, he urged me to rise to my feet and turned me to face him.

My dragon was so beautiful on his knees in front of me, sitting on his heels with his wings outstretched, eyes glowing, and glistening cock arching up toward his stomach.

He drew me closer, kissed my abdomen, and clasped my hands in his own much larger ones.

"Little mate," he said, gazing up at me. "I promised on all three of our wedding days that anything you need, I will do my best to provide it. That includes pink clouds."

I kissed his hair and managed a wobbly smile. "That's an awful lot of trouble to go to just to bribe me to take your knot in the sky, sneaky dragon."

With a chuckle, he rose. "Forehead kisses, orgasms, and pink clouds on request. Anything my little mate wants, she will get. I made that promise too." He bent to wrap me in his arms. "A dragon keeps his promises," he murmured in my ear.

"To the clouds, then," I said, snuggling into his embrace. "Before they blow away."

Not that I thought they would. The night had stilled, and those beautiful, fluffy clouds looked like they would stay that way for a while.

My dragon wrapped his tail around me and carried me up into the sky.

We flew in widening circles around the station as he gained altitude. I pressed my lips to his chest and drank in his scent and the way he rumbled just for me…and for Luvia and Adrea whenever one or both lay on his chest to nap.

Higher and higher we climbed as I stroked his cock and he murmured into my ear how much he loved me. For all his impatience to give me his knot, he seemed to be savoring every moment of this flight. Maybe he thought we might not be able to do this again for a while, or maybe he wasn't thinking any farther ahead than these perfect moments.

When I took his beautiful cock inside me, he held me to his chest and thrust gently until his knot bumped against me. And then he carried me up into the pink clouds.

The thick mist smelled sweeter than I expected, with a hint of what I would have sworn was a smoky brandy scent if I didn't know better. Surely Ardruc couldn't have found a way to blend his scent into the clouds?

Nothing was impossible on Vorsa World, though—not even pink clouds that smelled like my mate.

He guided me on his cock until I came with a soft cry, my nails digging into his shoulders in the way he liked so much. And then he cooed. I rested my head against his chest and let him hold me as he gave me his knot in three gentle thrusts. It swelled inside me, a perfect fit.

I whimpered with need. "Ardruc," I gasped, my voice muffled by his hot skin and the thick cloud around us.

He'd already claimed me so many times, and so thoroughly, but there was something about this moment that made me say, "Dragon. Claim me, *please*."

He filled me with snarls and growls, his movements and sounds bringing me to a second climax that was even more satisfying because he made a low sound deep in his chest that I never heard unless I was coming on his knot.

Warm and content and so full of him, I pressed my lips to his Vorsa mark, closed my eyes, and breathed him in.

Strange how improbable it seemed for a human mycologist

from Fyloria to be married and mated to an atmospheric scientist from Fortusia, and yet how inevitable too. When I looked back down our paths, every step—even the stumbles, falls, and lost ways—had led to this moment in the clouds.

Science and logic could explain it, but it was miraculous too.

"Elena," Ardruc said, cupping the back of my head. From his tone, I thought that wasn't the first time he'd spoken. "Little mate?"

"Sorry." I kissed his chest. "I got lost in thought."

"As my brilliant wife is known to do, even while flying in miraculous pink clouds with her mate's knot inside her." He nuzzled my hair. "What thoughts are filling your head tonight, my love?"

"I was thinking about a stuffy dragon," I said, and tapped his nose so it would twitch adorably. "And all the reasons I married him three times."

"*Three* times," he mused. "You must love that stuffy dragon."

"I do." I cupped his face with both hands. "What should we do now?"

He considered. "We could return to the roof so I can hold you until my knot eases, or fly farther out into the valley, or…"

"Or?" I prompted.

He squeezed me. "Or we could fly to our forest refuge and take a little more time away."

When Ardruc and I returned from our first visit to Fortusia three years ago, we'd discovered the Nyvoran research stations were already gone. We'd lived in a capsule home during the construction of the new labs, and Vorsa World made us a beautiful, almost cathedral-like forest refuge in place of the small shelter they'd created for us first. As much as I'd loved that little secret place, our new refuge was a true masterpiece of pure Vorsa design and our first real taste of their beautiful natural architecture.

Nearly two years ago, Ardruc and I had made Luvia and Adrea on the refuge's giant mossy bed. When we were ready to add to our little family, I planned to do so in the very same place…or in the sky above it.

"Well, we *do* have someone watching the girls tonight," I mused. "I could be persuaded to take some more time away with my mate...*if* he was in the mood to teach me a lesson or two."

His eyebrows went up. "Or *two?*"

"I've been very disobedient, Dr. Husiorithae," I said, and he made an absolutely delicious rumbly sound. "No lab reports for a month, so much data not filed properly..." I lowered my voice and whispered, "And I haven't obeyed your lab dress code all week."

He puffed smoke out his nose and fixed me with a golden stare.

"There is only one proper response to that level of irresponsibility, Dr. Regis," he growled, and gods above I quivered around him. "This rises to the level of willful insubordination. Will you never learn to follow my policies?"

"No, Doctor," I said, and gave him my biggest, widest, most innocent eyes. "I really don't think I will."

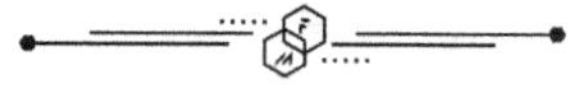

*DON'T FORGET TO JOIN MY READER COMMUNITY TO RECEIVE FREE **SFW** and **NSFW** art of Elena and Ardruc and other books and stories in the Fortusian Mates universe!*

Join at LisaEdmonds.com.

THANK YOU FOR READING

Thank you for reading *Claimed in the Clouds*, the third book in the Fortusian Mates series! I hope you enjoyed the story.

More novels featuring Fortusian males and the fierce human women they love are coming soon.

Reviews are very much appreciated by all indie authors, if you have the time to share your thoughts.

ABOUT THE AUTHOR

Lisa Edmonds was born and raised in Kansas. She studied English and forensic criminology at Wichita State University. After acquiring her Bachelor's degree in English, she considered a career in law enforcement as a behavioral analyst before earning a Master's in English from Wichita State and then a Ph.D. in English from Texas A&M University.

For ten years, she was an associate professor of English at a college in Texas, where she taught a variety of writing and literature courses.

Now a full-time author, she shares a cute Victorian-style home called The Storybook House with her husband and their pets, and enjoys writing, reading, traveling, spoiling her niece and nephew, and singing karaoke.

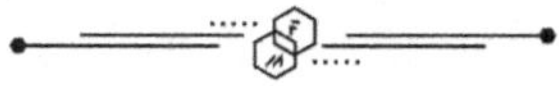

Don't miss new releases, commissioned art, and sneak peeks at works in progress! Join Lisa's reader community at LisaEdmonds.com.

www.ingramcontent.com/pod-product-compliance
Lightning Source LLC
Chambersburg PA
CBHW060605300726
48975CB00005B/1459